Elizabeth Cooper

The Life of Thomas Wentworth, Earl of Strafford and Lord-Lieutenant of Ireland

Vol. 2

Elizabeth Cooper

The Life of Thomas Wentworth, Earl of Strafford and Lord-Lieutenant of Ireland
Vol. 2

ISBN/EAN: 9783337323783

Printed in Europe, USA, Canada, Australia, Japan

Cover: Foto ©Raphael Reischuk / pixelio.de

More available books at **www.hansebooks.com**

THE LIFE

OF

THOMAS WENTWORTH,

EARL OF STRAFFORD

AND

LORD-LIEUTENANT OF IRELAND.

BY

ELIZABETH COOPER,

AUTHOR OF LIFE OF "ARABELLA STUART," "POPULAR HISTORY OF AMERICA," ETC., ETC.

IN TWO VOLUMES.

VOL. II.

LONDON:

TINSLEY BROTHERS, 8, CATHERINE ST., STRAND.

1874.

LONDON:
BRADBURY, AGNEW, & CO., PRINTERS, WHITEFRIARS.

CONTENTS TO VOL. II.

CHAPTER I.

CHAPTER II.

CHAPTER III.

PAGE

CHAPTER IV.

CHAPTER V.

CHAPTER VI.

CHAPTER VII.

CHAPTER VIII.

CHAPTER IX.

CHAPTER X.

CHAPTER XI.

CHAPTER XII.

CHAPTER XIII.

CHAPTER XIV.

CHAPTER XV.

CHAPTER XVI.

Note.—The limits of the present work not allowing of those illustrations of special points which, for the relief of the general reader and the use of the student, are often referred to notes and appendices, all who desire a minute account of the Trial, and especially of the Bill of Attainder, are advised to study the Journal of the Long Parliament, by Sir Simon D'Ewes, and the folio of Rushworth devoted to the Trial alone. The MS. State Papers are singularly defective on this part.

THE LIFE

OF

THOMAS WENTWORTH.

CHAPTER I.

TOWARDS the middle of November Lord Wentworth returned to Ireland. The accession of good spirits which followed his cordial reception in England had died away long before his second departure from his native land. He returned to labours hard as ever, and which had lost their freshness. He, too, had no longer the prestige of novelty in the eyes of the nation, and the well-deserved honours which would have recreated it had been refused by the King.

Did Lord Wentworth ever ponder over the past, over the days gone by; when, with Pym and Hampden, with Seymour and St. John, and others of that immortal band, he pleaded and fought, and suffered imprisonment for the liberties of the people? Did he call to mind how gratefully those efforts had been received by those for whom they were made, and how, reflecting within the rapturous appreciations from without, he had cried, exultingly, "Our hearts are a gift fit for a king?"

Well, the King had the gift. And what was his valuation of it?

Alas! Such thoughts as these would never do. The Lord Deputy of Ireland must to work, to work. That alone was to comprise his life on earth from henceforth. Work without appreciation, without affection. "For, in good faith, George, all here below are grown wondrous indifferent!"

The first trouble that beset him on his arrival in Dublin was caused by the folly and injustice of the Protestant clergy.

The bigoted spirit of Laud was abroad; his determination to reduce every man in the three kingdoms to the profession of the ritualistic Church of England was well known. Everywhere this meddlesome old man was causing mischief and revolt. For if there was one thing in which the three kingdoms were united, it was in the resolution that he should not play the Pope. He had been a constant torment to Lord Wentworth during the last three years, by endeavouring to persuade him to enforce pains and penalties and exactions against the Roman Catholics and Puritans of Ireland. Lord Wentworth was a staunch member of the Church of England, but his mind was far too capacious to dream of conversion by persecution. And the only excuse for persecution now, was the conversion of the people for their own sake alone. For they had fully bought the right of exemption, and by paying the contribution, had swept away all excuse of fines for the needs of the country. Yet, the Lord Deputy found that the Protestant bishops and their chancellors had taken advantage of his absence, once more, to 1636. attempt the levy of the abhorred fine of twelvepence on every one who absented himself from Church on Sundays.

The whole nation was aroused. The priests and friars took joyful advantage of the opportunity to excite the people against the English, to persuade them they were betrayed, and enrage them with the apprehension of a terrible persecution. But for the wisdom and presence of Lord Wentworth, the rebellion of 1641 would have been anticipated. He instantly and indignantly stopped the Sunday fine, and at once wrote to Secretary Coke, to prevent any appeal against his decree. For this was one of his greatest difficulties. In dealing with the recusants of all sects, Laud, even, was against him and the King was with Laud. By his corrections of the scandals in the Protestant Church, Wentworth had made the clergy his enemies, and he well knew how dire a temptation to the King would be the money accruing from the renewed fine, and he hastened to put the matter in its true light before the English Council.

And, first, he pointed out the imminent danger of rebellion—a rebellion which would cost far more to put down than the amount of the fine.

"It is well known," said he, " what furious outrages and sad effects such rumours and fears have produced in this nation, and we that are upon the place do clearly see that with this people: *Quo quid crudelius fictum facilius creditur*, especially in anything where their religion is rubbed upon, or the English government concerned.

"It will be ever far forth of my heart to conceive

 that a conforming in religion is not, above all other things, principally to be intended.

"For, undoubtedly, till we be brought under one form of divine service, the Crown is never safe on this side, but yet the time and circumstances may very well be discoursed; and, sure, I do not hold this a fit reason to disquiet or sting them in this kind, and my reasons are divers.

"This course alone will never bring them to church, being rather an engine to drain money out of their pockets, than to raise a right belief and faith in their hearts, and so doth not, indeed, tend to that end it sets forth.

"The subsidies are now in paying, which were given with an universal alacrity, and very graceful it will be in the King to indulge them otherwise, as much as may be, till they be paid.

"It were too much, at once, to distemper them, by bringing plantations upon them and disturbing them in the exercising of their religion, so long as it be without scandal, and so, indeed, very inconsiderate, as I conceive, to move in this latter, till that former be fully settled, and, by that means, the Protestant party become by much the stronger, which, in truth, as yet, I do not conceive it to be.

"Lastly, the great work of reformation ought not, in my opinion, to be fallen upon, till all incidents be fully provided for, the army rightly furnished, the forts repaired, money in the coffers, and such a preparation in view as might deter any malevolent, licentious spirit to stir up ill-humour, in opposition to his Majesty's pious intendments therein. Nor ought the execution of this to proceed by steps or degrees, but all rightly disposed to be undertaken and gone through withal at once.

"And, certainly, in the meantime, since the less you call the conceit of it into their memory the better will it be for us, and themselves the quieter. So, as it there were no wiser than I, the bishops should be privately required to forbear their ecclesiastical censures till they understood further of his Majesty's pleasure therein."

These words of Lord Wentworth are well worth consideration, for other reasons as well as the events to which they especially relate. They are a fair measure of the influence of religion as taught by the Church of England at this time, and throw a great light on the cause of the rapid increase of Puritanism, independently of political motives.

Lord Wentworth was a stanch Churchman. In the Church of England he had been educated, and, amid his political changes, from her he had never swerved. He was the nearest friend of the highest dignitary, and was acknowledged by the English clergy at home as a faithful son. He regularly fulfilled the enjoined ordinances, and brought up his family to follow in his steps.

Yet, what an idea of the office of religion do his words present? The answer is easy. In his eyes, it is nothing but a *form*, and a form, too, of very inferior importance to many worldly matters. He is perfectly honest in his simplicity; and the result is altogether consistent. Recognising, as he does, the real consequence and weight of other things, it is quite impossible that a mind so clear as his should place the small before the great. He measures the magnitude of each by its consequences; he sees that if a rebellion breaks out, or the subsidies suddenly stop, incalculable evil must follow. But if the people do not go through this ceremony, each Sunday, that he honestly believes to be religion, no harm will happen at present. That it can injure their souls, evidently never once enters his head. He sees it in its triviality. It is not only a mere tool, but a very insignificant tool in his eyes. He himself goes through all its forms, not as a hypocrite, but as a believer in them, as he believes in the forms of State. One form is called Court etiquette, the other Religion. Large sums of money have been appointed for the expenses of both, and he finds that one sum has been grossly abused, and applied to private instead of the public use for which it was granted. Such abuses cannot exist under his government, and hence the reformation of the Protestant clergy, whom he rates with as little reverence when, as he tells one, "he deserves to have his rochet pulled over his neck," as he would a pilfering usher.

What a contrast to Laud! Both men are equally sincere in the belief of the reality of the thing. They differ only as regards their comprehension of its magnitude. To Laud it is proportionably great and important. It is the same kind of thing, made of the same material, and of the same shape to him as to Wentworth. Only, it is the largest thing in his life, and, consequently, all else is minute beside it. In his eyes, a war between Scotland and England is nothing in comparison to the Creed of the service being read in a surplice; and, for the life of him, he cannot conceive why his fellow-worshipper should hesitate at such a trifle as a rebellion, when there is a chance to enforce conformity.

The negative results are the same in both. Neither <u>1636.</u>
Wentworth nor Laud is influenced in the remotest
degree by his religion in his personal conduct. It
does not restrain Wentworth in his barbarity and injustice to Lord Mountnorris, or Laud from severing
the ears of Prynne. The first, though the Lord-
Deputy of a kingdom, can amuse himself with the
veriest gossip that ever poured from the lips of an old
washerwoman ; the last, though the holy Primate of
all England, can rail at his dead wife long years after
she has lain in her grave.

The joy and peace that crowns the true believer,
whose hope in a lofty ideal compels him to purify
himself, even as the bright object of his hope is pure,
are to these, all unknown, undreamed of.

And so they pursue their course ; each throwing his
life into the greatest object of his existence.

That the limited capacity of Laud never could have
comprehended an enlightened system of theology
seems very probable. His ideas of the Deity have
already been alluded to, and when we remember that
he had the greatest opportunity, not only by having
the Scriptures, especially the New Testament, for his
daily study, with all the commentaries of the greatest
minds, but that he had intercourse with Jeremy
Taylor, whom, to his credit, he greatly aided and made
his chaplain, and yet could attain no conception of
spirituality, his case seems hopeless. He patronised
Jeremy Taylor on account of the strong leanings
of the latter towards episcopacy. But Taylor was
then a young man, and, though he always remained
true to his first opinions, they could not bar or
swamp the soul that shines through his works—

 works which would have been mysteries to the archbishop.

But for Wentworth! Was not a spiritual religion the great want of his life? To all intents and purposes he was a pagan. Not only did he accept the husk for the grain, but he was ignorant of any other grain—so ignorant, that it never occurred to him to search for better things. And there was no chance of another offering them. The very fact of his great intimacy with Laud would be quite sufficient to keep aloof all men of an opposite persuasion. Laud claimed to be his ghostly father. Wentworth was entirely satisfied with him; none else would presume to touch on sacred subjects with so high a personage. Then, too, by his residence in Ireland he was deprived of the chance of meeting those whose accidental conversation in the houses of his friends might have awakened new chords in his soul.

Beautiful instances did happen in those unsettled times, when some rich man, wearied with the strife and tumult around, by chance, caught the quickening words of some great preacher whom he recognised as a heaven-sent friend. Such was Dr. Hammond, who, preaching by accident before the Earl of Leicester, was by him taken to Penshurst, where, among his hearers, was the young Algernon Sidney, then a boy. And such, some years later, was Jeremy Taylor to John Evelyn, who, hearing him discourse in St. Paul's Cathedral, besought his instruction, and found in him a spiritual adviser in joy, a consoler in sorrow, and a helpful guiding mind in all things, while the riches of Evelyn helped to soften the biting cares of poverty in the days of Taylor's distress. There are few more beautiful friendships of this nature—friendships of the soul,—than that of Jeremy Taylor and John Evelyn.

And this it was that Wentworth needed. Some may consider him to have been incapable of it. With the two most learned Protestants of Ireland in his rule, Usher and Bedell, he had no communication except such as related to official duties. But Laud had a prejudice against Bedell, and though Wentworth always spoke with respect of Usher, yet there was no sympathy between them.

Another obstacle was the want of time. Wentworth's whole life was absorbed in the work of this world. He thought, indeed, that by going at the appointed times to church he fulfilled all that was ordained. Had he recognised or been taught the solemn duty of constantly seeking for food for the spirit he would have fulfilled it; and who shall say with what result? Many a lonely being, hungering vainly for high communion with the living has, by the ceaseless study of the works of the great dead, alighted on words that have kindled thoughts and hopes such as have opened new worlds to their delighted view, and changed the whole current of their lives.

What feelings, for example, might not the works of Philip Melancthon, or Luther, or Hubert Languet have awakened in him? A half hour with the divine old monk, Thomas-à-Kempis, might have sent him to the beatitudes of the Sermon on the Mount. If once he could have dreamed there was a religion beyond his visible Church—once have brought himself to ponder and set his mighty intellect to seek—what might he not have found?—perhaps the missing spring, the lost chord of his life! Alas! that the story should

1636. still be so common, that men with capabilities far beyond the average, with powers to feel, should yet pass on, their noblest capabilities deadened, because they look upon the most vital of questions as " settled " for them, as if unconscious that every day a new thought is born into speech, that those who will not seek, cannot find !

One thing is certain.   Had the feelings of Lord Wentworth ever been fairly roused and deeply interested, his soul would have rested in no narrow limits. Even in the pitiable form of his own ideas of religion he, at a bound, passes before all his contemporaries in one thing—he clearly recognises the utter impotency of persecution to produce conversion.

" This course, alone, will never bring them to Church, being rather an engine to drain money out of their pockets than to raise a right belief and faith in their hearts."

Could he have dreamed that " a conformity in religion " was not a petty cause, instituted by the commands of a man, with the equally petty object of " making the Crown safe on this side," but a result anticipated by the first founders of Christianity, of the truth they taught,* which should voluntarily crown the perfected civilisation of the whole world, and therefore a dream to be realised only after countless ages on ages have rolled away in futurity, but a dream to which, nevertheless, the humblest worker who made that end his object may contribute, how different would have been his system !

Still, in that age of bigotry, it was an unconscious

* " There is one body and one Spirit, even as ye are called in one hope of your calling."—St. Paul.

aid, even towards this, to recognise the folly and evil _1636._ of compulsion. If he did not thereby teach positive good, he left the road free to others to drop the seed, nor, in the common stupidity of the time, trod it underfoot. Time alone is the test of the virtue of the plant. In the beginning, the wheat and tares are too much alike. Wisdom has declared they must be allowed to grow together until the harvest.

A fit of illness attacked the Lord Deputy almost immediately on his return from England, and it was perhaps no injury to him to receive various letters consulting him on the private affairs of his friends. His reputation for wisdom and influence seems quite to have overpowered the remembrance of his incessant occupations, and very little consideration was shown in the continual interruptions on his time— leisure we cannot say ; that was to him an unknown word. Still, it may have been well to divert his mind.

Among other petitioners, was one for his counsel and influence from the Countess of Leicester, sister of his friend the Earl of Northumberland. The Earl of Leicester had been for some time ambassador extraordinary in Paris, and, like all the servants of Charles, had to complain not only that his salary was long in arrear, but that his expenses far outran his allowance. The Leicesters were poor, with twelve children, and the Countess was tired of the honour of serving on such terms.

Another constant correspondent was the poor ex-Queen of Bohemia. Her two sons were now in London, and she seems not to have felt such perfect confidence in her royal brother as to render it unwise to ask Lord Wentworth to befriend them, while the two youths themselves had their requests. All received patience and courtesy at the hands of their friend. It is almost a relief to read the lightness of his answers to them, as a sign of some subjects not overweighted with care.

Though he himself had been disappointed in promotion—and it most truly made no difference in his manner of fulfilling his duties—yet, it did not alter his opinion with regard to the necessity of rewards and punishments in the case of others. He thought it would be very advisable to stimulate the zeal of the Commissioners of Defective Titles by making their profits agree with their work. He, therefore, had written to the King recommending a grant of four shillings in the pound to the Lord Chief Justice and the Lord Chief Baron of Ireland on the first yearly rent raised upon the commission of defective titles.

The King had agreed, and the result was found to be so encouraging that he now advised the same plan to be pursued with the Chief Baron and Barons of the Exchequer in the case of the composition of the recusants, which at present failed to satisfy expectation. Except in his own case, Lord Wentworth was utterly sceptical as to the influence of love or honour in the fulfilment of service. "Reward," he said, "well applied, advantages the services of kings extremely much; it being most certain that not one man of very many serve their masters for love, but for their own ends and preferments."

He had, also, an especial repugnance to employing poor men in great services, and such as required any outward display. "If," said he, "his Majesty once found the advantage to his affairs and treasure that might be got by employing, *cæteris paribus*, men of blood and estates, the difference would quickly let him see how great it is betwixt a person that brings £12,000 a year to spend in his service, and one that will look for as much from him to bestow upon his own wasteful and vain expense, and be a means to make others press less upon his bounties; and when they have them, husband them better, after they shall observe that the King finds he may be served with as much honour and more profit by others for nothing, than by themselves to his excessive and, it may be, scandalous charge."

The King acceded to his request with regard to the percentages, which had the double effect of quickening the scent of the officers of the Crown and binding them to Wentworth, who had been the means of this unlooked-for profit.

Still, this affair of the defective titles, lucrative as it was, was wearisome work. The jurors who had decided in Lord St. Alban's favour against the King were still in prison for their verdict; but, not caring to waste away their lives in captivity, acknowledged themselves wrong, and wrote to St. Alban's, begging him to yield his lands and themselves to the King's mercy. He accordingly went to Secretary Coke and presented their request, begging him to apply to the King for pardon, seeing that they all yielded the disputed point.

But Coke took another view. He told St. Alban's that, to speak to the King without first speaking to the Lord Wentworth, would be an affront to the latter, whom he must first consult, and to whom he counselled him to write. But Coke took care himself, before the letter of St. Alban's could reach the Lord Deputy, to write a rather unnecessary letter, suggesting that it was scarcely consistent with the King's honour to pardon, seeing that the imprisoned jury yielded not to the King's justice, but his power. Besides, by a pardon the King would lose the all-precious fines due for contumacy. Of course Wentworth was of the same opinion. The unfortunate St. Alban's wrote a sad and submissive letter, pleading most pathetically for the jury; but in vain. They had committed the crime, in this world, so often irreparable, of conscientiously opposing those who were stronger than themselves, and who, therefore, could not yield without implying the possibility of their having been in the wrong.

The imprisonment and fining of the jury of Galway may stand by the side of the name of Mountnorris in the dark register of wrong. They are among the worst spots in Lord Wentworth's life.

Like the story of Mountnorris, too, it did not pass uncommented. Lord Holland was heard to remark that he feared the severity of the Lord Wentworth would disaffect the people of Galway, and possibly provoke them to call the Irish regiments in Flanders to aid in revolt. His words were reported to Wentworth, who was none the more disposed to mercy by them. The King, too, heard of them, but he soon received the good news that the forfeited lands of the Londoners at Derry would bring in £8000 a year instead of £5000, as had at first been calculated, and such good news was enough to cover any little unpleasantness in the other matter.

For money, always the King's greatest need, was 1636.
particularly wanted just now.   It was difficult for
matters to look more threatening everywhere but in
Ireland. The tyranny of Laud was goading the people
on to a religious war, both in England and Scotland,
and, but for his wiser friend, would have done so in
Ireland.

Lampoons and libels were everywhere published
about him. Some fell into his own hands, which he
sent to Lord Wentworth, first to read and then burn.
The aspect of foreign affairs was no brighter than that
of those at home. The death of the old Emperor of
Germany had given Charles some hopes that the disposition of his successor might be different. Accordingly, an ambassador was despatched, to endeavour to
persuade the new emperor to enter into treaty to
restore the young Elector Palatine to the throne of his
father. Any one might have predicted the result.
The miserable condition of England was well known.
All her military fame had been lost under the Duke
of Buckingham and the shabby little expeditions to
deliver the Palatinate. It was hardly likely that a
foreigner should yield for love what he had no motive
to give up for fear ; especially improbable that a strong
Roman Catholic should give up a kingdom to a weak
Protestant.

The embassy was a total failure. The ambassador
was coldly, almost uncourteously, received, and
dismissed with a mean present, and a quiet, firm
refusal.

Many a heart in England throbbed, many a cheek
burned with shame and humiliation at such treatment,
as the thoughts of Englishmen turned back to former

1636. days, and remembered what their country had been before the Stuarts came to degrade it.

Even Charles was moved—moved at the personal affront, and longed to avenge it. Like a child, he spoke of going to war, as if war were a trifle, a simple matter of inclination to be indulged at will.

Thus closed the year 1636.

CHAPTER II.

The new year opened with heavy rumours of foreign 1637.
war.

Hitherto, the King had refrained from consulting Lord Wentworth on other subjects than those relating to Ireland, or such as affected his own duties. He now for the first time enlarged his confidence.

He informed Wentworth that since the return of his ambassador from Germany, he had perceived the impossibility of restoring his sister and nephews to their dominion by fair means, at least, without threatening. He had, therefore, formed a strictly defensive league with France,* and joining in confederation with Denmark, Sweden, and the States, he proposed that all should unite in their demands. If these demands were not complied with, or so long delayed as to amount to a denial, then the allies were to proclaim the House of Austria, with all her allies, enemies. But he had informed his friends that his share of the war must be performed on sea, not on land. He was resolved not to meddle with land armies.

When we think of the condition of his own kingdom, how he proposed to plunge into this war without even

---

* The treaty was not signed, but the King had no doubts of the willingness of the French.

1637. consulting or calling together the great council of the nation, we can scarcely be surprised at the blind recklessness with which he waived all dangerous consequences. He concluded his communication with the following remark :—

" What likelihood there is that, upon this, I should fall foul with Spain, you now may see as well as I. And what great inconvenience this war can bring to me, now that my sea contribution is settled, and that I am resolved not to meddle with land armies, I cannot imagine, except it be in Ireland. And there, too, I fear not much, since I find the country so well settled as it is by your diligent care. Yet I thought it necessary to give you this watchword, both to have the more vigilant eye over the discontented party, as also to assure you that *I am as far from a Parliament as when you left me.*"

Yes. Quite as far from a Parliament. The sea contribution that he spoke of as so surely settled was the ship-money. How soon it would have been followed by a *land* " contribution," but for the resistance already made, is pretty evident from the cool style of this letter. But for Hampden and his friends, we may be quite sure the King's resolution not to meddle with land armies would have been rather less decisive.

Lord Wentworth was dismayed at the news. War with Spain he had deprecated ever since his residence in Ireland. He had no confidence in the French. Their late behaviour about the pirates was quite enough to show how hollow must any profession of friendship be on their side. They were much more likely to draw the English into a trap or make a tool of them. Lord Wentworth was not alone in his distrust. Sir Henry Vane gave it as his opinion, that, 1637. " if the French join with us for the Palatinate and that Prince's restitution, we shall be engaged certainly into a war. But my opinion is that they will suddenly undertake the same with us by conjunction, but make peace by themselves, if they can attain it, and that this offer of ours will facilitate the same with the House of Austria, if it be not already done."

Added to this disbelief in the good faith of the French, was the general conviction of the inability of England to undertake her own part.

Lord Cottington wrote to Wentworth : " The common people in London and Madrid do believe the peace will break between the two crowns. What the league with France and some other things concerning the Prince Elector may unwittingly produce, no man knows, nor doth any man understand better than your lordship, how unfit we are yet for a war." The Earl of Northumberland, who held his office of admiral of the fleet much against his own will, on account of the bad pay and bad management alone, was still more displeased at the prospect.

" Anjicer," said he, " is lately come from my Lord of Leicester with propositions, as is conceived of much advantage for us, if we will yet enter into a league with France, to which the King is much more inclined since the coming home of my Lord Marshal,* who hath fully represented unto him the disrespect offered unto his Majesty by the House of Austria and the impro- bability of getting anything from them by treaty.

" The assistance of our ships, and some levies of men, are the demands of the French, for the which we

* The Earl of Arundel, who had been the ambassador.

 require the share of all their conquests, and that no peace may be assented unto by them, until the Prince Elector be restored to all his possessions and dignities.

"About this matter the Foreign Committee doth often attend the King, and, on our part, all things are almost absolutely resolved of.

"The general opinion is that we shall break with Spain.

"To speak freely to your lordship, although I look upon all these things but at a distance, yet I can perceive full of confusion, and those who are the principal managers of them do not well know how to form or digest designs of that nature.

"The Prince Elector seemed lately desirous to put himself into action, and was by some led on with a belief that if he would go to sea and undertake anything against the Spaniard, he might have many adventures with him and large contributions from the people of England. My Lord Craven, for a pattern, was to furnish the Elector with ten thousand pounds. But the backwardness of everybody else in following this example hath quite dashed those designs."

The following piece of intelligence is ever memorable as recording one of the greatest disgraces ever incurred by the English Bench :—

"For the better enabling his Majesty to perform these great undertakings, the judges have all of them (not one dissenting) sent this day unto the King their opinions of the legality of taking the shipping money. So, as now, those that are refractory will, by a legal proceeding, be brought to conformity."

It needed not these opinions to impress Lord Wentworth with the imminence of the danger of war under

1637

present circumstances. Besides the risks in other ways, there was one that touched him very nearly.

It was not possible that he should have bestowed such profound thought and labour on Ireland, and not feel a proportionate interest in his work. He was becoming attached to the country, and, notwithstanding his severity, had really her prosperity at heart. Anxiously he had sought to remove the obstacles likely to check her growth in the shape of the taxes on coal, cattle, and horses. He had fought several battles to prevent her from being pillaged of her revenue, and to apply it to her own good.

If, in the matter of the prohibition of the manufacture of wool, he had inflicted a heavy injury, it arose more from the ideas of the age he lived in than from any tyrannical intention. Free trade, and the right of every land to develop to the utmost every grain of its natural resources, was then a theory unknown. That it could be best for all in the end was undreamed of. Woollen cloth was the great English staple, and had Wentworth promoted its trade in Ireland, he would have been overwhelmed with outcries from home. And the compensation he made in etablishing the cultivation and manufacture of flax he believed to be an ample compensation. If needed, he would have prohibited flax in England as much as wool in Ireland, as an article of profit. Now, he thought each had her share.

As yet, the great scheme for victualling the Spanish navy was waiting fulfilment. Next to that of the flax, it was the best promise of wealth to Ireland; for, once established, it would never stop at the navy, but Spain

 would be the highway through which the productions
of Ireland would pass to the adjacent countries.

All this would be upset by a war. And the worst
of it was, this war was sure to be fruitless. Small was
the chance of the Elector ever regaining the throne of
his father. Everything was against him. His kingdom
was but a few years old, and his family had had no
time to root themselves into the hearts of the people
deep enough to draw forth that passionate loyalty that
at last becomes superstition, and will support the most
unbearable tyrants from no other cause than attachment to traditional usages. He himself had neither
money, talent, or bravery.

And in a renewal of the attempt that had so often
failed to accomplish this task, what precious progress
was to be sacrificed! Happily, the warnings of Wentworth were enough, seconded as they were by two
other circumstances.

One was that the reports of approaching war, at
once, put a stop to the profitable sale of the land in
Galway and other royal possessions in Ireland, touching the King in the most tender point. The other
was that the French themselves began to give proof
of the justice of Lord Wentworth's estimation of their
good faith. They delayed the signing of the treaty
on every pretext, till, at last, Charles himself lost confidence, and resolved to follow the advice of his wiser
minister, and Wentworth had the satisfaction to receive
not only an assurance from Mr. Secretary Coke that
there was to be no war with Spain, but the following
lines from the King himself :—

" I thank you for your considerations concerning

war and peace, but, by your favour, ye mistake the
question.

"For it is not whether I should declare a war to the House of Austria or not, but whether I shall join with France to demand of the House of Austria my nephew's restitution and state, being, as I judge, in a very good and ready way towards our own defence."

On again preventing the duty on coal Lord Wentworth thus expressed his pleasure :—

"It contents me much to hear that the coal business is settled without prejudice to this people. For I foresee the kingdom is growing apace, and a thousand pities it were by bringing new burthens upon them to discourage those that daily come over, and must (or nothing will) make it flourish. Especially when but by a short forbearance till they have taken a good and sound root, his Majesty may, at after, gather five times as much from them without doing any hurt, where a little pulled from them at first, breaks off their fruit in the very bud."

This last sentence is most painful as showing how the highest and best of the speaker's ambitions, that of making Ireland a prosperous and happy country, was poisoned by the same venom that entered all his other ideas—the thought of how the King should gather the fruit, not how he should cultivate it for the good of the country.

But he most carefully warned those who were waiting, that nothing must be expected till conformity of religion was established, or, at least, till the major part of the Irish were Protestants. And it is quite likely that seeing this to be impossible, at least, in his own day, that while it would not have been safe to

1637. declare the justice and necessity of applying the results of Irish industry to her own good, that he used this as an argument to gain the necessary time to develop her prosperity.

"The plantations," said he, "must take their full effects, and the nature of the people be wrought to delight themselves under the sweet and moderate government of the Crown, and so, by degrees, to study the good husbanding of their grounds, the beautifying their seats, and the procuring to themselves those accommodations and comforts of life, which might be as so many living pledges of their future obedience and fidelity. Whereas yet they have nothing to lose that with reason they can set their hearts upon."

The desperate illness of Captain Plumleigh, which had completely incapacitated him for his duties, added to the unfortunate mistake of Wandesforde, and the attack on Plymouth during the absence of the Lord-Deputy from Ireland, had thrown back matters greatly in St. George's Channel, and proved the need of un-remitting vigilance. The pirates were ever ready to take advantage of the least neglect, and the scandalous state of the English Channel, which allowed them to arrive freely enough so near to the better ruled waters, called for new care on the part of Wentworth.

Trade had greatly fallen back during his absence. The protection afforded to the Moorish pirates in the French ports, where they were said not only to be "nearly lodged," but to be "made much of," so frightened the merchants that trade threatened to sink back into its former state. Slavery was a still greater terror than robbery. The evil that had been put down in the shape of foreign privateers and pirates

personating them, seemed half replaced by the safe
lurking places afforded by the French.*

Wentworth begged the Lords of the Admiralty to hasten the guard-ships and also to add to their usual strength.

"It is," said he, " a most reproachful condition and horrid perspective from shore to see our people robbed and their bodies carried away for slaves, and their souls endangered under our beards, as it were, and we not able to deliver or help them; it being most certain that the ' Swallow ' and ' Whelp ' alone will not possibly be able to drive forth this *canaille* before us.

" My heart is so filled with disdain and detestation to apprehend this barbarous usage of his Majesty's subjects, as it hath awakened me to offer all the best means I can, in present, bethink myself of how these pilferies and ravishments may be prevented for this next year." †

Hitherto, after performing their summer work, the two vessels had been sent to England to winter, and thus were a constant source of anxiety to Wentworth as to the time and condition of their return ; the Admiralty at home being so wretchedly managed that most things emerged in a worse condition from the hands of the Lords.

But now it was arranged that, for the future, .the vessels should winter in the Irish ports. Directly this change was settled, Wentworth gave orders to have an inventory taken and a price set upon all the cordage, sails, anchors, and other stores in the naval magazines in England belonging to the coast-guard, in

* Letter of the Lord Deputy.   State Papers, Ireland, MS. (original).
† Letter of the Lord Deputy.   State Papers, Ireland, MS. (original).

order to see what he could furnish cheaper in Ireland, instead of sending home for all that was wanted.*

This was not to save expense alone, but to see whether these vessels might not be made to help in another design in addition to that of keeping the seas safe. This object was one ever present to the mind of Wentworth, and was never lost sight of in connection with his other plans, namely, to render Ireland as productive as possible, and make it profitable to others to encourage her productiveness. Only had this great and beneficent idea to yield when some counter-purpose crossed it, such as the fear of taking the wool trade from England, or of rendering Ireland so prosperous and powerful as no longer to need the sister country, whose affectionate caresses resembled rather the hugs of a bear than the embraces of generous kindness.

The following estimate, drawn up by Lord Wentworth, is very valuable, as showing the prices in that day. Hitherto, also, the men had cost 8*d.* a day for provisions :—

Estimate of the St. Patrick, *burden* 300 *tons, for eight months.*

	£	s.	d.
The ship, with her equipage, trimmed and fitted to sail at 100*l.* per month's charge	800	0	0
For the wages of 60 mariners, with the officers, at 20*s.* each man, one with another, 60*l.* per month	480	0	0
For the victualling of 60 mariners and 40 musketeers, at 6*d.* apiece, 75*l.* per month	600	0	0
For the gunners' store of powder and shot	100	0	0
	£1980	0	0

---

* Letter of the Lord-Deputy. State Papers, Ireland, MS.

Estimate of the smaller ship of sixty tons.

163.

	£	s.	d.
The ship, with her equipage, fitted to sail at 25*l.* the month, for eight months	200	0	0
For 30 mariners, with the officers, at 20*s.* apiece the month wages	240	0	0
For victualling of 30 mariners and 10 soldiers, at 6*d.* apiece per diem, being 30*l.* per month	240	0	0
For powder and shot	40	0	0
	£720	0	0

" So that the charge of the two ships for eight month's service amounteth unto the sum of £2700, allowing only 6*d.* per diem for each man's diet; and no pay for the musketeers in regard they are allowed his Majesty's pay in their several companies.

" Upon better advice, I find the lesser ship to be undermanned at twenty mariners. And therefore, it is thought fit to make them up thirty. And accordingly you will find the estimate to be rated.*

" WENTWORTH."

Not content with the improvements made, the Lords of the Admiralty expected more.

Formerly, when the coast-guard was a mere name, the same vessels that " protected " the shores of Ireland served also for the coasts washed by the Severn. And this was now required.

But Wentworth, at once, pronounced it impossible. First, he pointed out that when this was done, the cost of the vessels was defrayed by England. But now that Ireland paid it, it was not right she should include English expenses.

* State Papers, Charles I. Ireland, MS. (original).

1637.   Secondly, the trade then was so small, Dublin being
the only frequented port, that there was little to do,
even for a pirate. But, now, there was a harvest in
every haven to be watched over. Such an extent of
water could not be covered by the vigilance of a single
ship. It would be much better for the English vessels
which had so little to do to cruise from the Severn to
the Land's End.*

Another piece of old economy had again been at
work. The new sailors sent this year to Sir Beverly
Newcomen were of the old cheap, bad kind. He was
positively afraid to go to sea with them. Yet neither
he nor Wentworth had power to dismiss them, they
having been sent by the English Lords.

"It were not only a pity, but great shame," said
Wentworth, "to have the ship endangered for want of
able and good mariners." And he begged for a commission for Sir Beverly to press new men at Bristol,
where the best seamen were to be found in plenty.

Suddenly, a terrible and unexpected loss befel the
Lord Deputy and Ireland. Already, Captain Plumleigh had been taken from his work by hopeless
disease, and, too soon, the brave and good Sir Beverly
Newcomen was to follow.

On the 28th of April, by Lord Wentworth's request,
he had set sail for Waterford, in order to sound the
depths of the river, that he might be able to give his
opinion as to whether it would afford safe anchorage
for the two vessels during the winter. While engaged
in this work, the pinnace was suddenly seized by a gale
and overturned. Of sixteen on board, five only were
saved by a fishing-boat; the rest, including Sir Beverly,

* Letter of the Lord Deputy. State Papers, Ireland, MS. (original).

his only son, his lieutenant, and master carpenter, all went down. The whole sixteen were washed off by the same wave, after which, by that mournful fate that leaves the living to perish and saves the inanimate, the pinnace righted herself and was safely towed ashore.*

Lord Wentworth at once sent her to Bristol to refit and obtain a new captain.

But Sir Beverly was hard to replace.

"Indeed," said Wentworth, "this gentleman is generally lamented in this place, and his Majesty's service will, I fear, suffer awhile by his death. For he was, I am persuaded, the ablest seaman the king had on this coast, very hardy, but vigilant and well affected in the employment.

Besides, some years' experience will be required, I assure you, to make up such a man for the guard of this kingdom."

But Wentworth begged the Lords to send him, at least, an able man, and that at once. And also one who would reside in Ireland. It was miserable management when, according to previous usage, the public servants resided in one country while their work lay in another.

But good news arrived just now from the expedition to Sallee. Since its departure, both the English and Irish coasts had been safe from the Moorish pirates. By blockading their ports, Captain Rainsborough not only kept them from sallying forth, but there was every prospect of obtaining the liberty of the poor English and Irish captives who had been sold as slaves, and of restoring them to their homes.

---

* Letter of the Lord Deputy. State Papers, Ireland, MS. (original).

One great disappointment ensued. Hopes had been entertained of finding large quantities of saltpetre in Ireland. A patent had been granted and a company of men sent over to dig and manufacture it ; it was then to be forwarded to England to be made into gunpowder, for Lord Wentworth, not deeming it safe to manufacture that dangerous article in Ireland, had expressly warned the King to prohibit it. His warning proved needless, for, after a rigid search all over the kingdom, no saltpetre could be found, and the attempt was one of the few useless expenses incurred by the Lord Deputy.

But most other things prospered. The rumour of war had prevented the usual tenants from leasing the fishing of Deny, which had brought to the King a rent of £1000 a year. So Lord Wentworth at once set fishermen to work for the King, and with the result of 240 tons of salmon, which he sold at 15*l.* a ton, and calculated that when the cost of fishing, salting, packing, and casks was deducted, he should clear £1400 instead of the £1000 hitherto gained by letting. Enormous sums were also gained by the imposts on tobacco, wines, pipe-staves, and the licences of ale-houses, yarn, &c.

Exultingly he pointed to the results of his measures : " Howbeit, my Lords, the then justices, and with them this whole council, informed his Majesty, before my coming into this kingdom, it was impossible to improve his revenue here, save only by imposing twelve-pence a Sunday on the recusants ; yet all these particulars, leaving that penal duty untouched, make up the increase of threescore and ten thousand pounds by the year, whereof the better half is already actually settled. And most confident I am the rest will also be so shortly."

As he intended to take a short excursion into the country, before going, he held a review of half of the whole army, with the object of seeing the troops exercise in large bodies as well as in the private companies. Another reason was that the sight of so large a number of soldiers confirmed the feeling of security among the loyal, and overawed those inclined to rebel. Though satisfied on the whole with their progress, when he considered their condition on his first arrival, they were still below his standard. The revenue and the army were the two great objects of his care and pride.

" I will never rest," said he, " till, by God's help, the army contain as ready and well-armed men as shall be possible, and nothing be wanting unto them but only the experience of fights themselves, which yet I trust there will be no occasion to bring them unto."

With the officers formerly so wretchedly inefficient, and standing towards their regiments somewhat as the clergy did to their churches, he was now quite satisfied, pronouncing them a company of gallant gentlemen not inferior to any in other armies.

Indeed, his resolution to bring the whole army together, once every year, in Dublin, there, with his own eye, to take account of the manner in which both officers and men performed their duties, had a wonderful effect. Both were moved to do their best by that fear of punishment and hope of reward on which the Lord Deputy depended. Beneath his immediate eye none could think to pass unnoticed.

Nor were the men themselves the only objects of his care. He was most particular with regard to the horses, and hated nothing more than the sight of a scraggy, undersized, or timid animal in the regiment. He was at present very dissatisfied both with the horses and their training.

"The horses," he said, "must be of much greater value, and made bolder than now they are; an assurance which they can only be won unto by much labour and custom; yet, if they want it, shall sooner disorder themselves, than an army. A horse impatient of drum, colours, or fire being altogether in a manner unserviceable, and therefore, once made, there should be an order that no horseman should change or put away his horse without the licence of the general."

Next to his fear of the revenue being appropriated to English uses, was his dread of the army being lessened or removed. Indeed, the fruits of his labours were so tempting, that there was a constant danger of their being gathered by others. Hence, he was constantly obliged to sound the warning notes of poverty and peril in the ears of the King, and to keep him off the present by the hopes of future and greater gatherings. False economy he dreaded quite as much as extravagance. With the army, as with the revenue, he referred to the blessed time of conformity of religion as the only safe hour for reduction; "for, if ever it be resolved on sooner," he declared, "it would occasion mighty disorders and insolences in Ireland, and, consequently, great unquietness and charge to England." The greatest care was to be taken that the troops should, if possible, be British, but in any case Protestants. He absolutely distrusted the Roman

Catholics, and deemed it altogether unsafe to invest _ 1637. _
them with any responsible office; and this not at all
from bigotry, but because his own observation convinced him of its necessity. The Roman Catholics
owed allegiance to a foreign power hostile to England.
They were completely in the hands of the priests, who,
at the least sign of disobedience to their commands,
threatened them with excommunication, while the
boldest breach of the laws of their country met with
absolution and encouragement.

While Wentworth was guilty of the most despotic
acts to the wealthy, and, above all, to landowners,
there is ample evidence of his care for the prosperity
of the labouring classes.

His maxim was to pay well, exacting good work for
good pay. Both soldiers and sailors found the benefit,
not merely in the increase, but the punctuality of their
wages. The same system was carried out to all he
employed. "*Thorough*" was his maxim in work as
well as in politics. And not merely did he guard the
interests of the people by his care that the public
revenue raised by taxes, customs, &c., should not go to
England, but he applied the same arguments to the
rents arising from the Crown lands.

Thus the King, having yielded on the former point,
thought there could be no objection to receiving·the
rents of the lands of Londonderry, forfeited by the
poor Londoners.

But, at once, Wentworth sent over reasons against
this. He said he held it most prejudicial that these
rents should be paid into the English exchequer.

First, there was the great want of coin in Ireland;
secondly, to carry the rents over in money rather than

 goods would be to lose at least a hundred pounds out of every thousand in the customs; thirdly, it might be lost at sea or robbed by land,—in which case, it was gone for ever. If sent by letters of exchange, there would be a loss of twelvepence in the pound.

It would create the greatest discontent among the people to see the money raised in their country carried to England to be spent. They would say, as they had done formerly, that unless the expense was kept up to the income, they and their posterity should become beggars by the carrying away the coin into England.

Instead of this, Wentworth's plan was for the whole amount of the rents and profits derived from these lands to be spent in Ireland in paying the King's creditors there, and in purchasing such commodities as should benefit the people as well as the Crown. If these were then carried to England, they would, by means of the customs, still farther benefit the King.

This was always his policy. He never advocated the advantage to be all on one side. Thus, in his great scheme of carrying Irish goods to Spain, he proposed not to bring back the money in coin, but in the shape of such goods as should be profitable to the Spaniards to sell and the Irish to buy. And, always, by this plan there was the advantage of the customs for the King.

Charles appears to have been wonderfully tractable at this time. Though he said this question of the rents of Londonderry required consideration, yet he agreed to everything else named by Wentworth. The war was given up. He promised to leave the revenue

in Ireland, and also that he would listen to none of 1637.
the petitions for land there, with which he was constantly pestered.　He declared the army should in no
way be lessened.　Lord Wentworth was to have his
way about religion; and, in fine, nothing could exceed
his satisfaction and pleasure with the works of the
Lord Deputy.　It is wonderful how great an impression a few words of this kind from the King seemed to
make on Lord Wentworth.　Charles knew it, and made
them serve in place of more solid recompense.　At
present, therefore, all things seemed prospering.　The
revenue, the army, the plantations, all went on well.
New lands were gained for the Crown, under the Commission of disputed titles.　The nation at large, which
gained rather than lost by these forfeitures, seemed
contented, and Lord Wentworth found himself at
liberty to taste the autumn in a little country excursion.

CHAPTER III.

 An exquisite susceptibility to the effects of the air was as is, indeed, the case with all highly nervous constitutions, a marked characteristic of Lord Wentworth. It was unfortunate that his duties compelled him to a city life. In London, he had always felt the bad influence of the close-packed houses and population, which, if immeasurably smaller than at present, were yet still more deleterious, owing to the entire absence of all the sanitary arrangements which render a moderately well-ordered workhouse in our day, a much safer spot than a palace two hundred years ago. Dublin was, probably, not so bad as London ; at least, it seems to have been far less subject to the plague and similar diseases, but, still, to a delicate person it was not like the country.

Among the many most unjust reproaches that were cast on the Lord Deputy was that of his " building up to the sky."

He had found it necessary to provide himself with a retreat, where he could, from time to time, escape from Dublin by a short journey, and there recruit his exhausted frame by a purer atmosphere and a change of scene.

Travelling on business connected with the Crown lands, into the region of the Byrnes, he was astonished and delighted with the, to him, hitherto unknown beauty of the country.   He pronounced the mountain scenery to be the finest he had ever seen, while game of all kinds sported in the richest abundance.

At once, he gave orders to erect a hunting seat, surrounded with a park, where he might, at any time, run down for a few days.

In addition to this, he built, at the cost of £6000, a country palace at the Naas.   It was of immense extent, and altogether on a magnificent scale.   Though erected at his own expense, it would have been, as he himself avowed, a most ridiculous structure for the use merely of a private nobleman or gentleman.   But he had another object in view.   With the exception of the shattered old castle which, as we have seen, he was forced to repair to render it barely safe as a dwelling, there was no royal residence in Dublin, and none at all in the country.   It was needful that there should be one worthy the dignity of his office for the Lord Deputy (whoever he might be) and his family to use. He had undertaken to build this on such a scale as, should the King be satisfied with it, he could at any time purchase it at cost price ; if not, as Lord Wentworth said, he must be content to keep it himself and smart for his folly.   It was fitted up with state-rooms, and furnished royally, according to the magnificent taste of the owner, in accordance with the purpose for which it was intended.

Here, and at his own little dwelling in Wicklow, which cost no more than £1200, he by turns sought a little repose. He well knew how it was grudged him.

"But," said he, "gnash the teeth of these gallants never so hard, I will, by God's leave, go on with it, that so I may have a place to take my recreation for a month or two in a year, were it for no other reason than to displease them, by keeping myself, if so please God, a little longer in health."

These short intervals, interrupted, as even they were, by State affairs, were yet the only pleasures of his life. Here, as he expressed it, he used to play the Robin Hood. Here, in the country of mountains and woods, he hunted and chased all the outlying deer he could light upon, and heartily did he enjoy the sport, notwithstanding the opposition of myriads of tiny enemies in the shape of midges, who bit him till he was disfigured for a week at a time. Often, he laughingly declared, did these little wretches, younger brothers to the mosquitoes of the Indies, tempt him to play the shrew soundly, and scratch his face in six or seven places, to gain relief from their venomous bites.

Fishing, also, was a favourite amusement, and he seems to have been as well acquainted with the best methods of preserving and cooking the spoils of the chase and the waters as any professional artist.

From the country he dashed off the following sprightly letters to Lady Wentworth, repeating his delight in the beauty of the scenery that greeted him on his tour.

It is a great pity we have none of the letters to the children so frequently alluded to.

*Lord Wentworth to his Wife.**   1637

" SWEET HEART,

" We are thus far gotten in health, God be praised, thereon the best country, indeed, I have ever seen since my coming into Ireland. Yet, am I not so much taken with it as that I could not be content already to be with you at Dublin. For Will, his coming to Cork, I leave it to yourself; but, in my opinion, it would be over troublesome and toilsome a journey for him, so I rather wish he might meet us at the Naas. Commend me to Nan and Arabella, and tell them I wish them some of the good plums we meet with here, and some of the partridge we kill in abundance with our hawks every day.

" And so I will bid you good night after that I have told you that I am very perfectly.

" Your truly loving husband,

" WENTWORTH.

"CLONMEL, *this* 13 *of August,* 1637."

Lord Wentworth to his Wife.†

" SWEET HEART,

" We have despatched all our business very happily, and after a noble entertainment we had from my Lord of Ormond at Carrick, are this morning going towards Limerick. I had the grace to remember your service to my Lady of Ormond, but, in truth, had not the memory or my wits about me so far as to remember

---

* Lord Houghton's Collection, p. 19.
† Lord Houghton's Collection, p. 20.

 it to the rest, for which I humbly beg your pardon. For, albeit, the first is more than I had in charge from you, yet out of good congruity and implicit complacency to what I might judge to be your will, I ought to have done the one as well as the other. Yet to obtain your remission I must tell you some news fit and reasonable for ladies. My Lady of Ormond is not so inclined to be fat as we thought she was at Dublin. My Lady MacCarthy, to my eye, improves not in her beauty. My Lady, sister to Castlehaven, if she be not the handsomest of the company, her ladyship is much mistaken; yet be it spoken to you in private without profanation, nevertheless, to her beauty, my Lord of Ormond's younger sister seems to me much the handsomer; only if I were of her counsel, I should desire her to beware lest she grew fat too soon.

"My Lady Thurles hath the mien of a lady of wit and spirit. So you have all I have to trouble you with, so as you have no more to do but to give my title the reading—

"Your very loving husband,

"WENTWORTH.

"I beseech you pardon me, for in truth I was so blockish and amazed in good company as I am able to give you no relation of what they were or how they were dressed.

"CLONMEL, *this Friday*, 1637."

*Lord Wentworth to his Wife.**

" SWEET HEART,

" Thus far we are got forwards from you, or rather backwards towards you, for now, the further we go, the nearer we are our return.

" I have not seen anything so noble since my coming into this kingdom as is this place. And a very fine, sweet country all along. Here, the town hath entertained us with the force of oratory and the fury of poetry, and rather taught me what I should be, than told me what I am. And yet, for all this, I find not myself the prouder, nor out of love so with my own, but that I desire to be back to see my house at the Naas, and after, as fast as I can, to Dublin, when I shall begin again, and so to the end constantly go on in the resolution of my being

" Your loving husband,

" WENTWORTH.

" KILKENNY, *this 16th of August,* 163 7.' '

Lord Wentworth to his Wife.†

" SWEET HEART,

" Through foul weather and ways we draw nearer you, and this day are for Cork, where I purpose, if the weather serve, to stay till Saturday, come seven-night; then to the Naas, where, having stayed a few days to order my business, then I am, God willing, for Dublin.

* Lord Houghton's Collection, p. 21.
† Lord Houghton's Collection, p. 22.

1637.   " We are all in good health ; only left James drunk
at Kilkenny, and have here Captain Southworth with
only half-a-crown in his purse, which makes him something grave ; and that the more that, unless it fall to
my share, not one man of the company will lend him
a crown.

" If this week have been as foul with you as with
us, I am persuaded you will be soundly weary of your
Connaught journey, and then you will see I am good
in the perspectives as well as in the prognostics ; for,
according to my confidence, against all other men's
opinions, Sir Thomas Wayman, we hear recovers.

" Little have I more to say, but that which, in deed,
is a very great deal, so with that, in full truth and
purpose, I am to continue always

" Your loving husband,

" WENTWORTH.

"CASTLEHAUGH, *this Friday morning.*"

Lord Wentworth to his Wife.[*]

" SWEET HEART,

" I shall desire you not to come hither at this
time. For being wrangling and busy with my work-
men, I am extreme ill women's company. But when
the house is ready to receive you I shall in no place see
you more gladly. Besides, those hoyting journeys back-
ward and forward, of all things I love not; they are good
for nothing but to disorder companies and spoil houses,
and therefore I pray you let us have as few of them as

* Lord Houghton's Collection, p. 23.

may be. My business here dispatched, I will come with all speed to you; nor shall you need to meet me on the way, being to come into town with much company, and the sword before me. In which case you will find the Deputy's wife never came; nor, indeed, decently can in her coach without being either sooner or later than were fit.

"I am glad Nan is so well, and conditionally that I may have the happiness to find you both so, I will dispense with your meeting of me no sooner than in the presence chamber, where, as in all other rooms, you shall undoubtedly find me,

" Your loving husband,

" WENTWORTH.

" NAAS, *this 12th of September*, 1637.

"Pray you remember my service to my sister Dillon, and, by your next, let me hear how she doth."

To his sister, the Honourable Mrs. Dillon, who was in delicate health, he frequently wrote, and we have her acknowledgment of his " lines so full of nobleness and affection." *

Poor little " Mrs. Ann " seems to have inherited the weak constitution of her parents, for we often find allusions to her ill health in the various letters. Thus Mrs. Dillon regrets she cannot "go to wait on her," and "trusts in God she mends."

There was also another person, at least, as much if

---

* Letter to the Lord Deputy, 2, 103.

not more interested in these expeditions than the chief himself. And that was the Archbishop of Canterbury who seems to have borne a strong resemblance to the abbots of old in other matters besides Ritualism. What these matters were the following extracts from the epistles of the Right Reverend Father to Lord Wentworth will show :—

"I find by your letters, as I said, you are gone on hunting. I hope you will find a time to go on fishing too. For I mean to be a very bold beggar, and desire you to send me some more of the dried fish (I do not know what you call it) which you sent me the last year. It was the best that ever I spent.

"And now you cannot say but I give you warning enough. If it prove not too much, 'tis well. For I doubt you will go near to hunt it out of your memory, and then think to stop my mouth with some of your hung beef out of Yorkshire, which, to your skill and commendation be it spoken, was the worst that ever I tasted, and as hard as the very horn the old runt wore when she lived. Nor would I have you think that I go against any old proverb in this. For 'tis one thing for a man not to look a gift horse in the mouth and another how gift beef relishes in one's own mouth.*

"But since you are for both occupations, fish and flesh, I wonder you do not think of powdering or drying some of your Irish venison, and send that over, to brag, too."

Laud seems to have felt a profound affection for all species of fish. Thus again he writes :—

Laud was fond of a pointless jest.

" Your Ulster eels are the fattest and fairest I ever saw, and 'tis a thousand pities there should be any error in their salting, or anything else about them. For how the carriage should hurt them I do not see, considering that other salted eels are brought as far and retain their goodness. But the dried fish was exceedingly good."

Again. "'Tis well that your hunting hath not made you forget your fishing, but I sometimes fear if it be yet to come from Galway, it will hardly get hither by Lent. And it is the best Lent provision that ever I met with, next to old Sir John Ling.

" As for venison, if you have any purpose to salt that the next year, your philosophy is very good. It will not take salt if it be heated, and therefore if you do make danger in the English-Dutch sense of *periculum facere*, you must do it upon such venison as is shot dead in the place, otherwise, all, both labour and charge, are lost."

No one would think any the worse of the writer for heartily enjoying a good dinner; on the contrary, there is a good-humoured tone about these anxieties with regard to the creature comforts that would, alone, be rather harmlessly contagious than otherwise.

But when we find, in the same letter, side by side with the gloating description of the fat Ulster eels, the following complaint, that too much mercy was shown to the wretched victims of the hangman's shears, then the whole becomes inexpressibly brutal and revolting, and Laud stands forth in all the coarseness of his cruelty.

" But what say you to it, that Prynne and his fellows should be suffered to talk what they pleased

1637.   while they stood in the pillory, and win acclamations from the people, and have notes taken of what they spake, and those notes spread in written copies about the city, and that when they went out of doors to their several imprisonments, there were thousands suffered to be upon the way to take their leave, and God knows what else ? "

Little did Laud dream that his own notes on this event would be also " spread in written copies," and altogether to the honour of the English poor, who never showed themselves in so bright a light as on this occasion.

Just at this period, he was much annoyed by the reports circulated that he and Lord Wentworth had quarrelled, and that the latter had greatly diminished in his esteem for him. It was certainly a pure invention. No quarrel had ever taken place, and Wentworth hastened to assure him of his " love and service," which he declared he should carry with him to the grave.

Laud was so much consoled and so grateful for this assurance, that for the moment it subdued even his bigotry with regard to Ireland, and he expressed his conviction that it *was* a pity that a constant forbearance should not be shown there, so that the English might be induced to settle; and he voluntarily promised Wentworth to promote his wishes with the Irish committee in every way in his power.

No sooner had Lord Wentworth returned to Dublin, than the slight improvement in his health disappeared, and the gout seized him with its former malice. As he painfully expressed it, while it made him able to do less, it gave him time to think more. To his ghostly father he complained that his enemies were trying to make the

King believe that he was making too much money 1637.
for himself, and had two or three and twenty thousand pounds a year coming in. As he justly said,
there was no crime in the bare fact, even were it
double as much. He had six thousand a year of his
patrimonial property in land, a share for a short time
in the farm of the customs, which he acknowledged had
proved to him a greater profit than ever he had
dreamed of. But then, as the enormous rise in the
customs was owing to his own good management alone,
this profit was merely a necessary consequence. It
would have accrued to any other farmer, but as he
was the means of the increase of over twenty thousand
pounds a year, he surely had a greater right to the
farm than a mere stranger. This was all he had in
addition to the same salary and privileges accorded to
his predecessors in office, while, on the other hand, his
expenses were far greater than theirs. His horse
troop alone consisted of a hundred, where previous
deputies were content with forty; and while they were
enabled to save five hundred a year out of the pay
allowed, he was forced to spend out of his own pocket
several thousands more than he received.

Another charge was the immense amount of land
he was buying constantly in Ireland. Here, he acknowledged that appearances were against him. On
his own account, he had not invested more than
thirteen or fourteen thousand pounds in land, but he
had been seeking good purchase both for the King
and Lady Carlisle, and his enemies at once concluding
it to be all for himself, had raised an outcry accordingly. So far from giving the King any real cause
of jealousy, he had closed his eyes to bargains that

1637. would have been most profitable, and which he would fully have been justified in securing for himself, in order to save them for the King : one, especially, which costing fifteen thousand pounds only, he calculated to bring in two thousand five hundred pounds a year, and double as much when the present leases were expired. " Let them," he cried, " set beside me, first, *one of themselves* that hath turned from himself to the advantage of the Crown a bargain of so mighty a profit, which honourably and justly he might have brought to the help of his own private fortune, as I might have done this, and then, at after, let them burthen me with my greediness of purchasing.

" In the mean space, let them for shame hold their tongues, however the malignity of their eye pursue me still. I am content; if I grow not the richer, I trust to grow the better, living thus under their discipline."

Then came the general charge of about as much value as general and vague charges usually are.

The King was told that the Deputy grew " monstrous rich."

But said Wentworth most justly in answer :—

" Have I in the least falsified or neglected the trusts of my most gracious master ?

" Have I corruptly or oppressively taken from his people ?

" Have I been a burden to his coffers more than for those his princely entertainments * which others have before had, and others must again have after me in these places ?

---

* " Entertainment," like many a word still in common use, had then a different meaning. It signified salary, or payment for work. Thus the " entertainment " of a soldier, &c., was his pay.

"Have I lived meanly, below that which I owe to the honour of his Majesty and dignity of the place I exercise?

"If so, let them show wherein. I defy them, every mother's son."

None of these things had been done. Those who accused him—according to the invariable method of cowardly slanderers, whose object is not to set right a public or private abuse, but to injure or ruin another—took care to avoid all hint of an impartial and minute investigation. Knowing that money was the weakest side of the King, they hoped, by persuading him that Wentworth was in reality making the royal interests subservient to his own, to deprive him of the credit of so largely increasing the revenue. As the thought came over the Deputy of how much he had sacrificed, how he had suffered and was suffering in his health, how dimness of sight threatening blindness had arisen from his care in writing long despatches by night in order to preserve the King's secrets from other eyes—how he had made this very matter of money, in which he was now accused of selfishness, the first object for the good of the King, his indignation rose to its height—indignation mingled with grief.

"Alas!" he cried, "if his Majesty have any suspicion I am not to his service as I ought; let there be commissaries of honour and wisdom set upon me, let them publicly examine all I have done, let me be heard, and after covered with shame if I have deserved it!"

Most touching is what follows, and most just, had his estimation of Charles been the true one—could he only safely have rested his conscience in the honour and judgment of the King. But who can do that with another? What mortal is high enough for us to cast all our cares, all our responsibilities upon him?

"I am none of those insolent servants," said Lord Wentworth, "that shall strictly call upon myself my master's justice without any grain of his favour. To him with all reverence and humility, I seek for his remission, his compassion of all my defects, all my infirmities, in the pursuit, in the fulfilling of his good pleasures, the rather in regard of the uprightness, however, of my heart to his person, to his affairs.

"But," he added, with a burst of passion, "I will break to fitters, die before I take from any so affected towards me, a better being, nay, indeed any being at all!"

"Well, then," he continues, in bitter soliloquy, "thus I am become rich, able, I hope, in some reasonable time, I praise God and his Majesty, to pay every man his own.

"Was I not, in some measure, so before I had the honour to serve his Majesty? Or shall that be a crime in me which they so heartily desire themselves—nay, perchance, in their grudging souls, lay it already as a great and grievous fault upon his Majesty, that he hath not made them so likewise!

"Or can it be any other than pleasing to any gracious, noble, or generous master that his honest and faithful servant grows rich under him?

"I confess, I am so great lover myself to have my servants thrive, as I believe all others like minded." This was quite true. Lord Wentworth was a good and generous master—not one of those who indulge idleness and negligence by allowing work to be ill done. He exacted the full measure of service; he returned the full amount of reward, and always showed an appreciation of faithfulness, and took a personal interest in the welfare of his dependents, that greatly endeared him to them. So far from showing any mean jealousy, he was always ready to aid them in any good plan for their prosperity.

He declared that up to the present time he had only increased his original estate by thirteen thousand pounds. Certainly, not an unreasonable addition, when his capital, his wonderful talent for improvement, and the just and fair opportunities of his position are considered. Indeed, setting aside the last, there is little doubt that as a private gentleman at full liberty he would, as he declared, have been able to have " put more crowns into his purse at the year's end than at present."

No doubt the severe pain of the gout helped to sharpen his mental sufferings. Certain it is that the intelligence of the intrigues that were going on in England to shake the confidence of the King, had a miserable effect upon him. It was in vain he wrestled with his spirit and tried to be calm. He found it impossible.

" How to digest this, how to turn it to good nourishment, to my health; this," mourned he, " is the difficulty. The humour which offends me is not so much anger as scorn and desire to wrest out from amongst them my charge. For, as they say, if I might come to fight for my life, it would never trouble me, indeed I should then weigh them all very light, and be safe under the goodness, wisdom, and justice of my master."

" Again," he sadly murmurs, " howbeit I am resolved of the truth of all this, yet to accuse myself is very uncomely. I love not to put on my armour before there be cause, in regard I never do so but I find myself the wearier, and sorer for it the next morning."

Profoundly tragical is the condition of feeling here revealed. Many an innocent sufferer will here behold reflected the struggles through which he has passed. How many have been the victims of slander either utterly false, or, a thousand times more villainous, based on some distorted fact—who are made to feel that the strong, unscrupulous enemy is retailing his falsehoods in all directions, in the ears of those who perhaps for years have professed friendship, and of others whose esteem they value and merit, who, probably, if they knew the real truth, would spring with horror from the liar to the side of the injured. But no public accusation is made, no chance is given to disprove. The victim, uncalled for, feels it impossible to volunteer the proof of his innocence, and has silently and without the power of defence to rest under the knowledge that everywhere the poison is being scattered. For the reticence by which he is bound is not needed by the destroyer. The same auditors who would stare amazed at an unasked defence, complacently receive an accusation. And not one in ten thousand, even of professed friends, while unhesitatingly retailing the evil word, have the bare justice to go straight to the absent and ask the truth.

And this was what Lord Wentworth felt. He knew that the false charge was being uttered, not only to his friends, but to the King. But not one, not

even the King, had either driven away the accusers
with scorn and disbelief—or demanded a full explanation, that Wentworth might clear his name. No.
They had all listened and talked, and had he remonstrated, would perhaps have answered: " We did not
believe it "—but of that he was not sure.

The silence of Charles was the worst ; and more
than ever did his faithful minister feel the withholding of that public recognition of his worth, which
would have crushed all slander to the ground.

Laud, with all his faults, was a true friend, and to
him it was that Wentworth, sick in soul and body,
turned for the sympathy his heart craved.

" Therefore," he said, " altogether to seek in myself
what to do, I have here opened my grief, and do
most humbly beseech of your advice and counsel what
were best to be done."

If, there be one thing pre-eminently pathetic
among the myriad sorrows of human life, is it
not the weakness of the strong, the humility of the
proud ?

Can it, indeed, be the haughty Deputy who says:
" Indeed, my lord, you know that I have not had anything of late from his Majesty which might give a
public testimony that I am graciously accepted in this
employment (albeit, private ones I humbly thank his
Majesty I have), which, in good faith, I think is one
occasion which emboldens them thus to fall upon
me.

" And I wish, through the opinion that I stand not
full to his Majesty's liking in my service in this
place, his Majesty's affairs may not suffer as well as
myself. But fall that as it may, I am resolved never

to stir that stone more. Dead to me it is to be for ever. Indeed I neither think of it, nor look for it.

" I have had a sharp fit of this. So soon as I am able, I will answer your last letters, but indeed I am at present weak and extreme weary with what I have done already." *

Weak, weary, overladen with work, saddened with slanders, in addition to merited rebukes, he failed to ask why should the King balk his own clever plan for putting the odium of royal breaches of faith and other wrongs on his minister, by giving public proof of his approbation of him? On the contrary, it would be reversing his own policy.

But Laud did his best for his friend, though not quite in the wisest manner, as he incautiously named matters better in every way to have left out. He read the whole of Wentworth's complaints of his enemies' charges, to which the King, as usual, replied in the cheap way of a few words of praise. Thus, knowing it would be repeated, he told Laud that Wentworth was a brave servant in his place. He approved the offer to sell him the new palace, but took care to give no decisive answer. He said he was satisfied with Wentworth's service, advised him to treat all *false* reports with contempt, to remember his own metaphor, and not to weary himself with putting on his armour till worse charges were made against him than had ever been yet, which he was confident would not happen. He denied that he had listened to the revilers, who, however, told a very different tale. As to Wentworth's private income, it mattered nothing to him how

---

* The Lord Deputy to the Archbishop of Canterbury, 2, 109.

rich so good a servant became, so long as it was not
taken wrongfully either from himself or his people.
Only when Laud let out that the Deputy had made
much more than he ever expected from the farm of
the customs, the King's tone changed to one of grudging impatience, and he said: "But he doth not tell
you how much," which at once led Laud to fear the
effects enough to remind Charles that he had formally
granted the farm to Wentworth and Radcliffe, and how
well they deserved it. And though the King hastily
assented with a " Yea, God forbid else," still his tone
so belied his words, that Laud thought it needful to
put his friend on his guard, and to warn him that there
had lately been some mutterings about these same
customs at Court, and that it was to be feared some
new applicant was nibbling at them.

The resolution to apply no more for a title or any
public recognition of his services by the King was
highly approved of by Laud. He said he was sure
that it would come in the end, but it was better to
leave the King to his own time. He could not understand that it was not at all as a gew-gaw, but as a
protection under so many heavy responsibilities, that
Wentworth desired it.

He also strongly advised him to adhere to his determination that whatever his enemies might say in
secret, by no means to defend himself or take any
notice till they spoke openly. He also counselled him
to thank the King for his present gracious messages,
and to ask his Majesty to let him know if any more
charges were brought against him, and call him to
account, so that he might thereby have a chance to
speak for himself.

1637.

Laud always gave him honest replies to his applications for advice in difficulty, never flattering him by words likely to please and yet injure. In the present case, he concluded his rather painful confirmations of Wentworth's unwilling submissions by saying, very truly :—

" You have made me bold to give you counsel, and so I challenge from you that you pardon all defects in it. And where you find it weak, as I doubt 'tis all along, that you forget not it proceeds from a faithful heart, though an understanding of no great reach." *

The Lord Deputy's spirits were now probably a little revived by the first earnest of success in his flax speculation, which, however, none besides himself appear to have worthily appreciated.

He despatched his first cargo to Spain. It was indeed an object that well merited his self congratulation. He had sown the seed, erected the looms, and now laden a ship with the perfect linen. With it he sent a letter to the Duke of Sidonia, informing him that this was his own private design at present, but that he hoped hereafter to extend it into a national interest. He had taken especial care that this first export should be of first-rate quality, and he hoped to leave behind him, in a prosperous linen trade, a monument of the honour and good affection he always professed to the Spanish nation.

As far as the return of these feelings went, he obtained but little gratitude at the hands of the Spanish. The miserable intrigues of the Roman Catholics in

---

* The Archbishop of Canterbury to the Lord Deputy, 2, 127.

Ireland were an incessant source of anxiety to him.
Nothing could be worse than the continued behaviour
of the Irish priests and their ingratitude to the Lord
Deputy.

Most truly could he say that since he had held office
in Ireland, not the hair of any man's head had been
touched for the free exercise of his conscience, nor
was there any difference made between Protestants
and Catholics in the administration of civil justice.
All that was required of them was equal obedience to
the laws. It has also been amply shown how much
care the Lord Deputy had taken to protect their
liberty, and how many a battle had been fought by
himself alone in their favour.

The return made by the priests was to attempt, by
every means in their power, to incite an insurrection in
Ireland, and to cause war between England and Spain,
by obtaining the help of the latter. Bitterly disappointed at the staving off of the, by them, hoped-for
war made by the King of England, and of which they
trusted to take a bloody advantage, these men, professed servants of the Prince of Peace, tried to bring
it about by other means.

"There is," said Lord Wentworth, alluding to these
priests, "a nation of the Irish the whilst that wander
abroad, most of them criminous, that forth of an unjust
yet habitual hatred to the English Government, delight
to have it believed and themselves pitied, as persecuted
forth of their country and ravished of their means, for
their religion only ; stirring and inciting all they can to
blood and rebellion, and keeping themselves in countenance by taking upon themselves to be Grand
Seigniors, and boasting and entitling themselves to

1637.

great dignities, and territories whose very names were scarcely heard of by their indigent parents." *

At the head of these men was the Archbishop of Cashel, who, with an income of £2000 a year, was said to be a pensioner of Spain. He with his agents abroad were constantly at work to incite the Pope and the King of Spain to restore the Roman Catholic religion as the state religion of Ireland. They were said to have declared, that if Spain would furnish them with arms for twelve thousand men, all the rest they would be able to do themselves. Their landing place was to be near Coleraine or Derry.

Though Lord Wentworth had no doubt of frustrating their plans by prompt and stern measures, "Yet," said he, "by my faith, this danger not timely and well prevented, may, I assure you, put the Crown of England to much trouble and mighty charge." The danger was fortunately conquered for the present by the vigilant watchfulness of the Lord Deputy, and his careful management of the foreign ambassadors.

But a new trouble arose in England.

In two points especially, the King and Lord Wentworth differed. Whenever the first found the people generous and yielding, it was his invariable rule to press and wring them to the utmost, treating them as if both their pockets and their patience were inexhaustible. Lord Wentworth, on the contrary, esteemed nothing more dangerous than this abuse of a conciliatory spirit. Where opposition was shown to his first demands, none could be more quick to exact both obedience and punishment for rebellion or refusal, as

---

* Letter of the Lord Deputy to M. Con, 2, 112.

in the case of the jury of Galway. But when his wishes were readily met, he always advocated forbearance, and dwelt on the need of keeping good faith to those who relied on his promises. While the illegal demand for ship money had been refused in various places, the northern counties under his presidency had complied to the utmost. Their reward, therefore, was to be called on to pay in addition certain levies which were due in other places. The North Riding of Yorkshire especially was ordered to pay a contribution for the carriage of ship timber within the bishopric of Durham.

At this even Wentworth stopped, startled at the endless prospect of taxes, which, as a rich native of Yorkshire, would fall heavily on himself.

At once he addressed a remonstrance to the Privy Council of England. He said, indeed that the sum demanded was not much, it was therefore not on account of the amount, but of the precedent such a payment would afford to the future, that he protested. He pointed out that Yorkshire having never received any help or advantage from the bishopric of Durham, it was most unreasonable that she should be called on to pay an imaginary obligation which Durham could well afford herself. When a palace was built for the King at York, the county unaided had to give no less than £12000 all at once for the expenses of the carriage of materials of wood, stone, and lime for the building. She never dreamed of calling on other counties to help pay for what took place entirely within her own domain. Why, then, should these other counties not do the same? There was not only no precedent for this demand, but no need for it: the

1637.   sum was quite inconsiderable and the bishopric able easily to pay it.

Moreover, it was peculiarly hard, seeing how prompt Yorkshire had been in complying with all previous orders. That every year, in obedience to the English Council, she had levied between five and six hundred pounds, in order to refurnish the magazines with powder and shot, and although this largely contributed to the defence of the neighbouring counties, they were not called upon to give a shilling. Then, with what cheerfulness and readiness had the call for ship money been answered. As much as were equal to six subsidies had been given in a single sum and had been one of the first payments. (Wentworth here spoke of Yorkshire alone—some demurring having been made in the other parts of his presidency.)

He, therefore, did most earnestly desire that the Council would countermand the order they had given, which, he again repeated, was dreaded, not on account of the amount, but as affording so perilous a precedent for the future.*

Nothing could be more just and clear than this. But what is still more worthy of notice is the exact parallel it presents with the objections formed by Hampden with regard to the ship money. Both were taxes illegally levied. Both were protested against on that very ground. It is difficult indeed to understand how the author of such words, so strongly expressed, could see any harm in the same thing in another. Only in the miserable inconsistency of human nature is the cause to be sought.

* The Lord Deputy to the English Council, 2. 110.

Laud had written to his friend that Hampden's case
was now before the court—adding that it was the
most important news of the day. It was to this that
Wentworth made his celebrated reply—one that has
perhaps done him more damage in the eyes of posterity
than any other of all the reckless utterances to be
found in a correspondence, which, had the writer ever
dreamed that it would be published to the world,
would have been more cautiously worded.

"Mr. Hampden," said Wentworth, "is a great
Brother (Puritan), and the very genius of that nation
of people leads them always to oppose, as well civilly
as ecclesiastically, all that ever authority ordains for
them. But in good faith, were they right served,
they should be whipt home into their right wits, and
much beholden they should be to any that would
thoroughly take pains with them in that kind."

And again—

"In truth I still wish (and take it also to be a very
charitable one) Mr. Hampden, and others to his like-
ness, were well whipt into their right senses. If that
rod be so used that it smarts not, I am the more
sorry."

After a low and ribald jest, he continues :—

"As well as I think of Mr. Hampden's abilities, I
take his will and peevishness to be full as great ; and
without diminution to him, judge the other, howbeit
not the Father of the Country (a title some will not
stick to give unto them both,* to put them, if it be
possible, the faster and farther out of their wits)."

We have here a striking illustration of the singular

* Wentworth here alluded to one of Hampden's fellow-sufferers in
the fines for ship money.

1637. deficiency in Lord Wentworth's great intellect that has already been alluded to, viz., his inability to comprehend the nature and disposition of others.

We have the description of Hampden, not only in the acts of his life, his own letters, and the words of his friends. But even his foes have added their testimony that, if ever there existed a man to whom the charges of self-will and peevishness were inapplicable, absolutely ridiculous in their application, it was John Hampden.

Long since have his claims to the possession of a " flowing courtesy to all men," a remarkable calmness and sweetness of temper, been conceded to him on all sides. Indeed, with a most happy natural temperament, with good health, with perfect domestic happiness, and the highest and safest condition of worldly prosperity—that of a rich country gentleman living on a large and beautiful estate of his own—it would be a miracle, indeed, if he had been peevish.

And it is the most profound testimony to his exalted worth, that he was willing to sacrifice this most happy life, rather than quietly to rest in that selfish enjoyment miscalled peace, that—safe itself—turns a deaf ear to the wrongs of others. A more beautiful example of the truth that they who are the most ready to sacrifice their own happiness for the welfare of others are in every way the most worthy of it, has never yet been witnessed than that given by Hampden.

Such a nature as his was peculiarly incomprehensible to the unhappy Wentworth, who was capable of quite as great sacrifice in a cause that he prized, and had virtues of his own which cannot be too highly rated. He had also obstacles in his path from which Hamp-

den was joyfully free.   The incessant anguish inflicted   1637.
on him by his bodily diseases, increased by a naturally
fervent and excitable temperament, kept him in a constant fever that rendered calmness, such as was the
natural heritage of Hampden, impossible, even with
the best and most persevering efforts on his own part.
Then the amount of unnatural overwork of the hardest
kind to perform would have weighed down even a
healthy man.   The ceaseless anxiety attendant on such
tremendous responsibility would have saddened and
rendered irritable at times the most cheerful.   And
the want of appreciation and affection in the man to
whom he had devoted all things—pledged all things,
must of necessity have produced a restlessness and
gloom in proportion to the depth of his feelings ; while
the complete ingratitude with which his best attempts
and those most honestly made were received by the
people who reaped the benefit, could not have failed to
generate a bitterness in the sweetest nature.

Often has the contrast been drawn between Hampden and Wentworth, invariably to the glory of the first
and the shame of the second.

But Hampden himself would have been the very
first to see the utter impropriety and injustice of con-
trasting them and judging one by the other, from
no better ground than that both went into Parliament
at the same time and with the same opinions.   ·

Supposing both to have been exactly equal in all
the highest moral and religious principles that gave
the law to Hampden's life, and all the other differences
to have remained, still must they have been as far
apart, as different in results at the end of life, as beings
of two opposite species.   Hampden in Wentworth's

1637.   position, with Wentworth's trials, would have left as different an image from his present one to posterity, as Wentworth, in the position of the great patriot, has done in his own allotted sphere.

Nothing is more common in criticism than to reverse the appointed paths of men, and glibly to point out how such a one would have acted in such a place. But true, to a certain degree, of common minds, how ineffably more so of those great originals who have left their stamp on the sands of time is it, that each has its distinguishing character, which, however modified by circumstances, never can be exchanged with another. And the first great step to justice, from the lightest verbal comment to the sternest sentence of national law pronounced at the highest tribunal, is to weigh those surroundings which press on individual humanity on all sides, and from which it cannot escape. Only thus can real responsibility be truly measured—only by so doing can the critic and the judge escape the guilt of cruelty and wrong.

It is not for his passionate temper, for his gloom, his decision, his wealth, his magnificence, even his change of party in politics, that Lord Wentworth is to be condemned.

Neither is it for his sweet temper, courteous manners, preference of the cause of the people and clearness of vision, that Hampden is to be lauded. The great, the marvellous difference between these two great men rests on the same simple cause that in all ages has separated the few exceptional good from the mass of the world.

It is the difference in the height and innate power of their moral standard.

Lord Wentworth's conscience was scarcely worthy the name.

To Hampden, Conscience was the law of life. Were it not for the fact that in his youth and freshness he withstood the first trial, and really did undergo fine and imprisonment in the cause of right, it could scarcely be considered that Lord Wentworth had a conscience at all. At the most, all that can be said was that it was born, it lived a short and sickly youth, it flickered at last into an unnatural and deceptive, probably self-deceptive, brightness, and then sank down to rise no more. Henceforth there was no barrier to arrest the most unlawful trespass— no prop to support the most perilous weight of responsibility; and not, alas! what in happier destinies has occurred, a friendly grasp to seize and draw back into the right and narrow way. The intellect, bereft of its guard of honour, had to trust to its own strength for guidance, and though, by dint of its clearness of vision alone, it was able to distinguish much that was beautiful, good, and useful, its very length of range led it to fix its eyes on the distant treasures that a weaker sight could not reach, while it overlooked the mire of the road visible to humbler travellers.

But with Hampden, the very strongest and highest point in his character was this very virtue of Conscience. Like a Spirit of Good through life it preceded him, heralding the path lawful to be trodden. It grew with his growth, and however lofty his progress in mental graces, in this it was higher and more rapid still. Like a fair bow of promise, it spanned every action, shedding a celestial beauty on all below it.

It is remarkable that in Wentworth the highest time

1637. of his moral life, when he was really best, was the time of his youth.

With Hampden the same number of early years was the only period to which even the shadow of censure is applied. Up to the age of twenty-five there are hints of dissipation, thought venial enough in those days, but which he recognised as opposed to his higher nature, and from the age of twenty-five he refused to submit. It makes his character none the less noble and interesting to find that he had passed through the fire, that his virtue was not the imitative and negative kind that comes from the lack of temptation, but was the reward of successful struggles.

Hampden never could have been in the position of Wentworth, from this great feature of his character alone. He might as honestly have changed his opinions, and become even a superstitious loyalist. But nothing could have persuaded him that it was right to support a man in falsehood, cruelty, dishonesty, and perjury. He knew it his duty to support the right, to oppose the wrong. He knew that, without constant examination of the circumstances under which he was called to act, he could not judge between right and wrong. But his high standard of right and his clear intellect was a sure guide given to him for use, not rust. After the King, by his coronation oath, had sworn in the sight of God to govern only by the laws of the land, and received his crown on that condition alone, if one of these laws was that the people were only to be taxed by their own consent, and the King did tax them without their consent, it was useless to tell Hampden that was not perjury which it was a sin against God as well as man to support.

Patience and forgiveness were Christian virtues. 1637.
They were needed towards the King as well as towards
other men.

And most truly were they shown. Repeatedly had
the people forgiven his breach of promise. Again
and again had he obtained large sums of money by
solemnly declaring, " on the word of a King," that he
would raise money only by lawful means; that he
would not quarter the soldiers on the people ; that he
would consult his Parliaments. In every single instance he had, after obtaining the money, broken this
word, till, by the deliberate breach of the Petition of
Right, he had opened the eyes of the most blind, who
held it their duty to see. Not till every effort had
been exhausted, did Hampden give up efforts to reform
by peace. The wonder, indeed, is that it was left to
the King to begin the civil war. Nothing but the
universal ignorance of the people, and the absence of
newspapers—those greatest agents in the correction of
abuses—could have made them endure the long years
between the Parliaments of 1638 and 1660.

And again, it was conscience that made it impossible
for Hampden to look on unmoved at the poor, who
did the hard painful toil of their country, and, in return,
needed the protection of those who alone had time to
consider what was their rights. Helpless as children,
it was not for noble minds safe in their own wealth
and rank, to see them plundered of their little earnings
by the bare word of a King, and these very earnings
applied to maintain a brutal soldiery who should per-
petuate this horrid tyranny, and even press their own
children into the service of wickedness.

As to the tests of the Bible by which it has been

1637.

sought to uphold despotism, Hampden was a firm believer in the Bible, and there he read the duty of the King's councillors was not to support him in wrong, but boldly to tell him of his crimes. There was plenty of precedent there for the deposition of false kings— none whatever for the infallibility of a single one. There were the examples of men in power torturing the spiritual teachers who held it a crime to be silent in the presence of crime; but the rebukes he found to be administered to the torturers, not the sufferers. And so, setting aside his natural feelings of humanity, and looking simply at the Bible, which both King and people professed to take as their law, Hampden dared not rest while good men were hacked and seared in Cheapside simply for denouncing deeds which could logically, as well as morally, be proved to be vile in themselves and in deliberate disobedience to the authority they confessed.

Let the whole career of Hampden, from the age of manhood, be examined in this light, and its real greatness and glory will be found to consist in these:— That he took nothing for granted; he used his powers and the best materials he could find to discover what was right in all things, and, having obtained this standard, he did his utmost to act up to it, regardless of consequences, regardful only of what he professed to consider the law of God. Many a time he turned back from a road pleasant and prosperous to himself and others, because it would have involved a breach of this law to follow it. Often did he pursue a painful path, of which the end was hidden in clouds, simply because the voice within said, "Go."

Long and sadly must he have pondered and weighed

the results that might be possible before he took those steps that were to sever the past and future by the gulf into which, however, like the hero of old, he did not hesitate to spring when once it yawned before him.

A gentleman of noble lineage, educated in all the traditional reverence for royal authority that was so deeply stamped on the aristocracy of England, his loyal feelings were so well known that twice he had been considered as a fit representative of their expression. Once, when young, with Laud, to write the Latin ode congratulating the Elector Palatine on his marriage with the Princess Elizabeth ; and a second time when he was considered the fittest person to undertake the education of the Prince of Wales.

We cannot but imagine such an office held by Hampden under such a king as Alfred. How his whole heart would have gone out to that noble King, and how he would have striven with joyful enthusiasm to train up the heir in the steps of the father. The impulse to prayer, so characteristic of a " brother," sneered at by Wentworth, might then with heartfelt fervour have poured itself forth in the words of the most beautiful and sublime petition that ever portrayed a real king of the people, such a king as, after more than ten centuries, the English fondly revere in Alfred :—

"Give the king thy judgments, O God, and thy righteousness unto the king's son.

" He shall judge thy people with righteousness and thy poor with judgment.

" The mountains shall bring peace to the people and the little hills by righteousness.

"He shall judge the poor of the people, he shall save the children of the needy, and shall break in pieces the oppressor.

"They shall fear thee as long as the sun and moon endure, throughout all generations.

"He shall come down like rain upon the mown grass, as showers that water the earth.

"In his days shall the righteous flourish and abundance of peace as long as the moon endureth.

"For he shall deliver the needy when he crieth, the poor also and him that hath no helper.

"He shall redeem their soul from deceit and violence, and precious shall their blood be in his sight."

Alas! Such words would have been nothing less than falsehood and blasphemy in the mouth of the pious and reverent Hampden. But none the less earnest and most solemnly appropriate were his dying supplications.

"O Lord, save my bleeding country. Have these realms in thy special keeping.

"Confound and level in the dust those who would rob the people of their liberty and lawful prerogative. Let the King see his error and turn the hearts of his wicked counsellors from the malice and wickedness of their designs. O Lord, save my country! O Lord, be merciful!"

Ever sacred must be the last words of so brave and beautiful a soul.

The true test of a lofty nature is less what it does than what it refuses to do. In so many cases do our interests and duty go hand in hand, that it is not possible always to trace a deed to its real motive. Happily also for the human race, the impulse to produce good is so natural, that not the vilest criminal, or the most ignorant barbarian but has the power, and uses it to promote some unselfish end. To say that a man is without this, is to deny his claim to humanity—almost to existence—it is the seed from whence has sprung the civilisation of the human race.

But to refuse not merely a pleasant evil, but a seemingly great and beneficent gift, because we must in return make some apparently slight concession of principle—this—this is the rarity and the difficulty. Not to play the sophist and look on a good end as sanctifying base means, not to make excuses for what is in itself intrinsically wrong—who that thinks knows not that from the cradle to the grave there lies the trouble. What horse panting for the victory will place the bit in his own mouth and turn away from the race-course, because his turn is not yet come.

Of all the great objects of popular applause, the monarchs, presidents, statesmen, soldiers, wealthy merchants, and the rest, how many have reached their eminence by an unsullied ascent, and how often does success mean more than unscrupulousness? Therefore in the often drawn contrast here deprecated let it also be asked, whether the difference did not consist in the immeasurable superiority of Hampden to the mass of mankind, in acting up to his moral standard far more than the descent of Wentworth below it? A little consideration, a little examination of the lives of well-known public men, and possibly a few honest individual internal glances will render the answer to the question not very difficult, and Lord Wentworth, while no better than he was in reality, still much less of a a monster than it has been the fashion to consider him.

These considerations, which may by some be looked upon as a needless divergence, are yet offered both with a view to justice in judging of the character before us as well as of other subjects of biography.

There can be but one law of right and wrong, in reality, however mistaken man may be in its interpretation. The nearer he is to the true interpretation and obedience of this law the higher and more glorious does a human being become. Judging of his true rank as a created being, therefore, we must to the best of our ability measure him by the nearest approach we can conceive of this standard of height. Who was the real king among men, Newton or Nero?

But there is also another measure in regard to which the fair question is not what a man *is*, but what we have a right to expect him to be according to his opportunities, contemporaries, and the level reached by civilisation in his day. To be greater than the average we have no right to demand of any, or to call him bad if he reaches that, low as that average may be. But in an honest biography, the object of which is neither to brighten or blacken the subject, but to show his career in order that others may follow his good and take warning by his evil deeds and errors, both of these must as far as possible be told. While, therefore, we do not hesitate to expose his greatest failings and all such as are constantly hidden in the lives of the obscure, in gratitude for the lessons thus painfully afforded, if not from higher motives—let us strive to be just, and constantly to guide our criticisms by such weights as, if not exact, may at least help us to hold the balance more truly.

CHAPTER IV.

Among the intelligence conveyed to Lord Wentworth, this autumn, by the Reverend Mr. Garrard, were the following items.

"Ben Jonson dead in England.

"At the siege of Breda, Peter Apsley is shot through the mouth, the bullet grazing upon his tongue and carrying a small part away. The King laughed heartily at it.

"Complaint hath been made to the Lords of the Council of a sheriff of West Chester, who, when Prynne passed that way through Chester to Carnarvon Castle, he with others, met him, brought him into town, feasted and defrayed him. Besides, this sheriff gave him a suit of coarse hangings to furnish his chamber at Carnarvon Castle. Other presents were offered him, money and other things, but he refused them. The sheriff is sent for up by a pursuivant.

"Strange flocking of the people after Burton when he removed from the Fleet toward Lancaster Castle. Mr. Ingram, sub-warder of the Fleet, told the King that there was not less than one hundred thousand people gathered together to see him pass by, betwixt Smithfield and Brown's Well, which is two miles beyond Highgate. His wife went along in a coach,

1637.   having much money thrown to her as she passed
——— along." *

Wonderful was the blindness that failed to read such signs of the times in their true and simple meaning. Wonderful was the obstinacy that threw such palpable warnings away. In the present day, we see often enough mobs of frantic enthusiastics follow a well-paid dancer, singer, or player whose only claim to their homage is the amusement she has afforded them at their own expense and her most exorbitant remuneration. For to amuse the world is to win its highest applause and reward. But here thronged a vast multitude, stretching far as the eye could reach for no purpose of frivolity, pleasure or profit, simply to show their boundless sympathy and reverent love to a humble dissenting minister, who, disfigured and disgraced by the State and Court, was on his way to imprisonment, of what kind it could be little doubted.

Mobs may easily be gathered by the most unworthy who choose to flatter them in evil doing, bribe them with impossible baits of hopeless equality, or in any way excite their selfish or animal feelings. Burton had made no show, he did nothing to stimulate even curiosity. He preached *against* vice, vanity, and worldliness. He demanded purity of life, honour and truth in all things, and himself set the example. And when the *people* of a nation can be stirred to the very depths by such themes as these—then let oppressors beware. Such a nation as England was then, might have resisted the power of Rome in her greatest days, led by such leaders as were the natural results of the spirit that fired them.

* Rev. Mr. Garrard to the Lord Deputy, ii. 114.

Among the statues erected to the heroes of the 1637
Commonwealth, we do not find those of Burton,
Bastwick, Prynne, and Leighton. Yet they were
among the first to rouse the people to that religion
which, shaking off the husk of form, makes the form
itself solid by the diffusion of the spirit through every
fibre of its growth. To the dissenting ministers of
this nature who shall calculate the obligations due?
Innate power was their characteristic—a power which
they imparted to their disciples by words and example
alone. Not to be confounded with men who came
after them, assuming their name, these had neither the
will nor means to enforce their doctrine by other than
legitimate method—the power of persuasion. They
were the manliest of men. Fops and fools might
sneer; but an innocent man who, standing bleeding in
the pillory for conscience' sake, could repress the
physical agony he *must* feel—could yet smilingly rejoice
that he could thus prove to his people his sincerity in
a holy cause—could say, like Bastwick while his ears
fell to the ground: "This is my collar day—my
day of honour," carried within him an irresistible
and contagious might that could have no other
effects than those recorded. From whence has
the mightiest republic in the world sprung but from
them?

Whether Lord Wentworth held the philosophical
theory of disbelief in everything that, as yet, has not
been experienced by mankind, or not, we do not know.
But it is certain that he had not the slightest idea of
the forces that were slowly gathering to shatter, like a
dream, the fond traditions, and loyal prejudices, and
ancient precedents, and all the words that are blown

1637. into vapour the moment they are opposed to a real concentrated power, charged with vital and solid truth.

He listened to the feeble complaints of Laud and idle-toned gossip of Garrard, who, perhaps, ignorant themselves, unwittingly deceived him, and concealed from him the momentous nature of the tidings they sent, by means of the flimsy expressions in which they wrapped them.

"These occurrences," said Garrard, "are so ancient and stale, that I will enlarge no farther," and then passed on to the mighty important subjects of a joke of the King, and a quarrel of the royal couple.

But though Lord Wentworth felt rather disturbed, he thought the mistake lay, not in the provocation given by the torturers, but in thus allowing the people to express their hatred unpunished. He thought the King erred on the side of mercy. He would not have persecuted the victims for their religious opinions as far as they related to what he called religion, viz., a mere profession of belief. But it was precisely because these Puritans looked on religion as a matter of every-day life, by which every man, high or low, rich or poor, was bound to regulate his conduct, that he was so confounded at their inso-lence. Wrong or right, he thought it mattered little whether a man believed in transubstantiation or no, whether he wore a surplice, or made himself vulgar by preaching in plain clothes—all these kind of things did not interfere with the government. For though he did not express it in so many words, he certainly held the opinion of some of the most celebrated and greatest philosophers of modern times, that religion

had nothing to do with politics. And he looked on
Laud almost in two separate lights—as two men who
had nothing to do with each other. The politician and
the priest lay as far apart in Juxon, for instance, as
the private country gentleman, Lord Wentworth and
the Lord Deputy of Ireland, representative of the
King's Majesty, lay in himself.

The extraordinary idea of the Puritans, that so far
from religion unfitting a man for a public office, it was
the only thing that could fit him for anything at all,
public or private, by inspiring him with the solemn
desire to do all things, high or low, to the glory of
God, and thus do his best in every conceivable act
without regard to consequences,—this was a mystery
he had not penetrated.

Consequently, when the Puritans called attention to
public abuses in their sermons, and without mincing
matters, boldly pointed out how opposed they were to
those Scriptures which the whole nation, from the
rulers downwards acknowledged to be the law of God
—here was high treason indeed. St. Paul and St.
Peter, especially deprecated all beyond simple and
modest dress in women, and here were the great
ladies of England thinking of little else. While
thousands were in misery and poverty, and more in
sin needing conversion by grave examples—here were
masks at Court and immodest plays in which the
Queen herself acted—spiritual wickedness indeed in
high places. Besides, such little matters as perjury,
lying, &c., &c., were solemnly denounced in the New
Testament. And as for the history of the Kings of
Israel, what awful warnings did not their lives give!
All these things, these ministers persisted in bringing

 before the people. They could not, and would not rest content with merely telling the poor to order themselves lowly and reverently to all their betters; but while they certainly did this, they sternly admonished those betters as to how they were bound to order themselves to the poor. They did not rest at convenient general charges, which each person could comfortably apply to his neighbour alone, they specified the precise deeds that were evil. For example: among other anecdotes related by Mr. Garrard to Lord Wentworth was the following, the events occurring at the very time the " necessities " of the King were " obliging " him to exact the detested ship-money.

"Here are two masks intended this winter. The King is now practising his, which shall be presented at twelfth-tide. Most of the young lords about town, who are good dancers, attend his Majesty in this business.

"The other the Queen makes at Shrovetide, a new house being erected in the first court at Whitehall, which cost the King twenty-five hundred pounds, only of deal boards, because the King will not have his pictures in the banqueting house hurt with lights."

Now, however harmless these amusements may appear, there is another side to the question. The Puritans held them to be wicked, and had they been acted by poor people, not as an amusement to themselves, but to gain a livelihood, they would have denounced them as selling their souls for their bodies. And in so doing they would have been left alone. But by these things being done in the highest places, the ministers looked with tenfold horror at their effects.

For there, they not only endangered the souls of the royal actors, but by their encouragement and example, multiplied the evil, and especially among " those young lords about the town who are good dancers." Consequently, the sermons were launched forth with all the eloquence that a sincere belief in the terrific danger could impart.

And then came the fines and imprisonments and nose-slittings, and ear-loppings, and cheek-brandings, all of which were cheerfully endured, rather than remissness in the tremendous duty of warning the falling souls.

Prynne, who as a lawyer as well as Puritan, was able to point out and explain how the rights of the people were trampled on, how, out of regard to the Queen, the Roman Catholics were permitted, in defiance of the law, to practise their rites, while the dissenting ministers were mangled for keeping it, was an especial object of hatred to the court party. Laud could scarcely write a letter to Wentworth without some malignant sentence against Prynne, and some solicitation of sympathy from Wentworth for the grief he had to bear on account of the indulgence shown to this man, and the people who thronged around his pillory. His object was to arouse the fears of the Lord Deputy at the contempt shown to the King by the popular disapproval of the royal conduct and orders.

And here he touched the weak point of the Deputy. For Wentworth simply placed the King in the place of God. Could he but have realised that what he insisted on as due to the King from all men, the Puritans deemed due to the *Most* High alone, possibly a new light might have dawned upon him. But even that little window was closed, and there was no hand to draw the curtain and let in the light. The Deity to him was a far distant abstraction, a name. But the King was real—a being he had seen and touched, and, consistently enough, had not much valued till he had seen him and had material communication with him.

It is not too much to say that he had no firmer realisation of Charles than these Puritans had of Him, they reverently loved to call the King of Kings. His command, as written in what they believed His book, were to them as imperative mandates as a royal despatch to Wentworth.

It is not to be wonder at that neither the Deputy nor any that did not share their belief could comprehend them. So rare in all times, in all creeds have been their reality. In our own day, among the tens of thousands of self-deceivers, how many are there who, realising to themselves what they profess to others, that the eye of God *is* ever on them, act with as much care in secresy and solitude in their hidden plans as when in the presence and with the knowledge of one weak mortal?

But this it was that was the strength of the Puritans, this absolute sincerity to themselves. This made them terrible in war, industrious in peace, moral and pure-minded in word and deed. Such a spectacle as they presented the world had never seen, so solid and compact a body bound together neither by authority, nor interest, nor custom, but religious principle. The incessant squabbles that took place between Laud and his laity were unknown between them and their ministers. Contrast, for instance, the feelings of Burton's congregation with a curious story told by Garrard. Though Laud had shown such a spirit to Burton for speaking against royal masques, yet it chanced that some players set up their bills and opened the theatre in Blackfriars during the first week in Lent. Laud hearing of it, at the next Privy Council, bitterly complained of the impiety of such scenes in Lent, and declared that unless the King ordered the contrary, he would " lay the players by the heels " if they played again.

The Lord Chamberlain, who was present, immediately and angrily rose and said that the Archbishop of Canterbury and himself served the same God and the same King, and he hoped that his Grace would not meddle with his place any more than he did in the archbishop's. The players were under his command.

Laud, however, refused to yield unless the King commanded. The King then decided in his favour, the Lord Chamberlain was defeated, and the theatres ordered to be closed during Lent. It is difficult to imagine anything more calculated to make a bad impression on the people than this. It told in various ways.

It gave proof that the head of the Church of England placed the authority of the King above that of God Himself. For he was willing to sanction what he declared to be impious, if only the King commanded him. Then he placed the Roman Catholic festival of Lent above the Sabbath, for he had tried to enforce the Book of Sports on the latter. What he thought wrong in Lent alone, others were persecuted for thinking wrong at any time. And this was the system of religion which the people against their consciences were to be compelled to support!

It was very unfortunate that Lord Wentworth should have been so distant from the scene as not to be able

1637.

to judge of its effects in England. Had his duties remained in his native land, it is very probable that the same spirit that enabled him to see the need of religious toleration in Ireland might have had due power at home. And Laud had learned to put the conduct of the Puritans before him in the light not of religious bigotry or stubbornness, even, but of political rebellion. And there was this difference between Laud and Wentworth. Wentworth earnestly and sincerely told his troubles, and asked the advice of Laud, with the anxious desire of guiding himself in the most secure way. Consequently, he stated a thing as it really appeared to him in all its bearings. But Laud only required to be confirmed in what he did, and therefore so represented matters in the light most likely to obtain the expression he desired. He had only himself to thank that Wentworth, seeing by this false light, wrote the expected words. For example, " Mr. Prynne's case is not the first wherein I have resented the humour of the time to cry up and magnify such as the honour and justice of the King and State have marked out and adjudged mutinous to the government, and offensive to that belief and reverence the people ought to have in the wisdom and integrity of the magistrate. Nor am I now to say it anew (even there, where the right understanding and right use made of this mischief would be the only way to take off the ill it threatens to all), that a prince that loseth the force and example of his punishments, loseth withal the greatest part of his dominion. Yet still, methinks we are not got through the disease—nay, I fear, do not sufficiently apprehend the malignity of it.

" In the meantime, a liberty thus assumed, thus

abused, is very insufferable, but how to help it I know
not, till I see the good as resolute in their good as we
daily observe the bad to be in evil ways."

The close intimacy of Laud and Wentworth was
regarded with the strongest disapprobation both in
England and Ireland. Those who despised the abilities
of Laud knew that he could, if he chose, make use of
those of Wentworth, and gave the latter much more
credit than he deserved for the doings of the archbishop. They would have been astonished to have
seen how much it was the reverse. Always in proportion to the greatness of the intellect is the modesty
of its owner. A man of cultivated genius measures
the amount of his knowledge by his ignorance, and
ever, like the great Newton, finds the first a mere pebble
by the side of the undiscovered ocean. He knows,
too, how great has been the labour to gain even this
little, and is glad of any aid that can help him on the
upward way. The more reverent and considerate the
critic, the greater the proof of his fitness for his office.
But the inferior mind, poor in itself, knows not the
existence of treasures that demand many a lesser gain
before they reveal themselves. It has none of the cares
and anxieties involved in the search, it has found its own
little hoard easy enough to acquire, and, satisfied with
that, assumes an air of superiority and ownership that
will often mislead the humbler and greater mind, whose
very consciousness of the wonders beyond its reach
makes it credulous and ever-seeking, where ignorance
is insolent and sceptical. Hence, the often-witnessed
spectacle of the higher, led by the meaner, soul.

There is something infinitely touching in the
sight of Lord Wentworth seeking and following the

counsel of Laud, and equally ludicrous the patronizing yet honest pleasure with which Laud announces his opinions. Still, to the credit of Laud, he never abused the confidence of Wentworth. That a friendship so wildly unequal should have endured to the end is to the high honour of the lesser man. Faithfulness and steadfastness form the natural atmosphere of a high mind, and when a mean one breathes it and maintains its life through difficulties and temptations, then is the honour tenfold, and it asserts its claim to a higher dwelling place; it shows the germ of wings. At this time incessant efforts were again made to promote a breach between the two friends. The principal means used were cunningly to convey to the ear of Laud, by different channels, the intelligence that Wentworth despised his friendship, and spoke against him. Another method was to speak of their intimacy as a thing of the past. But Laud took the only true way in such cases. He at once informed his friend of all that was said. He allowed no poison to rankle silently, and received the just reward.

" There is a nation of people," said Wentworth on this subject, " which are ever to be found in the courts of great princes, which intend nothing so much as by false reports to wound the credit of honest men, and to breed, if by any means they may, jealousies betwixt persons better than themselves, and greater in power. The fairest revenge, and to those evil-disposed persons, the most grievous, is for those that are good, to knit themselves the stronger together. Whilst this art and ourselves are too well understood and known the one to the other ever to do either of us harm, yet in the mean space I cannot but laugh extremely at such a senseless impudence as could cast out a rumour of any unkindness betwixt your Lordship and me with hope to be believed by any reasonable men. But let them take their course : in the end no doubt they will have their reward.

" It is a great value and authority your Lordship's approbation sets upon anything I shall write or do. I confess if it like you, it moves me to think much better of it myself than otherwise I should. It comforts me likewise very much his Majesty still vouchsafeth so graciously to accept of my weak endeavours in his service. In good faith, my lord, I do as well as I can ; most glad I should be still to do better, and become most thankful to any man living that will show me a path which may lead me in a nearer and more upright line to the fulfilling of his good pleasure and service."

He thanked Laud for the good efforts he had made to preserve the Irish revenue for Ireland. He said if only they could maintain it thus until a good colony of English were settled in Galway, then all would go well.

To Laud, as to all others, he spoke enthusiastically of the hopes he had of Ireland.

" I shall not neglect," said he, " to preserve myself in good opinion with this people, in regard I become thereby better able to do my master's service. Longer than it works to that purpose, I am very indifferent what they shall think or say concerning me."

In words as well as all else did Wentworth allow his strange infatuation to show itself. He did himself wrong by this profession of no interest in Ireland beyond that of the King. True, the King's interest was first with him, but it was impossible for any man to be indifferent to a country for whose prosperity he had worked so hard, much less such an ardent nature as his.

He felt it, and could not help adding, " Howbeit, I cannot dissemble, so far as not to profess, I wish extreme much prosperity to them also, and should lay it up in my opinion as a mighty honour and happiness, to become, in some degree, an instrument of it, and thereupon preserve that intention second in my thoughts and care after the powers and profits of the Crown. Much I protest before anything of my own private fortune."

A curious example now occurs of how completely he had reduced all things to method—how nothing was allowed to form an exception to his absolute inability to leave anything unprepared for. As we have seen in the case of the late Lord Treasurer, it was easy for him to feign a grief he did not feel. But that he was capable of feeling the deepest grief is also beyond all doubt. He was greatly attached to the family of his second wife, and always treated her parents with the respect and affection of a son; always taught his children to think of them in the same way.

He now heard of the dangerous illness of the Earl of Clare, father to his second wife. He was announced to be near death, and reports were even abroad that he was already dead. Lord Wentworth had not received the final announcement. But he did not wait for that. He wrote a letter of condolence to the Countess on the supposition that she was a widow, and sent it to one of his cousins near her, with orders

to present it if the earl were dead. If not, then the   1637.
letter was to be returned to himself.

The earl died before its arrival, and the letter was
delivered.

The widowed Countess of Clare was very anxious
to have the children of Wentworth to reside with her;
and though their father, believing it to be for the
good of the two girls, tried to persuade himself to send
them to her for their education, yet, again and again,
did he defer it, finding it impossible to part from
them. Their portraits, in full length groups, painted
by Vandyke, may still be seen, and it needs but little
imagination to add the dark face of their father gazing
upon them with that passionate fondness, which compelled him to turn to their innocent solace for consolation, amid the hatred that from all sides fell upon
him.

But ever in English history, amidst the stormiest
times, do we find this domestic affection. It mattered
not whether the home were Royalist or Republican,
Episcopalian or Puritan, the strong feelings of nature
smiled in all alike, and a most beautiful literature
might be collected from the existing letters of warriors
and statesmen, who, to the world, seemed as iron as
their own harness. Nothing can be more ridiculous
than to single out this as a special virtue in any man.

The sums paid for ship-money this year amounted
to £196,400; every shilling unlawfully gathered. It
mattered very little to the English people whether they
were plundered at home or abroad, and even the
slavery of Sallee was parallelled by the press gangs of
the King and the compulsory foreign service.

It was well, however, that Lord Wentworth had a

gleam of light to cheer him, for, with slow but sure grasp, disease was binding yet deeper her fetters around him.

"I was," he says, sadly, "crept indeed a little out of the gout; but I am presently fallen worse again than I have been at any time before. I see infirmities, with years, grow upon me."

Blindness was his constant dread; but as no specific disease of the eyes existed, he set down his dimness of sight to the premature old age that had already commenced its ravages.

"Touching your Lordship's eyes," said Coke, "under favour, you cannot yet pretend to the infirmities of age. But we that are aged know that sight suffereth most by expense of spirits in watching and writing, which you may please again to think upon."

Other friends were of the same opinion, and warned him of overwork. But so much of his work depended for success on being performed by his own hand, that he felt he must either go on as he had done or resign. And to resign was to undo in a day all the past heavy toil. No, he must go on; no rest for him but the grave, which, at the longest, promised to receive him in a few short years. Yet, if time be counted less by years than work accomplished, already he was a patriarch, as he himself said in reference to his fate: "He lives more that virtuously spends one month, than some other that may chance to dream out some years, and bury himself alive all the while." Yet, with death ever staring him in the face, he appeared in no way awakened to the wrongs he had done, and was as obtuse as ever to the fact that they were wrongs. Thus, at the end of this year Lord Mountnorris was

allowed to leave Ireland, to take his trial before the 1637.
Star Chamber in England. Yet, his depressed condition elicited nothing but a cruel sneer from Wentworth, who told him he never wished ill to his estate
or person, further than to remove him thence, where
he was as well a trouble as an offence unto him. That
being done (howbeit, added the Deputy, through his
own fault, with more prejudice to him than was intended) he could wish there were no more debate
between them, and, if he wished, it would spare the
prosecution in the Star Chamber in England.

But Mountnorris proudly thanked him, and said
that he desired to meet the bill, that so by his oath, he
might satisfy the Lord Deputy how innocent he was of
having his hand in any such foul slander against him
as he was accused of. Lord Wentworth certainly
mistook his bearing when he said, " At his departure
hence he seemed wondrously humbled, as much as
Chaucer's Friar, that would not for him anything
should be dead."

The innocent who refuse a pardon, the proffer of which
implies their guilt, are never humbled.

It is to be feared that a naturally cruel or hard nature
is not softened by suffering. The pitiful become yet
more gentle, ever reflecting their own thoughts and
wishes on others. The very sternness of the Spartan
made him demand the like from all. It is the con-
sciously weak who know what it is just to expect. And
though it is eternally true that, in the words of the poet,

" Who best can suffer, best can do,"

it by no means follows they best can feel for others.
The red savage at the stake will, unmoved, meet death

1637.   under pangs that make another shudder to read of. But He who suffered for mankind shrank as the agony approached, and quivered at the thought. Nor does it take from the reverence due that He uttered a loud cry, where many a coarser nature has endured in silence. And it is very questionable whether that self-sufficient spirit that prides itself on hiding every outward sign of pain from the world, does not generally repay itself by scorning the pain of others, and treating the desire for sympathy as a contemptible weakness.

Lord Wentworth did not despise sympathy—his heart was too passionate for that—and he leaned more and more on Laud, because Laud offered it. But he did not seek it, nor did he grow merciful. The curtain that had hung between him and his fellows through life seemed to thicken and darken as his trials increased. Few were those with him on the other side. Still, to wish for their affection, and to appreciate it, was far better than being entirely alone.

Laud now began to be really anxious about his friend. He found his letters remain unanswered from the inability of the invalid to guide the pen. Intermittent fever again reduced him, and, after a long delay, Wentworth confessed to " much decay in sight, and, in truth, in the whole constitution of body and *mind*."

When a man so proud reveals so much, it behoves others to make allowance. In a paroxysm of pain we are often hardly conscious of what we do, and claim the excuse. Those whose life is a succession of paroxysms, which they are striving not only to bear, but to hide and to work beneath them, are in a state so unnatural, that it may well affect their every action. Cruel to themselves, they hardly recognise their cruelty

to others, and leniency in their own case might pro-
duce such results as to teach them leniency to others. 1637.
Nature ever avenges an outrage, and retorts her wrongs.

Under this " decay of body and mind and sight," the unhappy Deputy owned his desolation to Laud.

" Good and faithful assistance, in truth, I have here at the Committee of Revenue, but this goes no further than the private. For, as for the public enmity and malice contracted in the execution from persons pretended and interested, *that* I must take to myself—tread that crooked and thorny path alone.

" God help and sustain me, for assuredly it begins to press and pinch me shrewdly.

" I most humbly thank your lordship for your noble care and counsel tending to the preservation of my health. A free bounty it is of your love towards me, where otherwise of myself I am so wondrous little considerable to anybody else."

No! Bitterly he felt that. The tears that fell on the lonely grave of Eliot would have been worth having. The deep, the holy love of the people for the mutilated martyrs of the pillory and the prison—was it so despicable after all? One thing was sure, that as far as success or happiness was concerned, the Deputy had by some means missed that.

With mocking pain he avowed that " The Lady Astrea, the poet tells us, is long since gone to heaven, but under favour, I can yet find reward and punishment on earth. Indeed, sometimes they are like Dr. Donne's anagram of a good face,—the ornaments mis-set. A yellow tooth, a red eye, a white lip or so. And seeing that all beauties take not all affections, one

1637.
———

man judging that a deformity, which another considers as a perfection or a grace ; this, methinks, convinceth the certain uncertainty of rewards and punishments.

" Howsoever, he is the wisest, commonly the greatest and happiest man, and shall surely draw the fairest table of his life that understands, with Vandyke, how to dispose of these shadows best to make up his own comeliness and advantage." *

Without doubt, here is the true problem of life ; not for Lord Wentworth alone, but for all.

Laud did not approve of his quotations of Donne and Chaucer. He did not care for poetry himself, and did not under stand its attractions for others. With singular inappropriateness, after telling Wentworth how hard this symmetry was to find, he sent him not to hopeful utterances, but to the saddest, amidst all its beauty, of the books of the Old Testament.

" Once for all," said this cheering adviser, " if you will but read over the short book of Ecclesiastes, while these thoughts are in you, you will see a better disposition of these things and the vanity of all their shadows than is to be found in any anagrams of Dr. Donne's, or any designs of Vandyke. So to the lines there drawn I leave you."

Laud, whose petty-minded malignity towards the objects of his personal spite always tried to feed and excite the more heavily-weighted hatred of Wentworth, now, instead of rebuking his expressions towards Hampden, and, at least, as would have become a professed teacher of Christianity, exhorting him to charity, could not forbear adding :

" Your mention of Mr. Hampden (and *I must tell*

---

* The Lord Deputy to the Archbishop of Canterbury, 2, 158.

you I like your censure of him and the rest very well)   1637.
puts me in mind of the ship business."

While the Episcopalians were occupied in improving the fashion of their robes and increasing the number of their ceremonies, filling up their spare time with persecuting the Puritans, the Roman Catholic agents were keenly on the alert to take advantage of the present state of things. Without advancing any opinion as to the relative value of the creeds, it may be safely asserted that when any man begins to attach a religious importance to vestments, decorations, and ceremonies, he is some distance on the road to Roman Catholicism. At this period there was precisely the same excitement as in our own day on these questions. The Ritualists were a scandal in the eyes of the Puritans, who were then the only opposing body worthy of the name. The variety of modern sects, comprising men of all shades, from the Calvinist down to the hard Atheist, boldly professing his disbelief in a God and a future state, did not then exist. The only sneerers in religious matters were the fashionable, worldly, professed members of the Church of England, who showed their wit in jests on the plain dress and stern lives of the Puritans. But then, as now, were numbers whose feeble minds, unable to endure the fatigue of searching into religious questions for themselves, and yet dreading the final consequences of doubt, longed for that ignoble safety they thought could be obtained by throwing their responsibilities on others. This safety was promised by the Church of Rome. She undertook to relieve them from that duty of examination into *facts*, and their bearings on truth, which in every subject whatever is so repulsive to the common mind. Consequently, conversions to the Church of Rome became so frequent as to excite the hopes of her friends and the fears of her enemies, that the work of the Reformation was going to be undone, and England once more become a vassal of the Pope. A few extracts from letters of the day will present a most curious parallel to what is going on in our own times.

It has been said that mankind never apostatizes, never returns to a creed that it has once shaken off. And when we consider how near was the seventeenth century to the reign of Philip and Mary; how overwhelming the number of English Catholics then compared with the present time; how England was hemmed in with Catholic nations; how the mighty republic of the West, the great bulwark of Protestantism, was then unborn; and, above all, how barren was the condition of philosophy and science; and, yet, with all these things in its favour, the old creed failed utterly to stem the advancing tide, there will appear but small grounds to believe that such a miracle can be accomplished in the latter end of the nineteenth century. The following passages are given for the purpose of illustrating the fears which so greatly resembled what we daily hear expressed:

1. "Dr. Haywood, late household chaplain to my Lord's Grace of Canterbury, now the King's, parson of St. Giles's in the Fields, where he lives, brought a petition, directed to my Lord's Grace and the other Lords of his Majesty's Council, complaining that in a very short time a great part of his parishioners are become Papists and refuse to come to church.

"The wolf that has been amongst them is a Jesuit,

one Morse, who, since this complaint is, they say, by order, apprehended and committed to prison.   1637.

"Popery certainly increaseth much among us, and will do still as long as there is such access of all sorts of English to the chapel in Somerset House, utterly forbidden and punishable by the laws of the land.

"I wish, and pray to God with all my heart, that the bishops of England would take this growth of Popery into their considerations, and seek by all means to retard that, as well as punish by suspension and other ways, those called Puritan ministers. I love neither their opinions, and so I leave them." *

Such was the opinion of the Rev. Mr. Garrard, himself a clergyman of the Church of England. (March 23rd, 1637.)

In his next he says:

"Another of my familiar acquaintance is gone over to that Popish religion, Sir Robert Howard, which I am very sorry for." (April 28th, 1637.)

Again:

"Here hath been a horrible noise about the Lady Newport's being become a Roman Catholic. She went one evening, as she came from a play in Drury Lane, to Somerset House, where one of the Capuchin's reconciled her to the Popish Church, of which she is now a weak member. Her lord, upon knowledge of it, being much grieved and in an high passion, went over to Lambeth to make his complaint to my Lord's Grace of Canterbury, of those whom he thought had been instruments in the conversion of his wife." (Nov. 9th, 1637.)

In this instance, it appeared that ladies of high rank

* Mr. Garrard to the Lord Deputy, 2, 57.

had been the agents employed. Various remedies were suggested to put a stop to these conversions, about as reasonable as such suggestions usually are. But in no single instance was the calm investigation of the grounds of belief proposed. No appeal to the reason and common sense of the "convert" ever dreamed of. Perhaps the most unjust and absurd proposition was one made at the Council table in a kind of imitative and retaliative spirit. It was the plan of the priests, whenever they were able, to persuade the parents to send their eldest sons (and often the others as well) to a foreign school to be educated. There they received, not only instruction in the Roman Catholic religion, but in treason to their country.

It was now advised that the government should seize all the eldest sons of the Catholics, and, by force, educate them in the Protestant faith. It was proposed to begin with the sons of Lord Powis. Of course, the father indignantly protested; and, after some deliberation, this monstrous scheme was given up. Had it been carried into effect, we may safely say that no stronger power could have been placed in the hands of the priests than the argument of such unnatural interference with the rights of parents.

The next anecdote is of a curious nature:

"The Lieutenant of the Tower, Sir William Balfour, beat a priest lately for seeking to convert his wife. He had a suspicion that she resorted a little too much to Denmark House, and staid long abroad, which made him one day send after her. Word being brought him where she was, he goes thither, finds her at her devotions in the chapel. He beckons her out; she comes accompanied with a priest, who, somewhat

too saucily, reprehended the lieutenant for disturbing 1637.
his lady at her devotions, for which he struck him two
or three sound blows with his baton."

These specimens will serve to show the attempts
that were made to restore the old order of things. It
is difficult to comprehend the folly of those who,
objecting to the priests, could yet persecute the
Puritans, the great bulwark against them. Still, so
bold did the Ritualism in high places render the
Catholics, that they became too confident, and a priest
was caught boasting openly that the King himself was
a Papist at heart, and the Protestants nothing better
than devils.

This brought matters to a point. Charles was certainly not a Catholic, and in his present position could
ill afford to be taken for one. To let the priest go
unpunished would be to confirm his words. The
unhappy wretch was therefore heavily fined, set in the
pillory, and both his ears cut off.

By this act, the King merely alienated the Roman
Catholics. He did not draw to him the most bigoted
Protestant an inch the nearer. The people detested
these infamous mutilations of human beings. Was
not the body of man declared to be the temple of God,
and, as such, to be kept holy ?

A feeble attempt was now made by Laud to prove
that he was opposed to the Catholics; but it mattered
little that he sent a few to prison and made a few
speeches at the Council. His words went for nothing.
All England held his very name in abhorrence. If he
were not a Catholic, his practices had led to the present
state of things, and so slight was the difference between
Ritualism and Catholicism, that it was scarcely per-

1637. ceptible to men who looked on forms of every kind as a species of idolatry.

Such, then, was the state of matters in England, when the crisis that must have arrived even there before long, was precipitated in Scotland by an act, to the intense idiocy and ignorance of which it is difficult to find a parallel.

Laud himself it was that by his blind folly loosened the avalanche that was to overwhelm himself, his friend, his King, and his Church.

CHAPTER V.

It was not without cause that Lord Wentworth felt himself oppressed with the most mournful forebodings. As his powers of body and mind grew feebler, the stronger and more menacing became the dangers that on all sides threatened him. And yet, it was in none of the directions scanned by his vigilant eye that the fatal enemy lay couched. The cloud, no bigger than a man's hand at present, but which was to overwhelm him in final darkness, was rising in the distant horizon of another land, where he had all his life been a stranger. Not by those well recognised foes in Ireland and England was the peril to be first awaked. It was to be by Laud, by the trusted and really sincere friend that the train was to be laid, whose explosion should be the signal of doom. What malice and treachery and power failed to accomplish, the imbecile folly of a feeble brain was to bring about.

The wise tolerance of Lord Wentworth had placed a bridle in Ireland, on the elsewhere uncontrolled impulses of the Archbishop of Canterbury, to compel a conformity to the ritualistic ceremonies of the English Church.

He had repeatedly sent orders for its adoption in

1637.　　Scotland but had constantly been informed by his subordinates in that country of the impossibility of enforcing his orders all at once. It must, they said, be a matter of time. The great difference between the Scotch and English Protestants consisted far more in outward than inward matters. The English preserving their admiration for many of the beautiful prayers of the Roman Catholics, preferred to retain them in the form of a Liturgy. The Scotch, on the other hand, with much less liberality, rejected all that had been hitherto used, and, from the beginning, their Protestant services were conducted entirely by the judgment of the minister, unaided, except by the Bible and hymn-book.

James the First was much taken with the Liturgy on his arrival in England, and was the first to order its adoption in Scotland.

His orders, however, were disregarded, and it was reserved for Charles to persevere in his usual disregard of the feelings of a whole nation. Some difference there was between the Liturgy prepared for Scotland and that of England, on the ostensible ground of consulting the wishes of the people. But their wishes were opposed to a form of any kind. A Liturgy to them was like a mass-book, and Laud waited in vain for their prejudices to cool.

At length, plainly recognizing that his orders never would be voluntarily obeyed, the King, who always supported Laud in ecclesiastical tyranny, decided that the time was come to settle the matter. It is evident they were afraid of resistance, for instead of an open proclamation, beforehand, announcing the day that was to witness the inauguration of the Liturgy, private

orders were sent to the Scotch bishops to arrange, so
that the first announcement should be made to the
people by the actual reading of the Liturgy itself.

It was on the 23rd of July, 1637, that the congregation assembled in the church of St. Giles, in Edinburgh, were startled by seeing the Dean of Edinburgh
arrayed in clerical vestments, enter the reading-desk
and commence reading the Liturgy. A most aristocratic assembly was present, including the highest
dignitaries of Church and State, as well as other
persons whose prestige it was thought would be sufficient to maintain obedience to the new regulations.

It proved a strange error. At first, the people were
stupified with astonishment, and the Dean gaining
courage at the scarce hoped-for silence, continued his
reading. But the people soon recovered themselves,
and an old woman, now immortalised in history,
suddenly started from a three legged stool on which
she was sitting, and with the furious exclamation
of :—

"What, ye villain, do ye say mass i' my lug,"
hurled the stool at the head of the luckless reader who
very narrowly escaped the missile. This was the
signal for a general uproar. It was in vain that the
Bishop of Edinburgh, who was appointed to preach,
ascended the pulpit, hoping by his august presence to
appease the tumult. He was received with the
ominous cries of: "A pape! a pape! antichrist!"
and obliged to descend and with the rest of his colleagues to flee from the church to save his life.
Similar scenes were witnessed in other churches, and
again in the evening when the foolish attempt was
repeated.

The next day the Council of Edinburgh prohibited all public meetings on pain of death, and commanded the continuance of the Liturgy, promising protection to the affrighted clergy, who were naturally not very eager to encounter another such Sunday. But the danger was too great, and consequently divine service was suspended till the report of what had happened had been forwarded to England, and the pleasure of the King made known.

Of course, both Charles and Laud showed their usual obtuseness to the presence of real danger. It is a notable thing, that before resolving to enforce the Liturgy Laud did not consult Lord Wentworth. It was a thing he was resolved on and probably dreaded unwelcome advice. Neither in the present emergency did either he or the King consult the wisest and most experienced of their friends. Laud wrote to him even without alluding to what had occurred, as if it were a trifle not worth naming.

Garrard, indeed, in the midst of one of his long letters containing idle gossip before and after the news of an event that was to plunge two kingdoms in war, has the following sentence. "I mentioned before, an attempt to bring in our English Church service into Scotland, which made a great hubbub there, and was repelled with much violence by the common people, though women appeared most in the action, flinging their stools at the bishop and rending his episcopal garments off him, as he went forth of the church; others flinging stones at him in the streets, so that if the Earl of Roxborough had not sought to quiet them and receive him into his coach, they had stoned him to death.

" A second attempt has been made of which fresh news has come thence to the Court wherein they have sped worse. Besides, some of the noblesse and many of the gentry and better sort appear in it, who withstand it with greater violence than before, so that there is no hope that it will be effected."

Laud was of a different opinion. When he received the first intelligence, he wrote to the Earl of Traquair to say that the Church must persevere, and show to the world that she was the injured party. Restitution must be made her at the hands of the law. The King took it very ill, said Laud, that the business of the service book had been so weakly carried, and his Majesty expected that the Council of Edinburgh would establish the Liturgy peaceably. The clergy had not power enough of their own to do it, and the advice of the Council ought to have been first asked.

It was very weak to suspend the service till the King's pleasure were known; it looked as if the bishops disclaimed the work themselves and only did it in obedience to the King. And this, Laud thought to be most unworthy. He considered that the bishops ought to have identified themselves with it as the cause of the Church, taking all responsibility on themselves, and only appealing to the authority of the King as a legal sanction of deeds, delightful in every way from their own intrinsic beauty and good.

Laud had a vague idea that the clergy ought to be as zealous in his cause, as the Puritans showed themselves in the cause of their ministers. Ah! if only the good were as zealous for the good, as the bad were for the bad, was his constant theme! But his clergy were of different mettle. There was no power to enforce his mandates, and he and Charles received advice, that it would be well to defer compulsion till after the harvest.

However unwelcome this counsel, he was compelled to follow it, for as usual, he had issued his absurd commands without the means to enforce them.

By the 19th of October the harvest was completed, and Charles then issued two mandates to his Scotch subjects. The first was to forbid all meetings among them, and to order every man from the time the order was proclaimed from the Market Cross, to return to his home within twenty-four hours, unless he could prove to the magistrates that he had indispensable business not connected with the Church. All who disobeyed this, were to be put to the Horn, to be declared rebels, and, as the King's invariable rule was to extract money from the sins or misfortunes of others, their entire possessions were to be forfeited to him.

The second order, published on the same day, was to the effect that his Majesty having been informed that a book had been published, entitled, " A Dispute against the English Popish Ceremonies, obtruded upon the Kirk of Scotland," every one possessing this book was to bring it by a fixed day to be publicly burnt. And if, after the time appointed, any were found in possession of a copy, they should be punished in proportion to their crime.*

What Charles considered a punishment proportionate to publish an opinion not forbidden by law, but contrary to, or obnoxious to his own, was well-known to

* Nalson, i. p. 11.

consist of standing in the pillory, having the cheeks 1637. branded, the nose slit, and the ears cut off. But nothing could shake the indomitable Scots.

The twenty-four hours that was to find them trembling in their homes, saw them gathered in new multitudes, following the obsequious clergy with just and loud utterances of indignation. It was in vain that the shrinking priests sent for help to the magistrates. The latter returned for answer that they were in a similar state of siege, and that the people had got them so completely in their power, that they had turned their own weapons upon them and threatened them with death—unless they signed a paper immediately, containing three particulars—

The First—To join them in opposing and petitioning the King against the Service Book.

The Second—To restore Ramsay and Rollock, two ministers they had silenced.

The Third—To restore a Reader named Henderson, who had also been silenced.

And these, added the poor magistrates, they had signed from sheer terror.

We may not admire these acts on the part of the people, yet we must remember they were simply putting in practice, in a very mild degree, the lesson that had been instilled into them by their teachers. For they only bargained for freedom to practice their own belief: they did not insist on forcing that belief on the poor cravens who basely deserted them in their hour of need—of eternal danger. And it is well, at times, for mortals to taste the bitter cup they impose on others.

1637.   The subscription having pacified them, the Lord
Treasurer and the Earl of Wigton, who had stayed
with the bishops, now thought they might venture out.
But at once they were met with shouts of " God defend all those who will defend God's cause, and God
confound the Service Book and all the maintainers
of it ! "

In the struggle to escape, the Lord Treasurer was
thrown down ; his hat, cloak, and white staff rolled in
the dust, and himself nearly trodden to death.   At
length, in despair, the confounded officials sent for
some of the nobility and gentry, who, more faithful
than themselves, had upheld their country in the resistance of hypocrisy, and, guarded by these, they
reached a place of safety.

The next act of these civil restorers of temporary
peace was to draw up addresses to the King and
Council, couched in terms of deepest reverence, and,
in the name of the noblemen, barons, ministers,
burgesses, and Commons, representing that the books
ordained by this new rule for profession in religion were in their eyes sown with the seeds of
superstition, idolatry, and false doctrine, contrary
to the true religion established in Scotland by Act of
Parliament.

That the doctrines therein contained, by investing
a bishop or archbishop with power to excommunicate
and to pardon, opened a door for farther inventions, as
well as the revival of abolished superstitions and
errors.

That by allowing the construction and power of
punishment solely to depend on the word of a bishop,
they were placed between the two dangers of utter

worldly ruin or the breach of the law of God— 1637.
the last being to them far more grievous than death.

Out of their bounden duty to their God, King, and native country, they complained of the prelates who had so far abused their credit, and they begged that the whole matter might be tried by the law of the land, and the bishops no longer allowed to sit as judges till their right be tried and decided according to justice.

To this the King, after first ordering the removal of the Council and law courts from Edinburgh and sending them twenty-four miles off to Stirling, and forbidding the Scots to go there or anywhere in reach of the new temporary capital, told them how much he hated Popery, or anything not perfect in religion. But what *was* perfect they must allow *him* to decide. That their inferior intellects could by no means take in so many words, and that was why he had, " in his princely wisdom," ordered the whole matter to be reduced to a kind of pap for them.

And, to drive away all their fears, he said, that he had not allowed one word to be printed in their books but what he had seen and approved, the effect of which royal revision would be that " even the very book would be a means to maintain the true religion." And though those nobles, gentlemen, burgesses, ministers, and all who had ventured to discuss the matter and petition him on it, deserved very " high censure, both in their persons and fortunes," yet, as it must surely have been done " out of a preposterous zeal and not out of disloyalty to him," he would " graciously dispense with their appealing to any judge, and pass the matter over." Only they must remember that, if they repeated

1637. these errors again, or disobeyed him in the least, or dreamed of appealing to law, or ever went within twenty-four miles of the sessions house, they should be considered, without more ado, guilty of high treason. And to inflict its penalties, the King had entrusted full powers to his deputies.

It was in vain that these miserable dialogues went on. Their invariable effect was to raise to a greater height the resolution of the Scots. These now bound themselves by a solemn covenant never to yield in their convictions of religion. Every man, woman, and youth who was deemed worthy of anything like trust bound themselves by this oath, which was framed in the most terrible and solemn language, to allow no temptation of pain, pleasure, or fear, or anything that can tempt mankind to prove false, to influence them. This was an oath that bound them to God himself. Henceforth they were called the Covenanters, nearly resembling, and often blent with, the Puritans of England.

It is not needful to go into full details ; but it has been necessary to explain so far, in order to show how Wentworth became involved in the strife.

Charles, finding every order treated with no greater obedience than could be shown by the most complete anger and contempt of his mandates, at last resolved to endeavour to deceive by feigned concession, and thus throw the Scots off their guard, till in secret he had formed an army to enforce his will.

He now wrote to the Marquis of Hamilton, his commissioner in Scotland, who, himself a Scotchman, had advised the King either to grant the Covenanters all their demands, or send a fleet filled with soldiers to garrison Berwick and Carlisle, following swiftly with a 1637. powerful land force.*

"I expect," said Charles, "not any thing can reduce that people to obedience but force only. In the meantime your care must be how to dissolve the multitude, and, if it be possible, to possess yourselves of my castles of Edinburgh and Stirling, which I do not expect. To this end I give you leave to flatter them with what hopes you please so you engage not me against my grounds; and in particular, that you consent neither to the calling of Parliament nor General Assembly until the Covenant be disavowed and given up, your chief end being now to win time until I am ready to suppress them. I will rather die than yield to those impertinent and damnable demands, as you rightly call them."†

Again he says: "I do not expect that you should declare the adherers to the Covenant traitors until you have heard my fleet is set sail."

And yet another paternal sentence, on hearing from Hamilton that the Covenanters had explained they meant no rebellion against the laws or legal authority, but only to be true to the religion they professed:

"As concerning the explanation of their damnable Covenant, I commend the giving ear to the explanation or anything else, to win time."

Time, indeed, was needed. Nothing could exceed the muddle-headed condition of Laud, whose singular capacity for bringing matters into hopeless confusion was in no way counterbalanced by a talent for replacing order.

* Rushworth, 8vo, 2, 518.　　　　　　† Ibid, 519.

For the first time we find him alluding to the matter to Wentworth, but he does not venture to state the truth in all its menacing proportions.

He says: "The Scottish business is extreme ill indeed, and what will become of it God knows, but certainly no good; and his Majesty hath been notoriously betrayed by some of them."

None would have imagined from this that the writer had been the chief mover and prompter of all the mischief. He then casually added that he had been told that the Scots had secretly taken a list of their countrymen in Ulster, and had found its amount to be above forty thousand fighting men. He probably hoped for a contradiction from Lord Wentworth.

But he was likely to be disappointed, for intelligence reached the Lord Deputy from other quarters.

A committee to decide on Scottish affairs had been summoned. Of these, the Earl of Arundel, Secretary Windebanke, and Lord Cottington were for war. But the more experienced, Vane and Coke and the Earl of Northumberland, were quite against it.

The latter wrote to Wentworth, to put him on his guard. At this moment there was not more than £200 in the English exchequer, nor by all the means that could be devised could they calculate on raising more than £110,000 for the expenses of a war. The royal arsenals were empty of arms and ammunition. There were no great commanders to inspire the people with confidence, and the people themselves had been so long unused to bear arms that they were now untrained and unfit for enterprise.

Another and not the least consideration was that

the English all through the country were so discontented 1637.
on account of the number of unlawful impositions
they were called on to endure, that they were much
more likely to join the Scots than to take part against
them.

The Earl of Northumberland, therefore, weighing all
these things, advised the King rather to give them
their own conditions than begin a war without the
means of carrying it on.

But this distasteful advice was not followed. The
King was resolved to enforce his commands, and
preparations were at once ordered.

Lord Clifford, the brother of Lord Wentworth's first
wife, received orders to prepare himself in the best
manner he could, and to begin the training of both
horse and foot regiments in the northern counties.

He wrote to Lord Wentworth, begging his advice,
stating that as yet he was destitute of men, money,
and arms; and hoping that, if any Irish troops were
sent over, he might have a command among them.

At this time, also, Lord Wentworth received a
letter from the Marquis of Lorne. It is a curiosity
in its way, as showing the style, composition, and
spelling of the eldest son of the Duke of Argyll in
those days :—

The Lord Lorne to the Lord Deputy.

"My werrie noble Lord.

"My Dewetie to his sacred Majestie tyes me to late
your Lo. know that thair is zitt some few resting in
thiz Pairtes of the rebellious Race of Clandonald who
hes evir takine thair Adwantage of trowblesome Tymis

1638.

to execute thair Rebellionis. Bot now it seemis thair Intentionne and Intelligence goeth farther; for (as some of themselffes hes confest upone Examinationne) they have Intelligence with many *Irishree* in that Kingdome & lykwayes from abroade, that upone the leaste Sture in his Majesties Dominionnes (which I hope in God they shall never find) both Odoneill and Oneill with some of thair awne Race abroade, justlie so puneished, ar to joyne togidder with werrie great Confidence to find Freindes before thame at home that may mak thame one werrie considerable Partie. How far thair is any Probabilitie of this, or quhat may be the Consequence of it in his Majesties Service thair is best knowen to your Lo. Which I remit to zour Lo. wyise Consideratiomne and shall evir remaine

"Your Lordship's

"maist humble Servant

"LORNE.*

"KINTYR 25*th Julii* 1638."

So faithful a subject and so correct a scholar was the Marquis of Lorne under Charles the First!

The King now sent to Lord Wentworth to know what aid he could furnish from Ireland in the event of a war with Scotland.

Lord Wentworth replied that the forces in Ireland at present amounted to two thousand foot and six hundred horse, which was, if anything, too little for the defence of Ireland alone, and would afford none to spare for Scotland. The settling of the plantations of

---

* Strafford Papers, 2, 187.

Connaught and Munster and other parts of the kingdom was now going on, and consequently the people
more excitable than usual. There were great numbers
of Scots in Ulster of the same religion as their countrymen at home, and, consequently, likely to lend them all
the aid in their power. To lessen the little army in
Ireland would make matters worse by causing the
flame to break out there also: and as this would de-
crease the number of English, there would be fewer
to counterbalance them. But though it would not be
safe to diminish the present number of troops, he
thought it possible to raise three or four thousand
men in Ireland, mostly English. For though the
Irish were likely enough to fight well against the
Scots, having no tie of sympathy with them, yet it
would not be wise to have too many accomplished
Irish soldiers who, when the Scots were done with,
might turn their arms against their teachers, and impart their own knowledge to their countrymen.

The gentlemen most fitted to raise recruits, Lord
Wentworth said, were Sir Francis Willoughby and
Sir Robert Farrer. They were quite to be trusted.
And he would spare ten or a dozen active captains
or lieutenants of his present army to assist them in
training their men.

But all the arms for the recruits must be sent from
England ; he had none to spare.

He also begged the King would give him early
instructions what to do, so that he might as soon as
needed draw the greater part of his little army into
Ulster, as near Scotland as might be, and, perhaps,
cause some change there on account of its proximity.

He thus simply answered the King's questions and

offered no opinion, which, indeed, had not been asked. He told Northumberland that he had quite resolved to decline meddling or giving any counsel at all, further than he should be commanded and required thereunto by his Majesty on the matter of Scotland. But to Northumberland, as to a private friend, he had no objection to speak in confidence, to this effect.

This matter had certainly happened at a very inconvenient time, as there were neither men, money, nor ammunition to carry it through with the speed and force to be desired. It was also the more dangerous from being so unexpected, and this was occasioned by that most unhappy principle of State practised both by his present Majesty, as well as by his father, of keeping secret and distinct all the affairs of Scotland from the knowledge of the council of England, in so much that no man was entrusted or knew anything of Scotland but a Scot. This was, in effect, to continue them in the condition of separate kingdoms, and to lose the advantage of English vigilance in the affairs of Scotland.

But, on the other hand, it was most fortunate that all our neighbours abroad were " so soundly together by the ears one with another," so as to have no leisure to meddle with us. " And," added Wentworth, with too premature triumph, " without assistance from abroad, the gallant Gospellers shall not by God's blessing be able to bear up their rebellious humours against their King, or bring other than their own ruin upon themselves."

Another advantage was, that from henceforth it would make the Crown trust the Scots less and the

English more; if only in this matter the English would
carry themselves with their ancient virtue and faithfulness towards their kings. He was quite of opinion
that the insolence of the Scots, in the protestation they
had published in answer to the King's proclamation,
was not to be borne by any rule of monarchy. It must
be corrected, or else it would lead to yet more daring
boldness.

But as for the ways and means to put down this
peril, which he quite agreed with Northumberland
was much greater than if a foreign enemy were at the
door, he must deprecate a sudden and rash declaring
of war. Neither could he wish the King to sacrifice
his will and honour to their mutiny, nor entangle himself with acts of Parliament, oaths, or what not, which
would be sure to be demanded with the same rudeness
with which they now called for a Parliament. And to
grant them a Parliament, at present, were the greatest
meanness.

But he advised the King to state to them that,
though if they had in the first place moderately sought
and sued for what they wanted, it might have been
granted; but it was not the custom of the best and
mildest of kings to be threatened with Parliaments.
He could not comply on seeming compulsion. Let
them wait and trust to his affection to them, 'and
meanwhile recollect themselves better, and consider
the modesty, the reverence, wherewith they were to
approach God's anointed and their King, and so frame
their petitions and supplications as that they might be
granted without diminution to his height and royal
estate. Lord Wentworth thought they might be thus
persuaded. But, if not, if they did their worst, they

 yet could never compel him to concede their demands.

Meanwhile, he proposed with all speed and secrecy to put strong garrisons into Berwick and Carlisle, well furnished with all kinds of ammunition. Let the whole winter be spent in training recruits, not only in the garrison towns alone, but in all the northern parts of England. By this means there might be a very large army, horse and foot, ready by the spring without any charge to the King.

Supposing the Scots, melted by the proposed royal address, should show themselves penitent, then Lord Wentworth advised to treat them " with all lenity and sweetness."

But if they continued stubborn and refractory, then let their havens be prohibited from all manner of commerce, inward or outward. This, Northumberland, as Admiral of the Fleet, would well know how to manage —one of the chief points being to seize as much of their shipping as possible.

Also, every endeavour should be made to raise a party for the King in Scotland. The loyal were to be commanded to separate from the rebels on pain of being considered equally guilty. The rebellious Presbyters should be seized and kept in prison, but no farther injured.

The best part of the Irish army should be quartered in Ulster, to keep a check on their countrymen on both sides of the Channel. The clergy, both in England and Ireland, should be instructed to preach to the people against these disorders and rebellions, as fervently as the rebels do against the prayer-book and the ceremonies of the church.

Lastly, Lord Wentworth counselled an expedition against Leith in the spring, which, with the help of the fleet, he thought might be easily taken. At present, it was weak, but might be very strongly fortified. When taken, therefore, let it be held by a strong garrison of eight or ten thousand men, relievable by sea. If this were done, the King might give his law to Edinburgh, and soon after to the whole kingdom. That accomplished, let the garrison and fort of Leith be maintained at the expense of the Scots till they had received the Common Prayer Book used in the churches of England without any alteration, allowed the bishops to settle peaceably in their jurisdictions, nay, possibly, till Scotland conformed in all things, temporal as well as ecclesiastical, wholly to the government and laws of England and Scotland, governed by the King and Council of England in a great part— at least as much as the people of Ireland.

But where was the money to come from to carry out all this?

"In good faith," said Lord Wentworth, "every man will give it, I hope, from his children upon such an extremity as this, when no less, verily, than all we have comes thus to the stake. In a word, we are, God be praised, rich and able, and in this case it may be justly said: ' *Salus Populi, Suprema Lex,*' and the King must not want our substance for the preservation of the whole."*

Nothing could appear more simple than this plan on paper. But so strangely did it ignore the other side of the question and the possibility of the power of

---

* The Lord Deputy to the Earl of Northumberland, ii., 189.

resistance to this clever scheme, that it seems hardly to belong to the usually far-seeing and carefully-balancing mind of Wentworth. Possibly, his judgment was affected by the state of his health; but the great defect was his utter ignorance of the Scotch character.

Before going to Ireland he had formed his plans, and was now carrying them out successfully in detail. Why should not the same power that had subdued the far more unruly Irish manage the Scotch?

He had to learn the reason by experience. It is also remarkable how little he knew of the state of feeling in England. Again, Northumberland was the better judge, when he said the English were more likely to aid the Scots than to fight against them. How Lord Wentworth could possibly imagine that they would identify their own cause with that of the King, and come forward with voluntary offerings, is, to say the least, strangely opposed to his general cautious judgment of the multitude. But, possibly, he included only the aristocracy in his calculation of loyal offering. He had not to wait long to be undeceived with regard to his hopes.

The first disappointment was in his own Presidency of the North of England.

The King had sent orders to Sir Edward Osborne to muster all the forces of Yorkshire, and see they were in readiness. In obedience to this command, Sir Edward, who was the Vice-President under Lord Wentworth, summoned all the Deputy-Lieutenants of the county to meet at York, on the 27th of July.

Of these many were absent on trivial excuses, and of those that came none showed the least enthusiasm or appeared impressed with any special need in conse-

quence of the King's special order. They saw no 1638.
occasion for any hurry beyond the usual days for
reviewing the militia and supplying the vacant ranks.
One said it was harvest time, and the men could wait
till that was over. When Sir Edward stated his
opinion to the contrary, on account of the message of
the King, he was at once asked if he knew of any
more cause for hurrying the muster than they did, for
if not, they saw no reason for such haste. To this he
gave no reply, as the policy of Charles was to make
preparations for war, without stating his object, and
merely under colour of getting the army in a good
condition, for the general needs of the country.

Sir William Savile, not a member of the House so
inimical to that of Wentworth, but his own nephew,
openly opposed the Vice-President. Osborne had
given orders that all the cavalry of the West Riding
should come to York, to be trained, as he was detained
there on account of various matters, and it would be
more convenient for him to review them while the
drilling was going on. But Savile boldly told the Vice-
President that his horses should not come to York, but
be trained in some more convenient place in the West
Riding. Osborne dared him, at his peril, to keep back
his horses—all the rest were coming to York, and he
would find it somewhat dangerous to be the only
defaulter.

The Vice-President then, at once, wrote to the Lord
Deputy, begging him, in his capacity of President of
the North, without alluding to Savile, to send him
orders to call all the cavalry to York, so that after
each division had been drilled separately, they might
then be exercised in one complete body. He also

1638. begged Wentworth to command him to bring before the Council table the names of any who should refuse to comply.

Sixty pounds was the sum allowed for the expenses of training all the infantry forces of Yorkshire for this gathering; but it proved too little for the cavalry; and though Osborne was so loyal as to offer to pay out of his own pocket a share of the deficiency, if the other two captains of cavalry would do the same, he was met with a decided refusal. The Deputy-Lieutenant said the whole £60 was needed for the foot, and Lord Wentworth was therefore petitioned for a grant of £20 more, to be applied to the training of the horse troops alone. This he kindly proposed should be deducted from the salary of £100 a year of Sir Robert Farrer, the muster-master, on the ground that in all other counties the muster-master himself trained the men, till the officers were competent to relieve him of the duty. Osborne also begged that a trainer might be sent over from Ireland, probably having greater confidence in one who had performed his duty under Lord Wentworth than any other. *

Writhing as he was under the relapse of health lately mentioned, Lord Wentworth had made arrangements to spend a few weeks in the country, with a view to recovery. He rarely returned to the city unbenefited by a holiday with nature. The prospect of such an access of labour and anxiety as appeared in the Scottish troubles rendered it especially necessary that he should watch his health, though even he under-reckoned the strain that was to be put upon it. But before he

---

* Sir Edward Osborne to the Lord Deputy, ii.

could leave Dublin many arrangements had to be made, which compelled him to defer his departure.

The first thing to be done was to give a minute inspection of the condition of the army.

It turned out to be no idle report, but a bare fact, that Ulster alone did contain 40,000 Scots able to bear arms. "I do assure your Lordship," said Wentworth, in reply to Laud, "it is not to be kept secret. We hear the crack of it, if not the threat, every day in the streets."

This, alone, rendered it needful to increase the present small force which, happily, was in such good order, as to render it easy for the discipline to be extended to new levies. Now it was that Lord Wentworth had cause to rejoice that he had not waited till the hour of danger to remodel his army. The change in a few years was striking indeed. When he came to Ireland, the cavalry had no other weapons than staves and swords. He declared there was scarcely a good pistol among them, and scarcely an officer who knew how to order his men.

But now, without costing the English treasury a shilling, he was able to muster 609 horsemen, of whom 110 were cuirassiers, and the rest carabineers. The carabineers, formerly almost defenceless, were now completely armed with swords and pistols, helmets, gorgets, breast and back plates, short tasses, and though less completely mailed than the iron warrior of two centuries past, who was literally, not poetically, sheathed in steel, still, all the exposed portions of the body were protected by plates of metal, while those parts that needed it less, were spared the incumbrance and the weight. The wearers were totally unconscious of

122

1638.

the delightful romance to be associated in times to come by youthful minds with the very name of a knight armed *cap-à-pie*. The cuirasses were called, in short terms, "backs and breasts," while the helmets went by the most terribly prosaic name of "pots."

These troops were daily exercised, and Lord Wentworth declared, with honest pride, that they were so well advanced in knowledge that he trusted no men would be shown more ready or capable to serve than they. The only defect lay in the horses, with which he was still dissatisfied, but which he was unable to remedy for want of means.

He had also ingeniously contrived to add to the mounted troops by the revival of an old custom that had fallen into disuse.

The four Provost Marshals of Leinster, Munster, Ulster, and Connaught had anciently twelve horsemen each, allowed them in the martial list. These were of great use in suppressing revolts, robberies, and other dangers which the carelessness of the justices of the peace had allowed to grow to a dangerous height; the marshals, with their company, being always ready to pursue and seize the outlaws, who would otherwise have escaped the tardy measures of the justices. "They prevented," said Lord Wentworth, "very many violences and some murders done upon the people." Bands of robbers would swoop down on the English, who now, revived in courage, could appeal to the marshals as to the military for aid, without the troublesome formalities needed in the latter case. Thus, not only was there a kind of reserve of cavalry, but a most efficient little civil force,

especially useful when a spirit of revolt was sus-
pected.

The infantry soldiers were divided into half pikemen and half musketeers. They quite equalled the cavalry, in every respect, and Lord Wentworth pronounced that, for anything he could hear or believe, none in the Low Countries were readier in their movements, exacter in their postures, more even, close, and orderly in their marches. He was therefore very confident that, for so far as belonged to exercise, command, and order, he could at any time spare sufficient officers and experienced soldiers, under good chiefs elsewhere to be found, to train and lead twice as many men as their whole body comprised. There was, however, some deficiency still in their arms; but Lord Wentworth undertook to remedy this by Easter, and without any charge to the King.

"And thus," said he, exultingly, "I dare undertake to show and approve them as ready and as well armed men as serve a King, be the eye never so curious which shall overlook them.

"I had them all here under my eye this whole month. They marched hither forth of their garrisons without offering the least violence to the meanest soul of his Majesty's subjects.

"They continued here with so much quietness and civility as, in good faith, you could not have almost taken notice any such men were in town. And they are now marched back with the same peace and order they came: men, if I be not mightily mistaken, well pleased, well affected, ready with cheerfulness and courage to venture their lives for his Majesty's person and service wherever they shall be appointed."

Earnest in all things, perhaps the enthusiasm of Lord Wentworth culminated in the army. He regarded it as a child of his own. It was no abstract existence, and needed no arguments to demonstrate its being. There it was, imposing in appearance, certain in capability and power. Could the King only acquire and maintain an army of such material and education as this little force in Ireland, and increase it to a sufficient number of men, he would be irresistible. On this idea Lord Wentworth constantly brooded, but not so secretly as to conceal from all others what was the subject of his meditations.

And it was at the hour that he resolved on the increase of the army, not as hitherto, for the just purpose of maintaining order in Ireland, but to render her a store-house where a military power was to be reared for the service of the King, that he fixed his doom. This intention on the part of Lord Wentworth has often been denied by his friends, who justify his raising men in Ireland to send to Scotland, by the sudden emergency of the case, and declare the charge of Pym, that it was only a part of a system meant to coerce England, to be unfounded. It will, therefore, be better to give the words of Lord Wentworth himself. They occur in the letter in which he describes the present condition of his army, and are addressed to the confidential secretary, Coke, who was pledged to secrecy, even from his fellow officer, Wandesforde.

"Considering it is necessary that his Majesty breed up and have a Seminary of Soldiers in some part or other of his dominions, a truth which, perchance, the present time shows but over plainly to every eye, with-

out doubt, it cannot be settled in any other part where 1638.
the ordinary use of it could have produced greater
effects for the honour and perfecting the great and
needful services of the Crown on this side, with so
little charge, with more safety, removed or transported
with greater conveniency, to answer the several occasions of the three kingdoms. So as in my weak
judgment, it is a matter worthy the care of the great
ministers on that side to see, that the General, here, be
called upon in all times, as well peace as war, diligently
to attend his charge, and to be rendered deeply
answerable in point of state, if he neglect or slubber
over the duty he owes his Majesty in the good government of the army: To wit, that it be complete for
bodies of men, for arms and other provisions of all
kinds, for often exercise, perfect knowledge and use of
their weapons, and giving them as much as may be,
severally, the understanding of every duty belonging
to worthy officers and soldiers.

" And truly this is no small matter. For I dare be
bold to say, if this work had been attended and followed since the war broke up, as it ought to have been,
*the Crown might have taken hence, at this, worthy and
able officers of our own, to have led an army of twenty
thousand men in any part of Christendom, under the
conduct and direction of a gallant and brave chief
chosen there and appointed to that purpose by his
Majesty.*"

But even this design becomes almost safe by the
side of another which was now laid before Charles,
and which nothing but accident prevented him from
adopting. It was entitled:—

" A Design to extricate his Majesty out of these

1638. present troubles with the Scots, and at once to render him free from the Miseries of his Majesty's royal prerogatives in England." *

This was to draw an army of ten thousand men from Flanders, and land them secretly in England. It was considered that the fact of their being foreign, and accustomed to war, would render them much more terrible than a far greater number levied in England. These men were to be jointly commanded by their own general, and a subject of the King. The money was to be raised by the Roman Catholics, on condition of abrogating all the severe laws against the recusants, or, perhaps, granting full toleration to the Roman Catholic religion. There was little doubt not only of large contributions from the Roman Catholics themselves, but it was thought the Pope would contribute not less than six months' pay, and by the time that was exhausted, the Scots would be compelled to lay down their arms.

But then the question arose, that as these laws against the Catholics had been passed by Parliament, they could not be repealed except by the same power. What then was to be done? The remedy was quite easy, says the proposer of this precious scheme.

" As Charles V., having an army ready to attend the Diet, upon pretence to secure the Electors assembled about the choice of an Emperor, did so awe that Diet, as thereby himself was chosen Emperor, albeit, the electors had no inclination that way of themselves.

" Even so, might the King, having a foreign army on foot, subdue the Scots therewith, and at the same instant keep the Parliament in awe, that his Majesty might

* Clarendon's State Papers, ii., 19.

easily make them come to what conditions he pleased.   1638.
And by this means, confirm his royal prerogatives, and
repeal such laws against recusants, as were made, not
only with intention absolutely to root out the Catholic
religion, but to keep even his sacred Majesty from this
Crown.   Witness the death of the Queen of Scots, his
Majesty's grandmother, of happy memory."

Of course, the negotiations with the Pope must be
kept very secret, but there was a very good example
of how the matter might be managed.

When Henry IV. of France wanted to be reconciled
to Rome, he employed M. d'Ossat, then living as a
private priest.   Just so, might King Charles of England " employ in a private way some stout spirited
priest, who durst lay the cause home to his Holiness,
and give him such motives for this design as he should
no ways be able to gainsay."   Nay, there was a priest
of the name of Houlden just fit for the office, being
" dexterous, learned, wise, virtuous, and a most loyal
subject of his Majesty."

Was this, as one would be ready to think, merely a
wild idea that occurred in some weak brain which
could meet with nothing but indignation at the hands
of the King?   For Charles always professed himself
a strict Protestant, nor is there any reason to believe
that he was otherwise.   But then, what a pleasant
prospect it was to compel not only the stubborn
Scots, but the hated Parliament to bend to his will.
Charles was not much in the habit of asking himself
whether a thing was right or not—still here was the
example of the gallant Bourbon, who was, and still is,
held up as an object of such admiration to the world.
He had not scrupled to use the aid of the Catholics

1638. when he found his plans must fail without it. There
is, unfortunately, no room to doubt of the complicity
of Charles in this conspiracy to betray the liberties of
England to her worst enemies. It matters little who
was the first mover, it is certain it met with the approbation of the King. An English Catholic, named Gage,
a colonel in the service of Spain, was employed to
sound the Spaniards on the subject.* If they would
furnish the King of England with ten thousand armed
men, he, in return, would give them twenty thousand
unarmed.

But the Spaniards thought the exchange on too large
a scale. They did not like the English, and did not
care to have twenty thousand in their army. Neither
could they spare ten thousand trained soldiers. But
they had long been accustomed to employ Irish mer-
cenaries, whose very hatred to England made them
more trusted by Spain. Three mixed regiments were
a regular part of the Spanish army. Gage, therefore,
proposed that the King of England should enable
them to keep up these three regiments to the amount
of 2000 men in each, making in the whole 6000
Irish, added to 4000 English, the latter being thus kept
subordinate in number to the Irish. In exchange, they
might send 4000 foot and 400 horse troops to
Charles.

This proposal came much nearer their wishes. But
the Spaniards seem to have had no more trust in his
Britannic Majesty than his own countrymen, as they
desired his part of the treaty should be first performed.

* Letter of Col. Gage, Clar. State Papers, ii., 21.

As a rule, State Papers are not of interest to the general reader. But so terrible a light does the following throw on the real character of Charles, so completely does it justify the jealousy of the Puritans, and so impossible is it to transmute the document into clearer, simpler language, that it is better to copy it from its original text in the handwriting of Windebanke, the King's Secretary of State.

" Instructions for our trusty and well-beloved Colonel, Henry Gage, now in the service of the Infant Cardinal in Flanders. *

" You shall immediately upon the receipt of our letters of credit which go herewith, procure access to the Infant Cardinal in private. And you shall deliver our said letters, with such professions in our name of our desire to continue a friendly intelligence with the King of Spain and him, as you in discretion shall think fit.

" You shall then acquaint him with a proposition lately made to us, wherein both our affairs and his are highly concerned, which is for some number of soldiers ready armed to be sent from thence for our service, in exchange for a greater number unarmed, to be levied here for the completing of their English and Irish regiments there.

" You shall represent to him that the number which we desire for the present service is 6000 foot and 400 horse, which, considering the number they are to have in exchange from hence yearly, being likely to continue, is not great; it being probable that the number of their recruits every year, which they are to have

* Clarendon State Papers, 2, 23.

 from hence, will amount to as many. Whereas we are not likely after this present action to have occasion to demand any from thence again.

"Of these 6000 foot, we expect 4500 shall be Harquebussiers, and the rest Pikes. And if the whole number shall be less than 6000, then the division of Harquebussiers and Pikes to be according to that proportion. These forces of horse and foot you are to procure to be embarked at Dunkirk in vessels of the King of Spain, and to be transported at our charge to the rendezvous. And they are to be there by the 1st day of April next ensuing, according to the foreign computation. And you must acquaint them that if they shall fail to be there at that time, they will be of no use, and the service be utterly lost. And you shall further make known to the Infant Cardinal that they shall be safe conducted to the rendezvous by our ships. And you are to procure that victuals be shipped there for these forces for one month at the least, at his Majesty's charge, assuring the Infant Cardinal that our ships which shall be sent to safe conduct them, shall bring ready money with them to pay for those victuals and their freight, and for the defraying of all other incident and necessary charges.

" As soon as they shall be embarked, they are to enter into our pay, according to the pay of Flanders, and to continue for six months, or as long as there shall be cause to use them; only deduction is to be made for their victuals.

" You are to take special care that the men be able, and their arms complete and serviceable; and the like for the horse.

" You are to acquaint the Infant Cardinal that they

shall be commanded in chief by some person of the nobility, being our subject. But that we expect your personal service herein, as one in whom we shall much confide, and therefore do desire him to authorise you by commission accordingly.

" In consideration of these forces thus armed, we do hereby engage ourself, that as soon as you shall have concerted and agreed this business, and given notice of it hither, he will instantly give warrant for the levying of such numbers of our English and Irish subjects as shall be sufficient to recruit and complete all such English and Irish regiments and companies in the King of Spain's service in Flanders, as at any time have heretofore been recruited or completed. And we will suffer or permit them to be sent from hence into Flanders for the service of the King of Spain, without any let or hindrance. And this, you are to assure the Infant Cardinal, we do promise and bind ourself in the word of a King, punctually to see performed. You must use great secresy, dexterity, and expedition in this business, and take care that it be not divulged; seeing if the party in Scotland should come to the knowledge of it, it would be utterly overthrown. And, therefore, the better to disguise it, when the forces shall fall down to Dunkirk to be shipped, you must advise upon some rumour to be cast out to amuse the world, that they are designed for Biscay, Italy, or some other parts, and give it out that they are victualled accordingly.

" You must be very cautious, especially if you shall find this proposition not like to succeed, that you deliver no paper thereof, nor engage his Majesty by any writing, lest there be use made of it hereafter to

1638. our prejudice and disservice. But if you shall find a willingness in the Infant Cardinal to assist us upon these conditions, then you are necessarily to treat by writing, but still under profound secresy and promise on their part not to disclose it.

"Now you see the great trust we repose in you; we doubt not but your diligences shall be answerable and according to the weight of this important service.

"You are to press a speedy resolution herein, and to give advertisement thereof hither within fifteen days at the furthest, letting the Infant Cardinal know that, unless expedition be used, the service will be lost."

Thus was to be solved the difficult question of troops for the royal service. Had Charles committed no other crime against his country than to have entered into this plot, the revolution would have been quite justifiable. What greater treason could a King of England commit than to bring in foreign troops paid by the Pope to crush the religion of Scotland, to force the Parliament to abrogate the laws of the country, to let loose the Roman Catholic priests to prey upon the land, and finally, in return for the aid lent in crushing his own country, to send English and Irish men to uphold the tyranny of the Spanish inquisition, and trample down the Protestant religion in those very lands where Queen Elizabeth lent her aid, and Sir Philip Sidney shed his blood to uphold it.

Charles had, indeed, good cause to "use great secresy." Quite necessary was the wicked lie about the expedition being designed for Biscay. He did not in the least exaggerate when he said: "if the party

in Scotland should come to the knowledge of it, it 1638.
would be utterly overthrown." Had this proposal
to the Pope been discovered either in England or Scotland, it is scarcely likely that the people would have
waited for the day of Nottingham.

Fortunately, a sudden reverse of the Spanish arms
rendered it impossible for them to spare their trained
men. The Dutch had obtained too great an advantage
over them, and the number of soldiers lost, put an end
to this miserable negotiation. The King, therefore,
had to renounce all hopes of coercing the Parliament
for the present, and to concentrate all his efforts on the
rebellious Scots.

Lord Wentworth was prepared for a struggle; but,
at the same time, justified the King in his usual insolent
style towards the defenders of liberty. He spoke of
the Scots exactly in the same manner as of Hampden.

" Nor is it to be expected," he said, " the King
should bear so great a disobedience, so high indignities
offered by subjects. Nor that they will, at after, be
brought into their right minds till they be well and
thriftily cudgelled back into them."

Having well examined into all needs, he sent an
agent to Holland to buy new arms, as they could be
obtained there better and cheaper than elsewhere.

Then, utterly worn out, he left Dublin, to endeavour
to snatch a little strength for the threatened troubles,
by passing a few weeks in the country. Nor did he
consider his own health alone.

" The plain truth is," he said, " I go to be quiet,
and cast up my accounts, that whilst the father is
light set by, I may at least be thought to have some
regard to the poor children."

CHAPTER VI.

1638.

THE present opportunity was taken by Lord Wentworth, to attend to matters individual and personal: the coming year gave promise of little time for anything but public matters.

The death of the Earl of Clare had given rise to disputes in his family concerning the division of the property. One of the sons had written about it to Lord Wentworth, who, as his brother-in-law, was likely to take an interest, and whose affection to the memory of his second wife never allowed him to pass by with neglect the least trifle relating to her family.

The matter in question is only of present interest as showing how unfading was the feeling he treasured towards the 'Lady Arabella. He besought Laud to call on the discordant family and endeavour to mediate. His message is couched in these words :—

" From my brother Holles, I understand of the unnatural suits like to spring up in that family, whence I had my late dearest wife, and forth of her those children God of his goodness lends me. To be a party I must not; to wish right understanding and unity amongst them is my duty to the memory of that blessed saint, how great a stranger soever I have been made to all that concerns them ever since.

Therefore, let me very humbly beseech your Grace to employ your pious and wise endeavour to piece them again if it be possible.

" I fear you will find them unruly, loving themselves on both sides something further than moderation, without that equal respect which we ought all to observe towards others."

Poor Laud may well be pitied for the task that Wentworth desired him to perform, though the quality he was desired to bring to its aid, was one that he possessed in perfection.

" Be something obstinate," continues Wentworth, " let not a little beat you off so good a work, and finally, overrule them to be friends, whether they will or no. You will say that is a hard matter. And indeed, I am persuaded less will not do it. They are *propositi tenaces*, which way soever you turn you." To overrule antagonists to be friends in their own despite, may be safely said to be an impossible matter. Nevertheless, it cannot be doubted that many a discord remains unhealed for lack of a wise and good third party, who, in the interests of justice and as a part of that most solemn duty enjoined to each, to do all the good in his power, shall at least make the attempt. The quarrels that are incurable and finally deepen into hatred, are those where there is determined wrong on one side—generally the stronger side. And while it is the rarest thing in this world, for a spectator to brave the distasteful task of pointing out to the powerful wrong-doer his evil position, and endeavouring to convince him of the real nobility of forsaking it, never are wanting a whole swarm of parasites and those interested in keeping open the breach, to en-

1638. courage and flatter and confirm injustice; till, before
long, it persuades itself of the merit of its own deeds,
and views them with complacency only more settled
by time.

But there are, nevertheless, quarrels, and very bitter
and painful ones too, that only wait the voice of
the mediator to vanish into air. They are, when two
souls of high order split on a mistake that has arisen,
it may be accidentally, it may be one of the tares
purposely sown by some wicked enemy who designs
to plunder the wheat. If the parties in question are
not old associates, and have lived apart, they may
separate with the wildest mistakes, the most extrava-
gant misconstruction of each other's character. Once
on a wrong track, every circumstance which really
points the opposite way but serves to misguide; and
farther and farther apart they go, till those who by
unity might largely have increased their own happiness
and that of mankind, live asunder, maimed both in use-
fulness and the enjoyment of life. But, it is here that
a third person, resolved, as Lord Wentworth says, to
" let not a little beat him off so good a work," may
prove the good physician. Let him take pains to
ascertain the exact truth, let him state this truth to
each of the opponents, let him point out the error
under which either or both are suffering, and if they
really be men of lofty souls, his task is done, his reward is gained—it is of such, that the Great Teacher
declared ' Blessed are the peace-makers.'

Laud was about the last person to fulfil these conditions. The most he was likely to do was, without
any inquiry into facts, without troubling himself
as to who really was right or wrong to address

himself to the weaker party, and advise him not
to quarrel but to show his love of peace, by
yielding unconditionally, perhaps his very honour
and truth, to the stronger, and he would then
counsel the stronger who might be altogether in
the wrong to accept the mean submission. Should
this equivocal mode fail, he would be likely to
maintain a pleasant friendship with the strong and
evil, utterly deserting the weak and just as an obstinate wrangler, foolish and perverse who deserved his
fate.

Laud's manner of commencing his task was not
promising. He announced as his sole motive for calling on the antagonists, the wish of Lord Wentworth
that he should try to make peace between them. As
for himself, he had quite work enough of his own to
attend to, and should be very glad if Lord Clare would
refuse his interference. Still, as it was a good work,
and his friend desired him to perform it, he would not
refuse the trouble.

His success was in proportion to his zeal. Yet
Lord Wentworth again wrote :—

"I still beseech you be pleased to settle a peace, if
possibly it may be, in the house of my late Lord Clare,
which I shall most humbly acknowledge. Howbeit,
perchance this is more than either I or yourself shall
have from anybody else. But I owe so much to the
memory of the wife I had from them, that it gives me
infinite contentment when I am able to further anything I think would have pleased her."

The attempt proved a total failure.

Meanwhile, another and much more entangled suit
was progressing.

Up to the year 1637, the strongest of all Lord Wentworth's supporters in Ireland, independently of his two personal friends, Radcliffe and Wandesforde, was Adam Loftus, the Lord Chancellor, who had been one of the Lords Justices previous to the arrival of the Deputy. Wentworth had on every occasion especially acknowledged his help, and it will be remembered on his late visit to England, procured him the honorarium of £3000 in acknowledgment of his good services.

Yet, shortly after this, for some unknown reason, the good feeling between the Deputy and Chancellor began to decline and show its decay in various insignificant matters. At length the smouldering fire burst into an open blaze.

Sir John Giffard brought an action against the Lord Chancellor on behalf of Sir Francis Ruishe for breach of contract. It appeared that the eldest son of the Chancellor had married the daughter of Ruishe, and at the marriage an agreement was made, that in return for a portion of £15,000 brought by the lady, the Chancellor should settle £300 a year on herself and £1200 a year in land on her children. The marriage being completed and the portion paid, the Chancellor refused to perform his part of the contract.

On this, the father of the lady employed Sir John Giffard to bring an action against the defaulter.

The case was tried before the Lord Deputy and Council, and decided against the Chancellor, who, on this, loudly protested against the sentence, challenged the authority of the Court and bitterly accused the Lord Deputy of having secretly instigated the proceedings against him. Lord Wentworth in return burst into one of his diseased and undying rages, and immediately sent his report to England. He soon received a letter from Mr. Secretary Coke, to the effect, that his Majesty was highly displeased that the Lord Chancellor, so great and ancient a judge, and who best understood how to make perfect answers, should now by three imperfect answers to the Lord Deputy and Council, have shown disrespect to justice and dishonour both to the Lord Deputy and the State.

In order to prevent any farther scandal to the government by so eminent an example of contempt, the King requested the Lord Deputy, in case the Chancellor persisted in denying his authority and that of the Council, to take the seals from him and use such compulsory means as law and justice required. But considering his long service and present old age, if he at once submitted, his offence was to be passed by and he was to retain his office, which otherwise was to be elsewhere disposed of.

To this message of his Majesty, Coke added the following scornful comment of his own.

"The Lord Chancellor is in your hands, which, I am persuaded, will support him better than his own, in this infirmity of his age and passion."

But right or wrong as might have been the Chancellor in the main cause, it was unjustifiable to treat him like a child in this manner, and he very properly refused to submit. He accordingly petitioned the King for leave to come to England and lay the case before him. As long ago as the year 1628, permission to come to England whenever he pleased had been granted him under the great seal, it was therefore a mere matter of form to apply for it now. However, his request was well taken. In granting it, the King used these words : " Our said Chancellor, having occasions of importance requiring his present repair hither, hath humbly besought us to give him leave to come over hither, as not presuming to adventure to come without our pleasure and direction therein, notwithstanding his former grant, which we do not only take well from him, but are now graciously pleased to grant unto him this his suit."

A letter was therefore sent to Lord Wentworth directing him to license the Chancellor's departure. It was one of the constant double-faced ways of Charles. First, he had given the Deputy absolute power over the defendant. Then, without the least reference to this, he had made the defendant absolutely independent of him.

It was not likely that with the King's license for his departure, the Chancellor should submit, nor was it more probable that with the King's warrant to commit him, Wentworth should forbear. In such a case, the strongest must win the day, and accordingly, Sir Adam Loftus was deprived of his seals of office and committed to prison by the Lord Deputy and all the Council for contempt of court. An account was sent to the King, who thereupon fully confirmed his committal, but at the same time declared his intention of hearing the appeal of the Chancellor, on condition that he apologised to the Court for his contemptuous behaviour. If he did this, he was not to come to England at once, but to stay in Ireland till he had stated all his grounds of appeal, and answered all the charges of the Lord Deputy and Council in full. But he still refused to apologise, and this being reported to the King, a royal message was sent to the Lord Deputy and Council, expressing the most complete approbation of their conduct to the unlucky Chancellor, " Only," said his Majesty : " we mislike your overmuch forbearance and patience, in permitting such scandalous disrespect to be cast by him both upon you, our Deputy, and upon the Board ; which reflect upon our authority and the government very much, and are not to be passed over.

" We do, therefore, require you to call him again before you, and represent unto him his miscarriage in such sort as it appeareth by your said letters and our great mislike thereof. And withal, let him know, that for reparation of the honour due to us and our government there, we require him to submit himself, and to acknowledge his fault before you, and to petition for pardon in that behalf; without performance whereof you are to keep him still in his restraint ; and we are resolved not to admit him to our presence ; which otherwise (that and such other things being performed as our former letters required) we are pleased to grant, and that with such expedition as you desire." *

What was the use of resistance after such a warning as this? Nothing but the consciousness of innocence and the resolution to suffer rather than gain relief by ignoble means, could have sustained the Chancellor in continued defiance. Of one of these he was certainly deficient.

Lord Wentworth and the Council both declared that he had so grossly misrepresented matters that

---

* The King to the Lord Deputy and Council, ii., 196.

1638.

nothing less than a public hearing of the case should satisfy them, as the only way to vindicate the honour of their proceedings, and their own good name to the world.*

They charged the Lord Chancellor with "foul transgressions in the exercise of his place, to the great scandal of his Majesty's catholic justice and oppression of the subject, as well as to his lordship's own particular benefit." If they were not able to prove their words, then would they have abused the King.

They "imputed to the Chancellor his insolent breaking through even all his Majesty's directions for the government of this kingdom (Ireland), and that, by his vast assumptions and universal irregularities, he hath invaded and disordered the whole frame of justice and all the other courts of judicature throughout the kingdom, and do all to a man advertise that, in our poor opinions, that lord, the peace and prosperity of this State and his Majesty's affairs cannot any longer stand together."

The style of these general charges are so manifestly exaggerated that it would be quite unjust to condemn Loftus from them. The fact that the whole of the Council joined against him is also no proof of guilt. Innumerable have been the cases in which a large number have joined to condemn an innocent person. Nothing but a knowledge of the whole of the facts can enable us to judge this or any other case justly. And these we do not possess, as, unfortunately, the great events that so rapidly followed prevented a rigorous revision of the trial of this case.

* The Lord Deputy to Sir John Wintour, ii., 227.

A vague report, given by Lord Clarendon, ascribes 1638. the interest of Lord Wentworth in behalf of the payment of the marriage settlement of the young Lady Loftus to a scandalous intrigue between himself and her, some letters " of a tender nature " having " been said " to be found in her cabinet after her death. But of this, also, there is not the slightest proof. Neither the letters nor a single sentence from them were ever given, while the defendant made not the slightest allusion to such a cause. But as Lord Wentworth's brother had married a Mrs. Ruishe, there was a very simple reason for the Deputy taking a special interest in this case.

The strongest argument is furnished by the Lord Chancellor against himself. To gain his release, he signed a mean petition for pardon, with a confession, which, if false, tells more against him than if it were true, and exhibits one of the most painful pictures of humiliation and cowardice, while, at the same time, an old man compelled to such an utterance by fear alone cannot but excite our pity for himself and disgust for those whose lack of mercy and forbearance forced him into such a position, using the helplessness of old age as a tool of crime.

Notwithstanding this confession, he did not gain his liberty. His neglect to comply with the orders of the Council in several matters—such, for instance, as sequestrating a portion of his estate to pay the sum sued for—furnished cause for detaining him in prison, and it was not till the 19th of November, 1639, that his appeal against the judgment was heard before the King and the Privy Council of England. He gained nothing by it, as the Irish sentence was fully confirmed in every article, and he was compelled to pay the portion according to his agreement.

As far as we can judge, he appears to have been in the wrong. No reason is assigned for his breaking the contract he had voluntarily made, and the error of Lord Wentworth appears to have been not in deciding the cause against him, and compelling him to keep his word, but in the fierce and merciless manner he maintained to a man who, if in the wrong, was old, and had been a faithful servant to both the King and his Deputy, and who, while compelled to do justice, might have been spared the petty indignity of a public apology.

A more pleasant occupation during the time was the consultation of Lord Wentworth with Lord Clifford. Clifford, as has been already stated, had been ordered to hold himself in readiness, and he had written to Wentworth, to ask his advice.

To him Wentworth spoke openly, and expressed himself with less confidence than hitherto. He said he should never meddle with the affairs of Scotland unless compelled—one kingdom was enough for him to attend to. If the Marquis of Hamilton, who had been sent as King's ambassador to them, should fail them, Lord Wentworth thought the effect would be in every way most troublesome and distracting. The inward rent was more to be feared than any outward enemy, so long as they were all united against the latter. But blows, he felt sure, must be exchanged.

To his brother-in-law, Clifford, who had always been greatly attached to him, he gave the following counsel :—

"You may be sure you are to have your share.

And a business, indeed, worth your looking unto, as an occasion wherein you may not only express your virtue and the ancient faith of your house to the Crown, but make it a great and ready step to your own honour and fortune. And therefore, in my judgment, you are with all cheerfulness and diligence to attend and execute such commands as his Majesty may honour your Lordship with."

He then advised him strongly to see to the training of his men with his own eye, assuring him that the presence of the commander had a wonderful effect on the progress of the men. He especially advised him to be a proficient in the use of pike and musket, as when soldiers saw their officers well acquainted with the commonest duties, it encouraged them greatly to learn them themselves. This plan would make him quickly master of work which, if trusted to inferiors, would be drawn out to a mighty length.

"I wish myself at your elbow for an hour a day next week," said Lord Wentworth, kindly, " in which time if I made you not the best musketeer Trent North, you should never trust to my assumption at after."

He then warned him to be very careful in choosing only able-bodied men, licensing all aged and decrepit persons to go free, and send strong ones in their places.

Also after he had carefully trained men for service, not to allow them to exchange without his special warrant, or that of some responsible officer. The trained men should, as far as possible, be either householders themselves, or the sons of good yeomen, with settled places of abode, so as not to be tempted to flit about.

 He was to accustom his men to bear the weight of their armour and weapons, so that it might as soon as possible become easy. Above all, let him win the King's confidence in his fidelity, and deserve it. And as it was likely there would be a garrison placed in Carlisle, he could not too soon use the interest of his friends to be made governor of it. It was all the more worth Lord Clifford's trial, as Wentworth believed that when once the garrison was there it was not likely to be removed again.

At present, he believed the King would surely send Clifford some able soldier to aid him in his task; but, if not, he himself would let him have a practised officer from his own army, who should teach his men the use of arms, and that "better perhaps than one of your great colonels, who many times vainly think it an inferior thing for them to know anything that belongs thereunto."

Fervently did Lord Wentworth endeavour to raise up friends for his master, and inspire them with loyalty against the struggle he began too plainly to see could not be avoided.

To the Marquis of Lorne he wrote, thanking him for his warning, and calling on him to support the King. "In a time so uncertain and declining towards disobedience," he told him, "it becomes us all, especially persons of your lordship's blood and abilities, actively and avowedly to serve the Crown. A perfunctory duty is less, by much less, than can acquit us either in ourselves or to others, never to stand in judgment before the clear discerning eye of our great and wise master. To be lazy lookers on, to lean to the King behind the curtain, or to whisper forth only our allegiance, will not serve our turn."

His next argument was artfully directed to the self interest of Lord Lorne, of whose disinterestedness he had many and grave doubts. He himself truly needed no such argument to serve the King as the following :—

1638.

"Much rather ought we to break our shins in emulation who should go soonest and furthest in assurance, and in courage to uphold the prerogatives and full dominion of the Crown, ever remembering ourselves that nobility is such a grudged and envied piece of monarchy that all tumultuary force offered to Kings doth ever in the second place fall upon the peers, being such motes in the eyes of a giddy multitude as they never believe themselves clear sighted into their liberty, indeed, till these be at least levelled to a parity, as the other altogether removed to give better prospect to their anarchy."

Now follows a striking illustration of Lord Wentworth's views on religion. He is perfectly honest in what he says :—

"But most lamentable it is to hear that religion should be once mentioned to patronise the disobedience of subjects towards their King; that it should be preached in a Protestant Church, against so excellent and Christian a prince, is most scandalous, and inflames and heightens the madness of it beyond all example.

"Could Bellarmine, Mariana, with all the rest of that rebellious college do more? Nay, did they ever so much? Certainly, no. For they never absolved subjects of their allegiance, but when the King in their opinion was heretick in fundamentals.

"But to shake off that strait bond for discipline, for

 ceremonies, *for things* (let Mr. Bloyer and his Presbyters rage never so much to the contrary) *purely and simply indifferent*, is more, in truth, I think, than the Church of Rome itself can justly be convicted or accused of.

"May God, therefore, in his goodness avert that mischief, that great impiety from amongst us, and give us the grace with modesty and humility to look into and discern those better duties which all law of God and man exact of us in these exigents."

If these things were indeed purely and simply indifferent, why should the King force them on a nation at the expense of war. Certainly Wentworth himself would not have done it. He now supported the King not to uphold his religion but his authority, even in such trifles. But to the Scots they were no more trifles than the great idol to which Nebuchadnezzar bade the prophet bow. All through the Old Testament idolatry was stamped as the greatest of sins. All through the New Testament Christ and the Apostles had marked their worship by its absolute simplicity and absence of form. Christ himself preached anywhere. On the heights of the mountain, by the waves of the sea, even amid the fields of corn his voice was heard. The very strongest of his denunciations was reserved for the Pharisees, who, leaving the spirit, rested all on the empty form of religion. Paul had not hesitated to denounce the superstition that imagined the Lord of Heaven and Earth could narrow his dwelling-place to a temple made with hands.

What possible precedent or authority could be found in the acts of the first disciples for enforcing the wearing

of a surplice, the turning to the east, the bowing at 1638.
the name of Christ in a creed, while the name of God
himself was passed over without notice ?

To obey the orders of Laud and the King, with
regard to these things was, in the eyes of the Scots,
to become idolaters. In religion, no single thing was
a matter of indifference to them, and that any " exi-
gence " could compel them to place the law of the
King above that of God they denied.

If it be objected that they were wrong in thus endeavouring to act up to a code of laws founded for
another people in another land long ages ago, the
answer is plain. The King, equally with themselves,
professed to make this volume his law. To measure
him by it, therefore, was simply to judge him by the
standard he himself had set.

Having done his best with the Lords Clifford and
Lorne, Lord Wentworth had now the disagreeable but
imperative duty of admonishing his nephew, Sir William Savile, for refusing to obey the commands of his
Vice-President, Sir Edward Osborne, to send his horses
to York. That any one related to himself should be
so mutinous was especially grievous, and, knowing how
great must have been the annoyance of the writer, the
tone is all the more surprising. That a man capable
of administering deserved reproof in a manner so
courteous, dignified, and reasonable, should at other
times have given way to malignant abuse, and for a
mere trifle, is very lamentable. It is difficult to imagine
a more worthy and gracious reprimand to an obstinate and hot-headed young man than Lord Wentworth
administered. It must be remembered that Savile
was the son of Lord Wentworth's sister, orphaned of

1638. both his parents, and had been as a child committed to the care of his uncle by his father, who had been a close friend of Wentworth.

Such conduct as that of Savile could in no light be justified. Had he belonged to the popular party, he had no right to hold office and set the laws at defiance. As it was, he professed himself a loyal adherent of the King, and yet insulted his superior officer, and set a bad example of insubordination.

He showed great ingratitude to Lord Wentworth, by adding to his troubles as President. To disobey Sir Edward Osborne was, in fact, to disobey Lord Wentworth. The latter had always been a most kind uncle to Savile. He had proved a faithful guardian to him when left an orphan, and for many years had devoted a large portion of his time to the management of his nephew's estates. His letter* had no influence on Savile, who continued to oppose Osborne as before, and soon gave cause for a new remonstrance.

Lord Wentworth now received a letter from the Bishop of Down, warning him a justice of the peace in the country of Antrim, and a Scot of good property both in Ireland and Scotland, had secretly gone to Scotland, and there signed the Covenant. The Bishop believed that many other Scots in Ireland had followed the example of Adair; that all the Puritans in his diocese were quite confident that the revolt in Scotland would have the effect of procuring toleration for themselves. Many whom he had brought to conformity had now again broken loose. Scotch merchants coming to

---

* This letter will be found in the Strafford Papers. It is with much regret that I find my limits exclude it here.

Ireland on business openly avowed they had signed the Covenant, and boldly justified the Act.

To this Lord Wentworth replied by advising the Bishop to remain quiet till they had captured Adair. He told him to find out the names of all who had signed the Covenant and send them to him.

To this the Bishop answered, that there were many not only in his diocese but all over Ireland, who had signed, only he could not prove the fact. He had lately no intelligence from Scotland, as all his letters had been intercepted. But he sent a list of persons, with this remarkable assertion :—

"I daresay that these persons whose names I present to your Lordship are guilty, because they are notable Nonconformists, and have been lately in Scotland."

As for those who contemned his process and opposed his jurisdiction, they were more than would fill all the jails in Ireland. As in Scotland they had signed a bond to defend each other by arms, so in Ireland they had vowed to defend each other by oaths. They made him weary of his life.

It was quite true that the Scots in Ireland were growing confident. Charles had tried to deceive their countrymen at home by every kind of false concession, simply to keep them quiet till the spring.

But his acts were vain. There were too many in England to sympathise with Scotland to render it possible to hide from them his secret preparations for war. The Scots were kept well informed of what was going on, and refused to be deceived.

Charles, therefore, told Wentworth he was at full liberty to use his own judgment to make what preparations he thought fit in Ireland, and, though he could not afford to diminish the army there, still he hoped he would be able at least to spare him five hundred men to garrison Carlisle. He was to send an answer at once to this effect, and to be sure to observe the utmost secrecy in the matter. If he could manage the men, then some pretext must be invented for their leaving Ireland. Also the King hoped he would send him some good cannon.

To this Lord Wentworth replied that he would provide the five hundred men by the end of two months—earlier would be impossible, as they would have to be selected and brought together from various different garrisons.

They should be well provided for a twelvemonth with powder, bullets, and matches from the Irish stores. They and their officers should be of the firmest loyalty to the Crown; they should be men of great bodily strength, and perfect in the knowledge of their profession: in short, said Wentworth, proudly, " such as England itself, without sometime of exercise and practice, shall hardly be able to set beside them."

It is easy to imagine the busy care he would employ in sending out such a picked body as should call forth expressions of admiration from all beholders.

Any one might safely have staked his life on what the appearance of these troops was certain to be.

Then for the pretence which Charles had warned the Lord Deputy must be made for raising this force, Wentworth had composed a pleasant little fiction. He should say that, as he heard that the Marquis of

Lorne was fortifying the other side of the water without the King's orders, it seemed to him very suspicious, especially as the Scots were riding up and down the same part armed with the, for them, very unusual weapon of a sword. The Council should confirm this story, and thus prevent any idea of the real destination of the troops, who were publicly to be levied for Carrickfergus, Derry, and Coleraine.

A ship was to be in readiness to embark them at the appointed time, and the port of disembarkation Lord Wentworth advised to be Whitehaven, in Cumberland, within two days' march of their destination.

He advised that their pay, from the day of their leaving their present quarters, should be raised from sixpence to eightpence a day, in order to encourage them. Sixpence was the Irish, eightpence the English rate, and the soldiers might reasonably complain if, in England, they had not English pay. It was true this would increase the expense to £1500 in a year, but the cheerfulness and contentment it would give would be worth more than the money. As for the officers, he would trust to the King's princely bounty for such augmentation as they should merit. Still, he must remind his Majesty that the deduction of this force was very perilous at such a time, and, therefore, he begged permission to raise an equal number of men to replace it.

The next question was for a commander for the departing troops. Lord Wentworth thought they would prefer to serve under one they knew, and for that purpose he recommended Sir Francis Willoughby, who would accompany them to England. But if that were not convenient, then he suggested his own brother-in-law, Lord Clifford, already the King's Lieutenant on the Border. He was by nature secret, trusty, and loyal. Besides this, he belonged to a family of great honour and countenance in those regions, and, indeed, it might be an excellent thing for his Majesty's affairs if Lord Clifford were made Governor of Carlisle.

This suggestion was carelessly slipped in between the advice for the disposal of the men, which he now continued. It would be very needful to add to this Irish force at least fifty if not a hundred horsemen, who might serve also as scouts along the Border.

He then adverted to the King's demand for cannon. He had a sufficient quantity of ordnance, but strange to say, it was all at present useless for want of carriage. He had sent for seasoned planks to England to supply this want, but was answered, there was none in store. He then ordered wood to be felled in Ireland, but as yet it was not seasoned, the Irish timber being not only bad but cut at the wrong time. However, by Whitsuntide he trusted to have twelve field pieces, and eight pieces of battery ready mounted.

Having thus settled his own part, Lord Wentworth proceeded to advise the King for the future. By all means, he must fortify Dumbarton, and secure it by a strong garrison. The place was of the utmost importance, and three thousand men might be placed there to the best advantage, and by the help of the fleet be victualled from Ireland if necessary.

By the fleet, also, all the best harbours on the southwestern coast might be gained, and with the concurrence of Lords Nithsdale and Kircudbright, and other loyal Scots, all the ground between the two garrisons might be secured. Besides, " with such a cloud hanging behind over their backs," the Presbyters would hardly be able to preach far from home. And so, at least, they would be forced to keep the fire within their own borders, without bursting forth to the annoyance of their neighbours. If matters *should* come to extremity, it would be worthy of his Majesty's wisdom to think how at once he could seize all the shipping of the Scots both in England and Scotland, particularly to pounce upon as many of their ships coming laden from the vintage in France, and those fishing on their own coasts. " Perchance, taking from them their wine, it might render them more sober."

But the most important step of all was to seize Leith, to fortify it strongly and garrison it with ten thousand men. This would not be difficult by means of the fleet which should carry this force, and by commanding the line of coast, provision the town at pleasure.

Only let his Majesty cast his eye on the map and note how handsomely Leith, Dumbarton, Berwick, and Carlisle lie quartered to cut off all the lower and best part of Scotland from the rest.

The Scots were understood to be much excited with hopes of help from their countrymen in Ireland, and indeed there was so much arrogance among them there, that the conjecture was likely enough. Still Lord Wentworth was confident he could keep all quiet, on one condition, viz., he must have full authority to check the first signs of revolt and crush the serpent in the egg.

Then followed one of those repulsive outbursts of insolence which from time to time disfigure his correspondence. After many lines of wisdom, of thought, of foresight; after fond expressions of loyalty and friendship, suddenly do these most odious utterances start forth. It is quite possible that some paroxysm of bodily agony aroused the demon at these moments, and prompted words that in calmer feelings he might not have spoken. Knowing what at this very time he was enduring in the shape of the most racking internal disease that can tear the human frame, in addition to the gout, we may be charitable enough to suppose that possible. Meanwhile, justice reluctantly must be obeyed, and the words alluded to, literally given. "Let none magnify of these barbarous mutineers, as being above your Majesty's discipline to correct and reduce. For it is not possible in human reason, but they are without much difficulty to be bowed to right reason without adventuring of many blows. For, by the way, I should never advise to afford them the honour of striking a battle with the Crown, much rather to keep them in with strong garrisons by land, with your fleet at sea, and so watch, fast, and starve them out of this madness into their right wits.

"Undoubtedly, sir, there is nothing much to be feared, or indeed considerable, but the expense of treasure in the service. And first or last, sure they should forth of their own store defray the charge, that invited us to this drunken and surfeited banquet; and, in the mean time, be forced into large contributions to these neighbouring garrisons, procuring them to be spoken, withal, in the same rate Absalom, we read, did with Joab." Two days had not elapsed after this sentence was penned, when Sir Edward Osborne, for whose judgment Lord Wentworth had a high respect, sat down to send him an opinion altogether the reverse.

Osborne knew the Scotch better than Wentworth. 1638.
He had been near the Border, too, since these troubles
began, and had frequently conversed with the Scotch
commissioners in their passage to and fro. The Marquis
of Hamilton had just returned quite defeated in his
negotiations. All his attempts to put the Scots off
their guard had failed. Concession after concession
had been offered, and to those who knew nothing more
than the offers of the King, the Covenanters might
justly have appeared unreasonable and ungovernable.
But there was the old, old story behind the scenes—the
duplicity of Charles. So notorious was his character
by this time as a liar and a perjurer, that they would
have been weak indeed to have trusted to his word
without beating the ground on all sides. And the
Scots were about the last people in the world to neglect this. They were far harder to deceive than the
English. They kept their spies in all directions, and
had besides good correspondents among the discontented Southerners. Despite the " secrecy " and the
" pretexts " and the " caution " of the King, his movements and preparations were quite sufficiently known
to them to enable them to make counter-strokes in
return. And a murmur, rolling and growing louder
as it neared the Border, thrilled the whole frame of
many with a foreboding of a very different struggle
from that imagined by Wentworth. This opinion, Sir
Edward Stanhope, Colonel of the Train Bands of York,
ventured to express to the Lord Deputy, thus :—

" Give me leave to dissent somewhat from your
lordship. You do not think the lion is so terrible as
he is painted. Point blank against this I am not, and
yet think he is terrible enough to fear (frighten) us.

"That he is terrible enough to fear us, sure, though it cannot be but that we in number are more than twenty to one. Yet how often hath that failed both in the Roman wars, the Turkish, the French, and with us against them, besides a numberless number of more examples, more ancient, more modern, and nearer hand.

"It hath been, especially in places of advantage, by the greatest commander in the world, thought too many hands have as often done hurt as too few. And doubtless they are able to bring men enough to the field (though not to supply losses) yet to give battle to any prince in Christendom, and keep as many as may secure their own country, if there were need of anything but the country itself to kill them that assault it. Out of doubt, they may draw out above three score thousand strong, able, well-armed men, such as hardly will be terrified with any danger, and such as are inured to all the ills that war commonly puts soldiers to."

Stanhope here alluded to the numerous Scots who, under the command of their countryman, Lesly, had learned the art of war under Gustavus Adolphus. To have fought under the standards of this great king was to have obtained the highest certificate of competency and endurance. Stanhope well knew the King was arousing no mere barbarous mutineers, but veteran warriors, to be terrified with no danger, worn out by no hardship.

"Though in the first," he submitted, "we may equal them, as long as health and strength lasts, yet doubtless in the other we fall far short. It is most certain of such men, excellently well armed, they have in one shire thirty thousand. We are, questionless, far inferior to them in number of great and expert commanders within this kingdom. And I fear if it should come to that, which God avert, they would be too far within to be easily cast out again by those sent for from foreign parts.

"And I am persuaded—nay, it cannot be, but we shall have work enough to draw our eyes, hands, and hearts from them to guard more precious things."

Not only did Sir Edward differ from Lord Wentworth in his estimate of the power of the Scots, but he widely dissented from him in another equally important matter.

Lord Wentworth, strangely enough, was altogether blind to the sympathy that must needs exist between the English and Scotch Nonconformists. He looked on them as ancient enemies, who maintained the old feelings of hatred to each other; and, with a most incomprehensible lack of his usual caution, he wrote to the King:

"Let none persuade your Majesty to distrust the loyalty and cheerfulness of your English subjects on this occasion. For, upon my faith to God, I believe they will be found very ready and trusty in the pursuance of all your commands, and most unwilling to divide stakes with the other. And, as for this subject (the Irish), questionless, the English (and native in this exigent) are most assured no suspicion to be had of them at all."

So far from agreeing to this, Sir Edward Stanhope told him: "Doubtless, no part of his Majesty's dominions but would be infested more or less. Nay, which is worse, *who can tell how many hearts they have* (God pardon and turn the hearts of such) *in this kingdom? Who, though they may be drawn to the field, may fight so faintly as they had better run away.* Nay, perhaps if fortune smile on them in any one conflict, false cowards may prove fatal and bloody butchers to their own side."

Notwithstanding the harsh words he applied at times, perhaps to testify his own loyalty, it is quite evident that Stanhope not only fully understood the character and appreciated the power of dogged resistance in the Scots, but that he did not conceal from himself that their course was a just one, and that the feeling of its justice would inspire them with as much strength as all their weapons, and that both together would be likely to make them irresistible. He plainly disapproved of the King's measures, and pointed out every obstacle to his success; perhaps in the hopes of converting Lord Wentworth to his own opinion, and of obtaining his influence in renouncing all persuasion of the King to the war.

"If," said he, " it should come to so great a mischief as a winter war, if they were able to lie in their trenches and have store of provision (as I believe they would have, for doubtless they will make these parts the seat of war), they scarce would ever need to fight, but would find cold nights and ill weather their familiar friends; and we, I mean the common soldier, would be found dead under every hedge.

"Doubtless, in point of enduring hardiness and fighting in blood, the courage of the peasant is as great as of either the gentlemen or noblemen, quite contrary to them of France, and as now effeminated."

The attention of the reader is especially called to

the next words of Sir Edward Stanhope. They are in 1638.
every way remarkable, not only for the sentiments
they contain, but as coming from a man whose position
was altogether opposed to that of the 'men of whom
he was speaking. They must have fallen strangely on
the thoughts of Lord Wentworth.

"Neither," says Stanhope, "is it a small encouragement to the common soldier to fight for victory,
liberty, maintenance of their laws and privileges,
besides booty and riches.

"Whereas we have but one of these, the glory of
the victory, which of how mean estimation it is, and
how insensible the common people (our strength in
respect to number) are of it, we may by experience
daily find.

"Nor is it not to be unregarded that these will have
less courage to fight against such as intend us no ill,
but in their own defence, and perhaps will seem to
take nothing from us but that the necessity of war
compels them to."

Stanhope did not think the Irish could be depended
on. They were more likely to take advantage of a
time of trouble to turn against the English.

At last, he pointed out to Lord Wentworth the real
key to the supposed ingratitude of the Scots.

"The late Proclamation, doubtless, was a very
gracious satisfaction to their demands, yet they think
it such a thing as is void of all reality, and rather a
snare than a declaration of liberty from surmised
grievances, only published to gain time, and lose the
advantage supposed now in their hands. The confession and bond lately published (by the King) and
enjoined to be sworn to by all people of all estates and

1638. degrees within the kingdom is suspected to aim at no other end, but as a bait cast out among dogs to set them together by the ears, and rather to annihilate and break asunder their former covenant."

Stanhope was not the only man who recognised the real blackness of the approaching cloud. Other intelligence also reached Lord Wentworth, such as made his first confidence of an easy victory begin to fail, and to show him matters in their real light. His health continued to decay. After his excursion into the country, he returned to Dublin much less benefited than usual, and had scarcely reached the castle before a relapse swept away what little increase of strength he had gained. Again we meet with the melancholy apologies in his letters for his shortcomings on account of his health. Thus to the King:

" Having already been three days and three nights in a sharp pain of the gout, I do most humbly desire leave to borrow the pen of my secretary," &c.

" My indisposition hath so hindered this despatch, as before I had freed my hands of it, I am overtaken with your Majesty's," &c., &c.

" I write in much pain and in a very untoward posture, be your Majesty therefore pleased to pardon the disorder of the discourse and the badness of the character," &c.

" I caused myself to be taken forth of my bed and to be set in this chair, that so I might humbly write these lines to your Majesty," &c.

" If your Majesty knew the pain I here bear in writing thus much, your goodness would pardon these scribbles," &c.

To the Earl of Newcastle.

" You will be pleased to admit a lame man's answer forth of his bed, by the hand of his secretary, that is not able for the present to move any way but by the help of others," &c.

To Sir John Wintour.

" This will be in answer to yours of the 5th of November, nor could it be any at all without the help of my secretary's pen ; in regard the gout hath so lodged me in my bed as disables me in present to write myself," &c.

Thus did the year draw wearily to its end. Yet so resolved was the stern sufferer to be in no doubt as to the condition of the five hundred troops promised to the King, that frequently, when the least movement was torture, he insisted on being lifted into a litter and carried to the parade-ground, there to see the men go through their exercises, and assure himself of their perfection by the time of departure.

CHAPTER VII

1639.

GLOOMILY, and charged with ruin and death, broke the year 1639.

The autumn had been consumed in vain discussions and proclamations by the King, that he was willing to grant every desire of the Covenanters, and assertions that the charge that he was only striving to gain time in order to raise a force against them, was a report " than which hell itself could have raised none falser." *
His denials of his preparations did but the more exasperate the Scots, who were kept constantly informed of the truth, and by the new year they were in open revolt. By order of their Assembly, soldiers were levied, and taxes imposed for paying them ; fortifications were raised. Edinburgh Castle was seized, and the whole nation awaked. Everywhere, the ministers of the Covenant harangued the people to join in the holy war against Popery and in defence of their own religion. Believing every word of the Old Testament to be literally inspired, and that every prayer there recorded to have been uttered by David or any other eminent chief of the chosen race, was a Divine example for them to follow, the imprecations breathed by the King

* Rushworth, vol. ii., 559.

of Israel against his enemies chimed in remarkable
harmony with their own excited feelings at this instant,
and as they had lawfully the pick and choice of the
whole sacred volume, which, it must be acknowledged,
comprises texts of sympathy for every conceivable state
of mind, it is not to be wondered that an assembly of
elders of the Church, who, " after sermon, sat down,
not a gown amongst them all, but many had swords
and daggers," should infinitely have preferred the
Psalms, which declared the Lord to be a man of
war, filled with hatred towards his enemies, to the
precepts of mercy and forgiveness set forth in the
Gospel.

Consequently, it was not uncommon for pious men to
pray publicly for vengeance on their enemies, independently of deliverance for themselves, as, for example :
One minister said from the pulpit, that as the seven
sons of Gibeon were hanged before the Lord, so the
wrath of God would not depart from them till twice
seven prelates (the number of the Scotch bishops was
fourteen) were hanged in the same manner. Another
refused to pray for the provost of Edinburgh on his
death-bed, because he had not signed the Covenant.
Another wished in his sermon that he and all the
bishops were at sea in a bottomless boat together, as
he would gladly go down if they might perish at the
same time.

It is all very well to hold up the hands at these
uncharitable utterances, but for those who maintain
the same belief—in the 109th Psalm, for instance—as
the Puritans, and treat all who look on any part of the
Bible as mere human utterances, as wicked heretics,
it must be difficult to deny the celestial right of these

 honest preachers to follow their authority for such sentiments.

In every shire of Scotland a committee of war was appointed.* Merchants were sent abroad to purchase arms and ammunition, and in a very little time there were arms for thirty thousand men.

Edinburgh was strongly guarded; and Leith, on which Lord Wentworth had cast so greedy a glance, was fortified, fifteen hundred people, including women, setting heartily to the work. And wherever the labour was .the hardest and most difficult, there were the ministers to exhort and help with their hands as well as their lips.

What had the King to oppose to all this enthusiasm? The Earl of Northumberland, who was one of the best informed men on public affairs in England, spoke in the most desponding manner.

"I assure your Lordship," said he to Wentworth, on the 2nd of January, "to my understanding (with sorrow I speak it) we are altogether in as ill a posture to invade others or to defend ourselves as we were a twelvemonth since, which is more than any man can imagine that is not an eye-witness of it.

"The discontents here at home do rather increase than lessen, there being no course taken to give any kind of satisfaction. The King's coffers were never emptier than at this time, and to us that have the honour to be about him, no way is yet known how he will find means, either to maintain or begin a war without the help of his people."

Cottington sent the pleasant intelligence to Ireland : " Our business of Scotland grows every day worse,

* Rushworth, 8vo. iii., 2.

so as we are almost certain it will come to a war, and that a defensive one on our side. And how we shall defend ourselves without money is not under my cap. My Lord, assure yourself they do believe they shall make a conquest of us, and that an easy one. . They speak loud, yea, even they that are here, and do despise us beyond measure.

"No course is taken for levying of money. The King will not hear of a Parliament, and he is told by a committee of learned men that there is no other way."

Lord Wentworth, whose anxiety was now thoroughly awakened, in order to obtain the most exact intelligence, sent a spy into Scotland of the name of Willoughby, a young ensign of good family. He returned with intelligence that was anything but re-assuring. He told Lord Wentworth, that a few days before his arrival, the Scots had received two ship-loads of arms of the best quality from Sweden. There were nine brass drakes of taper bore, six culverins and demi-culverins, all of brass, and upon their carriages, ready to march, four thousand corselets and eighteen hundred muskets, as good as any he ever looked upon. And these were merely in addition to what Scotland already possessed and could procure in other quarters. Willoughby told Wentworth he had never seen a country so stored with arms in all his life. Drill masters went up and down, and, calling the inhabitants of several towns together in one spot, there trained them to arms.

The Covenant had been sent abroad to all Scots in foreign countries, and generally obtained signature, especially in Sweden, where the Scots were said to be covenanted to a man.

   All disguise was now over, and various councils were held in London as to the best means of opposing the Scots, whose unanimity was sadly contrasted with the lukewarmness of the English.

"The military preparations that are here intended do make a great noise," said Lord Northumberland, "but advance slowly. I have had the honour to be present at many debates for the ordering of this work, where I find so much want of experience in those who manage this business, and such regards to private ends, that I have little hope to see any design prosper that may tend to the public good, honour, or safety of this land."

At length, something like organisation was fixed upon. The English Council sent orders, in the name of the King, to the Lords-Lieutenants of the counties, to cause a view and muster to be made of all the arms and trained soldiers within each county, and for all the forces to be in readiness to join their colours at a day's notice. All able men, from the age of sixteen to sixty, were to be enlisted, besides the train-bands and lists returned to the Council; that each county should provide its due proportion of powder, match and lead, and store it in the magazines; the beacons were to be trimmed ready for the alarm, and well watched; all vagrants and suspected persons were to be apprehended.

The King next addressed a circular letter to the nobility, informing them of the rebellion of the Scots, which, his Majesty stated, was begun upon the pre-text of religion, but in reality was caused by factious spirits, and fomented by particular persons to shake off monarchical government, though he had repeatedly

assured them he would maintain religion as established   1639.
by law.

That as they had now raised considerable forces, he was resolved to repair in person to the North, there to resist any invasion, and for that purpose he must raise a considerable body of horse and foot.

He therefore summoned his nobles to attend him at York, on the 1st of April next, in such equipage and with such forces of cavalry as their birth, honour, and interest in the public safety obliged them, and to certify to him, within fifteen days, what help he was to expect from them.

Writs were also directed to the Lord William Howard, Lord Clifford, Lord Wharton, Lord Grey of Wark, and Lord Lumley, requiring them to repair to the North, with their households and retinues, well armed, under the penalty of having their lands, goods, and chattels in those counties seized by the King, and used by him to pay the expenses of guarding other parts.

Writs were likewise sent to the Mayors of Hull and Newcastle, to fortify those towns at the expense of the inhabitants. Levies were ordered of raw troops, to go to Holland, in the place of trained and experienced soldiers there, who were at once to return to England. All the Lords-Lieutenants were ordered to their respective counties, the Earl of Bridgewater to his presidency of Wales, and all governors of islands, forts, and castles to their respective commands.

Archbishop Laud now came to the aid of the King, and sent letters to all his clergy, to inform them of the traitorous conspiracies of the Scots, under the pretence of religion, which, he said, was always the cloak to cover the designs of factious spirits. But he did not doubt that the bishops and clergy in general would give freely to the common defence. He also wrote in the same style to Doctors' Commons, expressing his conviction that the judges and others of the common law would contribute to the King's necessities.

The next person to the rescue was Queen Henrietta Maria, who addressed the Roman Catholics. She told them she had always believed in their loyalty and affection to his Majesty, and she now called upon them to verify her words—that she had undertaken his Catholic subjects should equal all others in help at the present moment. Often had she solicited favours for them, and she now begged them to show their gratitude by assisting his Majesty with a considerable sum of money, freely and cheerfully presented. And as she presumed this sum would not be unworthy her presentation to the King, so she should receive it as a particular mark of respect to herself, the merit of which she would try to improve to their advantage.

It need hardly be said that one of the first to respond to the King's appeal was the Lord Deputy of Ireland. At first he thought of sending the King the half of his picked guards; but second thoughts told him of the danger of diminishing his force in Ireland at present. He therefore gave orders to his steward, as his rents came in, to pay into the hands of the King's treasurer of war the sum of £1000 at Midsummer, and another £1000 at Christmas, as his contribution; and he added, what was rather dangerous, " If this be not sufficient, I do most humbly beseech your Majesty to command all I have there to the last farthing."

Wandesforde and Radcliffe also sent the King £500 between them, and Lord Wentworth's younger brother £100.

This was all they could do at present, being unable to furnish soldiers as yet from their own families.

"Our sons," said Wentworth, "are all children; but if they were able to bear arms, I would send the young whelps to be entered in your Majesty's militia. Judge it to be their greatest honour, it might be so; and for a conclusion, so it might be better for your service, hang up the old dogs."

He then told Charles, in answer to his question as to the possibility of provisioning Carlisle from Ireland, that it was too late for the present season; but by next winter he could, at cheap rates, send beef, butter, corn, biscuit, and herrings. Cheese was a deficiency of Ireland. Even the five hundred men just ready for starting had to wait for that till their arrival in England, and be content with bread and beef till then.

Having done his best in the way of money, Lord Wentworth now exerted his influence in the King's behalf. He wrote to his Deputy Lieutenants in Yorkshire, exciting them to do their utmost in the present crisis. They had indeed responded already in such a manner as to give him great satisfaction, and enable him to express his "joy and contentment" with their conduct.

Had the cause been a good one, it would have been impossible not to enter with sympathy into his rousing words:

" Proceed on, then," he cried, " in the name of God, suitable to these beginnings and becoming yourselves. And I wish from the bottom of my soul I might be there to fight by and with you, with that kindness in your particulars, with that faith towards my King and country, that I trust you have ever observed in me. Believe me, it is the relation I stand in to his Majesty's affairs on this side, and not my heart, that could have denied me to you at this time."

He then obtained from the King authority to depute the whole of his power in every branch in England to Sir Edward Osborne, who, though Vice-President, was hitherto limited in many ways. But Wentworth fully trusted him, and enlarged his power to the utmost, making him his Deputy Lieutenant-General, in order that he might hold due rank in military matters.

It will scarcely be credited that, after the munificent contribution of Lord Wentworth, his zeal and activity, that in the present most dangerous hour, when it was needful beyond all things to maintain strict discipline and trust, and support so faithful a servant, that the King again began his former habit of countermanding Lord Wentworth's orders, of giving away places at his disposal, and pardoning offenders condemned at the Castle Court. Lord Wentworth, patient as he was under anything that came from the King, found it hard to restrain his feelings at conduct that must paralyse his power to help the foolish prince, who could thus trifle with such important influences, and at such a time.

For example, Lord Wentworth would state the circumstances of a case, and before passing the final act would ask the ratification of the King, in order that

all might be clear. This he would obtain, and then 1639.
pass sentence. Suddenly, some time after, he would
receive an order from England, ordering him to revoke
the sentence, and set the defendant free. Sometimes,
this reversal was obtained by the friends of the defendant, sometimes by enemies of Lord Wentworth. But
in either case it was an insulting arraignment of the
justice of the Lord Deputy and Council of Ireland, and
a most gross breach of the conditions on which alone
they had consented to accept their anxious and responsible office. And it was not as if the reversal were
obtained by a fair trial, in a court of appeal—it was
simply by the bare word of the King, gained by personal influence alone.

Two special instances of this royal breach of contract now occurred.

A lieutenant in the army, of the name of Smith, was
tried before the Castle Court, for what was recorded
as "a most abominable and malicious conspiracy to
ravish Sir Arthur Blundell of his estate, life, and good
name, aggravated by this circumstance, that Mr. Smith
then served as lieutenant, where Sir Arthur Blundell
commanded him as captain."

The case was proved against him, and he was sen-
tenced to imprisonment and a fine of a thousand
marks, and the payment of costs to Sir Arthur
Blundell.

The fine, much reduced by Wentworth and his
Court, and costs, were paid, and the rest of the sentence had scarcely been put in execution, when an
order arrived from Mr. Secretary Windebanke, by whose
very hand the King had ratified the sentence, ordering
it to be revoked and the fine remitted. No reason

1639.

was assigned beyond the mercy of the King. Not the slightest proof was offered or assertion made that the decree was unjust. And that any Court, with its president, could be expected to submit to such interference as this, was too much. It made justice a mere child's play.

If the Court or judge were convicted of wrong, let them be replaced by a better; but while they sat the public and acknowledged administrators of justice, it was monstrous that their decrees could thus be blown into air by the mere word of the King, and that too passed without the least notice or consultation with any member of the Court.

With all his king-worship, Lord Wentworth felt, if this went on, ruin must be the speedy result, and so he informed Windebanke.

He said he could not choose but bemoan himself that he was forced to revoke the performance of so many directions sent him under the King's own hand, and begged the secretary to read the copy, which he now enclosed, of the conditions promised to be observed towards him when he accepted the government; and of these conditions he also besought him to remind the King. If these were continued in such disregard, then the affairs of the country must go back much quicker than they advanced. Such acts as this last added most painfully to his difficulties and unpopularity, as it seemed as if he were always the cause of harshness, and the obstacle to the King's natural clemency. "Indeed," he exclaimed, "it *is* overhard I should be put to give all the negatives single and alone. I shall willingly take my share, but too much is too much."

The case in question was one of especial difficulty.

A fixed fraction of all fines went towards the revenue 1639. and without a new process how could he take out of the exchequer by his authority the sum paid, and, still harder, force the plaintiff to give back the just compensation he had received for his wrongs.

No case had ever been more clearly proved than this of Smith, and if, after all, he was to escape with impunity, then the sentences of the Court would become *Bruta fulmina;* and Lord Wentworth confessed he knew not the innocence that could promise itself security. So indignant was he that he almost forgot that he was speaking of the King, and declared, " Such favour granted to delinquents is commonly scandalous to public justice, discouragements to the judges that gave the sentence, and the Court itself thereby becomes despised."

The other most aggravating performance of the King was a repetition of the same thing, of which we have already given many specimens. This was to give away in England honours and offices within the gift of the Lord Deputy only, and which were of incalculable importance for the latter to retain entirely under his control, in order that he might be able to reward his faithful officers and servants.

The death of the Earl of Kirkcudbright had left the command of a troop of horse vacant. Without the least warning or consultation of Lord Wentworth, the King gave the captaincy to the Earl of Desmond, and the first intelligence Wentworth received of this was a letter under the royal signet commanding him thus to dispose of the commission.

Again he was brought to the very verge of despair. This was even more exasperating than usual, for this troop happened to be wholly Scottish, and in the present state of affairs not to be trusted. The death of the captain had afforded Lord Wentworth an unhoped-for opportunity of disbanding it and distributing the men among new regiments apart from each other. In place of the old troop he intended to form another of men on whom he could depend. But the arrival of a new captain, an absolute stranger, who must necessarily be entrusted with the delicate task of "quietly and insensibly framing the new one," was fraught with all the obstacles of ignorance of place and men and circumstances, as well as depriving Lord Wentworth of the power of appointing a man he knew, and who was well acquainted with the Irish army. And the affront offered to him not only lowered his authority in general, by showing men that they could give commands without consulting him, but left those unrewarded who really merited promotion, and whom he had promised should obtain it. In fact, these two last acts of Charles went a long way towards treating the Lord Deputy as a mere cipher.

"I do," said he "most humbly beseech his Majesty might be pleased to command that excellent provision, *settled by his own orders*, might be strictly observed on all sides, that no suits be absolutely granted there till the Deputy and Ministers here be commanded humbly to certify what they shall in their judgments find fit to be understood there for his Majesty's service."

So often, however, did this miserable interference continue to occur, that Lord Wentworth, as a last resource, addressed a long letter on the subject to Windebanke. He not only felt the King's conduct as an obstruction to the fulfilment of his duties in every way, but he was stung by the want of consideration for himself as a man. The following words are most extraordinary as coming from him, though in every way much less severe than was merited by the King :—

" His Majesty may command all that ever I have, and break my sleep very small, it being accustomed with me so entirely to attend his Majesty's service, as I am verily persuaded few men in the world think on, or consider their own private so little. Besides, it is in my fate to find few that are pleased to remember or mention just and equal things, which might persuade for me; yet feel many hands injuriously tearing from me not only the rights of my place, my innocent and peaceable conversation, the candour of my good repose among men (all this under the sun and with impunity), but even the capacity also of serving here with that advantage to the Crown I otherwise might."

He then proceeded to argue his case with an energy that must awaken sympathy in all who, holding positions of high responsibility, are deprived of the means of fulfilling it, while nevertheless they are called upon to answer all consequences.

In judging of the arbitrary acts of Lord Wentworth it has been too much the fashion to ignore all these difficulties by which he was surrounded, and how often he was deprived of the lawful engines of power by the fickleness of the King. There was no remedy but to renounce the King's service, or to serve him in defiance of justice ; both could not reign, and Wentworth had made his election. He simply acted what so many, even in the present day, most loudly preach. But let us listen to his own words :—

" Should those great offices incident to the disposal

 of a Lord Keeper, a Lord Treasurer, a Lord Chamberlain, a Lord Marshal, a Lord Admiral, a Master of the Horse, a Captain of the Guard, &c., become the suit of every young courtier, those noble persons would quickly in their own case find themselves aggrieved, and yet some of them, perchance (by what rule of justice I know not), shall move, press, and importune the whilst that the like liberty may not be afforded unto me, that they respectively challenge and enjoy themselves.

" As if I were the only servant of my master unworthy to have the dues of my place, howbeit, an employment, verily, they would think a great prejudice to have put upon them in any sort with all the great advantages belonging unto it.

" Yet is the difference very great, for with all these (except the Lord Admiral) the inability of these subordinate Ministers may be supplied by a Deputy, however himself only like to answer ; the Giver no ways liable to answer the transgression.

" But in these cases the duties of the Captains are not to be done by proxy. Their ability or weakness may be unto a General the loss of the cause, his life and honour ; nay, insensibly wrest forth of the thoughts of the inferior officers and soldiers all respect and obedience, and so the very soul of all action cast into a dead sleep.

" Nor, indeed, can it with reason be expected or hoped for otherwise, but when the power of punishment and reward is entrusted with their persons who are chief in command."

Passionately he asserted :—

" If I were guilty to have executed this power

greedily to my own lucre, not to have therein intended
the good of the army above all other respects, to have
thought of advantaging myself one groat in the
disposal of the late four new raised troops of horse,
there were something inwardly might quiet me, tell
me, I were rightly served if the army were not,—I
speak it with confidence and truth,—in all respects
infinitely more fit for service than I found it, there were
something outwardly might tell me the privilege were
justly denied that I had negligently abused.

" If the liberty had not, as I humbly conceive, at
first been granted unto me; were not his Majesty's
orders for me, and they, such as being observed, have
brought the greatest prosperity upon these affairs that
hath been since the English Conquest; I should conceive reason might well advise to try some other way
in the moulding and bowing this State more to his
Majesty's advantage.

" If my poor endeavours had taken less effect, if I had
lived in a condition below other Deputies before me,
or the dignity of this government, ever of more regard
with me than my own quiet or benefit, it were but just
that not only the power to gratify worthy and fit persons for the service of the Crown, but even the entertainment and profits themselves were taken from me,
which others had the happiness not only to enjoy, but
to have their labours rewarded besides; my Lord
Chichester with land at one gift worth at this day ten
thousand pounds a year; the Lord Falkland ten thousand
pounds in money at once. However, I never coveted
more than the inherent rights and honours belonging
to the place, and yet I modestly persuade myself my
pains have been equal, my expense far beyond either

1639. of them, and his Majesty's revenue advanced in my short time ten times as much as in both theirs."

This was entirely true. The popular idea that he was the recipient of incessant favours and bounties and bribes at the hand of the King, was utterly false. Equally false and slanderous was the report that he abused the opportunities of his place to his own advantage. When we remember how completely monopolies, either by gift or purchase, were the custom of that day, Lord Wentworth, so far from being singled out as a criminal for his share in what almost all who had the chance partook, deserves rather praise for his great forbearance in not far oftener profiting by the advantages of his place to largely increase his income by these means. Constant prominence is given by his enemies to the fact of his monopoly of tobacco, while they quietly pass by the large amount he spent from his private purse on public expenses, and especially the great founding of the linen trade, which he might justly have monopolized, but which he was most anxious to impart to others.

It was these omissions that helped to make his life more bitter. He saw that not only was every fault catalogued, and, when possible, magnified, but never by any chance were his most earnest efforts for good recognised by his countrymen. Even the King signified his approbation merely in cold general terms. Not a soul ever cared to measure the amount of pain and labour that his efforts had cost him. And this lack of appreciation had an unfortunate effect on his character. As has already been noticed, he had that child-like side to his character which is generally a part of a great mind. And though nothing could stop

his energy or make him do his work with less care, still 1639.
he missed the kindly words of encouragement to whose
influence he was as open as a child, and chilled by the
frozen atmosphere around him, himself grew colder,
sterner, and harder to others.

Kind friends, also, were not wanting to impress the
fact of his unpopularity upon him by special means.
Lord Cottington took the trouble to write to him that
his enemies in England spread the report that he was
universally deserted in Ireland; and Willoughby, his
spy in Scotland, brought back the news amongst his
other matters, that he was hated " most extremely " by
the whole Scotch nation, who even threatened to do
him personal mischief.

At the English Court, Lord Holland, who had
written to him to assure him of his esteem, was his
greatest enemy. Not a noble open enemy, to himself
expressing his disapprobation, but a man smooth and
smiling to his face, and losing no opportunity of injuring him behind his back. And that he constantly had
the ear of the King was one of the secret cares that
gnawed at the heart of Wentworth, who had been well
warned of the real feelings of Holland towards him.

Mingled with his natural and just reasons for objecting to place the troop of Lord Kircudbright under the
young Earl of Desmond, occurs a most extraordinary
statement, referring to his own personal safety in the
matter.

That he should often allude to assassination as a by
no means impossible fate, is not to be wondered at; or
that the names of Ravaillac and Felton were so often
on his lips. But that he should associate such an idea
with the chance of the arrival of the Earl of Desmond

in Ireland, is indeed too remarkable to be passed over without notice. He can scarcely have had any just ground for so horrible a suspicion, and in all probability it is to be traced to the condition of his nerves, strung to a pitch of sleepless fever, the result of incessant mental and bodily pain and toil. Alluding to young Desmond, he says :—

" I esteem it were in me to betray these affairs, should I not by all means possible avoid the bringing of young and unexperienced persons to be captains in this army in a time thus conditioned; or, which is far less, neglecting the just care I owe my own family, *to venture my honour or my life with I know not whom. My life shall be as freely laid down for my gracious master as any that lives, yet I am not weary of it neither; should be very unwilling to die like a fool*, or, to deal clearly, desirous to fight but in the company of such as understand their profession, such as I should in some measure take to be as well wishers to my person as to the cause."

These words are, to say the least, equivocal, as if he hesitated to utter his real meaning, which yet he could not altogether withhold. And what follows is so unlike his general haughty disregard of his own perils, so tottering seems the usual fixed resolution, that the condition of the writer speaks through it more than anything else. Again and again, he returned to the subject of Desmond.

" I beseech you, what can I hope for from the tender years of this young nobleman? Experience tells me what to fear. I will name no man to his prejudice; but I protest by one youth, whom his Majesty commanded me to make a captain here, I have had more trouble, the King's payments more *1639.* scandal, than from the whole army besides.

" It is a condition below a gentleman to be put to deny all, and not to be allowed to gratify some; very hard to my seeming, that by strictly observing his Majesty's orders I should procure so many enemies, and not be admitted to keep them when I might oblige one friend, and he a person in all respects abler to discharge the duty to the public.

" Only I shall crave leave that a tenderness to my own private, may not silence me to the public, interest; but that therein my lines may be read without prejudice."

Many a time had Lord Wentworth been forced to remonstrate, but never before had he spoken as at present. It is evident that, for the time at least, his confidence in the King was beginning to fail, and a feeling of hopelessness was creeping over him that he could not subdue. Never does he appear to have been so desponding. He could not repress his complaints, could not conceal his despair of success, nor his conviction that the King would destroy faster than he could build.

" It discourageth a servant," he said, " in his own confidence, seeing himself not allowed the upright credit and benefit of his labour and watches, but that others must make and obtain suits of those things which of custom and right reason are assigned him.

" Nor can I in any time, much less in this, promise myself any ability to execute the commands of his Majesty, unless the power not only of punishing, but of rewarding fit persons also with such places as belong to the Deputy be left unto me; to the end that, as I displease many, I may at least engage some few to undergo with me the hazard of all events ; bring up others in hope of preferment, desirously and attentively to execute what I shall direct for the good of the service."

The change in him is to be noted by another circumstance. Of the two Secretaries of State, Coke and Windebanke, it will be remembered the former had been chosen by himself and the King as the one to conduct whatever part of the correspondence was especially private and confidential. Three years ago, not even to Coke would Wentworth have thus expressed himself about the King. But now he uttered the whole of his discontent to Windebanke, and that too by the hand of his secretary. It may, therefore, be concluded that he intended the King to know his feelings, and, perhaps, indulged a faint hope of alarming Charles into different conduct by giving his opinions the chance of support at the hands of a third party, who, unprompted, might warn the King of the effect of his worse than folly.

Perhaps the intense stupidity manifested by Charles at this moment, annoyed Lord Wentworth more than his constant breaches of his privileges and rights. He made requests impossible to be granted, gave orders that could not be obeyed, and offered suggestions that a schoolboy would have known better than to follow.

Thus, not content with the splendid troop of horsemen that Lord Wentworth had raised for him entirely at the expense of Ireland, and with the knowledge that even in peace, Ireland had needed all her own money, he desired Lord Wentworth to send him a good sum from thence, and if he could get it no other way, he was to borrow five thousand pounds.

With Charles, to wish for a thing was to ask for it, no matter what might be the circumstances. Lord Wentworth had speedily to put a stop to his hopes in that quarter.

" As for borrowing the sum his Majesty desireth," said he, " I should, I protest to the Almighty, pawn all my estate to the uttermost farthing to effect it; but that which is truth will be heard. I do not believe that, to save my life, I were able to borrow five thousand pounds amongst all the merchants of this town. Generally, all people here turn their stock in a course of trading; the number of moneyed men are extreme few; and those altogether take mortgages of land for their security, and will in no sort meddle with any man's bond."

And " even if a hundred thousand pounds in coin could be raised, to send it over would be the utter ruin of Ireland, the stoppage of all trade, and cost the King in the end far more by the loss of the customs."

Wentworth was now again stung by the young wasp in Yorkshire—his nephew Savile. With spiteful impertinence he continued his efforts to thwart his uncle, and exerted his utmost influence to have another lieutenant joined with Lord Wentworth in Yorkshire. He probably either had some friend of his own in his eye, or possibly hoped for the appointment himself. But he over-reached the mark. Lord Wentworth at once consented to the appointment of another lieutenant of York, and obtained of the King that Sir Edward Osborne should hold the office. As the great object of Savile had been that the lieutenant should be an opponent of Osborne, and support himself in his opposition, his chagrin must needs have been great indeed. A side stroke was then aimed in revenge, as was believed, by Savile, who sought to wound his uncle by injuring his friend. Sir Christopher Wandesforde had held the commission of colonel of a Yorkshire regiment, which he retained yet. The orders of the King to all officers to join their regiments had necessarily been not complied with by him, on account of his position in Ireland as Master of the Rolls. Information of disobedience in him and neglect in Lord Wentworth for allowing this disobedience was therefore lodged against them.

Lord Wentworth was deeply moved by this conduct in a nephew whom he had cared for as a son. But, violent as he could be when he himself was in the wrong, here, where his anger was most justly provoked, he still bridled it in an unwonted degree, though he did not refrain from rebuking Savile as he richly deserved.

Lord Wentworth, not contented with writing himself, applied to his old friend and tutor, the good clergyman, Mr. Greenwood, who was living in Yorkshire, to speak with the unruly Savile, and bring him, if possible, to a sense of his unbecoming conduct. Unlike Laud, Mr. Greenwood did not commence the task of a mediator by telling the offender that he hoped he would refuse his interference. On the contrary, he at once remonstrated with him, and when Savile showed him the letters above quoted, Mr. Greenwood pointed out kindly the value of Lord Wentworth's remarks. He did his best, and wrote word to his old pupil that he thought Savile's next letter would give him good satisfaction, as he had promised to join peaceably with Sir Edward Osborne in doing good service. And as we hear no more of his opposition, we may suppose he kept his word. The last great matter of personal trouble to Lord Wentworth was an action for libel, which he brought against Sir Piers Crosby, and which came off at this most inopportune time.

A working man of the name of Esmond, who was engaged in the building affairs of the Castle, was summoned for neglecting his work and refusing to carry timber according to contract. On being brought before the Court, the Lord Deputy shook his cane at him and told him he would teach him better manners. The man was sent to prison and shortly after died. A report was then set abroad, that he had died of terrible blows on the head given him by the Lord Deputy. The story spread, of course, with the usual amount of exaggeration, and Lord Wentworth, greatly annoyed, traced the tale to Sir Piers Crosby. He accordingly prosecuted him with several others for repeating and spreading abroad his words.

The case was heard before the English Council and decided against the defendants.

Crosby was fined £4000 to the King, and ordered to give such satisfaction to the Lord Deputy as the Court should direct, and the rest of the defendants ordered to pay £1000 damages to the Lord Deputy.

CHAPTER VIII.

On the 27th of March, the King left London for York.

The appeal to the nobility and gentry for contributions had met with rather a lukewarm response. Some had given liberally in various sums from £100 to £10. But many more had allowed the letters to remain without response, and among these ominous defaulters were the names of Noy, Godolphin, Denzil Holles, and Sir Francis Seymour. However, there were the ship-money, the money raised by monopolies and heavy taxes on all the bare necessaries as well as luxuries of life. The clergy gave more liberally than any, and some of the principal nobles raised troops to accompany the King, who calculated on accumulating an enormous force on his journey. A letter was despatched to the Vice-President and Council of York, requiring them to make known to all the northern counties that whosoever would provide provisions of corn, meal, butter, cheese, or other fare for soldiers, or hay, oats, pease, beans, or straw for their horses, for supply of the army, which was intended to lie there for their defence, should be duly paid at the market price, notwithstanding what ill-affected persons might say to the contrary.*

* Rushworth, iii. 27.

A Commission was then issued under the Great 1639.
Seal of England, constituting Thomas, Earl of
Arundel, General of the Army to be raised, and Robert,
Earl of Essex, to be Lieutenant-General, and Henry,
Earl of Holland, General of the Horse. And in order
that all the best horses might be preserved for the
officers of the King, orders were issued, that no horse
courser should be permitted to buy any horses at the
approaching fair of Wooburn, till the last day of the
fair, and no man was to sell his horse to a horse
courser for a less price than had been offered by the
King's agents.

A fleet was also rigged and put to sea under the
command of the Marquis of Hamilton, and containing
five thousand land troops who were to attempt to regain Edinburgh, Leith, or Dumbarton.

The five hundred men from Ireland had been despatched to Carlisle, and Lord Wentworth strongly
urged the addition of seven hundred foot and two
hundred horse to complete the garrison. He had a
very great idea of the importance of cavalry, and told
the King how necessary it was to send small bodies
of horsemen to the border, to be continually moving
up and down the frontier in order to prevent any
sudden incursion. The three pinnaces employed on
the coast, were now absent with the troops, but on
their return in a few days, Wentworth said he would
victual them, and then send them to the north-east of
Ireland to beat to and fro about the head of Cantire
and Dumbarton Frith. Two pinnaces he calculated
would be quite enough to capture all the Scottish
boats trading from Ayr, Irvine, and Dumbarton ; still,
with his usual caution, he added another.

And as Charles had given orders that they might take any good opportunity to land and plunder the Scots, Wentworth, with somewhat needless humility, thought permission necessary to prey upon Scotch barks, and especially the long boats of the Earl of Argyle.

He also sent orders to all the troops and companies garrisoned in Ulster, to be ready to march at five days' notice, and he informed the King he had now three hundred men ready for the relief of any pressing necessity.

On the 30th of March, Charles arrived at York. There he was met by the mayor, who received him with a speech of such disgusting flattery, as ought to have awakened either the laughter or anger of any man above the level of an idiot.

The mayor begged his Majesty's pardon that they had caused him, their bright and glorious sun, to stand still in the city of York, a place now so unlike itself; once an imperial city, where the Emperor Constantine Chlorus lived and died; in whose tomb a burning lamp was found many centuries of years after; a place honoured with the birth of Constantine the Great, and with the noble library of Egbert, and afterwards twice burned. And yet the births, lives, and deaths of emperors, were not so much for the honour of York, as that King Charles was once Duke of York,* &c., and so on continued the nauseous stuff.

The Scots in the meantime had proceeded vigourously with their preparations. Poor as was the nation, that mattered little when all, save an insignificant

* Rushworth, iii. 34.

minority, were ready to peril life and limb and property in defence of a just cause. They little needed enforced taxes when voluntary contributions from the poorest poured in. All who could bear arms gladly learned their drill. Their most experienced veterans, who, like Lesley, had practised the art of war on the continent under Gustavus Adolphus, returned to give their countrymen the benefit of their experience, and the most aristocratic of the nobles mustered their clans against the common enemy. The recreants consisted of the episcopalians, a few courtiers, and that class, everywhere to be found, who secretly betray a good cause for their own personal profit, while a few honestly hung back as true believers in the divine right of kings.

But so prompt had been the Scots, that before Charles arrived at York, Edinburgh, Dumbarton and Leith had been secured in addition to Dalkeith, a place of less importance, but notable as containing the regalia of Scotland. This had been committed by the King to the Earl of Traquair, who, unable to defend it, had given a pompous warning to the Scots to beware how they touched the regalia. They replied, with a sneer, that Dalkeith was not worthy of such treasures, and they would take them to the capital, and accordingly sent them to Edinburgh.

When Lord Wentworth heard of these rapid successes, his heart misgave him; and when he received intelligence that the King intended to march to Edinburgh, he looked upon it as nothing less than surrendering himself a prisoner. Charles had professed his intention of holding a Parliament in the Scotch capital, but Lord Wentworth had seen enough to be quite certain that the Scots recognised no divinity as hedging a King, and trembled for the consequence. His real attachment to the person of Charles showed itself in his anxious petition to him, not to go.

"It was writ me," he wrote to the King, "your Majesty intends to go to Edinburgh, and to be present at their Parliament. Sir, the reading of it went as cold to my heart as lead, and the consequences of such an assurance fright me to think of them. But I trust God is not so angry with us, as to suffer your Majesty to be led into so apparent a danger."

He strongly advised the King to attempt nothing this summer beyond securing Berwick and Carlisle by strong garrisons, well training his army, and preventing any incursion into England. But let his Majesty by all means avoid fighting this year.

The King then desired Wentworth to have his cruisers ready by the 16th or 20th of April, off the north west of Scotland, as he wished them to take what they could from the coasts.

But this, also, was deprecated by Lord Wentworth. He pointed out to the King how small would be the advantage of plunder, how great the provocation that would thus be given. As to seizing their shipping, that could be done as well, if not better in August. There was also a strong objection against that.

If the war were with a foreign enemy, then, Lord Wentworth said, he should like well enough to have the first blow. But as the dispute was with his Majesty's own natural, though rebellious subjects, it was a tender point to draw blood first, for till it came to that, all hope of reconciliation was not lost. And the Scots would not have the least excuse for saying

that his Majesty had brought matters to such an 1639.
extremity.

An attack on their coasts might provoke them to
assault some part of England, and might at least, enable
them to prevent the placing of men and ammunition in Carlisle and Berwick, which at present they
had no excuse for doing. But if they did so, as
things stood at present, then it would be an act of
open and inexcusable rebellion which would justify the
King in turning his army against them.

Another effect of attacking them first would be to
overwhelm the King's party in Scotland, and would
also precipitate the war on England before she was
fully prepared, and, by depriving the Covenanters of
all hopes of grace, drive them to desperation.

Berwick and Carlisle were the two pledges of success
to the King. Therefore, nothing should be done till
they were secured. Perhaps, the summer would bring
the rebels to submission without any need of the
King to injure the trade of his kingdoms by falling on
the shipping.

The best employment for the pinnaces, at present,
was to cruise up and down the north-west coast of
Scotland, rather to secure the subjects of Ireland than
to attack the Scotch. Much was to be lost, little to
be gained. But, at any rate, it was best to do nothing
till August, as then the season would secure both
kingdoms till next spring, when all things would be
more forward than at present.

A letter from Sir Francis Willoughby, the commander of the five hundred men from Ireland, fully
confirmed Lord Wentworth's opinion. Though the
coming of these men had so long been known, not

the least preparation had been made to receive them. There was not straw enough even for them to sleep on, their first night at Whitehaven, and they had to separate and send a few two miles distance in search of quarters. Though a list had been previously sent of the conveyances required for the baggage, not a single one was in readiness. Not a soldier was yet placed in Carlisle, nor even a single piece of artillery.

However, the news of the arrival of the Irish troops soon spread abroad, and their splendid appearance awoke hope and confidence. As soon as Lord Clifford heard of their arrival, he hastened to receive them and send the needful conveyances. He also at once obtained two hundred men and sent them off to Carlisle, where they were soon joined by the Irish force. At the same time Lord Essex took possession of Berwick, with Sir Jacob Ashley; and thus these two important posts were at length secured, to the great joy of the people, who had been living in daily dread of an invasion of the Scots. The confidence of the King increased. The two Secretaries of State being left at London, he commanded Sir Henry Vane, Comptroller of his household, to act their part and transact his correspondence. In order to please the people and attract them to himself, he suddenly recalled all patents for monopolies of carriages, broken tobacco, butter, logwood, and various other articles. He also sent word to Lord Wentworth that, by the 1st of May, he expected to be encamped near Berwick, or at least, on the other side of Newcastle, and that, at the same time, his fleet would be on the coasts of Scotland with the Marquis of Hamilton and five thousand land troops, provisioned for three months. Thirteen pieces of

artillery were on their way to Carlisle. He desired to 1639.
express his great satisfaction and content with the
loyalty of his subjects under the government of the
Lord Deputy, and he looked on them with affection as
an effect of Lord Wentworth's care.

But, as for the Covenanters, it was but too well
known how they had proceeded, as far as in them lay,
to poison the hearts of his subjects throughout the
whole kingdom. And, as his grace and clemency had
met with a return of nothing but dangerous plots and
conspiracies, he resolved to provide for the worst, and
no further to be amused by treaty, but to make his
frontiers safe, so that by God's grace it should not be
in their power to break into the kingdom. He would
attack the Scots by sea, shut up their rivers and ports,
burn all upon their coasts, make descents into Scotland,
break off all intercourse and commerce with her people,
and infest them by all the means he could.

He, therefore, desired the Lord Deputy to draw a
considerable portion of his army to the north of Ireland
to be ready to join the fleet, even if they did nothing
more than terrify the Scots. Also to have in readiness
three or four thousand men, to be ready at four-and-
twenty hours warning to go to Scotland, either to Ayr,
Irwin, or the mouth of Clyde, in order to prevent the
Scots from sending all their forces to the English
border. For it was quite possible that unless something was done to divert their forces, they would all
concentrate in one body and enter England. But,
still, his Majesty was resolved not to provoke a battle,
only to remain on the defensive.

However, all the ships of the Scots in the port of
London, to the number of thirteen, were seized, and

1639. orders given to capture all their vessels in the English ports, also all their goods throughout England and Ireland. Letters were also directed to the United Provinces, desiring them to suspend all privileges enjoyed by Scotch merchants, as they were all Covenanters, and to protect them would be a wrong to England, with whom the United Provinces were in amity.*

The assertion of the King, that he meant simply to remain on the defensive, was sufficient to satisfy Lord Wentworth, who did not much heed his menaces to Scotland, so long as he waited to fulfil them till he was prepared. Lord Wentworth now arranged to send his faithful Radcliffe to York, there to settle the payment of Willoughby's men, and report on the general condition of things.

Wentworth took the greatest pride and interest in this regiment. He sent the members a kind message, and told them he would well care for their interests in Ireland. He sent word to the captains and under officers to take special care to exercise their men twice every week, if they expected any respect from him on their return to Ireland.

To the commanders, Sir Francis Willoughby, Sir Henry Blundell, and Sir Henry Tichbourne, he. addressed a few rousing words.

He expressed his confidence in their sense of honour, and of the fair field before them to show their merit. But two things he yet especially recommended to their care. The first was to keep their authority over the men they commanded; not only to maintain them in good order as a common duty, but because

* Clarendon State Papers, ii., 36.

they would thus better serve the King. The second was to examine carefully all the defects of the town and castle of Carlisle, and how they might best be strengthened and made tenantable. Also to calculate what provision they should need in case of a siege, and forward the estimate at once to the Secretary of State, and desire him to furnish what was needful, without delay.

Another piece of most excellent counsel he added on behalf of the privates. He advised the officers to find some employment for them, by which they could earn some money, and thereby be kept from riot and disorder.

He ended with the kind words :

"It is not easily to be believed how much I think of you, or how much I tender you ; and I promise myself so much from you all, as if you do not more gallantly than other men you meet with you shall not satisfy my expectation. And I pray tell Captain Weinmann, and Captain Blount, all the lieutenants and ensigns, as much from me. And so happiness and health accompany you each one."

After writing the above, Lord Wentworth received the pleasant news that they were looked upon as so superior to other regiments, that they would probably be sent to join the main body of the army, to train the rest. He, therefore, again most earnestly pressed them to keep their men to arms, and "never think them good enough, but still endeavour to make them better."

The most disheartening intelligence reached him of Scotland. Windebanke told him it could not be worse. The delay in garrisoning Berwick and Carlisle had given the Scots great advantage. For so many men

1639. were needed there, that there were too few in Scotland to make any way with the rebels. Treachery, too, was suspected in the French ambassador. Professing to have received orders from home, he intended to move to the seat of war, with the purpose, it was believed, of furnishing intelligence to the French. But intimations were given him that his presence was not desired, to which he was forced to pay unwilling heed.

Lord Wentworth now wrote to the King for instructions, and accompanied his requests with the most earnest advice. He thought the castle of Dumbarton had been very clumsily lost. He considered it of far greater consequence than the castle of Edinburgh; and had the fleet only sailed in time it might so easily have been secured. As it was, there seemed nothing to restrain the Scots from marching into England.

The seizure of their ships in the ports, he looked on as a great error. It quite set aside the policy he had so anxiously recommended, of not giving the Scots any excuse of attack. But, in consequence of this precipitate deed, all the circumstances were altered, and he now knew not what to do. He had arranged to have an oath put in form by which all loyal Scots were to abjure the Covenant. If they refused, he desired to know the King's pleasure as to the culprits.

Should he imprison the delinquents and seize their lands and possessions for his Majesty, " for the use of the public?" We may be sure the eyes of Charles sparkled at this proposition.

Should not a Proclamation be issued ordering all Scots resident in Ireland to return to their homes, under pain of forfeiting their estates? Was it the King's pleasure that all Scotch vessels out at sea

should be seized? And if so, how were their crews
and cargo to be disposed of? Would it not be well to
detain the masters, and make them serve as pilots for
English vessels along the Scotch coast? And many
other suggestions burst from the busy brain of Wentworth.

But he most decisively advised the King to fortify
Carlisle and Berwick in the strongest manner. To
increase their garrisons with powerful bodies of horse
and foot; to largely store them with every kind of
ammunition and provisions, and to place persons in
authority there of proved loyalty to the Government.
If this were done, he thought the cavalry alone would
secure England from invasion this year. Only let the
summer be spent in perfectly exercising the troops and
making both officers and men familiar with their duty.
A battle might be avoided for the present by strongly
and commodiously entrenching the army in some place
of advantage, so as to secure Newcastle, and have the
use both of that town and of the sea. All this was the
more needful, as Sir Francis Willoughby had reported
how unfit the country was to receive an invading
enemy. But thus safely entrenched and fortified, the
King might look calmly and without opposition on
the fury of the foe, till the strength of their outbreak
was exhausted, and then, perhaps, they might see their
wickedness and yield. And this was more to be
desired than a victory by arms. But if not, then there
would be time before next spring to collect money,
arms, and men, and all things needful, finally to crush
them.

But he did not rest satisfied with warning Charles
alone. He knew how dilatory was the latter in fol-

lowing the most urgent counsel. It was owing to this that all the great castles in Scotland had been lost. And it was impossible any longer to treat the Scots with contempt.

Wentworth, therefore, wrote to Sir Henry Vane, repeating all that he had said to the King, and adding other directions equally important.

He cautioned him against a mistake very likely to be made by Charles, viz., that of quartering his army in some inland district, where, being unable to obtain relief by sea, he might soon be cut off from provisions, as the enemy would surely lay waste the country round.

It was also of highest importance to command the strictest order and discipline of war to be observed in the severest manner. The captains should be commanded diligently to exercise their men, to teach them the perfect use of arms; drawing them into convenient spots for that purpose, thrice a week. Once a week, they should be drawn out in large bodies, brigades, at least, and then embattled and marched in whole regiments. Skirmishing and giving fire on each other was not to be neglected. In short, they must be rendered perfectly familiar with the active part of war.

Besides this, the whole army should sometimes march out in line of battle, if the ground would permit it, two or three miles backwards and forwards, the soldiers fully accoutred and bearing all their arms.

By these means, in addition to other advantages, the soldiers and officers would be kept from idleness, which was the general cause of armies growing dissolute and licentious.

All these duties the King should require to be put in execution by the chiefs of his army, commanding them in person to attend to those high commands and not to transfer these tasks to lieutenant-generals and sergeant-majors. Nay, if his Majesty in person would be pleased sometimes to be in the field himself, his affairs would prosper none the worse, but would make the officers more careful, give infinite comfort and cheerfulness to his men, be a noble recreation to himself, and his judgment attending upon the work in hand, still show him something worthy his knowledge.

Lord Wentworth said he was quite aware that all these cares were held to be little matters, beneath the attention of the chief commanders, and only fit to be deputed and entrusted to inferior officers. But those who held that opinion should certainly not command him.*

"It was by these apparently little things," he said, "that all the great actions of war were accomplished and perfected. Nay, besides that, if the chiefs neglected small duties, and held not a strong hand over their performance, but cast the reins loose on the neck of their army, it would run into a thousand outrages headlong, the discipline of war be utterly lost amongst them, and by the next spring their men be as ignorant and as useless as soldiers as at present.

" There was also one matter of supreme importance, and that was, that the soldiers be kept in their quarters to their night duties constantly; their watches, outguards, and all things incident to that particular of war as strictly observed as if the enemy were lodged within a mile. And it would be to excel-

* Letter to Sir Henry Vane, ii., 325.

lent purpose, if, when they went to exercise, the Master of the Ordnance were directed to his place, where to march with the ordnance, so that the ministers belonging to that part of the militia might be acquainted and perfect with what belonged to their duty."

Some apprehensions were entertained of the Scots rising in Ireland, and it is certain Lord Wentworth kept his eye fixed upon them.

" If they should stir," said he, " (our eight thousand arms and twenty pieces of cannon arrived, which I trust now will be very shortly) I hope to give them such a heat in their clothes as they never had since their coming forth of Scotland. And yet our standing army here is but a thousand horse and two thousand foot, and not fewer of them, I will a-warrant-you, than a hundred and fifty thousand ; so you see our work is not very easy. The best of it is, the brawn of a lark is better than the carcase of a kite, and the virtue of one loyal subject more than of a thousand traitors."*

Lord Wentworth now received information that the appointment of Desmond to the troop of Lord Kircudbright, which had so greatly excited him, had been made at the instigation of Queen Henrietta Maria. His anger was extreme at this piece of meddling on her part. It was not to be borne, at a crisis so dangerous, when all things depended on the army, that his disposition of the officers should be set aside by an ignorant Frenchwoman, even though called by the name of a Queen. There had always been a silent antagonism between her and him. He had a great respect for women of real talent and feeling, and had been singularly happy with all his three wives, each of

* Letter to Vane, ii., 328.

whom required but to know his wishes to fulfil them. Consequently, he was the more disgusted at the constant attempts of the Queen to " manage " her husband. She disliked Wentworth, because he did not flatter her and obey her whims; also, he did not sufficiently resemble a hairdresser's doll to satisfy her highly-exalted taste for manly beauty.   She thought him " vairy uglee," his sole redeeming quality being in her eyes " his preetie white hands," and on them she often expatiated.

He had a mean opinion of her intellect, none at all of her judgment, and was constantly irritated by her interference in the affairs of the Government.   He now sent off a message to Sir John Wintour, desiring him to inform her Majesty that he should receive it as a great and singular favour, if she would move no further in this matter of the Earl of Desmond.   It was a precedent which, if persisted in, would introduce a mighty disorder in the army, and disable him altogether from serving his Majesty as otherwise he trusted he should be able to do.   It was most pernicious in this time of general action, when the whole of Scotland was in revolt, and great numbers in Ireland were disaffected. He had need of the most experienced officers, and he trusted to be approved in the bestowing what of right and by practice had ever belonged to the place he occupied for such good and important ends and purposes.   He trusted rather to be sustained and strengthened for better duties in his Majesty's service, not thus disabled, and at length despised and neglected, in the course of his service even by those who, next to their Majesties, ought to respect and obey him the most, so

1639.

1639. long as his Majesty honoured him with the charge and power of General amongst them.

He wished the Queen to know that, if once these places of command in the army became suits at Court, looked upon as preferments and portions for younger children, the honour of the government of Ireland, and consequently the prosperity of affairs, would be lost.

We may be quite sure that the kindly feelings of Queen Henrietta Maria to Lord Wentworth were by no means increased by these plain words.*

He now received news of his regiment at Carlisle. They were the wonder and the admiration of all around. Attempts were made to exchange the men into other companies, and they were everywhere in request to help drill the raw recruits. All the orders of Wentworth had been exactly obeyed, and not a man had been lost since their departure from Ireland. Twice a week they were exercised, and "having their new clothes, made a brave show." But these fine soldiers themselves were disgusted with the comrades offered to them, as well as with the wretched improvidence and bad management, of which the careful training of Lord Wentworth had made them severe critics. On a rumour of their being distributed in various places, they with one accord, officers and men, joined Sir Francis Willoughby in requesting Lord Wentworth that they might either remain altogether and perform the service for which they were sent, or else be recalled to Ireland. They boldly declared they were jointly resolved not to sue for or accept of any other employment than that of guarding Carlisle. In that they would do their duty, and were ready to

* The Lord Deputy to Sir John Wintour, ii., 328.

spend their lives and fortunes in the King's service. But part they would not.

They found neither stores nor any storehouse nearer than Newcastle. Nothing was provided to replace their diminishing ammunition, nor any materials to repair the fortifications. The place was so weak that they were in constant dread of the approach of the enemy before it was ready. Only £200 was in possession of the Mayor, and with this they began to prepare their wheelbarrows and other tools. Food and lodging were very dear. The soldiers found it hard work to live on 3s. 6d. a week. The town itself pleaded poverty, and declared its inability to afford them either fire or light when on guard.*

At this juncture, when money was so urgently needed by the King as well as men, a document arrived in England which, had it fallen under the eye of Lord Wentworth, would probably have resulted in an explosion such as would have made the writer more modest for the future. For, however oppressive the acts of the Lord Deputy to his countrymen, there was not a man in the British Isles more jealous of foreign interference and insolence. The following is a copy of this delectable epistle :—

(ENTITLED)

" *Instructions from the Pope to his Nuncio in England.*

" You are to command the Catholics of England in general, that they suddenly desist from making such offers of men towards this Northern expedition, as we

---

* Sir Francis Willoughby to the Lord Deputy, ii., 330.

1639. hear they have done, little to the advantage of their discretion. And, likewise, it is requisite, considering the penalty already imposed, that they be not too forward with money more than what law and duty enjoins them to pay, without any innovation at all, or view of making themselves rather weaker pillars of the kingdom than they were before. Inform the provincials of every order, that it is expressly prohibited no more assemblies (of what nature soever) shall admit of the laity to have either voice or session in it, being what will be urged for a precedent is but only an usurpation.

"Declare unto the best of the peers and gentlemen by word of mouth, that they ought not to express any averseness, in case the High Court of Parliament be called, nor show any discontent at the acts, which do not, point blank, aim at religion, being in general the most fundamental law of that kingdom.

"Advise the clergy to desist from that foolish, nay rather illiterate and childish, custom of distinction in the Protestant and Puritan doctrine. And, especially, this error is so much the greater when they undertake to prove that Protestantism is a degree nearer to the Catholic faith than the other. For, since both of them be without the verge of the Church, it is needless hypocrisy to speak of it; yea, it begets more malice than it is worth.

"That the provincials are required to give a general warning through all orders that no religious person ought to be seduced by any noblemen, either officers of the Crown or the like, who pretend to be schismatic into a præmunire. For he that dares not follow the truth as his conscience directs him, is not worthy to be sought or followed by any of our faith. But, on the other side, we give the like command, that whosoever is thought inclining to God in his heart, let no man be so rash to boast and speak it abroad.

" All busy inquiries are forbidden, but especially into arcanas of the State. That none of the Church, whether lay brother or ecclesiastical, contribute so largely as they have done to the society; but dispose their charity that every order may partake alike."[*]

There is a great deal of common-sense in this letter. The repulsive part of the matter is, that a foreign ruler should take upon himself to issue orders in England. Still it was a good thing that the Catholics were held back from supplying funds for this wicked war. It was also a good thing that money was scarce in every direction. The Council were at their wits' end. Loan after loan was refused, and very cold answers came in from the gentry in answer to a new appeal.

" Though they be not direct refusals," said Windebanke, " they are almost as ill, for they bring us no relief, nor no hope of it. Some petty sums, and those very few, have been offered. So that my Lords begin to apprehend it may be of dangerous consequence. Upon the whole matter, my Lords have commanded me to represent with all humility to your Majesty that they see no possibility of procuring such supplies to your Majesty as are expected till the end of October."

The higher classes were not the only recreants. The King had sent letters to the citizens of London demanding a heavy loan.

On the 10th of June the committee appointed to procure money for the King met at Whitehall, to

---

[*] Clarendon State Papers, ii., 47.

 receive the Lord Mayor and Aldermen of London and
place before them the needs of the King. The Recorder
first read aloud the King's letter. After this, Archbishop Laud made a speech representing the needs of
the King, and the danger of the whole kingdom if he
were not supplied. The only place where ready money
was to be had was the city, which, hitherto, even in
times of less peril and necessity, had been ready to
serve the Crown. His Majesty demanded nothing by
way of gift or contribution, but a loan upon good security of repayment both of principal and interest, by
which they would be no losers, but gainers. On such
terms they seldom refused any applicant, and of course
it was impossible they could make the least difficulty
to the King upon so urgent an occasion, and where
their own safety was so nearly concerned.

His Grace was warmly seconded by the rest, and
the Lord Privy Seal told the listening Mayor and
Aldermen that when he was Recorder in the time of
King James, the city had lent £100,000 for a-year at
three days warning, and had it repaid punctually to
a day.

But still the Lord Mayor required time to consider
with his friends as to the wisdom of following this
bright example.

To this the committee replied that though the business was very weighty, yet it needed no such deliberation. The greatest difficulty lay in the manner of
doing it; for they must know it must be done, and
that being yielded to they should have time to advise
upon the rest. It would therefore be quite enough to
consult together privately on the spot, and give the
result to the committee before their departure.

The committee then withdrew, leaving the Lord Mayor and Aldermen in the Council Chamber. After the lapse of an hour, these disloyal citizens informed the committee that considering the present scarcity of money and damp of trade, they held it impossible to give his Majesty satisfaction.

"My Lords" of the committee replied, they durst take no excuses or refusals, and advised the Lord Mayor and Aldermen to be careful how they gave his Majesty such just cause of indignation, which must be of dangerous consequence to the city in general, and to every one of them. And Lord Cottington went so far as to tell them, they should have sold their chains and gowns.

This eloquence having no effect, they were left to consider the matter again, and a proposal made to raise so much a month.

But before the time arrived for their answer, its necessity was superseded by events which will shortly appear.

Among the Scots who had settled in Ireland were the usual per-centage of traitors and cowards in a good cause. These, instead of the pride in the valour and independence of their country that the majority avowed, trembled with abject fear lest they should be thought to share it, and thereby endanger their worldly possessions. And to ensure their own safety they drew up a petition, which has stamped the names of all who signed it with shame and dishonour.

It was addressed to the Lord Deputy and Council, and written in the names of "divers lords spiritual and temporal, knights, gentlemen, and others of the Scottish nation, inhabiting the kingdom of Ireland."

1639.

The petitioners stated that they had with inward sorrow, hitherto, observed the disorders in Scotland, occasioned by the covenant entered into by their countrymen there without his Majesty's regal authority or assent.

And as the petitioners altogether disliked those courses, and feared lest they might be suspected of being a party thereto, notwithstanding their perfect innocence, they desired to vindicate their loyalty. And to enable them to prove themselves perfectly free from " so great a blemish, from the contagion and malignity of the lewd and desperate transgressions of that faction," they begged the Lord Deputy and his Council would prescribe some test by oath, or other means by which they could show how free they were from any suspicion of consent to these proceedings of their wretched countrymen.

Nothing could be more opportune for the King than this request. It was exactly what Lord Wentworth needed, and took from him all the odium of suggestion. Of course he complied, and by order of the Lord Deputy and Council, the following oath was ordered to be administered to every Scot in Ireland. All who refused to take it were to be sent before the Council.

" I do faithfully swear, profess, and promise, that I will honour and obey my sovereign Lord, King Charles, and will bear faith and true allegiance unto him. And defend and maintain his royal power and authority. And that I will not bear arms, or do any rebellious or hostile act against him ; or protest against any his royal commands, but submit myself in all due obedience thereunto. And that I will not enter into any covenant, oath, or bond of mutual defence and assist-

ance against any persons whatsoever by force, without
his Majesty's sovereign and regal authority. And I
do renounce and abjure all covenants, oaths, and bonds
whatsover, contrary to what I have herein sworn,
professed and promised. So help me God in Christ
Jesus."*

This oath was so satisfactory to the King, that he
ordered it to be taken, also, by all the Scots in England above the age of sixteen, and a commission was
accordingly issued to that effect.

Meanwhile, the King found almost as much difficulty
in obtaining privates for his army, as in finding money
to pay them.

In England the Marquis of Hamilton, and in Ireland
the Earl of Barrymore, were compelled to press their recruits; few, indeed, came voluntarily to their standards.
So detested was the service in Norfolk, Suffolk, Essex,
and Kent, where Hamilton sent his press-gang, that
men were found to mutilate their feet causing lameness
for life, and even to hang themselves rather than serve.†

In Ireland, where the Earl of Barrymore took the
King's commission to raise a thousand men, he pursued a system the opposite to that of Lord Wentworth.
He took no money either to pay the troops or provide
for their necessities. The old scenes of former times
were soon revived. The houses of honest labourers
were invaded, and the tenants with their sons pressed
into the royal service. The recruiting parties were
composed of the most brutal ruffians. Wherever they
appeared, the inhabitants took to flight as at the approach of an enemy.

* Nalson's Collections, i. 219.
† Mr. Garrard to the Lord Deputy, ii. 357.

1639.

Lord Wentworth was highly disgusted, and begged that if a levy must be made in Ireland for the Scotch war, that it might be managed by the Irish ministers of the Crown.

On the 29th of April, the King left York on his journey to Berwick. Before leaving, he expressed his great satisfaction with his reception at York, saying, that he had never found the like true love from the city of London, to which place he had given so many marks of his favour. On the first night after his departure he was lodged at Raby Castle, the seat of Sir Henry Vane, where he was magnificently entertained; and from thence he proceeded to Newcastle, where he met with a similar reception at the hands of the mayor and citizens.

As he approached Berwick, his army was drawn up in line of battle, and at its head he marched to the Tweed and pitched his camp at a place called Birks, two miles west of Berwick.

On hearing of the King's arrival at Berwick, Lord Wentworth wrote to him to entrench his army with all possible strength and diligence, always taking care to leave a free passage between the camp and Berwick, and also the sea free. And by no offensive act to provoke an invasion till the end of August. If this could be managed, and the cavalry meantime strengthened as much as possible, he thought it not unlikely that the King might with great success suddenly march with all the cavalry to Edinburgh, spoiling and burning all the corn of the champagne country, and seizing all the shipping, fishing, and commerce, disable them for the winter. And not less than two thousand men should be left in Carlisle.*

<hr>

* The Lord Deputy to the King, ii. 356.

This last plan is hardly consistent with the usual 1639.
clear vision of Lord Wentworth. If the Scots were in
sufficient force to allow of any danger of their boldly
marching upon an entrenched army, and attacking two
well-fortified garrisons, it would scarcely be likely they
would keep so poor a watch as to admit of a great
surprise, or allow an enemy unchecked to ravage their
lands.

But there was also another impediment to this plan.
Neither army could afford to wait. The English were
discontented and mutinous; the Scots could not so
long neglect their work, submit to the loss of trade
and fishing by the blockade of their ports, for Lord
Hamilton had now arrived off the coast with the
fleet.

"It was our great desire," said the Chaplain of the
Scots army, " to have at once been at handy strokes,
well understanding that our poverty could not long
permit us to keep the field together. If the ships
should keep us besieged by sea, and hold us from all
trade; if on our border an army of strangers should
force us to lie in camp long before them, till our countrymen, even from the North, came on our backs, till
the Irish came on the west and English on the south,
we saw at once that this would undo us without stroke
of sword."

The faithlessness of Charles gave the desired opportunity. The Scots, with strange imprudence, had
agreed not to come within ten miles of the royal camp
so long as Charles did not cross the border.

But on Sunday, the 2nd of June, a council of war
was called in the English camp, and intelligence
was brought that the Scots were in their quarters

1639.

at Kelsey, about six miles' distant and about 1,500 strong.

It was then resolved to attack them, and, accordingly, the next day, the Earl of Holland, with 2000 horse and 2000 foot crossed the Tweed, and marched into Scotland.

The day was one of sultry heat, such as had not been known within living memory, and the infantry, though cooled by wading through the shallow river, were too fatigued to be able to overtake their cavalry, which had now advanced three miles ahead of them, and come in sight of the enemy. As they came on, the Scots sent a trumpeter, demanding what men were they who thus, in warlike array, entered their country. As he uttered this challenge, a large body of horse troops came rapidly behind him, and suddenly all the hedges became alive with Scotch soldiers. It had been a mistake, indeed, to dream of catching them sleeping.

From behind the little hills new troops sprang up, and surrounded the English horsemen on every side. The surprise was to the English, who had fallen into their own trap, and, without striking a blow, they ignominiously turned back, re-crossed the Tweed, and fled to the royal camp.

But the truce had been broken, and there was now nothing to fetter the action of the Scots, while this miserable adventure had but too plainly revealed the condition of the English.

On the following day, the King commanded all the nobles, gentlemen, and his own train to muster before him. Having obeyed his order and " made a gallant show," though unfortunately nothing else, they dismounted, and having all sent their horses to their respective quarters, were about to retire. Suddenly the alarm was sounded that the enemy was among them. It was given by Sir John Byron, who, rushing into the royal pavilion, brought out the King and showed him the Scots marching upon the camp, with colours flying and fully prepared for battle. The King took out his field-glass and went to the side of the Tweed. There was no mistake. The main body of the enemy was all on the nearest side of Dunse Hill, and none ready to oppose them.

The King uttered an oath. " Have not I," said he, " good intelligence! that the rebels can march with their army, and encamp within sight of mine, and I not have a word of it till the body of their army give the alarm ? "

He then sent for the general, who blamed the scout-master, and he, in turn, accused the scouts. No shame, and no regret were manifested by the troops. Instead of any eagerness to redeem their neglect, they began to murmur about the badness of their provisions, that their biscuit was mouldy and they could get no drink in the camp. They could find no better subject of conversation in sight of the Scotch army, than abuse of Sir William Savile, for furnishing his own regiment the best, complaints that no food could be had out of Scotland now beyond a few lambs that had been bought, &c., &c.

While in the midst of this pleasant state of affairs, the King was holding a hasty council of war, the Earl of Dumfermline, preceded by his trumpeter, advanced from the Scotch camp and came to the pavilion of the King.

He brought with him the oft repeated petition for liberty of religion, and the declaration that only to defend that and keep the laws of God, and by no means to rebel against the King, had they taken arms. If only their rights, according to the laws of the land, were granted, they would instantly return contentedly to their homes.

It was utterly useless to contend with them now, and Charles was forced to yield what otherwise they had the power to take. With the hope of saving his pride, he caught eagerly at the word " laws," and pretending to have misunderstood the Scots before, and to have thought they wished to set aside the laws, he soon came to terms, and on each side the following articles were agreed to.

On the King's part:

1. That all matters ecclesiastical shall be determined by the assembly of the Kirk, and matters civil by the Parliament and inferior judicatories, which assemblies shall be kept once a year, or as shall be agreed on by the General Assembly.

2. That a free General Assembly be kept at Edinburgh the 6th of August next, where the King intended to be present, and a Parliament held there the 20th of August next, for ratifying what shall be concluded in the said Assembly, and setting such other things as shall be necessary and therein an Act of Oblivion to be passed.

3. That upon the Scots disbanding their forces, discharging their tables, restoring his honours, castles, forts, and ammunition, and to his subjects their liberties and estates, he will retire his fleet and land forces, and restore what ships and goods are detained.

4. That as he intends no alteration of religion or laws, so he expects obedience of his subjects, and if any shall continue disobedient, the calamities that ensue are occasioned not by him but by themselves.

The articles were afterwards put in this form :

1. The Scots to be disbanded within forty-eight hours.

2. His Majesty's castles, forts, ammunition, and royal honours to be delivered up.

3. His ships to depart after the delivery of the castles.

4. His Majesty to restore all persons, goods, and ships arrested since the 1st of November.

5. No meetings or convocations but what warranted by Act of Parliament.

6. All fortifications to desist.

These articles were then signed on both sides, and both armies were disbanded.*

Thus ended in utter disgrace and deserved shame this expedition against the Scots. Happily for the honour of the English name, it was impossible to call it a national cause. The Scotch lords who had taken part with the King were everywhere the objects of scorn and execration to their nobler countrymen. When the Marquis of Hamilton, by the orders of the King, went to put Lord Ruthven into the Castle of Edinburgh, and see it furnished with provisions and ammunition, as he passed along the streets of the capital, he was overwhelmed with such hootings and hissings, that, in terror, he called on some of the covenanting lords to attend him to the castle, as a guard against the people, who hurled at him the

* Rushworth, 8vo. iii. 64.

1639.　epithets of " pirate," " traitor," " enemy to God and the country," &c. And the Earl of Traquair, Lord Treasurer in Edinburgh, who was also obliged to visit the city, met with a similar reception. His white staff of office was torn from his servant, and on a rebuke offered to the people by the council, all the apology was the bare act of returning the staff.*

* Rushworth, iii. 64.

CHAPTER IX.

WHEN the news of the pacification reached Lord Wentworth, he regarded it, as indeed it truly was, merely as a truce which the weakness of the King had compelled him to make. To a man so faithless as Charles, it was apparently a great advantage. It not only afforded him time to prepare new instruments of compulsion, but gave him possession of all the fortresses of Scotland, which before were in the hands of the Covenanters. Indeed, it is much to be wondered at, that the castles, or some of them, should not have been retained as hostages by the Scots.

Wentworth, little heeding the jealous eyes that were bent upon him in England, even more than in Scotland, now rapidly proceeded on that course which could not fail to strengthen and confirm the suspicions of all the friends of liberty. Though the peace declared should at once have put a stop to all warlike preparations, he continued them more vigorously than ever. He administered the oath to the Scots in Ireland with the same rigour as before. He filled his arsenals with arms sufficient for ten thousand foot and one thousand horse, with all other stores in proportion. And he most earnestly counselled the King to maintain his full garrisons in Berwick and Carlisle, and perfect the fortifications of Leith as well as garrison it strongly with loyal troops.* He still deprecated the plan of the King's holding a Parliament in person at Edinburgh. But if his Majesty persisted in this intention, he begged him, at all events, to secure his return, and take such measures, that no advantage might be taken by the Scots of his being on the spot, to constrain him to comply with anything which might in the least "press upon his honour," or embolden either the Scots or any other of his subjects in the future.

Three principles Lord Wentworth said must be granted :

1. That it was the knowledge the Covenanters had of their own weakness, not their better affections, that inclined them to seek an accommodation.

2. That nothing is to be yielded there, which by way of precedent, may encourage to protest or contest the royal commands or the laws already established.

3. That England and Ireland ministering to the King's sovereignty—as Lord Wentworth said, he felt confident they would, if rightly handled—there was abundantly in the King's power, suddenly and safely to conform Scotland to his will in all just things.

It was well that the little word "*just*" came in the right place in the last sentence. But even then, Lord Wentworth deemed it advisable to ask the King to burn the letter containing such equivocal matter.

But the Scots, on their side, were equally cautious. They insisted that the terms of disbanding both armies included the discharge of the garrisons of Berwick and Carlisle, and they loudly protested against any addition

* The Lord Deputy to the King, ii. 372.

either to the fortifications or the number of men in
the royal castles of Scotland.

This unexpected stroke of the Scots completely
thwarted the cunning designs of the King. How to
carry them out, he could not devise. His preparations
could not be carried on secretly, and if attempted
openly, they would be met with counter forces that
might lead to a result like the last. And yet, to allow
the Scots to remain in possession of the victory, was a
humiliation he could not endure.

In this predicament he resolved to send for Lord
Wentworth personally to confer with him. But even
by this he feared to awake new suspicions. He therefore wrote to Wentworth, telling him to come to
England but be sure to hide the cause. "I have,"
said he, "had too much to desire your counsel and
attendance for some time, which I think not fit to express by letter more than this. *The Scots Covenant
begins to spread too far.* Yet, for all this, I will not
have you take notice that I have sent for you, but
pretend some other occasion of business, as to be
present at the hearing of the Chancellor's Appeal, or
what you will."

The King was too little in the habit of seeking
timely counsel of his ministers, not to show that he
was profoundly embarrassed at this time. But anxious
as Lord Wentworth was to obey him, and at once
proceed to England, some delay was unavoidable, in
order to arrange the government of Ireland during his
absence. And most unfortunately, too, he was now
suffering from one of those attacks of illness that were
becoming ever more frequent and violent. He thus
wrote to the King :—

" Verily, Sir, my foot should this very morning have been in the stirrup towards your presence, but, that the condition of this great charge doth necessitate me to have powers from your Majesty so to do, and settle also this government in such a manner as in these cases is required.

" Howbeit, in sadness, my health is not very good, and such a lameness fallen into my knee, the remainder of my last year's gout, as is very troublesome to me now, and hath been ever since the last winter."

He was in great apprehension lest he should lose the use of his limbs at this juncture. But with stern resolution, he immediately began to look for some remedy, and arranged to be carried to England on a litter rather than be wanting to the King.

And, at once, he ordered Sir George Radcliffe to see that all forms were prepared for the transfer of his duties to a lieutenant during his absence. While these were being made ready, Lord Wentworth rapidly selected his deputies and made his domestic arrangements.

His two little girls he resolved to send to their maternal grandmother, the widowed Countess of Clare. She had often asked him for them, but he never could persuade himself to part from them for so long a stay and at such a distance. But as separation was now inevitable, he settled at last, to entrust them to her.

It was on this occasion that he wrote the following beautiful letter :—

The Lord Deputy to the Countess Dowager of Clare.

" MAY IT PLEASE YOUR LADYSHIP,

"My Lord of Clare having writ unto me, your Ladyship desired to have my daughter Ann with you for a time in England to recover her health, I have at last been able to yield so much from my own comfort, as to send both her and her sister to wait your grave, wise, and tender instructions. They are both, I praise God, in good health, and bring with them hence from me no other advice, but entirely and cheerfully to obey and do all you shall be pleased to command them, so far forth as their years and understanding may administer unto them.

" I was unwilling to part them, in regard those that must be a stay one to another, when by course of nature, I am gone before them, I would not have them grow strangers whilst I am living. Besides, the younger gladly imitates the elder in disposition so like her blessed mother, that it pleases me very much to see her steps followed and observed by the other. Madam, I must confess, it was not without difficulty before I could persuade myself thus to be deprived the looking upon them, who, with their brother, are the pledges of all the comfort, the greatest, at least, of my old age, if it shall please God I arrive thereunto.

" But I have been brought up in afflictions of this kind, so as I still fear to have that taken first that is dearest unto me; and have in this been content willingly to overcome my own affections, in order to their good, acknowledging your Ladyship capable of doing them more good in their breeding than I am. Otherway, in truth, I should never have parted with them, as I profess it a grief unto me not to be as well able as any to serve the memory of that noble lady in these harmless little infants.

"Well, to God's blessing and your Ladyship's goodness I commit them, and have of sorrow in my heart till I see them again, I must, I know it right well. And I believe them so graciously minded to render themselves so the more, the more you see of their attention to do as you shall be pleased to direct them, which will be of much contentment unto me. For whatever your Ladyship's opinion may be of me, I desire, and have given it them in charge (so far as their tender years are capable of) to honour and observe your Ladyship above all the women in the world, as well knowing that in so doing they shall fulfil that duty, whereby of all others, they could have delighted their mother the most, and do infinitely wish they may want nothing in their breeding, my power or cost might procure them, or their condition of life hereafter may require.

"For, madam, if I die to-morrow, I will, by God's help, leave them ten thousand pounds a-piece, which I trust, by God's blessing, shall bestow them to the comfort of themselves and friends, nor at all considerably prejudice their brother, whose estate shall never be much burthened with a second venture, I assure you.

"I thought fit to send with them one that teacheth them to write. He is a quiet, soft man; but honest, and not given to any disorder. Him I have appointed to account for the money to be laid forth, wherein he hath no other direction but to pay and lay forth as your ladyship shall appoint, and still, as he wants to go to Woodhouse, where my cousin Rockley will supply him. And I most humbly beseech you to give order to their servants, and otherwise to the tailors at London, for their apparel, which I wholly submit to your ladyship's better judgment. And be it what it may, I shall think it all happily bestowed, so as it be to your contentment and theirs. For cost I reckon not of, and anything I have is theirs so long as I live, which is only worth thanks, for theirs and their brothers all I have must be, whether I will or no, and therefore I desire to let them have to acknowledge me for before.

" Nan, they tell me, danceth prettily, which I wish (if with convenience it might be) were not lost, more to give her a comely grace in the carriage of her body, than that I wish they should much delight or practice it when they are women. Arabella is a small practitioner that way also, and they are both very apt to learn that or anything they are taught.

" Nan, I think, speaks French prettily, which yet I might have been better able to judge, had her mother lived. The other also speaks; but her maid, being of Guernsey, the accent is not good. But your ladyship is in this excellent, as that, as indeed all things else which may befit them, they may, and I hope will, learn better with your ladyship than they can with their poor father, ignorant in what belongs women and other ways. God knows, so distracted, and so a-wanting unto them in all, saving in loving them; and therein, in truth, I shall never be less than the dearest parent in the world.

"Their brother is just now sitting at my elbow, in good health, God be praised; and I am, in the best sort I may, accommodating this place for him, which in the kind I take to be the noblest one of them in the King's dominions, and where a grass time may be passed with most pleasure of that kind. I will build him a good house, and, by God's help, leave him, I think, near three thousand pounds a year, and wood on the ground as much, I daresay, if near London, as would yield fifty thousand pounds, besides a house within twelve miles of Dublin, the best in Ireland, and land to wit, which, I hope, will be two thousand pounds a year, all which he shall have to the rest, had I twenty brothers of his to set besides me.

"This I write not to your ladyship in vanity, or to have it spoken of, but privately to let your ladyship see I do not forget the children of my dearest wife, nor altogether bestow my time fruitlessly for them. It is true, I am in debt; but there will be, besides, sufficient to discharge all I owe, by God's grace, whether I live or die.

"And next to these children, there are not any other persons I wish more happiness than to the house of their grandfather, and shall be always most ready to serve them, what opinion soever be had of me. For no other usage can absolve me of what I owe, not only to the memory, but to the last legacy that noblest creature left with me when God took her to himself.

"I am afraid to turn over the leaf, lest your ladyship might think I could never come to a conclusion, and shall therefore add to all the rest this one truth more,

that whenever I be happied through the occasion,   1639.
there is not any more

> " Your Ladyship's

> " Obedient and most humble

> " Son and Servant,

> " WENTWORTH.

" FAIRWOOD PARK,

> " *The 10th of August*, 1639." *

There was another reason, also, for sending away the children. The son of Sir Edward Osborne had lately been killed at York by the sudden fall of a chimney, and, ever since, the fear of a similar accident had beset the little Wentworths.

Alluding to this miserable calamity, Lord Wentworth wrote to Laud :—

" The sad news of the death of the Vice-President's son was very grievous unto me, the rather that my friend should come to such a misfortune there where I had placed him. But it hath scared all the women and children in the house most seriously, and, to say truth, with reason. For I do not think there are anywhere so many rotten chimneys as are in this Castle, and so dangerously high and weakly set, as if they had been so done purposely for mischief. These late great winds frightened them sufficiently; but I do not think it will now be possible to keep them in their beds, when boisterous Boreas shall swell his cheeks

---

* The Lord Deputy to Lady Clare, ii., 379.

 next.   God bless the young whelps, and for the old dog there is less matter."*

Just at this time the Lady Loftus, in whose behalf Lord Wentworth had decided against the Chancellor, died.   The manner in which he spoke of her after her death is a great argument against the miserable scandal attached by his enemies to his friendship for her. Thus to Lord Conway he expressed his grief: "We have sadly buried my Lady Loftus, one of the noblest persons I ever had the happiness to be acquainted with.   And as I had received greater obligations from her ladyship than from all Ireland besides, so with her are gone the greatest part of my affections to the country; and all that is left of them shall be thankfully and religiously paid to her excellent memory and lasting goodness."

And later he spoke of her as that "gentle person, who to have procured the whole world could not have moved a dishonourable or unrighteous thing to me ; no, though she had known aforehand that I would have yielded thereunto."

By words and deeds, Lord Wentworth endeavoured to arouse a feeling of loyalty towards the King.   The arguments he used are remarkable for their plausibility, and afford a striking example of the possibility of placing a bad cause in a good light.

Sir Richard Hutton, one of the judges who decided in favour of Hampden in the famous trial on the ship money, was a relation of Lord Wentworth by marriage, and frequently corresponded with him.   Just at this time, before his departure for England, Lord Wentworth thought it well to express his opinion on this

* The Lord Deputy to the Archbishop of Canterbury, ii., 251.

course; but very different is his manner from the flippant tone in which he spoke of Hampden to Laud. The following argument, in favour of arbitrary taxation by the King, may well impress minds really as shallow as Lord Wentworth was in the habit of considering those of the taxed people to be :—

"I do conceive that the power of levies of forces, at sea and land, for the very—*not the feigned*—relief and safety of the public, is such a property of sovereignty, as were the Crown willing, yet can it not divest itself thereof. *Salus populi suprema lex;* nay, in cases of extremity, even above acts of Parliament. And I am satisfied that the monies raised for setting forth a fleet was chastely bestowed that way, not at all vitiated by any application otherwise, nay, satisfied that it was necessary that it should be so, and that our fleet at sea were in these times of mighty honour to the King, most fit to preserve the rights of private subjects, the peace and safety of the commonwealth.

"And, considering it is agreed by common consent that in time of public danger and necessity, such a levy may be made, and that the King therein is sole judge, how or in what manner or proportion it is. to be gathered; I conceive it was out of humour opposed by Hampden beyond the modesty of a subject, and that reverence wherein we ought to have so gracious a sovereign."

The second part of his argument is still more impressive :—

"The prospects of Kings into mysteries of State are so far exceeding those of ordinary common persons, as they be able to discern and prevent dangers to the public afar off, which others shall not so much as dream of till they feel the unavoidable stripes and smart of them upon their naked shoulders. Besides, the mischief which threatens State and people are not always those which becomes the object of every vulgar eye; but then commonly of most danger, when least discovered; nay, very often, if unseasonably over-early published, albeit, privately known to the King long before, might rather inflame than remedy the evil.

"Therefore, it is a safe rule for us all, in the fear of God, to remit these supreme watches to that regal power, whose peculiar indeed it is; submit ourselves in these high considerations to his ordinances, as being no other than the ordinance of God itself; and rather attend upon his will with confidence in his justice, belief in his wisdom, assurance in his parental affections to his subjects and kingdoms, than feed ourselves with the curious questions, with the vain flatteries of imaginary liberty, which, had we even our silly wishes and conceits, were we to frame a new commonwealth, even to our own fancy, might yet, in conclusion, leave nothing ourselves less free, less happy than now, thanks be to God and his Majesty, we are, nay ought justly to be reputed by every moderate-minded Christian."

That Lord Wentworth, at least, persuaded himself of the truth of these words there can be little doubt. According to the principles adopted by him, the money spent on the fleet sent out to crush the Scots was " chastely bestowed." But once admit the ground that the King is responsible to God alone, and that regal wisdom is supreme on earth, and it is difficult to see why the whole legal establishment should rest on any other basis than the royal will, or to recognise in the coronation oaths anything but an insulting, if not an impious, farce. The whole of Lord Wentworth's arguments vanish into air when opposed to the fact, that in England a king reigns solely on certain conditions accepted by himself, and by which he confesses himself to be a mortal, bound by precisely the same obligations of morality as the rest of mankind.

1639.

CHAPTER X.

It was not before the middle of November that Lord Wentworth was able to leave Ireland. When all his arrangements had been made, and even his baggage got ready, he was seized with violent paroxysms of two of the diseases that held him in their racking fetters. But desperately struggling with these most cruel enemies, he, nevertheless, set sail and crossed St. George's Channel. On disembarking at Chester he was obliged to pause, and while resting his shattered frame he wrote to his wife describing his bodily sufferings. After a few days he set out for London, and immediately on his arrival, probably to give that colour to his visit which the King had desired, the appeal of the Lord Chancellor Loftus of Ireland against the judgment of the Irish Council and Deputy was heard in the Star Chamber by the King in person. The appeal was vain, and the case a second time settled, and now by the Privy Council of England, against Loftus. Among those who thus decided were Vane and Holland, both enemies of Wentworth.

The late Pacification of Berwick had been the greatest mortification ever experienced by the King. Never was a defeat more complete than that. He writhed beneath the shame, and hated the Scots with tenfold hatred. The ease with which they had secured the victory opened his eyes, and showed him that if he meant to make a second venture he must oppose with a stronger force.

He could not forget the warnings of Lord Wentworth, and his cautions not to commence the war before spring. Those cautions he had disregarded, and struck the first blow by seizing the Scottish vessels. The fears of his wise counsellor had been verified. Had the King only followed his advice, how different had been his position now! At length, Charles began to recognise the value of the mind that had maintained the most dangerous portion of his dominions so long in peace. By his own management he had lodged himself in a Slough of Despond, and according to the custom of human nature in such circumstances, he looked to the man for cure whose advice to prevent the evil he had scorned. Wentworth now was to be his most trusty weapon. A new leaf must be turned over. Those aids to authority in the shape of worldly dignities that Wentworth had so much needed in his most difficult task in Ireland, and which he had been so coldly refused, were now to be granted. Not as a reward for his past services, not to make his path easier for himself, but to render him more useful to the King was a title to be bestowed. The new year of 1640 witnessed what Lord Wentworth playfully called " the death of that great person, the Lord Deputy of Ireland," and his transformation into the Earl of Strafford and Baron of Raby. Strafford being the name of the hundred or wapentake in which his paternal mansion was situated, he chose that for the name of his earldom. At the same time he was made a knight of the Garter, and his title of Lord Deputy changed into the higher one

1639.   of Lord-Lieutenant of Ireland—a name which had slept
since the days of the Earl of Essex. From this time
he was known no more as Lord Wentworth, but by
the name always applied to him in speech and history
that of the Earl of Strafford.

His first act in his new dignity was to join with
Laud and the Marquis of Hamilton in a secret council
to debate on the needs of the King. The affairs of
Scotland threw all else into the shade by their magnitude and importance.

With Strafford's views of royalty, the triumph of
the Scots was as unbearable as to Charles himself, and
he had an additional cause of anger that Charles did
not feel. To the mortification inflicted on his political
opinions was added the warmth of a partisan. His
affection for the King added the King's pain to his
own. Quietly to rest in this condition was impossible
to him. His King, his idol, was a mark of scorn to
the world. The enemies of his friend were triumphant. Could he, even at this late hour, have
recognised the real position of the two parties as they
stood in the light of abstract justice alone, and said to
Charles: " You are wrong in the whole matter. Terrible is the humiliation, galling the smart, unbearable
almost to speak of, while you look at it in the sense of
a vulgar defeat. But take the truly royal position of
a prince who desires the habitation of his throne to be
justice and judgment indeed, and you will rejoice in
having been prevented from perpetrating a wrong:
you will accept the stern lesson at the hands of a noble
people, and feel how far more glorious it is to rule
over a free nation than a horde of slaves. Let this
suggest to you the need of studying the spirit, the dis-

position that can prove itself so stedfast. Be yourself the first example of obedience to the laws, and rebellion will be all unknown in England. And for me, a loyal servant, a faithful friend, let me die rather than fail you in what is good, or serve you in what is ill;"—could Lord Strafford have suddenly awakened to a sense of whither his blind affection, his abandonment of all things to the desires of the King were leading him;—could he with devotion as firm have seen the star of Right, and steered unswervingly his course by that as chief—who can say what would have been the result? Not much, it is to be feared, to the good of the King, who would probably have dismissed him with rage and disappointment to a prison.

There are minds which need only the call of a noble and sympathetic nature to spring from darkness into light, which will joyfully grasp the outstretched hand that seeks to draw them from the mire into which they have been betrayed by guile or the force of a mighty temptation, which, even unaided by all, can never reconcile themselves to a base condition, and still grope and struggle and mourn for better things, even though they have never seen or known them.

And there are others whom no power can sustain on high. With a glorious upward path before their very eyes, with great work, fit instruments, and whatever can elevate and cheer, with a sphere waiting;—all—all are vain. The weight of worldly selfishness overbears all else; no wings are powerful enough to lift such a one in air; its strongest attribute compels it to grovel. Again and again attempts to raise it may be made, it cannot exist above the earth, it has no sympathy with those bright orbs whose mutual powers of attraction sustain them in their celestial sphere, and the artificial supports removed, it falls prone, once more, to perish and decay.

A more hopeless nature than that of Charles it is difficult to conceive. The wonderful patience of the people in, again and again, pardoning his broken faith awoke no desire of return in him. The vigour and prompt decision of the Scots suggested no appreciation of the importance of their worship in their own eyes; he looked upon their unity as conspiracy. Neither had he the temptation of strong passions to hurry him into folly, or the excuse of hopelessly difficult circumstances to drive him to dangerous despair. As a king and as a man, fortune was propitious to him. Fervent loyalty and friendship, such as the noblest men would have died to win, were his, and were as nothing in his eyes. His mind was essentially poor, barren by nature, and much less cultivated than is generally believed. This native poverty is his best excuse. It is by accrediting him with far greater powers than he possessed that the real injustice is done to him. The glamour of a royal name, a handsome face, a picturesque dress, have been most truly suggested as having a generally undreamed-of influence on his admirers, though it needs only to remember the boundless power of mere appearance and name over most minds to admit the possibility at once. That he was incapable of improvement is seen by the failure of all that could tempt a man to goodness to move him.

But with Lord Strafford it might have been otherwise. Had a truly good and great man felt for him such an affection as he felt for Charles, and used that affection to awaken him to conscience, none can say what might not have been the result. Unfortunately for him, the acquaintance of Pym and Hampden never reached to friendship, and outside the House of Commons, even in his early days, when he shared their political opinions, he was almost a stranger. Pym is said to have been intimate, but no trace of this remains. There are no signs of mutual visits, no friendly letters, no kindly mention even in the earliest days. It was a disadvantage to Strafford that those who really loved him, worshipped him in the same manner that he worshipped the King, and were, without exception, men who felt their inferiority. Yet from them he could bear to be told of his faults without offence, and frequently he promised them to try to subdue his passionate temper and haste—almost his only defects in their partial eyes. And it is this deference to their opinion, added to his wonderful devotion to the King, that vindicates his fitness for a loftier sphere than he found on earth. A soul capable of one unchanging love for another through his whole life, who ever puts the welfare, the happiness of that other before his own, who is unmoved by any unpopularity, who clings the closer for misfortune, sacrifices the more for need—no matter how erroneous may be the manner in which he shows this feeling—so long as it is true in itself and its object more to him than himself; such a man has other possibilities hidden within, seeds waiting only for that warmth which is their right atmosphere to bring them to life. And among the other lessons taught us by the career of Lord Strafford may not this be one? That when we see another armed with such powers, yet seemingly deficient in the one thing that can render them a blessing to humanity, those gifted with a keen and lofty moral sense shall not be content to blame the defect, but hold it among their duties to endeavour by influence to supply it, or rather to kindle the flame hidden and lost in the flint for want of the friendly contact of what, at first sight, seems the alien steel. Had Hampden, for instance, dreamed of the possibility of striking the first spark of conscience in Wentworth's soul, of feeding the flame with affection, it is vain to say that the noblest results might not have followed. But this is only one of the many dreams of "what might have been."   Not the faintest effort was made by the patriots to retain Strafford—not a single timely remonstrance was heard. Unaided in his hour of weakness, the hatred with which he had ever since been pursued rendered return next to impossible.

War with Scotland was again resolved on.   Ever since the pacification, commissioners had passed to and fro between the King and the Scots, consuming the time in weary arguments that deceived neither.   The Scots were perfectly convinced that the moment they laid down their arms and rendered themselves helpless, the King would pour down his forces and compel them to receive the hated, and in their eyes unholy liturgy, and any other matters he chose.   His own breach of the treaty, in filling the Castle of Edinburgh with troops, gave them a fair excuse for not completely disbanding, and amidst mutual recrimination both prepared for a new struggle.

But the King was again met by the terrible need of money that had proved such an obstacle before, and to supply that need was now the subject of anxious consultation.   A council was called to consider means.   A loan was first proposed, but it soon became evident

that this would go but a short way. It was, nevertheless, adopted as a means of immediate supply, while
more solid plans were forming. To this loan Lord
Strafford subscribed no less than twenty thousand
pounds out of his own private estate, as well to afford
an example to others as for its own substantial use.
Though the obsequious judges had declared in favour
of the King's claim to ship money, their decision was
so palpably opposed to the laws, that it rather increased
than lessened the difficulty of collecting it. And all
other illegal measures promised such poor results, that
the only safe chance of obtaining sufficient means to
meet the voluntary forces of the Scots was to fall back
on the nation, and once more summon a Parliament.
The delight of the people at once more seeing their
beloved assembly would, it was hoped, put them in so
good a humour with the King, that they would be
ready with open purses to support him. But if not, if
a Parliament should refuse, then the council considered
the King, having exhausted all lawful means, would be
fully justified in taking the matter entirely into his
own hands, and raising money for the war in the
manner that seemed best to himself.

But England was not alone to be called upon. Lord
Wentworth had such confidence in the goodwill of the
Irish towards the King, and their total lack of all
sympathy for the Scots, whose hatred of Popery was
not likely to attract them, that he proposed to call
another Parliament in Ireland for the express purpose
of laying the subject before them.

Matters were then settled accordingly. Writs were
issued in England, summoning a Parliament to meet
on the 13th of April, and Lord Strafford took his

 departure from England to hold the same august assembly in Ireland.

Meanwhile, in each of the three countries were seen again the preparations for a renewal of the civil and most wanton strife. The Earl of Northumberland, Lord High Admiral of England, was also appointed Commander-in-Chief of all the Forces against the Scots, and Lord Strafford named Lieutenant-General under him. The navy was to be largely increased, twenty new ships of war to be ready by the 10th of April. The city of London was ordered either to furnish a ship of war, or the money to enable the King to fit out one of his own vessels. The citizens preferred the latter alternative, and guaranteed the sum required. Letters were sent from the Privy Council to the Lords Lieutenants of the counties, with orders to raise a certain number of troops, to whom the Earl of Northumberland would send officers to train them. On the 10th of May they were all to meet at one general rendezvous, and thence march to Newcastle. For the present all their expenses were to be paid by the country, which was afterwards to be repaid out of the exchequer. Men for the navy were to be raised in a similar way.*

On the arrival of Lord Strafford in Ireland, the King sent him a formal letter directing him to make certain statements to his good subjects in Ireland. Among these was an account of the wickedness and ingratitude of the Scots. In this most pathetic document Charles related to the Irish how he had hitherto tried to conceal from all others the manifold distempers and ill affections shown towards his government and person

* Rushworth, 8vo, iii., p. 127.

by the Scots; how he had endeavoured out of his princely clemency silently to reclaim them, and equally bow their judgments and consciences to right reason and that natural allegiance God required of them for him.

Yet, he said, his gracious inclination had not wrought in them that clear sight and sense of their disobedience he trusted would have been the case, and which must have happened had his goodness and compassion towards them been looked on and received with such reverence and thankfulness as these qualities deserved. But at length he was forced to expose the culprits. They had grown worse through his forbearance and moderation, and now, under the mask of religion, had shown so little regard to the rights of his Crown, and the dignity of his person, that he could no longer neglect to put his affairs and armies in such a condition as should enforce their obedience and conformity.

For this reason, therefore, he had resolved to call a Parliament, both in England and Ireland, to consult on these matters, and to offer to his well-affected subjects the honour to endeavour with him the joint safety of King and people.

And, in particular, Lord Strafford was to tell the people of Ireland that through the disorders of others, the King looked with delight upon their great and continued expressions of affection and loyalty; and, what was more, he assured himself with all confidence of their fit supply and personal assistance in the execution and accomplishment of his just and pious intentions.

And therefore Lord Strafford was to demand of

1640. them, in these pressing and urgent occasions of the King, the grant of six subsidies, to be paid in three years. At the same time, he was enjoined to tell them that if God should give that misguided faction in Scotland grace to submit, then the King would remit two of the six subsidies, and employ the other four for improving the revenue, so as to be no further burdensome to Ireland, *unless some great and pressing occasion should enforce him.*

But the six subsidies were not all. People do not maintain a character for generosity for nothing. Lord Strafford was further enjoined to declare that the King had that well-grounded opinion of the Irish faith and courage, that he purposed to have a levy of eight thousand foot and one thousand horse of them, to join the rest of his forces at Berwick, to reduce Scotland to obedience.

And, in return for these loyal gifts, the King said he had given Lord Strafford charge to advise with the Council for the framing of such laws as should conduce to their happiness; and these being sent for his approval, should be returned to be passed by their Parliament.[*]

But these delightful messages were threatened with a delay which nothing but the unconquerable spirit and endurance of Lord Strafford could have prevented. On his journey back to Ireland, he was seized at Beaumaris with one of his paroxysms of pain, which he thus describes to Secretary Coke :—

" Paper grows scarce, as are the winds, so you must be content with half a sheet.

" Nevertheless, though it blows something westerly, I will this morning on board. God grant us a good

* Strafford Papers, ii. 393.

passage. That which makes me hasten the more is in regard having had a great pain all night in one of my ancles ; I am so lame this morning as I stir not without much anguish ; and I should grieve extremely to be bound up here to my chamber in a season wherein his Majesty's service requires me so much in Ireland.

" I thank God it took me so late! for, had it fallen upon me three days sooner, it would have been impossible to have got me hither. But now the next ground I touch, by God's help, shall be Irish. There within two or three days, I shall either be well, and cease my gout, I trust, for this year, or 'else be able to tell where I may be found for three weeks, or a fortnight at least. Howbeit, one way or other, I hope to make shift to be there and back again hither in good time. For I will make strange shift, and put myself to all the pain I shall be able to endure, before I be any-where awanting to my master or his affairs in this conjuncture. And, therefore, sound or lame, you shall have me with you before the beginning of the Parlia-ment. I should not fail though Sir John Eliot were living.

" In the mean space, for love of Christ, call upon and hasten the business now in hand, especially the raising of the horse and all together, the rather for that this work now before us, should it miscarry, we all are like to be very miserable. But carried through advisedly and gallantly, shall, by God's blessing, set us in safety and peace for our lives at after, nay, in probability, the generations that are to succeed us. *I'y à faute de courage, je n'en aye que trop.* What might I be with my legs, that am so brave without the use of them ?

    "Well, halt, blind, or lame I will be found true to
the person of my gracious master, to the service of
his Crown, and my friends."

These illnesses had now become so frequent that
Lord Strafford was obliged to take them into calculation in all his plans, and so arrange for them to be
as little hindrance as possible. In the present instance,
he had directed the Parliament to assemble by a
certain day, and he found it already sitting on his
arrival. The Council had made a very sensible
alteration with regard to the subsidies. As the last
had been six in number, they feared that a precisely
similar demand would cause the people to take alarm
and imagine the first was now to be taken as a precedent. The Council, therefore, asked for four, with
a promise of the other two if his Majesty should
urgently need them. To this amendment Lord
Strafford heartily agreed, and, on the 23rd of March,
the four subsidies were voted in the most cheerful
manner. Nothing could exceed Lord Strafford's
delight at the ease with which they were obtained.

It raised his spirits by giving him a proof of popularity that was so rarely experienced by him. Work
and pain without encouragement, without gratitude,
was too commonly his lot for this to pass unfelt and
unnoticed by him.

"This" (cheerfulness), said he to the King, "I take
to be of more advantage to your Majesty in itself, and
in the consequence, than the grant of six subsidies
would have been. And, amongst other reasons, which
may convince it to be so, I dare undertake (as little
beloved as some will needs have me to be by this
people) that if your Majesty would, it were in my

power to persuade them after Easter to give you four 1640. subsidies more, payable the next two years after the former levied.

" In one word, your Majesty may have, with their free good wills, as much as this people can possibly raise. Next, your Majesty may as safely account yourself master of their lives and fortunes, as the best of Kings can promise to find amongst the best of subjects. And that if those in England comply with the like alacrity, and minister to your Majesty's princely designs and purposes, you will be at an end of the war before it begins."

Nothing now remained but to raise the troops and furnish all their requirements and baggage. In this Lord Strafford declared he would not lose an hour, nor let the zeal of the Irish nation cool. To him their zeal seemed on fire to serve his Majesty. This done, he would return with all speed to England.

The assurance of Irish loyalty did not rest on the word of Lord Strafford. Not content with their professions to the Lord Lieutenant alone, the Parliament of Ireland in their address accompanying the offer of the subsidies, spoke of Lord Strafford in a manner that certainly justified his belief in their satisfaction with his Government. Particular attention is called to their words, as it will be hereafter necessary to refer to them. They were as follows:

" In that his Majesty hath provided and placed over us so just, wise, vigilant, and profitable a governor, as the Right Honourable Thomas Earl of Strafford, Lord Lieutenant of this your said kingdom of Ireland, who by his great care and travail of body and mind, sincere and upright administration of justice without partiality, increase of your Majesty's revenues, without the least hurt or grievance to any of your well-disposed and loving subjects, and our great comfort and security, by the large and ample benefits which we have received, and hope to receive by your Majesty's commission of grace for remedy of defective titles procured hither by his Lordship from your sacred Majesty. His Lordship's great care and pains in restoration of the Church, the reinforcing of your army within this kingdom, and ordering the same with singular good discipline. His support of your Majesty's wholesome laws here established; his encouragement to your judges, and other good officers, ministers, and dispensers of your laws in the due and sincere administration of justice; his necessary and great strictness for the execution thereof, his due punishment of the contemners of the same, and his care to relieve and redress the poor and oppressed.

"For this, your tender care over us, showed by the Deputy, and supporting so good governors, &c., we, in free recognition of your great goodness towards us, do for the abbreviation of some part of your Majesty's inestimable charges, most humbly and freely offer to your Majesty four entire subsidies," &c.*

Not content with this, they wrote a long letter to Mr. Secretary Windebanke, "expressing, even with passion how much they abhor and detest the Scottish Covenanters, and how readily every man's hand ought to be laid on his sword to assist the King in reducing of them by force." Then, as a contrast to the ungrateful Scots, they declared, "that their hearts contained mines of subsidies for his Majesty, that twenty

---

* Nalson's Collections, vol. ii. 180.

subsidies, if their abilities were equal with their desires,   1640.
were too little to be given to so sacred a Majesty,
from whose princely clemency, by the ministration of
the Lord Lieutenant, so many and so gracious favours
are derived unto them." *

On their side, the Scots made every effort to prepare
for the coming struggle. The preachers exhorted them
to patriotism from every pulpit, and, as a bitter clergyman of their enemies expressed it, " turned their lungs
into bellows to blow the fire which melted the plate
and rings and jewels into current coin." Loans were
eagerly volunteered, and the energy of the previous
year, if possible, was increased.

But the feelings of Lord Strafford were much
changed from what they had been the year before.
The reluctance that he had then manifested, had given
place to a restless activity that found full occupation
in his last preparations for departure. The language
as well as the conduct of the Irish Parliament had
excited him to a condition of feverish exultation.
Popularity was to him so strange a thing that he could
not conceal his delight or maintain his calmness. In
spite of all his reputed haughtiness, the approbation
of his fellow men was dear to him as to any, and he
insisted that the rare tribute should be acknowledged.

" It is my desire," said he, "his Majesty will judge
betwixt those that have scandalized this Government,
to have proceeded with so much severity as had
rendered me a most hated person, indeed, a Vizier,
Basha, or anything else that might be worse, and the
humble assurances given by me to his Majesty that

* Nalson's Collections, ii. 182.

1640.   this people were infinitely satisfied and joyed under
the shadow of his protection and justice, and that
they did not distaste me so much as willingly to
change me, or to desire any new Deputy in my
stead." *

He strongly advised that the loyal Declaration of
the Irish should be read at the English Council, and
after published to the nation, both for the purpose of
awakening an emulation in England and of dis-
couraging the Scots. So much did he hope from this
that he pronounced the Declaration to be of more
value than ten subsidies.

With regard to the levy of troops, an equal willingness was found; and here, too, he saw new cause of
rejoicing. There is something very pathetic in the
way in which he dwells upon his new experience of
sunshine.

"As in their purses," said he, " so also in their
persons, I find them most earnest to venture them in
his Majesty's service, so as there will, I trust, be no
want of men. Nay (howbeit I have been reported by
some to be a person hateful to God and man, as if it
were not sufficient I should be so wretched as to be
thus hardly thought of by them, unless I were so
believed and taken by others), I held it, I say, much
conducing to the quickening of their zeal to let them
know that I would go along with them myself, and if
the game came to that, be found amongst them as
near the strokes as another man, which I find they
take extreme kindly from me, that they have me in
their reasonable good opinion, and that if it were left

* Letter to Mr. Secretary Windebanke, ii. 398.

to their choice, they would not have any other general 1640. than myself. Most certain it is that none of them will be less forward to put himself into the action, because to be commanded by me." *

As the result of this favourable disposition of the Irish, he counted on being fully prepared by May, to march from head-quarters in Ireland with an army of a thousand horse, eight thousand foot, thirty pieces of ordnance, and all other necessaries for transportation, ammunition, victuals and pay for eighteen months, without costing the English treasury a shilling during that time, on the sole condition that his stipulations should be complied with. For he was careful to warn the King that unless good faith were kept with him, all his plans must fail.

These stipulations to which the King had already assented, during the last visit to England of Lord Strafford, were as follows :—

1. Fifty thousand pounds of the loan borrowed on security of subsidies to be granted immediately to pay for the outfit of the army, which was to be procured in the Low Countries, at that time the cheapest arsenal and military store in Europe. Ten thousand pounds were at once to be sent there, and the rest of the money to be ready as Lord Strafford should call for it.

2. The rents of the Crown lands of Londonderry and Coleraine, or money forth of the exchequer of England to their value, to be paid into the Irish exchequer towards the war, so long as the Irish army should be in service.

3. All the gunpowder served free from the magazines of England.

* Letter to Mr. Secretary Windebanke, ii. 399.

4. A sufficient number of the King's ships to guard the coasts and serve as a blockade against the Scotch ports.

5. Pay for the two thousand foot and five hundred horse, arranged to join the Irish troops in Cumberland, the money to be advanced to the Irish treasurer at war for three months beforehand, precisely as Lord Strafford had hitherto paid the force sent under Sir Francis Willoughby to Carlisle.

This was a very needful stipulation, nothing being more likely than for Charles to send on his English troops to join Lord Strafford's men, and leave Lord Strafford to pay them as best he might.

6. A release from the heavy charge of the Irish troops in Carlisle, and repayment of a month's advance to them made by Lord Strafford.

These conditions had been drawn up some time before, and absolutely guaranteed by the King. But Lord Strafford again sent them to the Secretary of State, warning him how much depended on their strict fulfilment. He also told him that though of little use in England, and never more needed in Ireland than at present, still, in obedience to the King, he had arranged to conclude all his preparations, and would embark for England on Ash Wednesday.

But as if the memory of the manner in which Charles had so often broken the conditions on which he had undertaken the government of Ireland, could not be stilled, on the same day that he thus warned the Secretary of State, Lord Strafford wrote to the Marquis of Hamilton to the same effect, recounting anew the promises, and begging Lord Hamilton to dwell on them to the King, and enforce on him the need of keeping

the covenant he had made; and boldly to remind him
that if his given words in this matter were not punctually performed, then Lord Strafford would hold himself
released from his charge, as he deemed it altogether
impossible to carry out the royal will without the needful succours.

At the same time, he dispatched his agent to London
to receive the ten thousand pounds with which he was
at once to go to Holland, and there buy the arms and
such stores as could not be obtained in Ireland. But
whatever could be furnished by the latter country, was
to be taken in accordance with the policy of spending
as much money there as possible, in order to encourage
trade.

Never had Lord Strafford cause to write so many
pleasant letters as now. It was astonishing how
zealous the Irish were in this—one of the worst causes
ever embarked in. All obstinacy, difficulty, or reluctance seemed to have vanished, and the military and
civilians having shown their goodwill so heartily, were,
after all, to be outstripped by the clergy. These
zealous members of the church now came forward as
they had never done before. Enthusiasm in persecution and abuse of heresy have been common at all
times to both Catholics and Protestants, Church people
and Dissenters. But they have generally been contented with inflicting pain and bad language on those
who differed from them in their interpretations of
Scripture, or the mode of public worship, or the question of religion. But liberally to advance money to
the best of causes in their own estimation has been
another matter by much less common.

In this instance it was different. Three subsidies

1640. yet remained of the old grant by the former Parliament to be paid during the next three years. To these three the clergy of Ireland added six more, to be also paid in the same time. So that for the next three years, in addition to what the Parliament had just granted, the King had nine subsidies to count upon.

Nor did they rest here. Besides this, they consented that a tax should be laid on all the ecclesiastical livings in the kingdom of Ireland, to be rated and set in the King's book at the sixth part of their full value. And this tax when fully gathered, it was calculated would quite double the amount of their contribution by equalling their subsidies.

Certainly, if Lord Strafford looked on all these munificent grants, in addition to the loudly uttered commendations of the representatives of the Parliament, the army and the clergy, as a proof of the general satisfaction with his government, he cannot be blamed. If the Irish were dissatisfied, they could show it as well as the Scots, and with the advantage of the sympathy and probable aid of the Catholics abroad, an encouragement of which the Scots were destitute.

Incredulity or scepticism was not a feature in Lord Strafford's character. Firm in his purposes, resolute in the preparation and carrying out of his plans, he was very ready to believe the words of others, and to listen to reports and affirmations, though neither his actions or opinions might be changed by them. And, indeed, it was hardly in human nature to turn a deaf ear to the welcome assurances that were now made to him. That they were unexpected is true. He had so steeled himself to the hatred of enemies, so accustomed his mind to work without encouragement, that he was

bewildered by what he was told was the truth after 1640.
all. And knowing how many efforts had been made
to injure his credit with the King, he was overwhelmed
with the sudden change. Formerly, he had constantly
to beseech the King not to listen to stranger enemies.
Now he had to persuade him to believe in friends as
strange.

But faithful to the great sentiment of his heart, his
chief joy was the success this unlooked-for encouragement promised him in fulfilling the wishes of Charles.
In one kingdom, at least, the cause of the King was
triumphant, and he had been the cause of it! The
thought fired him with redoubled zeal. This was his
highest reward, to be able, as he believed with literal
truth, thus to address his King:—

"Sir, your person and authority here is infinitely
honoured and reverenced. This people, abundantly
comforted and satisfied in your justice, set with exceeding great alacrity to serve the Crown the right
way in these doubtful times, and much trusting and
believing us, your Majesty's poor ministers; all this
in as high a measure as your own princely heart can
wish.

"And if all this be not literally true, let the shame
be mine, so wretchedly to have misinformed your
Majesty. But if it be (as indeed it will be found) most
true, then your Majesty in your wisdom will find how
those persons are to be trusted hereafter, who, forth
of their personal spite to me, go about to have it
thought by your Majesty, and all the world besides,
to be quite otherwise. God forgive them their
calumnies, and I do."

But the body could not keep pace with the mind.

The empire of disease was too firmly established to be touched even by the strong healing power of a cheered and hopeful spirit.

Adverse winds had prevented Lord Strafford from sailing on Ash Wednesday, according to his first intention, and by the time they changed, his illness, ever increasing with every new attack, again seized him. Besides the gout, which, latterly, was the invariable companion of whatever form his various maladies assumed, he was now held for seven days with an internal seizure so " violent and ill-conditioned," as he says he never had before. This last assertion was now a constant and mournful truth. Still growing worse in health, rest of body and peace of mind were luxuries for which he sighed in vain. " This illness," said he to the King, " has brought me so weak as, in good faith, nothing that could concern myself should make me go a mile forth of my chamber. But this is not a season for bemoaning of myself, for I shall cheerfully venture this crazed vessel of mine, and either by God's help, wait upon your Majesty before that Parliament begin, or else deposit this infirm humanity of mine in the dust."

He tried to keep his word. Torn and shattered with bodily agony it was still less his powers of endurance that he feared than that the physical weakness consequent on such torture should gain the day and render it impossible for him to be moved. He would die in the struggle if need be, but fail the King, who was so anxiously expecting him, never. He ordered himself to be lifted into a litter, and thus carried on board his ship. When this was accomplished, the wind again threatened a change, and

another long delay. But though the gale rose so high,
while the vessel was yet in port, that the captain
declared it dangerous to put to sea, all his remonstrances were in vain. The channel must be crossed
before the wind settled from the east. That very
night the Lord Lieutenant sailed, and, in spite of every
obstacle, arrived safely at Chester. But the ghastly
visitation of sea-sickness had now left the tokens of
its presence, and with the gout in both feet and the
" ill habit of health brought from Dublin," there was
no possibility of performing the journey to London
without some respite. However, the channel was
crossed, and east winds were divested of their most
formidable terrors. The physicians were therefore
enabled to enforce a rest of twenty-four hours on the
patient, whose inclination to disobedience arose neither
from the diseased nor the stupid obstinacy that so often
besets the invalid subject, but, in his case, was the
result of anxiety as to the effect of delay on the welfare of others.

But even *he* now felt delay to be inevitable. He
conquered his weariness and pain sufficiently to write
both to the Secretary of State and to the King to explain the cause,—also to his wife, to whom he was as
ever a constant correspondent in absence. His letters
all bore the burden of one sad theme, a subject tedious
and provoking to the robust and healthy, but one that
cannot fail to awaken the deepest sympathy and compassion from those who like himself have writhed beneath the agony of direst bodily pain, and the still
worse torture of the nameless restlessness of the nerves
that forbid repose and consume the hours and long
periods of life—so anxiously longed to be given to high

1640. enterprise and worthy labour—in " the constant anguish of patience."

The following is his sad letter to the King :—

" May it please your sacred Majesty,

" With some danger I wrought through a storm at sea, yet light on a greater misfortune here in harbour, having now got the gout in both my feet, attended with that ill habit of health I brought from Dublin.

" I purposed to have been on my way again, early this morning, but the physician disadviseth it ; and, in truth, such is my pain and weakness, as I verily believe, I were not able to endure it.

" Nevertheless, I have provided myself of a litter, and will try to-morrow how I am able to bear travel, which, if possible I can do, then, by the grace of God, will I not rest till I have the honour to wait upon your Majesty.

" In the meantime, it is most grievous unto me to be thus kept from those duties which I owe your Majesty's service on this great and important occasion. In truth, Sir, in my whole life I never desired health more than now, if it shall so please God. Not that I can be so vain as to judge myself equally considerable with many other of your servants, but that I might give my own heart the contentment to be near your commands in case I might be so happy as to be of some small use to my most gracious master in such a conjuncture of time and affairs as this is.

" God long preserve your Majesty.

" Your Majesty's most faithful and most humble
Subject and Servant,

" STRAFFORD.

" CHESTER, *April 6th*, 1640."

For the very first time during the whole of their 1640.
acquaintance, the King is to be found willing and
voluntarily offering to make his own convenience
secondary to the welfare of his friend. It is true that
he now so completely rested all his hopes on the genius
and devotion of Lord Strafford, that the health of the
latter was of the very first importance to him, and
this most precious aid would be lost without the
greatest care. Nevertheless, it is just that Charles
should have the benefit of the best construction that
can be put upon his words with any probable assimi-
lation to the truth; and, amid a crowd of mean and
selfish despatches, this little note of the King stands
out in too pleasing contrast to be omitted here. Lord
Strafford had been detained for some days at Chester,
when the King thus wrote to him :—

" STRAFFORD,

" Having seen divers letters to my Lord of Canterbury concerning the state of your health at this
time, I thought it necessary by this to command you
not to hazard to travel before ye may do it with
the safety of your health. And in this, I must require
you not to be your own judge, but be content to follow
the advice of those that are about you, whose affections and skill ye shall have occasion to trust unto.

" If I did not know that this care of your health
were necessary for us both at this time, I would have
deferred my thanks to you for your great service lately
done, until I might have seen you.

" So praying God for your speedy recovery, I rest,

" Your assured Friend,

" CHARLES R.

" WHITEHALL, April the 12th."

1640.

Strafford was forced to obey this kindly order, but even during his delay at Chester, he transacted a curious piece of business.

While approaching Nesson, on his voyage from Ireland, he had observed a Scottish ship of about seven score tons, and bearing eight or ten pieces of ordnance, riding at anchor. On inquiry he found that she was a merchant vessel, and that the master was now in the town to receive for his freight about six hundred pounds. Though an embargo had not yet been formally laid on Scotch vessels, the day was so near, that to lose such a prize for a mere piece of formality was not to Lord Strafford's mind. If he could find some excuse to delay it till it could be lawfully seized as a prize of war, the matter would be easy.

Of all obstacles to evil the need of a pretext is the easiest removed. Lord Strafford privately advised the merchants to stay their payments of the freight, and then gave orders for the apprehension of the ship's master and his mate, and told the Custom-House officers to seize the vessel, " on pretence of cozening the King in his customs." The delay that an inquiry into this charge would cause, would be sufficient to last till the embargo was declared. " And thus," said Lord Strafford, exultingly, to the Earl of Northumberland, " will she lie fair and open for your arrest, and perchance prove your best prize of that kind; and really being manned with English mariners, which may be pressed for that occasion, be of all others the fittest vessel for the transportation of your men and ammunition to Dumbarton."

As was usual with Lord Strafford in similar moods to the present, he threw aside the caution of calmer hours, and recklessly flung around him such speeches 1640. as were calculated to do him irreparable injury.

They were eagerly caught up and carried, with the usual additions of reporters, to his enemies, and did him incalculable mischief.

Nor would any condemnation be too stern to pass upon them, if we were justified in forgetting the bodily anguish under which they were uttered, and which they partly represented.

Side by side with his passionate words, came the piteous bursts of pain: " My present infirmities enforce me by the pen of my secretary to answer your letters."

" I shall not delay one hour of putting myself in the way of London, after such time as I shall by the blessing of Almighty God be able to endure the journey, it being my exceeding great grief to be thus detained from the place where either his Majesty or any other might think me capable to serve him."

" Will my weary hand be able to carry on my pen not one line farther."

" Such hath been my weakness that I have not had hitherto strength to answer yours."

Notwithstanding his struggles, he was unable to realise his wish of reaching London in time to be present at the meeting of Parliament. Though the worst pangs of the gout began to leave him, such was his debility that he was unable even once to cross his room, and as in Ireland so in England, the great council was to assemble ungraced by his presence.

CHAPTER XI.

THE 2nd of March, 1629, witnessed the abrupt closing of the last Parliament. Eleven years of discord, poverty, and gloom, had elapsed since then. Despotism had not vindicated the choice of the King by the success of his personal government. The new Parliament met.

On the 13th of April, 1640, the King, with all his train, rode to Westminster Abbey, and having there listened to a sermon by the Bishop of Ely, proceeded to the House of Lords.

The new peer was not there. Fretting in torment at Chester, he had been unable to take his seat.

When the King had ascended his throne, and the Prince of Wales was seated on his left hand, the Commons were summoned, and the Lord Keeper, Sir John Finch, was commanded to address the assembly on behalf of the King. With Scotland in its present condition, and the knowledge of the spirit abroad in England, it might have been supposed that a special modesty would on this occasion have marked the opening oration.

But a very few words were enough to show that as far as language, at least, went, the failures and blunders of eleven years were to manifest none of the wisdom of experience. Boasting, flattery, and the most monstrous assumptions on behalf of royalty, formed the chief points of the speech.

1640

The members present were informed that though his Majesty's kingly resolutions were seated in the ark of his sacred breast, and it were a presumption of too high a nature for any Uzzah uncalled to touch it, yet his Majesty was now pleased to lay by the shining beams of Majesty, as Phœbus did to Phæton, that the difference between sovereignty and subjection should not bar them of that filial freedom of access to his person and councils. Only they must beware how, with the son of Clymene, they aimed not at the guiding of the chariot.

Then followed a catalogue of the blessed condition of England under the King, with the assertion that the Queen was not to be paralleled for her person and virtue, and a touching allusion to the "sweetest pledges of their love," and after that the real business of the day.

This, of course, was the crimes of the Scots. With accuracy worthy of the King, a short abstract of the doings of these "men of Belial" was now submitted to the listeners. In this they were stated to have led a multitude into a course of disloyalty and rebellious treason, such as former times had left no parallel, or the present furnish an equal. They had taken up arms against the Lord's anointed, and invested themselves with regal power and authority. Only the last summer, his Majesty at his own charge, and at the vast expense of many of his faithful and loving subjects of England, went with an army against them.

1640.   But they took upon them the boldness to outface and brave his royal army with another of their own raising. Yet for all this his Majesty's goodness was not lessened by that, nor could his gracious nature forget what he was to them, nor what they were to him, but out of his piety and clemency he chose rather to pass by their former misdoings, upon their humble protestations of future loyalty and obedience, than by just vengeance to punish their rebellions.

But since then, he had discovered that they did but prevaricate with him to divert the storm which hung over their heads, and by gaining time, to purchase more advantage for pursuing their rebellious purposes.

Then came a glowing description of the opposite conduct of the Irish, who certainly deserved a very handsome compliment for their loyalty, and their zeal against the Scots was warmly eulogized.

The King's intention of coercing the Scots by means of a powerful army was next announced, and all present were warned that no attempt at mediation between the Scots and the King must be made. Such a thing would be very presumptuous to offer, as if any one could possibly by solicitation make the King more merciful than he was, and ever would be out of his own spontaneous grace and goodness. But the Parliament had been summoned to provide him with the means for this war, and therefore he desired them without delay to vote him the necessary subsidies.

The speech concluded with an allusion to tonnage and poundage, which the King said, he desired not to claim but by grant of Parliament, and an assurance that, after the money was supplied and the war over, he would listen to any just complaints.

No sooner was the Parliament fairly opened, than 1640.
petitions for the removal of grievances began to pour
in from different counties. And these petitions, and
not the urgent need of the King for money, occupied
the attention of the House. It was useless for the Lord
Keeper or anyone else, to promise in the King's name,
that after he had obtained his subsidies he would
redress every wrong. The people desired the redress
to come first, and their complaints were faithfully set
forth by their representatives in the Commons, and
especially by Pym, a man who possessed the entire
confidence of the people. He offered " a model of
the grievances which afflicted the commonwealth, and
which had disabled it from administering any supply
till they were redressed." These he divided into three
kinds :

1. Those grievances, which, during the past eleven
years' interval of Parliaments, were against the liberties
and privileges of Parliament.

2. Innovation in matters of religion.

3. Grievances against property.

In all these, Pym declared he should take care to
maintain the great prerogative of the King, which
was : " That the King can do no wrong."

This last emphatic statement boded mischief to the
friends of the King. The two last articles were especially
aimed at Laud and Strafford. Indeed, the latter was
charged with the first, unjustly enough. For the hatred
of Parliaments was inherited by Charles from his
foolish father, and, notwithstanding the axiom regarding
the immaculate nature of Kings, the government without Parliaments was the peculiar and personal crime
of Charles. But Laud cannot be freed from the

1640. second, nor Strafford from the third charge. The stories of Prynne and his fellows are enough to prove the first, that of the seizure of Connaught and the jury of Ulster to prove the second. After dwelling on the first order, Pym proceeded to the second, and complained of the encouragement given to the Roman Catholics by the suspension of the laws against them. His words on this subject are worthy of note, as placing in a different light what otherwise seems an act of bigotry and injustice.

"I desire," said Pym, "not to have any new laws made against them (the Roman Catholics), God be thanked, we have enough. *Nor a strict execution of the old ones, but only so far forth as tends to the safety of his Majesty; and such a practice of them, that that religion, which can brook no co-rival, may not be the destruction of ours by being too concurrent with it.*" *

It is always most interesting, when we find the circumstances of the present resemble those of the past, to turn to the past and see how they were regarded by our ancestors.

The tendency of the ritualism introduced by Laud, was watched with the most jealous care by the English Parliament. The maintenance of an officer of the Pope, whose avowed purpose was to give his master intelligence of the progress of popery in England, was publicly noticed.

"There is," said Pym, "an intention of a nuncio from the Pope, who is to be here to give secret intelligence to Rome how we incline here, and what will be thought fit to win us thither."

He then pronounced ritualism a grievance.

* Parliamentary History, ii., p. 547.

" I observe," he said, " as a great grievance, there are   1640.
divers innovations in religion amongst ourselves, to
make us more capable of a translation, to which
purpose popish books have been published in print.
Disputations of popish points are, and have been, used
in the Universities and elsewhere with privilege;
preached in the pulpit and maintained for sound
doctrine, whereby popish tenets are maintained.

" The introducing of popish ceremonies, as altars,
bowing towards the east, pictures, crosses, crucifixes,
and the like; which of themselves considered, are so
many dry bones, but being put together make the
man.

" We are not now contented with the old ceremonies,
—I mean such as the constitution of the reformed
religion hath continued unto us; but we must introduce again many of those superstitions and infirm
ceremonies, which accompanied the most decrepid age
of popery, bowing to the altar and the like."

After more of this nature, the speaker then touched
on the third order of grievances, and his words must
have fallen heavily on Strafford.

Among these he named the fines for Knighthood,
which in his office as President of the North, Strafford
had rendered so profitable to the King. The gross
abuse and distortion of this ancient institution was
thus described :—

"In the next place of these grievances, I rank
knighthood, the original whereof was, that persons fit
for chivalry might be advanced. But this after was
stretched for another end, for money, and extended not
only to terre-tenants, but to lessees and merchants,
who were first to appear, and then to plead for them-

 selves at the Council board, but were delayed from day to day, to their great charge and inconvenience." *
It was to avoid all these ruinous delays and expenses, that so many were glad to close with Lord Wentworth's plan, and pay a composition which settled the matter at once and brought in " a good round fine " to the King.

But it was quite true that the fine, not the service, was now the object desired, and no worse principle can be imagined, than one that makes a punishment a matter desired for the profit it brings to the inflicter, instead of the reform of the defaulter.

Then came the rest of the grievances under this head, including the system of monopolies, military impositions, especially the seizure of horses by warrants of the deputy lieutenants alone.

It was in vain that the Commons were referred to the King's opening speech, that they were told, if their supplies were not speedy they would be useless, that the army was already marching and costing the King £100,000 a month. The Commons were resolved no more to be fed with false promises, but to have wrongs redressed before they advanced money.

The King then appealed to the House of Lords by the same arguments. The Peers proved to be more tender than the Commons, and agreed to invite that stubborn body to a conference, and see what their persuasion could accomplish.

Accordingly, by invitation of the Upper House, the Commons met their lordships, who at once opened the subject by the mouth of the Solicitor General. He informed the Commons that the war was already

* Parliamentary History, ii.

begun.   The Scots had pitched their tents at Dunse,   1640.
and threatened to invade Northumberland.   Then
followed the previous arguments, with the promise of
redress of grievances " on the word of a King."
Possibly some of the Lords felt this pledge less weighty
than might seem—for some of them added, " on the
word of a gentleman also." *

The conference had a most opposite effect to the
one intended.   The Commons warmly resented the
interference of the Lords on their special province, the
question of supply.   They voted the proposition of the
Peers to be a breach of privilege, and declined to be
influenced by their persuasions.

As a last effort, the King sent a message promising
that if they would grant him twelve subsidies, to be
paid in three years, he would renounce his practice of
levying ship-money.†

But the wary members were not so to be caught.
Amongst others, Pym and Hampden pointed out that
the acceptance of such a condition would acknowledge
the King's right to ship-money.

Deep, indeed, was the pit dug for a nation so
slavishly bound by precedent as England.

But while the subject was still in debate, the angry
impatience of the King rose to its height, and on the
fifth of May, he suddenly dissolved the Parliament.

The dissolution was followed by the most arbitrary
acts.   The houses of members of Parliament were
ransacked for treasonable papers, and members put in
prison " for undutiful answers to questions importing
his Majesty's service," and condemned, without trial, to

---

* Rushworth, vol. iii., p. 155.   † Ibid. 156.

1640.   remain in prison till his Majesty's further orders.
Sheriffs were prosecuted for lack of zeal in collecting
ship-money, and the train bands called out to prevent
any rising of the irritated people. Public assemblies
were forbidden, and the boats that passed down the
river stations were prohibited from carrying " idle
persons." * The consequences were merely to infuriate
the populace.

The treatment of the Puritan ministers was still
fresh in their minds, and Laud, who, as a member of
the Privy Council as well as Archbishop of Canterbury,
was principally blamed for these acts of the King,
was the chief object of hate.

A paper was posted up on the Royal Exchange, inviting the London apprentices to sack the Archbishop's
Palace. Five hundred men answered the call, and
had not the palace been strongly fortified and defended
within, the career of Laud might have ended there
and then.

The tumult was put down and the. ringleaders
tried, and one of them named Thomas Bensteed
literally hanged, drawn, and quartered.

Uninfluenced by this warning, the soldiers who
were on their march to Newcastle constantly mutinied
on the way. Their pay, which Lord Strafford was
always so careful to remit punctually whenever it
rested with him, was perforce withheld in the condition of the royal exchequer. Without pay, without proper rations, without the faintest interest in the
war, and with the knowledge of its utter unpopularity,
it was not likely that the soldiers could be kept in
good order.

* Rushworth, iii. p. 162, &c.

By the dissolution of the Parliament, the King had 1640.
thrown away his last chance of extrication from the
miserable entanglement in which he had netted himself.

He now resumed his former method of government
by means of his Council, who in his name summoned
the Lord Mayor and Aldermen of London to give in
the names of such of the citizens as were able to lend
money to the King. Several of the aldermen refusing
thus to aid in the sacrifice of their fellow citizens,
they were at once committed to prison, and the rest,
with the Lord Mayor, were ordered to find by a certain
day, such as could amongst them make up a loan of
£200,000 for the King. Should any refuse, the Lord
Mayor was to send in their names, and these, like the
aldermen already imprisoned, were to be prosecuted
by the Attorney General, in the Star Chamber, for
their contempt!

Meanwhile, the army as it marched northward was
maintained by billeting the troops on the inhabitants,
and especially in Yorkshire, where probably the great
influence of Lord Strafford was calculated by the King
to enforce any decree. But loyal as were the Yorkshire people, they had been too much abused, and on
the 28th of July, a petition was drawn up at York,
in which the people of Yorkshire stated, that only the
last year they had, in obedience to the King, expended
over £100,000 in military expenses alone, to their own
very great impoverishment, and far above what they
ought to have paid in proportion to other counties.
They declared the burden was so heavy, they could
bear it no longer. That they were oppressed with the
billeting of unruly soldiers, whose speeches and actions

 tended to the burning of their villages and houses, and to whose insolencies they were daily subject.

They prayed that as the billeting of soldiers against the will of the subjects, was contrary to the ancient laws, confirmed by the Petition of Right, the insupportable burden might be taken away, lest some sad accidents happen, which would be displeasing both to his Majesty and his subjects.

On the reception of this the King became desperate, and ordered the seizure of all the bullion which was lying ready for coinage in the Mint. And this order he would have enforced, but for a meeting of the merchants, among whom were many wealthy Spaniards, who warned him* that such an act would not only cause the loss of the coinage, and would ever after prevent the bringing of bullion to the Tower, but would ruin his Majesty's reputation, his faith being pledged to the merchants for their freedom to carry the bullion to the Mint and back again.

A compromise was then effected.

The merchants agreed to lend the King £40,000 (the value of a third part of the bullion) upon the security of the Customs.

Another plan for raising money was to buy up all the pepper on security, and sell it for ready money below its value.

The next scheme was to debase the coinage by a mixture of copper with the silver, and to coin £300,000 in silver threepences, which, with an addition of copper, were each to count as twelvepence. This money was to be declared current payment for all ex-

* Rushworth, vol. iii., 8vo.

penses incurred by marching army.* Some like that 1640.
of the pepper were put in practice, but most of
these miserable plans ended in propositions. Indeed
their absurdity soon became apparent. Had they been
all carried out to the utmost, it was palpable that they
would be but a drop in the ocean—a crumb towards
the necessities of an army that was intended to
subdue a kingdom.

But all were attributed to Lord Strafford, He had
been carried by slow journeys to London, in a litter,
and arrived in time to take his seat in the House of
Lords. The rest of his time was chiefly consumed in
efforts at recovery, or such a fraction of health as
would allow him to reach the North. Frequently he
was detained from the Council Chamber by sickness,
to which he was forced to yield, so direly did he dread
being utterly disabled in the hour of utmost need.

Among other charges, apparently without foundation, is that of his censure of the Yorkshire petitioners,
and of his declaration that their assertion of an ex-
penditure of £100,000 the year before was an exaggeration. †

This can scarcely have been the case, as we find
him writing to the King, on the occasion of the Yorkshire train-bands being called out, and thus remonstra-
ting against the heavy pressure placed upon his native
county :—

"Mr. Vice-President writes unto me from York,
that he hath your Majesty's order to march six regiments of the train-bands forthwith to Newcastle, and
that all the rest should be in readiness upon four-and-

---

* Rushworth, vol. iii., 185.

† It is Rushworth who brings this charge. See vol. iii.

 twenty hours' warning. This seems somewhat strange, as I perceive, to them there that, contrary to the former grace intended, the charge of this second year's war likewise is thus likely to fall upon that county, to their very great impoverishment, whilst the rest of the kingdom at home keep their fingers warm in their pockets. I confess, I am ignorant of the occasion, and, therefore, presume not to judge of the counsel. Yet, in truth, sir, methinks there might be more equality held in their cases, and your levies so disposed, as that the whole burden might not light commonly, as it doth, upon the best affected, whilst the worst disposed deride them for their forwardness in your service."

This was certainly written in no tone of censure to the people of Yorkshire.

But the King was driven to extremities. The question lay between giving up the war, or raising, by force, the means to carry it on. He preferred the latter. The most insulting demands were issued in circular letters to the people. Thus, the order for ship-money was accompanied by the following threat to the sheriffs :—

" If, through your continual neglect, all the ship-money be not timely paid, both this and the former admonitions given, you will add weight to your default and contempt. And if you pay not in the least one-half of the money payable by that county for the said service by the last of this month (May 11th), and the other half by the 24th of June next, you must expect to feel the smart and punishment due to so wilful a remissness, in a business of so great import and consequence."*

* Rushworth, fol., 2nd part, 2nd vol., p. 1182.

To keep down the people, who it was feared would rise in revolt against this hated tax, a provost marshal, with a band of soldiers, was ordered to patrol the city and all the train-bands were kept ready for any emergency. Laud by no means trusted to spiritual weapons. "I have got cannons," said his Grace, "and fortified my house as well as I can, and I hope all may be safe."

In every county, recruiting sergeants marched, by the King's order, to enlist the peasantry by force, if necessary; and when, as was often the case, an honest labourer refused to be torn from his family and peaceable occupation, to be butchered in a distant and unjust war, against a friendly nation, whom he believed to be in the right, the order was " to commit to prison such persons as, being liable to the said press, shall refuse to receive prest-money for the said present expedition for his Majesty's service."*

But not only men were seized, horses and waggons for the baggage, carters to drive them, and coat and conduct money were to be furnished, under penalty of fine and imprisonment. In short, nothing included in the Petition of Right was left unviolated.

In London, a levy of four thousand foot was ordered, together with coat and conduct money; and the Lord Mayor was sternly ordered to provide the best men for the North.

But all would not do. An army was indeed gathered together, but, as regiment after regiment was despatched, mutiny quickly followed the order to march. Officers were murdered by the men; and when the

* Ibid. 1174.

1640.

criminals were imprisoned, they were speedily released by comrades as rebellious as themselves.

As a contrast, the Scots were marching southwards, united by the same spirit that had proved so faithful the previous year.

But, by a strange infatuation, the King's generals appeared totally unable to realise the danger. In the beginning of July, Lord Conway, the commander at Newcastle, received intelligence that the Scots were within a few days of Dumfries, with seven or eight thousand men, with the intention of invading Cumberland. This he chose to doubt. He thought the Scots would not venture to invade England, but said he would, nevertheless, prepare, and wrote for reinforcements.

No better idea can be given of the condition of the King's army than the curt reply of Sir Jacob Ashley Major-General of Foot. It was as follows :—

"My Lord,

"I had order from my Lord General to send four or five thousand men to your lordship to Newcastle ; but, considering that there is not such a number yet come, and those that are come have neither colours nor halberds, and want drums, I forbear it, &c.

"There is come money but for seven days; and if I should send any of these troops in this case, you would be sufficiently troubled with them for want of pay, &c. Now, my lord, I am to receive all the arch knaves of the kingdom, and to arm them at Selby.

"Before I came, some 500 of them were brought

to Lieutenant Colonel Ballard. They beat the officers 1640. and the boors, and broke open the prisons, &c. Two days since, Colonel Lunsford's regiment comes, who, by the way, fought with all their officers, and, as they passed, abused all the country."*

Pleasant persons, certainly, to be quartered on private and defenceless families.

Following this agreeable intelligence came more letters from Sir Jacob Ashley, stating that a part of his own regiment, raised in Berkshire, came to Daventry, and there totally disbanded; that the lieutenant to Colonel Colepepper was basely slain by the Devonshire men; that three hundred more refused absolutely to go to Hull, for fear of being shipped. †

Of course, the Scots were not ignorant of this state of things, and by the 3rd of August Lord Conway began to alter his opinion. For, on that day, he received a letter from Sir Henry Vane, warning him that word had reached London of the march of the Scots with a powerful army, and begging him to do his best to keep the troops from mutiny, till money arrived, which the King was endeavouring to collect as fast as possible.

By the 10th of August Sir Henry Gibb arrived from Scotland, with intelligence that in three days the Scots would be in England with 30,000 men.

Terrible was the consternation of Conway. The foolish confidence, that the Scots would never cross the border, had left Newcastle unfortified, and pitiable was the condition of the commander.

* Clarendon, State Papers, ii. p. 101.
† Clarendon, State Papers, ii. p. 101.

1640.   The King told him, in emergency, to burn the
suburbs, but as the buildings were of stone, that promised little good.   What was to be done ?

"If I leave any number of men in the town," said
Lord Conway, "their arms will help to arm the Scots,
and they are in great danger to fall into their power.
If I quit the town and leave no soldiers, I am sure it
will be imputed to me as a most dishonourable thing,
when an enemy is master of the field that night, to
quit to him that which cannot be kept, and in such
manner as he shall receive least benefit by it.   I will
immediately give order that all the ships go out of the
river ; those that cannot, to be burnt or sunk." *

In this strain he wrote to Northumberland and
Strafford, who, strange to say, remained almost as in-
credulous as before as to the real power of the enemy.
But Lord Strafford, whose judgment was strangely
enfeebled—who was fitter for the hospital at this time
than the Council board, wrote back an angry reply to
Conway.   It is certain that Lord Conway had been
strangely misled, but now, at least, he fully measured
the danger.   It might be supposed that his former
supineness, not his present alarm, was the cause of
displeasure, and he must have been strangely astonished to receive the following extraordinary rebuke
from the Lieutenant-General :—

"My Lord,

"Yours of the 10th present was yesterday delivered
unto me as I sat at Board, and I understand that the
other to my Lord-General (whereof you favoured me
with a copy) gives much discourse at Court, and that
with no advantage to your Lordship.   It is observed

* Clarendon, State Papers, ii. 102.

that it is contrary to all that your Lordship hath 1640. formerly writ, wherein you still judged England secure of the Scots this year. And that to believe so mighty an increase of number above what you formerly mentioned, and in truth can probably be really so, upon no more ground than from the bare relation of Gibb, a known Covenanter at heart, and that, too, not of his own view, but on the credit and report only of the Lord Haddington, is a little wondered at.

" But above all, those who wish you not well, severely interpret to your prejudice that, upon so slight an advertisement, and from a person whom you had so little cause absolutely to trust in that business, you should so suddenly pronounce the town of Newcastle lost, and so early take into thought the quitting of the place.

" Besides, we all believe it to be but a mere northern crack in regard we do not as yet understand anything from the Governor of Berwick contrary to what he had formerly written in that behalf, which we conceive we should certainly have done before this day if the Scots had been suddenly increased twenty thousand men, as Gibbs reports, it seems, to you.

"Nevertheless, I have written to the Vice-President to have all the trained bands in Yorkshire in a readiness, and will to-morrow move that Colonel Goring and another regiment of foot, with all the horse may instantly be directed to march up to you. Which all together with the trained bands of Durham and Northumberland, with the town itself, I should think would be sufficient to make good the place, till the rest of the army march up to your relief.

" But, for the love of Christ, think not so early of

1640.   quitting the town, burning of suburbs, or sinking of ships. For, believe me, if any such thing escape you, there are those who would quickly misconstrue you therein to the King. And, with all my heart, I wish you had not writ that letter, it being most true Sir John Conyers mentions nothing of it; which makes me also believe Gibb's news either to be out of folly or malice, mistaken or misrepresented to your Lordship." *

What had become of all Lord Strafford's cautious foreseeing mind when he wrote this strange epistle? Hitherto, he had been the last man in the world to close his eyes to danger, and the very possibility of attack was sure to find him long before prepared. Now, like a child, he is angry at being told unwelcome tidings, and would fain turn away from the unpleasing sight. Nothing but the announcement that he will send to the Vice-President for reinforcements, sounds like his former self. Sorrow, pain, anxiety, and toil had begun too plainly to sap the fortress of this noble intellect, and in this letter the first signs of the breach become clearly visible.

The next day a Council was held, at which the chief subject of discussion was the advisability of the King's departure for the north. Charles wished to go. He thought his presence would arouse enthusiasm and bring out supplies. But Strafford was averse, and thought it premature. For once Charles was in the right in differing from him, and declared that his own fear was only lest he should be already too late.†

---

* Clarendon, State Papers, ii. 103.
† Hardwicke, State Papers, ii. 166.

It was therefore decided, that the King should march to York at the head of all the forces he could collect, and the 20th of August was appointed for his departure. On that eventful day, he published a proclamation of the usual kind. All the Scots who should enter England in a hostile manner, and all who should help such Scots were declared traitors. Yet the King would even at this hour forgive them if they would return. And he professed before God and the world, that he never did and he never would hinder his subjects of Scotland from enjoying their religion and liberties according to the ecclesiastical, civil, and municipal laws of their kingdom. And if they would yet acknowledge their former crimes and exorbitances, and in humble and submiss manner, like penitent delinquents, crave pardon for what was past, and yield obedience for the time to come, they should still find that his Majesty would be more sensible of their due conformity and obedience than he had been of their rebellions, and he rather desired their reformation than their destruction.*

On the same day, orders were sent to the Lieutenants of the counties of Cumberland and Westmoreland to keep strict watch on the Borders, to keep the beacons trimmed, and to search all the granaries on the Border, so that no person might keep such a store as should benefit the enemy should they seize it. And as it was usual to put nearly two thousand cattle to pasture in the summer with only a boy or two to watch them, it was now ordered that the owners of such cattle should send with them herdsmen enough to drive them from the enemy, should pillage be attempted. On this 20th

* Rushworth, fol., iii. 1221.

1640. of August, therefore, the King, with the Earl of Strafford and the Peers who formed his Council, set out for York.

On the self-same day, the vanguard of the Scotch army crossed the Tweed, and entered England under the command of the Earl of Montrose.

By the 23rd of August, the King arrived at York, where proclamation was made that he himself was come to lead the train-bands against the enemy. But the answer to this, was a petition from the chief persons in the county, reiterating their former complaints, and declaring their inability to accompany his Majesty unless fourteen days' pay was issued for the troops beforehand.

The Earl of Northumberland, General of the royal forces, still continuing too ill to travel, the Earl of Strafford, the Lieutenant-General, who was far worse in health, assumed the chief command.

By the 27th of August, the Scots had advanced within four miles of Newcastle, altogether unchecked. Lord Conway was powerless. The country refused to advance money to pay the train-bands, or the regular troops, and the men themselves were rather glad of the excuse of no pay to stay at home and guard their homes, quite as much from the protectors as from the enemy.

So feeble in frame that he was scarcely able to sit his horse, his nerves quivering with the internal torture of the most agonising of his maladies, his very eyesight dazed and blinded with the oppressive glare of the light, no one with any feeling of justice, much less of humanity, would judge Lord Strafford harshly at this moment. He might have followed the example of

Northumberland and saved himself not only from suf-   1640.
fering, but from danger and responsibility, by claiming
the privilege of his direful sickness. Better, in every
way, had he done so. But he would not leave his
friend in this extremity, cost what it might; so long as
he could totter to the front, there he would be found.

He now addressed the people of Yorkshire in behalf
of their King. But all his eloquence had vanished,
even the force with which anger alone will sometimes
charge its words was gone. Weakness marked his
speech. He told the people how they were bound to
help his Majesty at their own proper cost now that the
kingdom was invaded; that it was little less than high
treason in any man to refuse his aid; that they were
no better than beasts if they refused to attend the
King, when his Majesty offered in person to lead them
on. He warned them that it was a matter of prudence
to prevent the Scots from advancing further, as if the
enemy once tasted the sweetness of the land, he would
hardly depart. If they would only do this service
now, the King had promised him, that all demands on
them should be lessened for the future.

On the same day, he wrote another letter to Lord
Conway, bitterly complaining of his allowing the Scots
to march so far.

Unjust as the letter is, and without reference to his
own former most inconsistent epistle, blaming Lord
Conway for his alarm, still the opening sentence dis-
arms our justice, and compassion for the unhappy
writer in so sad a condition, compelled to perform the
most onerous duties of another man in addition to his
own, is the first sentiment awakened. Thus he begins.
" I purposed to have been moving towards you to-

 morrow, but I am so very sick and weak as the King will not permit me to stir hence till Saturday at the soonest. Your Lordship will admit me to deal plainly with you. I find all men in this place extreme ill satisfied with the guiding of the horse, and publish it infinitely to your disadvantage, that having with you one thousand horse and five hundred foot, you shall suffer an enemy to march so long a way without a skirmish, nay, without once looking upon him.

"And it imports you most extremely by some noble action to put yourself from under the weight of ill tongues. Your last letter then certified us that the enemy is intended to pass the Tyne at Hexham. If so, I shall advise that you, with all the horse and at least eight hundred foot, and all the cannons you have, march opposite unto them on this side the river, and be sure whatever follow, fight with them upon the passage. Indeed you look ill about you, if you secure not the river. If there be a bridge at Hexham it must be broken down.

"Dear my Lord, take the best men, and do something worthy of yourself." *

A sudden accession of bodily pain here stopped the hand of the writer; to use his own language, "so furiously assaulted" him, that he was "not able to write a word more."

How different to his former lucid arrangements for any purpose great or small, are these most vague and irritating orders! Formerly, for a man to do something worthy himself was, in the eyes of Lord Strafford, to do something to advance the end in view. None ever

* Strafford Papers, vol. ii.

thought less of empty glory, none were more minutely cautious in weighing intelligence; yet now, he, soon after, added a postscript, desiring Lord Conway, who had so long been on the spot, who must have the best means of knowing the truth, to surrender his judgment to the word of a solitary spy, who had gone from York and returned with the news that the Scots cavalry was "not considerable," and their foot "at most but 20,000."

Lord Conway became desperate on the receipt of this letter. Strafford was his commander, and as Conway truly said, though these words professed to be only advice, they were, in reality, a command for him to break his neck upon any disadvantage.

An accident fortunately settled the question for him.

The two armies were separated by the river Tyne, where, for a few hours, each watered their horses, and regarded without disturbing each other. Suddenly an English soldier fired on a Scotch officer as he was leading his charger to the stream, and this proved the signal for a general engagement. The English troops, raw and cowardly as well as hopeless, very soon threw down their arms and ran away, and their commander, after a vain attempt to rally them, was compelled to sound a general retreat. The Scots soon crossed the river, and very speedily convinced Lord Conway of the impracticability of holding Newcastle.

At midnight, on the 28th of August, therefore, the whole army marched to Durham, leaving the Scots in full possession of Newcastle. The King was at North-allerton, and Lord Strafford at Darlington, twenty-six miles from Newcastle, when this fatal news reached them. At once, the King retreated to York, while

 Lord Strafford sent messengers to the army to order the chiefs to rally their scattered forces, and to keep them in a compact body.* There was no remedy, he said, but retreat, and Hull appeared the best place. He now fully admitted that to fight with the miserable rabble, miscalled soldiers, that were all Lord Conway possessed, was out of the question. Nothing could be done till the King's forces arrived, which he hoped would number 20,000 men. He would use as much diligence as possible to provide bread, and £8,000 were already to meet them at Topcliff. Lord Conway was to assure the soldiers that in a few days £80,000 would arrive from London, which would "give every man his own royally."

The promise of payment for provisions was also by no means unnecessary. The Scots were so very exact in these matters, that unless the King was equally punctual, it was to be feared the disloyal peasants might prefer selling for ready money to the enemy to trusting their sovereign for his purchases.

Miserable was the condition of the country in the north. The coal mines of Newcastle, which employed ten thousand persons constantly, were utterly deserted. Of the four hundred ships that used to anchor in the river not one was to be seen; those that arrived at the mouth taking immediately to flight, without a cargo, on hearing the state of things. The shops were closed, and many houses precipitately deserted, leaving all the contents to the enemy. The city of Durham was almost depopulated, and a famine of bread was threatened, the King's army having devoured all in

---

* Rushworth, fol., part ii. vol. ii. p. 1240.

their march, while the country people were too terrified
to supply the market. Fear of the brutalities of the
royal troops was quite equal to fear of the Scots.

On the 2nd of September, the Lords of the Scots'
Covenant drew up a petition to the King. They professed themselves unwilling to shed English blood, and
of this reluctance, they said, they had given proof by
dismissing their prisoners with meat and money, notwithstanding their own men who had strayed from
headquarters had been massacred. In Newcastle, they
had paid for all they consumed; and now their sharp
sufferings had forced them to enter England, where
they lived on their own means and provisions, injuring
neither property nor person, till they were compelled
by force of arms to put down those who opposed their
passage. And they prayed his Majesty, at last, to
consider their pressing grievances, and provide reparation for their wrongs and losses, and with the advice
of a Parliament in England to settle a firm and durable
peace.

To this the King replied, on the 5th of September,
that as their petition was only in general terms, he
desired to know their special grievances. And for
mature consideration thereof, he had summoned the
peers to meet him at York on the 24th, that with their
advice he might answer the petition. He commanded
the Scots to advance no farther with their army,
which forbearance would be a way towards that reconciliation of which none were more desirous than his
Majesty.

To this the Scots replied :—" That the particulars
were contained in the conclusions of their last Parliament, already printed, and were briefly—

1640.　　　" 1. That the last Acts of Parliament be published in his Majesty's name, as well as that of the Estates.

" 2. That the Castle of Edinburgh and other strengths may be used for their defence and security.

" 3. That their countrymen in England and Ireland be free from censure for subscribing the Covenant, and from oaths and subscriptions contrary thereunto.

" 4. That the common incendiaries may receive their just censure.

" 5. Their ships and goods, with the damage thereof, to be restored.

" 6. Their wrongs, losses, and charges to be repaid.

" 7. The proclamation against them as traitors to be recalled. And that, by advice and consent of his Parliament, his Majesty would remove the garrisons from the Borders, and other impediments of a free-trade, and with their advice, condescend to all things which may establish a firm and well-grounded peace." *

A commission was now issued, authorising Laud and others of the Privy Council to provide in the King's absence for the safety of the kingdom, and writs were issued to the rest of the Peers to attend the King at York, on the 24th of September.

Meantime, the Scots played a masterly stroke. On the 9th of September, they wrote to the Lord Mayor and Aldermen of London, and, after referring to their published account of their wrongs, declared that their present occupation of Newcastle was necessary for their security, but was not meant to stop trade on the river. They knew how needful coals were for London, and they wished the trade in them to continue; and hearing that masters of ships were hastening away

* Rushworth, 8vo, iii., p. 205.

empty, they sent two noblemen to them to persuade 1640.
them to stay and load, and they renewed the assurance
to the city of London as a testimony of their respect
and goodwill for their affection and the peace of the
two kingdoms.

Hitherto, the Scots had paid their way, but the
maintenance of so large an army, coupled with the
stoppage of all their trade, began to render this impossible, and to reduce them to the expedient of all
victorious invaders, of levying contributions on the
inhabitants of the conquered districts.

Heavy murmurs now began to reach the King. The
people of Northumberland said they had to pay the
Scots £300 a-day, besides hay and straw in such quantities as threatened to leave their own cattle to starve.
The people of Durham were called on for £350 a-day,
and petitions to the King for relief began to pour in.
A Parliament was the only chance, and both London
and Yorkshire prayed his Majesty to summon one.

It was plain that something must be done. On the
25th of September, a great Council of the Peers was
held by the King at York, to discuss the means of
subsistence for the army. The Earl of Berkshire
proposed that Yorkshire and the adjacent shires, with
London, should advance the money on promise of
repayment.

To this, Lord Strafford at once objected. He said
that Yorkshire had already been at a heavy charge,
and was greatly impoverished. The men were now
licensed to go home, to be ready to return at an hour's
warning. They needed rather to be supplied themselves than to furnish others. He then offered to give
an account of the state of the army, which, he said, he

 had taken as he found it, and so could not be responsible
for former actions.

They were already a fortnight in arrear to Yorkshire
for food. Between 19,000 and 20,000 foot, and between twenty-two and twenty-three regiments of horse,
in addition to the Scottish reformed officers' regiments,
were in pay, which amounted to £60,000 a month,
and all this was short. If this army disbanded, with
the enemy in such a position, the country would be
lost in two days, and the fire go to the farthest house
in the street. No infamy named in history would
equal the desertion of their men at such a crisis. Two
hundred thousand pounds was the least they could
subsist on till Parliament met. He did not wish to
risk all by a battle; he preferred to wear out the Scots
by delay.

The Earl of Berkshire next suggested to draw up a
list of the chief towns, and to request contributions
from them. But the Earl of Bristol said he feared this
would fail; the city of London was the place to look
to, and if a Parliament were promised, he thought the
money would be forthcoming.

The Peers present then agreed they would all be
security to London if she would advance the money,
and it was settled to ask for £50,000, to be ready in a
fortnight, £100,000 in a month after that, and £50,000
a fortnight after that. It was thus settled :—

By October 12 . . .	£50,000.
By November 15 . . .	£100,000.
By December 1 . . .	£50,000.

It was also settled that the King should summon a

Parliament, to meet by the 3rd of November, and that 1640. commissioners from both Scots and English should meet at Ripon, there to discuss articles of pacification.*

When this was signified to the Scots, they expressed their delight, but stated a slight difficulty. The treaty would take up some time to settle; and, during the negociations, how was their army to be maintained? Unless the King would supply them with the means, it was not in their power to stand still even for so good an object as a final peace. Their men and horses must be fed. On being asked what sum would be required for this, they replied that nothing less than £40,000 per month would suffice.

On receiving this answer, the King, with the lightness common to him, quietly passed it over and sent word to the Scots Commissioners to meet him at York, in preference to Ripon, as the latter was an unhealthy place.

But the Scots were too wary for him. They had no notion of the most important preliminary being thus glided over, and sent back word that provision for the maintenance of their army was to precede the treaty. They had already stayed their march, in obedience to his Majesty's command, when they might have been better provided and have maintained themselves without hurt to the English nation, simply by confining their demands to the papists and prelates, with their adherents, and all other professed enemies, who, having really been the cause of these troubles, might most justly be made to suffer for them. Such was the financial policy of the Scots.

* Hardwicke, State Papers.

And, as to going to York at all, they said they could not conceal from themselves how dangerous that would be. It would be to surrender themselves to the army there commanded by the Lord Lieutenant of Ireland, against whom, as the chief incendiary, they intended to complain. He had, in the Parliament of Ireland, proceeded against them as rebels and traitors, and his commission was to subdue and destroy them, and he desired by all means and upon all occasions, the breaking up of the treaty of peace.*

To these objections the Scots' Commissioners adhered so firmly, that the King was forced to yield and allow the treaty to be held at Ripon. There, a treaty was at last signed by the Commissioners on both sides for a cessation of arms till Parliament met, and the King agreed to allow £850 a day for the Scotch army, meanwhile; the money to be levied on the northern counties. On hearing of the writs for a Parliament, the City of London accepted the security offered by the Peers, and agreed to advance the £200,000 required. Yet, so complete was the distrust of the King's word, that on some delay occurring in the writs for the Parliament, the lenders at once drew back, the remittances were delayed in like manner, and only freely tendered when the summonses to the members placed the matter beyond all doubt.

As the 3rd of November drew nigh, it was debated among the Peers at York whether it would be wiser for Lord Strafford to take his seat in the House of Lords, or remain at his post as Lieutenant-General of the royal army in the north.

The King most earnestly desired his presence in

---

* Rushworth, 8vo, iii.

Parliament, as he should have great need of his   1640.
services there, and placed the utmost confidence in
his ability and loyalty.

But the Earl himself, worn out with toil and disease,
shrank from new warfare and excitement.   His friends
in London had warned him that a storm was gathering,
and that Laud and himself were already marked out for
condemnation.

"The King can do no wrong," was still to be the
maxim, but it was a maxim fraught with terror for the
King's ministers, and this Lord Strafford clearly foresaw.   He was, also, too painfully aware of the hatred of
the Scots and their intention of charging upon him the
provocation of the late war, as well as the present.
And the old fire that once prompted him to seek out
and voluntarily face his foe was grown wan and feeble
now.

He pleaded to the King that " he should not be able
to do him any service in Parliament, but should rather
be a means to hinder his affairs, in regard he foresaw,
that the great envy and ill-will of the Parliament, and
of the Scots would be bent against him.*

" Whereas, if he kept out of sight, he would not be
so much in their mind as he should be by showing
himself in Parliament.   And if they should fall upon
him, he, being at a distance, whatsoever they should
conclude against him, he might the better avoid
and retire from any danger, having the liberty of being
out of their hands, and to go over to Ireland, or to
some other place, where he might be most serviceable
to his Majesty.   But if he should put himself into their
power, by coming up to the Parliament, it was evident

* Hardwicke, State Papers, ii. 196.

u 2

1640.   that the House of Commons and the Scots, with all their party, especially being provoked by his coming amongst them, would presently fall upon him and prosecute his destruction." *

But the King over-ruled all these arguments, and laid his commands on Lord Strafford to join the Parliament, assuring him at the same time, "that as he was King of England, he was able to secure him from any danger, and that the Parliament should not touch one hair of his head."

To this, the Earl at once submitted, adding "that if there should fall out a difference between his Majesty and his Parliament, concerning himself, that it would be a great disturbance to his Majesty's affairs, and that he had rather suffer himself than that the King's affairs should in any measure suffer, by reason of his particular."

The King was quite ready to accept the sacrifice, saying that "he could not want Lord Strafford's advice in the great transactions which were like to be in this Parliament."

And thus the matter was settled. The King took his departure for London in order to be present at the opening, and Lord Strafford remained in the north with the intention of following some time after.

But, previous to the departure of Charles, one man before others was resolved to turn the present hour to good use. This was the Earl of St. Alban's. Now was the time to get back his lands without a long law-suit. If ever Strafford was to be had at disadvantage, it was now. Boldly, therefore, St. Alban's

* Whitelock's Memorials.

appealed to the King, and, to use his own expression, 1640.
" Neither my resolution nor my memory failed me
to express what could be objected against such a
person, by one so much injured as I conceived myself
to be."　And the debate had this conclusion : " I have
recovered all my tenures and chiefryes, that were so
much threatened to be taken from me, and the King
will make good his former grant, and the Lieutenant
did engage himself to obey it and to give direction for
the despatch of it in Ireland.

" Only it doth stick upon this point : he, under
pretence of service to the King, would have Athleaf, a
principal manor of mine in the county of Roscommon,
and give me land for it to the full value, in the county
of Galway.　And the King (as I conceive), more out
of compassion to him in this conflict than any necessity
of his service, requires my promise of this before he
confirms his former order." *

This demand St. Alban's justly refused, plainly
seeing that if he admitted the King's right to compel
an exchange of possessions in one thing, he must do
so in others, and Charles, in no condition to struggle,
easily yielded the point.　It showed how the tide had
turned.

* Hardwicke, State Papers, ii. 205.

CHAPTER XII.

IT was on the 3rd of November, 1640, that that great Parliament, whose very name is a synonyme for the liberty of England, met. On that day, the Long Parliament was opened by the King in person. But, amid the brilliant assembly of Lords and Commons that thronged around the King, to listen to his opening speech, the real monarch of England, the man to whom every earnest eye was turned in appeal, was by no means the gorgeously robed occupant of the throne. The true King of England at that hour was John Pym, and it was for his utterances that the members were so impatiently waiting.

The speech of Charles so nearly resembled that of the previous April that it is not worth quoting, and the usual string of flattery having been administered in reply, the House proceeded to business.

The first week was consumed in receiving the petitions for the removal of grievances that poured in from all quarters, brought by troops of horsemen to the door of the House of Commons. Among these petitions were many from Ireland. These were eagerly seized, rather as affording a valuable text, than from any special desire to afford relief to the Irish.

On the 6th of November, therefore, it was moved by Pym: *   1640.

"That in regard the complaints of the King's subjects in Ireland were many, who had undergone great oppressions in that kingdom by mal-government there, and come to this Parliament for relief, they might be referred to a Committee of the whole House for that purpose only, to be appointed."

After some debate, the question was resolved in the affirmative, and the Committee appointed for next day.

Immediately, the friends of Lord Strafford sent post haste to him to Yorkshire, to warn him of the danger to be apprehended from this Committee, and advised him to weigh well whether he should remain in safety in the north or brave his foes in Parliament. If he decided for the latter, they suggested that he might turn the tables by being the first to impeach certain members whom he was able to accuse of inviting the Scots into England.

On receiving this intelligence, he resolved to go at once to England and " abide the test of Parliament."

His friends in the north, more alarmed for him than he for himself, anxiously protested against this step. They told him that both the Scots and the Scoticizing English had resolved on his destruction, and that he would do wisely to remain at his post, protected by his English army, who had begun to show some affection for him, or retire to his Government in Ireland. It might even be better still to go abroad for a while till

* Rushworth, folio, iv. 1.

 the storm was blown over. It would be no confession of guilt to flee from malicious foes, before whom innocence could avail nothing, and he might then live to do his royal master better service abroad than in Council at Whitehall.*

But he would not be persuaded. He believed that he would produce good evidence against his enemies of having invited the Scots, and thereby at one stroke expose them, and divert the blow from his own head. He, accordingly, took post-horses for the capital, and, on the 10th of November, arrived in London. But, on the very next day, Pym rose in his seat in the House, and announcing that he had matters of the greatest importance to reveal, he requested that all strangers should be dismissed, the doors locked, and the keys laid on the table. This having been done, he proceeded to address the assembly.

Judging by the stern laws of abstract justice and truth, by the same standard by which Lord Strafford himself has been condemned, it is difficult not to regret many of Pym's expressions. That he firmly believed Lord Strafford to be a most dangerous and unscrupulous man, there is no doubt, any more than that he considered his death necessary to the safety of the country. But, that he believed in the eulogy he passed on the King is impossible. It was enough to state the real facts and the real perils as they appeared to his own mind, without stooping to oratorical arts to prejudice the minds of his hearers against the object of his condemnation.

He began by lamenting the miserable state and

* Rushworth, fol., iv. 2.

condition of the kingdom, and drew a powerful picture 1640.
of the misgovernment of late years, which, notwithstanding the words of Lord Clarendon, it was scarcely
possible to exaggerate. The laws of the land, he
said, were now no more considered, but subjected to
the arbitrary power of the Privy Council, which
governed the kingdom according to their will and
pleasure, and " *these calamities were falling in the reign
of a pious and virtuous King, who loved his people
and was a great lover of justice.*"

It was certainly out of no respect for Charles that
Pym paid this compliment to him, but from hatred to
Lord Strafford, who could only be made a perfect scape-
goat by this absolution of the King.

The speaker then said, they must inquire from
what fountain these waters of bitterness flowed; what
persons they were who had so far insinuated themselves into his royal affections, as to be able to pervert
his excellent judgment, to abuse his name, and wickedly
to apply his authority to countenance and support
their own corrupt designs. Though he doubted there
would be many found of this class, who had contributed their joint endeavours to bring this misery upon
the nation, yet he believed there was one more signal
in that administration than the rest, being a man of
great parts and contrivance, and of great industry to
bring what he designed to pass; a man who in the
memory of many present had sate in that house an
earnest vindicator of the laws, and a most zealous
asserter and champion for the liberties of the people; but
long since turned apostate from those good affections,
and according to the custom and nature of apostates,

1640.
was become the greatest enemy to the liberties of his country, and the greatest promoter of tyranny that any age had produced.

This man was the Earl of Strafford, Lord Lieutenant of Ireland, and Lord President of the Council established in York, for the northern parts of the kingdom; who had in both places, and in all other provinces wherein his service had been used by the King, raised ample monuments of his tyrannical nature; and if a short survey were taken of his actions and behaviour, they would find him the principal author and promoter of all those counsels which had exposed the kingdom to so much ruin.

Pym then gave various instances of the haughtiness of Strafford, both in his own acts and in the advice he gave to others. He went still farther and repeated some of the scandalous reports that were circulated against the private character of Strafford, reports which had not the shadow of foundation, which Pym should have scorned to utter.*

He concluded with telling the Commons, " that they would do well to consider how to provide a remedy pro-

---

* The slanders by which the private life of Lord Strafford were assailed were precisely of the same value as those attached to the names of some of the best and purest public personages of our own day. There is not the shadow of proof to support them. It is lamentable, that in the performance of what he firmly believed to be his duty, Pym should have soiled his hands by the use of base and degrading weapons, or rather tools. Even *had* the private life of Strafford been faulty, it had nothing to do with his conduct in public, and it was an unworthy act to attempt to prejudice his judges.

As if in retribution for this, one of the few stains on his otherwise noble character, Pym, who was a Puritan, as austere in life as in name, was himself afterwards charged, and with equal falseness, with a dishonourable passion for the Countess of Carlisle, the very person

portionable to the disease, and to prevent the farther
mischiefs they were to expect from the continuance of
this great man's power and credit with the King, and
his influence upon his counsels.[*]

When Pym had ceased, the subject was caught up
by other members, and hours were consumed in " bitter
inveighing, and ripping up the course of the Earl of
Strafford's life before his coming to court, and his
actions after."   Not a single friendly voice is recorded
as uttering one word in his defence, not an isolated
memory recalled a thought of the undoubted benefits
he had conferred on Ireland, no merciful excuse
suggested itself by the recollection of his tremendous
difficulties, or the obstacles presented by his miserable
health.

The abrupt dissolution of the last Parliament had
left its members in a sullen and suppressed rage,
which now burst forth on one devoted head.   The
wretched sophistry still maintained that " the King
can do no wrong," for the present, diverted the storm
from the head of the King to fall with multiplied force
on those of his greatest supporters.

To all earthly things there is a limit, and among
others to the patience of an oppressed people.   The

whose name had been associated in evil report with that of Lord
Strafford.

Lady Carlisle was one of the most intellectual and fascinating women
of her day.   The delight with which the great men of her acquaintance
listened to her conversation, and, therefore, sought her society, had the
frequent effect in such cases of awakening the poisonous tongues of her
inferiors.

But she has rendered herself immortal in English history by the
timely warning she gave to the five members of their intended arrest by
Charles I.

[*] Clarendon, Hist. Rebel., vol. i.

 servility of the judges in deciding in favour of the King with regard to ship-money, had roused the nation more than the tax itself. And very justly. The English prided themselves on their obedience to the law. *That*, all must uphold. The King himself owed allegiance to it, and years of care and thought had been expended in the endeavour to make it the shield of liberty. But by the decision against Hampden, it had been perverted to the service of tyranny to which the nation must submit, or disobey the power for which it felt such reverence. And, too, things would not stop here.

Men who could wrest the meaning of the law to the defence of ship-money could interpret it to mean anything, to support anything. To have enforced the ship-money in the face of a legal decision against him, would have been a safer step for Charles than to claim it under such protection. There was something inexpressibly galling in the treachery of the Bench. And in this harassing predicament, with anarchy on one side and tyranny on the other, when every help was needed to steer safely between these terrible alternatives, it was wildly exasperating to see one of the clearest and most powerful intellects in the country throwing all its weight into the wrong scale. The very consciousness of all that he might have been to them, of the difficulties from which he might have saved them, had he remained their friend, embittered his countrymen as much as the positive injuries he had inflicted.

It was a great misfortune, too, for Lord Strafford, that his long residence in Ireland, and the circumstance of her shores being the scene of his energies, he had

no witness in his own country of the redeeming 1640
qualities he possessed. The safety he had gained for
St. George's Channel, it is true, was a great benefit to
the western coast. But this chiefly affected Ireland,
and the number of pirates that still infested the
southern shores, and the pitiful tales that reached
home from English slaves abroad much more than
covered this. The wonderful improvement in the
Irish army was an object not of praise, but hatred and
jealousy, from the belief that this army was not for,
but against England. In short, when the rancour
against an individual has reached the height of that
against Lord Strafford at this moment, whether it be
well or ill founded, his virtues avail him nothing, and
are looked upon, if at all considered, merely as
obstacles in the way of justice that are to be swept
aside with contempt.

The time had so far been consumed less in debate
than in the utterance of the charges to which every
enemy had some contribution to make, when a message
arrived from the House of Lords requesting a conference with the Commons that afternoon, in the
Painted Chamber, at three o'clock, in order to decide
on various points connected with the Scots treaty.*
Two judges were the messengers.

But the Commons were not to be disturbed, and
accordingly an answer was returned by the same
envoys : " that at this time they were in agitation of
very weighty and important affairs, and therefore they
did doubt they should not be ready to give them a
meeting that afternoon, as the Lords desired. But as

* Rushworth, fol., iv. 3.

1640.   soon as they might, they would send an answer by
        messengers of their own." *

This slight interruption over, the business of the day was soon brought to a point by a unanimous resolution to impeach the Earl of Strafford of High Treason. A suggestion was indeed offered by Lord Falkland, as to whether it might not be better first to arrange the charges against him systematically, and afterwards, when all was ready, to send up their accusation to the Lords.† But Pym objected, bluntly declaring that such a delay might probably blast all their hopes, and put it out of their power to proceed farther than they had done already. He warned them that Lord Strafford's power and credit with the King, and with all those who had most credit with the King or Queen, were so great, that if he discovered what was preparing against him, he would contrive to procure a dissolution of Parliament, and so save himself rather than undergo its justice, or take some other means, even at the hazard of the kingdom's ruin, for his own preservation, if only he had timely notice.

But if they impeached him at once, the Lords would be compelled to imprison him to await his trial, and thus he would be kept both from counsel and from the King. When once they had thus secured his person, the whole process against him could be carried out with the utmost despatch.

These arguments were at once decisive, and seven members were then selected to confer with the Peers. Their names were as follows:

* Rushworth, folio, iv. 3.
† Clarendon, Hist. Rebel., i.

Mr. Pym.	Sir John Clotworthy.	1640.
Mr. Stroud.	Sir Walter Earle.	
Mr. St. John.	Mr. Hampden.	
Lord Digby.		

The seven next proceeded to a committee room to prepare their address, and having agreed on this, they returned with it to the House.

CHAPTER XIII.

IT was on this same 11th of November, that the Commons were so fiercely debating, within locked doors, on a subject charged with such momentous interest for himself that Lord Strafford, wearied with his long journey of the previous day, had remained in-doors all the forenoon, in order to recruit his exhausted frame, before entering upon the new labours that he believed awaited him. By three o'clock in the afternoon, he felt sufficiently revived to go to the House of Lords, and see what was passing there.*

With rapid footsteps he advanced towards the door, where he instantly called for admittance. It was opened by James Maxwell, Keeper of the Black Rod, on which Lord Strafford, his countenance darkened with more than its usual gloom, advanced towards his place. But before he could take his seat, a sudden concourse of voices, whose tones of authority carried the power to enforce in their accents, bade him quit the House.† Bewildered with this unwonted reception, he attempted to remonstrate. But in louder utterance followed the stern command, bidding him be silent and

* Clarendon's Hist. Rebel., i. 245.
† Baillie's Letters and Journals, i. 217

obey. In company with Maxwell, he retired to an ante-chamber, whence, after a short interval, he was summoned to the presence of his peers. And not of his peers alone. At the bar of the House stood Pym, with three hundred of the Commons at his back, every one of whom was a foe to Strafford, and pledged to his destruction. Again the voice of command was heard. Before the majesty of the people of England Lord Strafford was ordered to kneel, and hear the charge against him.

Then Pym, standing in front of all the train of representatives, in a loud and clear voice, spoke as follows :—

" My Lords,

" The knights, citizens, and burgesses now assembled in the Commons House of Parliament have received information of divers traitorous designs and practices of a great peer of this House, and by virtue of a command from them, I do here, in the name of all the Commons of England, impeach Thomas, Earl of Strafford, Lord Lieutenant of Ireland, of High Treason. And they have commanded me further to desire your lordships that he may be sequestered from the Parliament, and forthwith committed to prison. They further command me to let you know that they will, within a very few days, resort to your lordships, with the particular articles and ground of this accusation."*

A slight discussion then followed among the peers, whether the earl should be imprisoned on a general charge alone, before any specific act was named. It

---

* Journal of the House of Lords.

1640.   was decided in the affirmative, and the Lord Keeper, turning to Strafford, who received the announcement still kneeling, thus addressed him :—

"My Lord of Strafford,—The whole House of Commons, in their own name, and in the name of the whole Commons of England, have this day accused your lordship to the lords of the higher House of Parliament of High Treason. The articles they will in a few days produce. In the meantime, they have desired of my lords, and my lords have accordingly resolved that your lordship shall be committed into safe custody to the gentleman usher, and be sequestered from the House, till your lordship shall clear yourself of the accusations that shall be laid against you."

Then Lord Strafford arose, and, in charge of the Usher of the Black Rod, quitted the chamber of the peers. Arrived in the ante-room, Maxwell demanded his sword, bidding him surrender it as a prisoner. The earl at once unbuckled the sword—his badge of honour and freedom—and placed it in the hands of the usher, who, with a loud voice, called his man to carry my Lord Lieutenant's sword.

The coach that had brought Lord Strafford from his house was still waiting outside, and the illustrious prisoner, not yet able to realise all the circumstances of his present changed condition, called his coachman to drive up ; but Maxwell interposed, and said, " Your lordship is my prisoner, and you must enter my coach." As they made their way to Maxwell's coach, the crowd, attracted by the unusual excitement, demanded what was the matter.

" A small matter, I warrant you," replied Strafford, contemptuously.

" Yes," was the reply, from some who knew more ; 1640.
" yes, indeed, High Treason is a small matter."*

Then the horses' heads turned, and before an hour was over the Earl of Strafford was a prisoner in the house of the usher.

His first act on his arrival was to write to his wife as follows :—

" SWEET HEART,

" You have heard before this what hath befallen me in this place, but be you confident that if fortune is to be blamed, yet I will not, by God's help, be ashamed. Your carriage upon this misfortune I should advise to be calm, not seeming to be neglective of my trouble, and yet so as there may appear no dejection in you. Continue on the family as formerly, and make much of your children.

" Tell Will, Nan, and Arabella I will write to them by the next. In the meantime I shall pray for them to God, that he may bless them, and for their sakes deliver me out of the furious malice of my enemies, which yet, I trust, through the goodness of God, shall do me no hurt.

" God have us all in his blessed keeping.

" Your very loving Husband,

" STRAFFORD."†

He was soon after transferred to the Tower, where, at first, his friends were freely permitted to visit him ;

---

* Baillie's Letters, vol. i., new edit., p. 273.
† Biographia Britannica, vol. vii. Art. Wentworth.

 where also, according to custom, he was allowed at his own expense to furnish his room as he pleased, and to walk about the precincts of the fortress under guard.

But this lasted only a few days. His accusers, perhaps fearing his escape, sent orders to Sir William Balfour, Governor of the Tower, to restrain his liberty to three rooms, and to allow none to visit him without special license of Parliament.

Meanwhile, orders were issued to open all the ports between England and Ireland which had been closed on account of the Scottish war, and all who had any grievance to complain of were to come forward and state it.

A committee was also formed to receive all petitions, complaints, &c., against Strafford, with power to demand any papers of any kind necessary for his trial.

And as Sir George Radcliffe was well known to have been his right-hand man in Ireland, and as his testimony might tell powerfully in the Earl's favour, it was decided to incapacitate him as a witness by sending for and impeaching him also of the same crime. This has been styled "a master-stroke of Pym." So it may have been, in one sense; but if, as asserted, it was made to deprive Strafford of a just benefit of evidence, not on account of Radcliffe's own guilt, it is not possible to denounce it too strongly.

The invitation to bring in grievances was most heartily accepted on all sides. Not only were real wrongs brought forward, but every pretext that could swell the charge, even the benefits conferred, were now perverted and dressed up as injuries. The very men who had succeeded in deceiving the prisoner by their specious praise and affected gratitude but a few

months before, now threw off the mask in the most   1640.
shameless manner. Foremost in this was the Irish
Parliament. No sooner had this precious assembly—
the very same that had voted the subsidies and sent
the loyal address against the Scots—heard of the fall
of the Lord Lieutenant they had described as the
blessing of their country, than they hastened to draw
up a paper full of the most bitter complaints, in direct
contradiction of their former address. They declared
their trading was destroyed, their industry disheartened,
new and unlawful impositions were imposed, and cases
decided arbitrarily at the Council table, " where," said
these loyal Irish, " no writ of error can lie, and the
King loseth a fine upon the original writ thereby."
Certainly, to charge Strafford with neglect of the King's
fines was somewhat unexpected.

Then they complained of the monopoly of tobacco,
the destruction of the plantation of Londonderry, the
exorbitant power of the High Commission, the prohibition to leave Ireland without license, and that, notwithstanding the many subsidies given, the King was
still in debt ! *

This curious mixture was styled " The Irish Remonstrance," and placed in the hands of the committee of
evidence against Strafford.

A committee of the House of Lords was then
formed to answer to that in the Commons, both meeting
.from time to time to consider the mass of matter that
poured in.

The impeachment of Strafford was to be no isolated
act, but the first of a new series of measures resolved

* Rushworth, fol., vol. iv., p. 7, ed. 1720.

 on by the Parliament indicative of an earnest resolve to root out the present system of government, and all who upheld it or were believed to have contributed to it. When Strafford fell, there could be no hope for lesser men. Before the year was out, Windebanke, Finch, and Laud were accused of High Treason. The two first fled, Windebanke to Calais and Finch to Holland. On the 18th of December, Laud was seized and lodged in the Tower, under precisely the same charge as his friend and fellow prisoner.

But though under the same roof, Laud and Strafford were allowed no communication with each other, and only permitted to taste the fresh air under guard, and in company of Maxwell or the governor. About this time, Lord Strafford wrote the following letter to his wife :—

" SWEET HEART,

" I never pitied you so much as I do now, for in the death of that great person, the Deputy, you have lost the principal friend you had there, whilst we are here riding out the storm as well as God and the season shall give us leave. Yet I trust Lord Dillon * will supply unto you, in part, that great loss, till it please God to bring us together again. As to myself, albeit all be done against me that art and malice can devise, with all the rigour possible ; yet I am in great inward quietness, and a strong belief God will deliver me out of all these troubles. The more I look into my case the more hope I have, and sure, if there be any honour and justice left, my life will not be in danger ; and for anything else, time, I trust, will salve any

* The son of Lord Dillon had married Strafford's sister.

other hurt which can be done me. Therefore, hold up your heart, look to the children and your house, let me have your prayers, and at last, by God's good pleasure, we shall have our deliverance, when we may as little look for it as we did for this blow of misfortune, which I trust will make us better to God and man.

1640.

> " Your loving Husband,
>
> " STRAFFORD."

On the 9th of December, Sir George Radcliffe arrived from Ireland, and was at once committed to the same close imprisonment in the Gate House, and orders given that all letters directed to him should be opened by the committee for Strafford's trial.

But yet another and equally important friend of the Lord Lieutenant would in all probability have been added to the number of prisoners but for a strange and most pathetic hindrance. This was Sir Christopher Wandesforde, whom Strafford had appointed his Deputy Lieutenant in Ireland during his absence.

But when Wandesforde heard of the calamity that had befallen his dearly beloved friend and master, he fainted. Unable to conquer his true and terrible forebodings, he sank beneath the agony of his despair and died the day after.*

When the sad intelligence was conveyed to Strafford, he could not restrain his tears—tears that must yet have had a mournful sweetness mingled with their grief at the thought of such fidelity.

---

* "So soon as the Deputie saw the articles of the Lower House, and heard of the Lieutenant's taking to the barre, he s(w)ounded and to-morrow died."—BAILLIE, i. 282.

    On the 30th of January, 1641, Lord Strafford was summoned to the House of Lords to hear the articles of his impeachment.

Under a guard of musqueteers he entered his barge, and came along the river from the Tower to Westminster. At the bar of the House he knelt, but was told to rise and be seated during the reading of the charge. At first it had been comprised in nine articles, but since the first engrossment so many new accusations had been made, that it had now reached the number of twenty-eight articles, filling two hundred sheets of paper, and taking three hours to read.

When the clerk had finished, the defendant asked for a month to give his answer—surely not too long a time for a matter so momentous, and not so long as his accusers had required to make the charge. But the request was promptly refused, and the present day being Saturday, he was only allowed till the following Monday to prepare his reply.

But Monday found him prostrate under an attack of the gout, which rendered it absolutely impossible for him to go to Westminster, as ordered. The following Wednesday fortnight was therefore appointed instead for him to give his response, either in writing or by word of mouth.

During this time he again wrote to Lady Strafford, as follows :—

" SWEET HEART,

" It is long since I writ unto you, for I am here in such a trouble as gives me little or no respite. The charge is now come in, and I am now able, I praise God, to tell you that I conceive there is nothing capital ; and for the rest,

I know, at the worst, his Majesty will pardon all, without hurting my fortune; and then we shall be happy by God's grace. Therefore comfort yourself, for I trust these clouds will away, and that we shall have fair weather afterwards.   Farewell.

" Your loving Husband,

" STRAFFORD."

While Strafford was preparing his replies, Parliament rapidly proceeded on the path of reform.   Peace was made with Scotland on terms most gratifying to the Scots; and if to cease the attempt at injustice towards another, and make the best recompense that remains for injustice already inflicted, be noble and brave, then the English had no reason to be ashamed of their concessions.   They, not the Scots, had been in the wrong, and when all books, libels, and proclamations against the Scots were ordered to be called in and a recompense for losses incurred in the war was voted to the amount of £300,000, and styled " a fit proportion for a friendly assistance and relief towards the losses and necessities of *our brethren* of Scotland," and the Scots not only thanked the Parliament for the money, but for calling them *brethren;* then hearty thanksgivings were offered in the churches. And when, also, the bill passed both Houses, and was ratified by the King, making it compulsory to summon a Parliament never at longer intervals than every three years, then were the people " exceeding joyful," lighting bonfires at night, and ringing the bells by day in honour of this new barrier against despotism. The Parliament seemed the very herald of hope to

1641.   all the oppressed. In their distant dungeons the brave Puritan ministers heard of it, and succeeded in forwarding their petitions.

Bastwick was the first to experience its power. His sentence was declared illegal, his fine revoked; he was set at liberty, and Laud, now by the most tremendous reverse of fortune, a prisoner instead, was ordered to make a recompense to Bastwick for all the losses he had caused him, and the pains inflicted by his wicked and unjust trial.

Such was the work that was progressing outside the Tower, whilst Lord Strafford was painfully preparing his replies to the articles against him. By the 24th of February they were ready, and sent in writing to the House of Lords, where they were read aloud.

Reduced to their barest forms, the crimes brought against Lord Strafford may be summed up under nine heads.

1. Obtaining and using illegal authority in general acts of government.

2. Uttering treasonable words.

3. Committing special acts of illegal tyranny against individuals.

4. Making illegal pecuniary gains.

5. Showing illegal favour to the Roman Catholics.

6. Giving illegal counsel to the King.

7. Secretly trying to kindle war between Scotland and England.

8. Raising an army in Ireland nominally to fight the Scots, but secretly to crush the English, and enable the King to rule without his Parliament, and subvert the laws.

9. Neglect of his duty.

How far the earl was guilty of these charges, the reader of the preceding pages will be able to judge for himself. For though the necessity of legal forms compelled his accusers to embody their charge under certain definite heads, it was really not for this or that article that he was called to answer, but for his whole political life, for his general influence and its results. For good or evil he was a tremendous power in the country, and how he had used that power was now to be called in question. If ill, could this be proved to such an extent as to be called High Treason ?

This object of the whole charge he at first failed to realise when he examined the details, and spoke hopefully of the result—as, indeed, looking at it from his own point of view, he was justified in doing. For nothing can be more manifest than the puerility of many, the glaring injustice of some, and the vagueness and looseness of others of the articles. Take, for instance, the words he was reported to have uttered, and especially his speech about the Irish troops.* If a man in his position, the governor of a kingdom and commander-in-chief of an army, could not praise his men for their loyalty in the highest terms without such praise being inserted among a list of high treasonable articles, then one of his very worst deeds, the imprisonment of Mountnorris, became almost justified by so stern a law. Again, who could dream of danger in the expression, " a conquered nation," as applied to Ireland ? Nothing but the desire of using it as a tool of mischief against the speaker could have dwelt on

---

* That in March, 1640, he had declared " that his Majesty was so well pleased with the army in Ireland, and the consequences thereof, that his Majesty would certainly make the same a pattern for all his three kingdoms."—ARTICLE 17.

1641.   such a phrase for a moment. It was certainly out of
no love to Ireland that it was caught up, as was shown
a little later by the accusation of leniency towards the
Roman Catholics of that kingdom. It will hardly be
admitted that the rights of Ireland were more recognised in 1641 than in the present day, yet one of the
most free-spoken and liberal-minded of modern writers,
the historian of Greece, curiously enough, is found to
utter the very same expression with regard to Ireland
that has told so hardly against Lord Strafford.*

On the 15th of March, Whitelock was sent up to
the House of Lords with this message:—" That the
House of Commons have considered the Earl of Strafford's answer, and do aver their charge of High Treason
against him, and that he is guilty in such manner and
form as he stands accused and impeached, and that this
House will be ready to prove their charge against him
at such convenient time as their lordships shall prefix."

The 22nd of March was then agreed on to open the
trial, exactly a week hence. A slight alteration was,
at the same time, made in the committee for the management of the trial, in order to introduce the Crown
lawyers, Maynard and Earle, and the committee was
now as follows:—

LORD DIGBY.	SIR WALTER EARLE, Knt.
JOHN HAMPDEN, Esq.	JEFFREY PALMER, Esq.
JOHN PYM, Esq.	JOHN MAYNARD, Esq.
OLIVER ST. JOHN, Esq.	JOHN GLYN, Esq.

* " Few ever laboured more strenuously to enforce an indulgent
course upon the Government on all matters bearing upon the sister
kingdom than the member for London, in bygone days. Yet he would
own—not, however, without a mournful tone and manner, in 1870—that
' I have arrived at the conviction that it will never be possible to govern
Ireland otherwise than as a conquered country!'"—PERSONAL LIFE OF
GEORGE GROTE, p. 313.

It was decreed that no counsel should be allowed
the defendant in matters of fact, but in matters of law
he was to have that assistance, the Lords reserving to
themselves the power of deciding which were matters
of fact and which matters of law.[*]

Witnesses were allowed the prisoner, but the warrants to summon them were only granted three days
before the trial. And that he might have full liberty
to defend himself, the King released him from his oath
of secrecy as a Privy Councillor.

Westminster Hall was appointed for the place of
trial, and orders were given to fit it up expressly for
the occasion, and worthily to contain all the most illustrious representatives of the three kingdoms.[†]

---

[*] Rushworth, fol., iv., 34.

[†] The trial of Warren Hastings was a mere imitation of that of
Lord Strafford. The dresses of the time of George III., as well as the
insignificant figure of Hastings, must have rendered it something like a
caricature of its great prototype.

CHAPTER XIV.

IT was not later than seven o'clock in the morning of the 22nd of March, when Lord Strafford left the Tower to meet his trial in Westminster Hall. A hundred soldiers, all armed with partisans, formed his guard, who, in six barges, rowed by fifty pair of oars, followed the earl up the river to Westminster. There they landed, and with their illustrious prisoner marched to the hall of justice.

Many a gorgeous, many a solemn scene had those old walls witnessed, but never one more imposing than the present.

At the north end, overhung by a lofty canopy, stood the King's throne, and by its side, the chair of state of the Prince of Wales. Before the throne, and seated on the woolsacks, were the Lord Steward, the Lord Keeper, the Judges, and all the great officers of Chancery in their scarlet robes, which were well contrasted and thrown up into a burning light by the black gowns of the clerks of the Parliament, who, with a dark line, divided them from the centre, where, in flowing vestures of heavy crimson velvet, lined with ermine, and barred on the right sleeve with the same to denote their degrees of title, sate the Peers of the Realm. Each side of the nobles rose a tier of seats, rank above

rank, eleven stages high, reaching almost to the roof. 1641.
These contained the stern accusers of the earl, the real
power in the state—the mighty Commons of England.
East and west of the wall they sate, and between them,
immediately behind the peers, was the Committee for the
trial. Rarely, if ever, were seen together countenances
so different, and yet so remarkable as those of the members of this Committee. Among them the eye of the gazer
could not fail to rest on the very embodiment of high
intellect and immovable resolution in the face of Pym,
of deep earnestness and suppressed emotion in the
quivering and mournful features of Oliver St. John, of
that devoted love for England which sanctified patriotism into religion that was written on the serene
brow and rapt expression of Hampden.

Between the peers and the Committee was the bar
covered with green, and the latter, drawing aside, left
the centre space for the prisoner.

Besides those officially employed in the trial, were the
spectators, who filled every available space. These
included the King, of course, incognito, who, with the
royal family, occupied an apartment at the back of the
throne, whence, himself concealed by a screen, he could
see and hear all that passed. In reserved seats were
the foreign ambassadors, whose ready pens were to
disperse the account of the proceedings to all parts
of Europe. Noblemen and gentlemen, and not the
least noticeable of the multitude, the very flower of the
aristocratic ladies, thronged the seats with pens and
paper, prepared to take notes of the speeches.

" It was, daily," says an eye-witness, " the most
glorious assembly the isle could afford." *

* Baillie, i., 326.

1641. Only one most important body was absent. That was of the bishops. To their high honour, they, with one accord, declined to be present at a cause in which they might be called upon to vote for the deliberate and violent death of a fellow creature, but took advantage of the provision in the canon law that released them from attendance on a criminal matter. A sad pity they had not always felt these scruples in Star Chamber proceedings! By eight o'clock the last preparations were completed, all the officers in their places, and the prisoner was called to the bar.

Then, his guards doubled to the number of two hundred of the train-bands, armed with muskets and halberds, the Earl of Strafford entered the hall, and with slow and stately step walked up to the bar, and having saluted the House with lowly and solemn reverence, he arose from his knees, and standing at the bar in silence, awaited the charge.

Never was the majesty of the mind more triumphant in its power of outward expression than in Lord Strafford at this moment. Dressed in deep mourning, with no other sign of his rank than his George, which he wore suspended by a gold chain, " his countenance manly black," as Whitelock words it, and pale and worn with sickness and suffering, his tall figure bowed from the same cause, still in the august expression the soul reigned supreme. Fallen from his high estate, and with three kingdoms for his enemies, there was not one of all that great assembly at that moment that was not enchained by his personal presence, and felt gazing on a true king of men.

A poet who was present exclaimed :

> " On thy brow
> Sate Terror throned with Wisdom.   And, at once,
> Saturn and Hermes in thy countenance."*

The rejection of his answers had fully awakened him to his real position ; and the mournful and solemn dignity, that was his present most striking feature, was simply the natural expression of a nature, that in its worst faults could never stoop to disguise.

After a short involuntary pause, the Earl of Arundel and Surrey, Lord High Steward of England, addressed him as follows :

" Your lordship is called here this day, before the Lords in Parliament, to answer to, and to be tried upon the impeachment presented to them by the Commons House of Parliament, in the name of themselves and all the Commons of England.   And that their Lordships are resolved to hear both the accusation and defence with all equity.   And, therefore, think fit, in the first place, that your lordship should hear the impeachment of High Treason read."

As Lord Arundel finished, he probably noted the intense weariness of sickness visible in Lord Strafford, for at this moment, what had not been previously provided for the prisoner, viz., a chair, was brought in by the gentleman usher, and by command of the Lords the earl was allowed to be seated.

Then the whole charge, with the defendant's answers, was delivered by Pym, as speaker of the Committee, to the clerk of the House to read ; and this being done, terminated the proceedings for the day.

It was on the second day that the trial commenced in earnest.   For then it was that Pym arose, and with

* Forster's British Statesmen, i.

1641. eloquence unprecedented within those walls,—eloquence noble, and yet with all its grandeur, miserable to follow, because, launched against the life of a countryman, it becomes painful in its very power over one so fallen and so great—opened the case.

Pym then ran over the articles of the charge, with the answers of the prisoner.

That the members of the Committee were perfectly convinced of the guilt of Strafford as a traitor to the liberties of the country cannot be doubted. That his whole array of talents would be used to destroy those liberties they firmly believed. That nothing but his death could relieve England from this fearful danger, and that, therefore, it was their solemn duty to compass his death, was as much an act of conscience with them as to die themselves in behalf of their country, must be fully granted. But, at the same time, we must be on our guard, lest our admiration of their personal characters, their spotless lives, their great abilities and overpowering eloquence, blind us to that high standard of justice, which is the right of the worst criminal who ever stood at the bar. And judging them by this, the very measure they applied to Lord Strafford, then it is not possible to acquit the Committee of using unfair means to obtain the condemnation of the prisoner.

As the trial lasted fifteen days, and occupies a thick folio volume, it is, of course, impossible to give the full details in the present account. They lie open in the pages of Rushworth, to all who are willing to pay the price of the thought and labour necessary to master the daily items and form their opinion from the original reports.

Not content with insisting on the articles formally

delivered, and with all the power and privilege of special
pleaders against the prisoner, bringing forward every
argument to prove and magnify his guilt, the members of
the Committee did not hesitate to advance the most
contemptible slanders forged by the lowest enemies of
Strafford, and which would bear neither investigation
nor proof. The real benefits that he had conferred on
Ireland were either denied or distorted into injuries ;
and he was painted as a monster incapable of a single
good deed or intention. The old miserable sophistry
that the King can do no wrong, afforded an ample
opportunity of loading Strafford with every crime of
the King, and if it was found impossible to deny the
introduction of any improvement, then this was at
once not only transferred to the credit of the King,
but the real author was accused of robbing his Majesty
of the just praise due to him.

And the more deeply is this to be regretted, seeing
that the real crime of which the prisoner was accused,
had been so sharply defined and passed by vote in the
House of Commons, viz. :

"That the Earl of Strafford had endeavoured to
subvert the ancient and fundamental laws of the
realm, and to introduce arbitrary and tyrannical government." To this, the accusers had to return at last,
having gained nothing by their unfortunate divergence
but sympathy for the prisoner, and a reaction in his
favour among the spectators of the trial, which made
his accusers tremble for his escape. And this, in their
eyes, was death to the freedom of the country.

But, also, it was the misfortune of Strafford, that
in addition to lack of scrupulous justice towards him,
the Committee really believed him guilty of much, for
which he was not only not answerable, but had opposed.

1641.

For instance, the war with Scotland was laid far more to his charge than to that of Laud, who was really the guilty party. But from nothing was Strafford more free than from religious bigotry and persecution. The war with Scotland was undertaken without his advice and against his judgment. His error in that matter was precisely of the same nature as nearly all his other mistakes, viz., it sprang from his blind belief in the duty of obedience to the King. He would never have counselled the imposition of the Liturgy on the Scots, but if the King insisted on it, then the Scots were bound to obey. And if both sides held out, he as a loyal subject was forced to support the King. The mistake of the Commons lay in the firm belief that he was the first cause and instigator of what in very truth, he only submitted to as an obedient professor and consistent follower of the doctrine of the Right Divine of Kings. That the King can do no wrong was a reality to Strafford. And it is difficult to see why he should be deemed criminal, for obeying the King's orders in gathering troops, &c., for the Scotch campaign, unless all other men who had marched against the Scots were considered equally guilty. Sir Henry Vane, the Earl of Northumberland, Lord Conway, Willoughby, Wilmot, &c., had all been active in the same cause, and nothing but illness had saved Northumberland from being in the very place of Strafford as commander against the Scots.

Yet amongst the articles most heavily dwelt upon was that of his being an incendiary against the Scots.

At the same time that these unfair and distorted charges were brought against him, some of his very worst deeds, and those completely in defiance of law

as well as justice, were passed over with very slight <u>1641.</u>
notice. Such, for instance, as the imprisonment of the
jury of Galway, and the prohibition of the wool trade.

These remarks are offered with no view of defend-
ing Strafford, or of reproaching the great men who
levelled his power with the dust. They are submitted
to show the necessity of a careful scrutiny of both
sides, before passing the too common judgment that
wholly condemns one and gives unmingled praise to
the other. For it was this negligence of the abstract
principles of justice that rendered the trial a failure
and its results a disappointment. By blaming him
where he was not guilty, and leaving his worse deeds
almost unnoticed, the great lesson of retributive justice
in those minor details which affect the very humblest
being was lost.

That he had been willing to do his very best to
support the King in a despotic Government was absolutely true. That he had committed despotic acts of
the worst character was also true. These should have
been produced as facts, with their attendant proofs,
and the law of the land, which he had violated, have
been opposed to its breach with the exhibition of its
decreed penalty.

A few extracts from the speech of Pym will illus-
trate the meaning of these remarks. Five objects
Lord Strafford declared he had endeavoured to attain
in his Government of Ireland. These were:

1. The maintenance of religion.
2. The honour of the King.
3. The increase of the revenue of the King.
4. The peace and honour and safety of the kingdom.
5. The quiet and peace of the people.

On these assertions, Pym now made the following comments :

1. " For religion, my Lords, we shall prove that he hath been diligent, indeed, to favour innovations, to favour superstitions, to favour the encroachments and usurpations of the clergy. But for religion it never received any advantage by him, nay, a great deal of hurt.

2. " For the honour of the King, my Lords, we say, it is the honour of the King that he is the father of his people. That he is the fountain of justice, and it cannot stand with his honour and justice to have his Government stained and polluted with tyranny and oppression.

3. " For the increase of his revenue : it is true there may be some increase of sums, but we say, there is no addition of strength nor wealth, because in those parts where it hath been increased, this earl hath taken the greatest share to himself. And when he hath spoiled and ravined on the people, he hath been content to yield up some part to the King, that he might with some security enjoy the rest.

4. " For the strength and honour and safety of the kingdom : my Lords, in a time of peace he hath let in upon us the calamities of war, weakness, shame, and confusion.

5. " And for the quiet of subjects, he hath been an incendiary, he hath armed us among ourselves, and made us weak and naked to all the world besides.

" (He saith) by his means, many good and wholesome laws have been made since his Government in Ireland.

" Truly, my Lords, if we should consider the parti-

culars of these laws, some of them will not be found
without great exception. But I shall make another
answer. Good laws, nay the best laws, are no advantage when will is set above law ; when the laws have
force to bind and restrain the subject, but no force to
relieve and comfort him.

" He says, he was a means of calling a Parliament
not long after he came to his government. My Lords,
Parliaments, without Parliamentary liberties, are but a
fair and plausible way into bondage. That Parliament
had not the liberties of a Parliament.

" (He saith) that he hath been a means to put off
monopolies, and other projects that would have been
grievous and burdensome to the subjects. If he had
hated the injustice of a monopoly, or the mischief of a
monopoly, he would have hated it in himself ; he himself
would have been no monopolist. Certainly, my Lords,
it was not the love of justice nor the common good
that moved him. And if he were moved by anything
else, he had his reward. It may be it was because he
would have no man gripe them in the kingdom but
himself. His own harvest crop would have been less
if he had had sharers. It may be it was because
monopolies hinder trade : he had the customs, and
the benefit of the customs would have been less. *When
we know the particulars*, we shall make a fit and
proper answer to them. But, in the meantime, we are
sure, whatsoever was the reason, it was not justice nor
love of truth that was the reason.

" (He saith) he had no other commission but what
his predecessors had, and that he hath executed that
commission with all moderation. For the commission,
it was no virtue of his if it were a good commission.

1641.   I shall say nothing of that. But for his moderation, when you find so many imprisoned of the nobility ; so many men, some adjudged to death, some executed without law ; when you find so many public rapines on the State, soldiers sent to make good his decrees, so many whippings in defence of monopolies, so many gentlemen that were jurors, because they would not apply themselves to give verdicts on his side, to be fined in the Star Chamber.

" Men of quality to be disgraced, set on the pillory, and wearing papers and such things (as it will appear through our evidence) can you think there was any moderation ? And yet, truly, my Lords, I can believe, that if you compare his courses with other parts of the world ungoverned, he will be found beyond all in tyranny and harshness ; but if you compare them with his mind and disposition, perhaps there was moderation. Habits, we say, are more perfect than acts, because they be nearest the principle of actions. The habit of cruelty in himself (no doubt) is more perfect than any act of cruelty he hath committed. But if this be his moderation, I think all men will pray to be delivered from it. And I may truly say that is verified in him, ' *The mercies of the wicked are cruel.*' "

Now, while many of these observations, and especially the principles therein contained, are wholly incontrovertible, there are surely mingled with them others of which no impartial mind can approve, especially with a life at stake on the question. Thus, in the suppression of monopolies, the speaker first denies the possibility of a good motive to the prisoner, and a moment after admits this possibility, but denies all merit because " he had his reward." Then he goes on to suggest bad motives, following his guesses on the matter with a free confession that he does not know the particulars, and ends by passing a wholesale condemnation on conduct which he avows he has not investigated.

So with regard to the commission of Strafford. The first article of the charge accuses him of obtaining an illegal commission. When he answers this directly with the assertion of its being no ways greater than that of his predecessors, Pym, instead of disproving the answer, or withdrawing the charge, scornfully dismisses it with the taunt of "no virtue of his if it were a good commission." Strafford made no claim to a virtue in it, but simply gave an answer to an accusation.

Again : the charge of setting men of quality in the pillory, making them wear papers, and whipping men in defence of monopolies, were merely idle slanders, doubtless reported to Pym, but which he made no attempts to prove, and which were as purely fictitious as if applied to himself. They were not inserted in the charge, the accused was wholly unprepared for them ; and to prejudice the listeners by the very suggestion of deeds odious and revolting, and utterly untrue, was unworthy of Pym, and great blemishes on his conduct here—which should have been altogether that of a noble foe incapable of using the petty stings manufactured by the swarm of wretches who ever burst forth to wound the fallen when they can do it with safety to themselves.

No wonder that as such language fell on his ear, Strafford at times lifted his hands and turned his eyes upward in mute astonishment and appeal.

Far more to the point, and completely just, was the

1641. denunciation of the theory so often brought forward, that the revenue is any real test of the prosperity of the nation. One of the great boasts of Strafford had been that he had made Ireland self-supporting, instead of being, as heretofore, a heavy burden and tax on England. One of the means he employed for this purpose, viz., the large increase of the customs, owing to the safety from pirates he had ensured to the merchants, was altogether noble, and worthy of the highest gratitude and praise. But this Pym left out, and passed on to the measures it was hardly possible to condemn too strongly, of the subsidies literally wrung by fear from the Parliament, and in defiance of the King's promise made in Lord Falkland's time, of the enormous sums obtained under the Commission for Defective Titles, by which men were enabled to secure an illegal title by paying a large sum, and could lose an inherited estate unless they chose to pay for having their right ratified. That he was guilty, that he used this Commission merely as a tool to obtain money for the King, is proved beyond a doubt by the fact of his bringing the disputed lands before a jury, accepting their decision when in the King's favour, and fining and imprisoning them when against the King.

It is marvellous that with so tremendous a power in their hands as this deed of Strafford afforded to his enemies, they should for a moment have had recourse to any engine beyond the simple truth to overthrow him.

Again : we have seen the steps that he took to reform the ecclesiastical affairs of Ireland. Very probably he honestly thought he had done his best. He restored the churches to their intended uses, and swept away the tradesmen who defiled the walls and precincts with their traffic. He had forced the clergy to reside on their benefices, and worked hard to put an end to the detestable trade they carried on by selling their offices and living on the proceeds. Without persecution, he had endeavoured to bring the people to attend to public worship, and, in short, as far as in him lay, to promote all those observances which formed his sole idea of religion. Under the commission of defective titles, too, he had found that many estates now in the possession of private persons " belonged" to the Church, and by " restorations" of this kind, or competitions for retention, had largely added to the ecclesiastical revenues.

He must, therefore, have been strangely moved when he heard himself accused of remissness as a true son of the Church.

Let the condition of the whole Irish coast, and especially of St. George's Channel, when Lord Strafford first came to the Government, be remembered and compared with its condition when he left it, and few persons will not regret the following words of Pym:

" I go to the 12th, and that is the great increase of trade; the increase of shipping one hundred to one. Truly, my Lords, in a time of peace, and in a growing kingdom, as that was, being formerly unhusbanded, it is no wonder that when land increases in the manurance, and people increase in number, both shipping and trade increase. But it is the advantage of the time, not the advantage of his government. For, my Lords, his government has been destructive to

1641.   trade (! !).   And that will manifestly appear by the multitude of monopolies that he hath exercised in his own person."

Then came a denial of Strafford's assertion that justice had been administered in Ireland during his rule without bribery or corruption ; and, lastly, a bitter reproach that his object in advising the King to call the last English Parliament had been to gain a surrender of the liberties of the kingdom.

Strafford had ended his written defence with the petition that he might not be charged with errors of his understanding or judgment, being not bred up in the law ; or with weakness, to which human nature is subject.

Seizing these words, Pym concluded his speech with the answer :—" Truly it would be far from us to charge him with any such mistakes.   No, my Lords, we shall charge him with nothing but what the law in every man's breast condemns, the light of nature, the light of common reason, the rules of common society. And that will appear in all the articles which my colleagues will offer to you."

Pym then sat down, and the first witnesses were called.   The same mixture of right and wrong, justice and injustice, that had marked the speech of Pym, was observable in the examination.   Thus, to prove that Strafford had tried to subvert the liberties of the Irish Parliament, evidence was given that Sir George Radcliffe had threatened two members who had voted against a measure supported by the Deputy, and when in defence it was urged that in the last case Lord Strafford was not even in Ireland at the time, Pym promptly answered, " That the spirit of my Lord of

Strafford could move in Sir George Radcliffe where- 1641.
soever it was spoken."

In proof of the prisoner subverting the laws and of corruption in government and justice in general, the Remonstrances of both the Irish Houses of Parliament were read.

Of these he had before heard nothing. We have seen the flattering epistle these two precious bodies had sent to the King, in which they specially declared their satisfaction with the Lord Lieutenant's " ministrations," and his faithful performance of all his promises to their entire satisfaction, expressed " with general acclamations, and signs of joy and contentment, even to the throwing up of their hats and the lifting up of their hands."

When, therefore, Strafford now listened to their present addresses to the English, his blood boiled, and he was unable to contain his indignation at those whose flatteries had lulled him into a false security only to turn and rend him the moment he needed the aid and support he surely merited, if their own words were true. He burst into an exclamation that he was the victim of a conspiracy. Not till his impeachment of High Treason in England had the Irish unmasked themselves. Faction and correspondence had followed on his troubles. Natural enough as this was, of course it could not be allowed, and he was in an instant called to order for charging the English Commons with conspiracy, and he immediately apologised, and explained that he only meant certain special persons, not members of the English House.

Even yet the articles of the charge were not formally reached, the present discussion being merely on the

1641.   statements made by Pym in his opening speech. And, as in the preamble to his written answers, Lord Strafford had made various general assertions with regard to his own conduct, Pym brought various witnesses to confirm his contradictions. New accusations thus cropped up for which the prisoner was unprepared—such as the Irish remonstrance—and Pym, anxious to reach the main body of the charge, requested the prisoner would on the spot answer all that had been previously said. Then Strafford arose, and pointing out the hardness of thus taking him unprepared, rapidly ran over the speech of Pym, denying or explaining away, till the Committee were driven back to the one great charge containing all others.

"My Lord," said Maynard, "my Lord of Strafford answered to very many particulars, yet to that main one he answered not. The main of our complaint is, his alteration of the fundamental laws against will, his introducing of new laws at his will and pleasure."

The twenty-eight articles, however, had to be formally gone through. As we have already noticed, they may be reduced to nine charges, and of these the third may be included in the first.

The question then amounts to this :—Was Lord Strafford guilty of these, and if guilty, did his guilt amount to High Treason ?

The first and third were not difficult of proof. The man who imprisoned a jury for giving an adverse verdict, was guilty of using illegal authority, even without going into the subject of Mountnorris and other cases. This exercise of unbridled power both for good and evil was the worst feature in the character of Strafford. And yet his complaint that he was charged with the

sole responsibility of deeds most fully shared by others 1641.
was true, and is constantly true in other cases besides his
own. Except in secret, it is hardly possible for one
man alone to be guilty of great crimes. There must
be others to support him, either by encouragement of
obedience or passiveness. And had not the Council
acted as it did, Strafford alone could not have convicted
Mountnorris. Still, as to the question of the defendant's
guilt, in the matter of illegal power there can be no
doubt.

The 4th and 5th were ill founded, so far as making
it a special crime in him to farm the customs or hold
the monopoly of tobacco. That the system was bad
was one thing, but it had not been declared illegal,
and had been openly followed by some of the most
popular men, who never dreamed of High Treason by
such a means of wealth. It was to raise a revenue
for the King, not for himself, that Lord Strafford's
reprehensible measures were employed. And these
may be placed under the first and third heads.

The 7th and 9th were altogether without foundation.
Strafford could not be blamed for the wretched state
of the English army and the entry of the Scots into
Newcastle, nor was the war with Scotland of his
causing.

So well did he plead these truths in his defence,
that his accusers began to lose ground. The stately
courtesy of his manner, and the marvellous control that
he maintained over his impetuous temper, and this, too,
while every nerve was suffering, both from mental
excitement and bodily torture, all told in his favour
with the spectators. His natural haste and irritability
were too well known for the wonderful victory he

1641.   had obtained over himself under such terrible dis-
advantages, not to compel a just tribute of admiration,
and draw forth a feeling of sympathy which threatened
to defeat the end in view. The accusers became
alarmed. Their hearts were untouched. This was
shown by their want of consideration for the state of
health of the prisoner. More than once he had nearly
broken down. Still, no notice was vouchsafed of his
condition, till, by the 26th of March, after a long
day's battle, he " declared his disability to endure the
toil, that he was ready to drop down, in respect of his
much sickness and weakness, and he desired their
Lordships to turn the case inwards and see if in their
own hearts there were not reason, that, being upon his
life, his honour, and his children, and all he had, he
should not be pressed further." Then the House
adjourned.

The next day, the prisoner stood at the bar as usual,
and struggled on till the 9th of April, when, for the
first time, he failed to make his appearance. The
Lord Steward then informed the House that the Earl
of Strafford had been taken in the night with so violent
an attack of illness as precluded his going out of his
room that day.

This was not sufficient to satisfy the jealous Commons, and the Lieutenant of the Tower was summoned,
who stated, that at eleven the preceding night, the
Earl had been seized with a fit of his worst complaint,
and, at six in the morning, had been unable to move in
his bed. That he trusted to go to the Hall on the
morrow, but at present it was out of his power.

This even was not enough, and not till the earl's
physicians, and even his foot-boy had testified to the

same, on oath, was the excuse accepted, and the Court 1641. sullenly retired with the parting notice that if the Earl were not well enough to appear to-morrow, they would proceed in his absence.

The House of Lords then ordered a deputation of their number to go to the Tower to inquire into the present condition of the prisoner.

They found him in bed, sick, and worn, but he promised to appear the next day—"even though he should be carried by four men" to the Court.* The next day, however, found him sufficiently recovered to attend as usual.

But this day occurred an event at the House of Commons which has been praised as a marvellous stroke of State by one side, and denounced as an unworthy piece of trickery on the other. It has been already said that, so far, Strafford had succeeded in carrying with him the sympathy of a large portion of the audience. Some of the charges he had so disproved that they were completely waived by the Committee. Others he had denied, and though they were still maintained, yet numbers concurred in his denial. But the great point was that even those proved against him did not amount to High Treason. And, unless he could be convicted of High Treason, his life was safe. And that in his life was contained the destruction of English liberty the Committee did most firmly believe.

That life of Lord Strafford must be quenched. What was to be done? That the charge of his attempt to bring in a despotic government and to subvert the laws of the land was true must be fully granted. But that

---

* " Journal of the House of Lords, 1641, April 9."

1641.   the means he had employed for that purpose did not amount to High Treason must be granted also. The law that specified any one of his acts as such remained to be made. And to condemn a man by an *ex post facto* law is an outrage in the face of all human justice. But this was now proposed to be done.

An old statute of the time of Edward III., declaring "that the Parliament only hath power to express and declare what is treason," was raked up, and, on the strength of this, a bill was brought in attainting the Earl of Strafford of High Treason.

This bill was read for the first time on the 10th of April. On the same day, the doors of the House being locked, it was notified that some new and most important evidence was in the possession of Pym. All members being ordered to keep their seats, Pym then arose, and, supported by the son of Sir Harry Vane, produced a paper containing a rough copy of notes of a Privy Council, held on the 8th of the preceding May, at which Strafford was present.

The following is a copy of the document which is, in itself, so scanty and incoherent, that it might scarcely be thought sufficient to form legal evidence. Plainly enough it does not give the words of the parties themselves, but rather signs by which such words could be recalled to the memory of the note taken.

SIR HENRY VANE's PAPERS, THE 5TH OF MAY, 1640.*

"*L. L. Ireland (Strafford).*

"No danger in undertaking the war, whether the Scots are to be reduced or not.

---

* Nalson's Collections, ii., p. 208.

"To reduce them by force, as the state of the king- <u>1641.</u>
dom stands.

" If his Majesty had not declared himself so soon, he would have declared himself for no war with Scotland. They would have given him plentifully. The city to be called immediately, and quickened to lend one hundred thousand pounds.

" The shipping money to put vigorously upon collection; those two ways will furnish his Majesty plentifully to go on with. Arms and war against Scotland.

" *The Manner of the War.*

" Stopping of the trade of Scotland no prejudice to the trade free with England for cattle.

" A defensive war totally against it.

" Offensive war into the kingdom. His opinion.

" Few months will make an end of the war; do you invade them.

" *L. Arch (Laud).*

"If no more money then proposed, how then to make an offensive war a difficulty.

" Whether to do nothing and let them alone, or to go on with a vigorous war.

" *L. L. Ireland.*

" Go vigorously on, or let them alone. No defensive war. Loss of honour or reputation. The quiet of England will hold out long; you will languish as between Saul and David.

" Go on with an offensive war as you first designed, loosed and absolved from all rules of government.

z 2

" Being reduced to extreme necessity, everything is to be done as power will admit, and that you are to do.

" They refused; you are acquitted towards God and man. You have an army in Ireland you may employ here to reduce this kingdom.

" Confident as anything under heaven, Scotland will not hold out five months. One summer well employed will do it. Venture all I had I would carry it or lose it.

" Whether a defensive war is impossible as an offensive war! Or whether to let them alone.

" *L. Arch.*

" Tried all ways and refused all ways. By the law of God you should have subsistence, and ought to have, and lawful to take it.

" *L. Cott (Cottington).*

" Leagues abroad they make and will, and therefore the defence of this kingdom.

" The Lower House are weary both of King and Church.

" It always hath been just to raise monies by this unavoidable necessity. Therefore, to be used, being lawful.

" *L. L. Ireland.*

" Commission of array to be public execution.

" They are to bring them to the borders.

" In reason of State you have power when they are there to use them as the King's pay. If any of the Lords can show a better, let them do it.

"Town full of nobility, who will talk of it. He will make them smart for it."

The manner in which these notes had been obtained is not pleasant to contemplate.

It appeared that the elder Sir Henry Vane, being in treaty for the marriage of his son with the daughter of Sir Christopher Wray, was called on to produce the title-deeds to his estates. But he, being in Kent, and the deeds at Whitehall, with many State papers, he gave the keys of his private cabinet to his son, telling him to take out the deeds and forward them. This order the young Sir Harry obeyed. But he did more. In the same cabinet he discovered the paper of notes of the Privy Council, endorsed, "Notes taken at the Junto," and, without scruple, at once perused them. But he did not stop here, which, for such a mirror of chivalry and honour as he has been represented, might be thought far enough. He immediately sought Pym, and showed him the paper, " with great expressions of a troubled mind, not knowing what way to steer himself betwixt the discharge of his duty to the Commonwealth and his faithfulness to his father."

Pym soon quieted his scruples, and at once took a copy of the notes which he now produced to the House of Commons as sure evidence of Strafford's treason.

A debate followed, and the new evidence was ordered to be laid before the House of Lords. Of course, it came under the head of treasonable language.*

Of the attempts to convict him of this, Lord Strafford had already bitterly complained. Not merely at

* Nalson's Collections, vol. ii., p. 103.

the Council Board or in Parliament, but in private and social conversation had testimony against him been sought. From the mouth of his own brother, at his table, his house, his bed, in every place, it was sought for something to convict him of that, he thanked God, he was never guilty of. To use his own language on the evil meaning attached to his mere conversational talk :—" If words spoken to friends in familiar discourse, spoken in one's chamber, spoken at one's table, spoken in one's sick bed ; spoken, perhaps, to gain better reason, to give himself more clear light and judgment, by reasoning : if these things shall be brought against a man as treason, this, under favour, takes away the comfort of all human society. By this means we shall be debarred of speaking (the principal joy and comfort of society) with wise and good men, to become wiser, and better our lives. If these things be strained to take away life and honour, and all that is desirable, it will be a silent world. A city will become an hermitage, and sheep will be found amongst a crowd or press of people, and no man will dare to impart his solitary thoughts or opinion to his friend and neighbour, but thereby be debarred from consulting with wiser men than himself, whereby he may understand the law wherewith he ought to be governed."

Nothing would be more unsatisfactory than the examination of the Privy Councillors, in whose presence the words referred to by the notes of Sir Harry Vane were said to be uttered.

Not one of the council could remember the exact words of Lord Strafford on that occasion, till Sir Harry Vane, the writer of the notes, was called upon for his

testimony. He began by declaring his dislike of un-   1641.
truth, which was stronger than ever in the presence of
such an assembly. As nearly as he could, he would
tell their lordships the truth in this matter. For the
time he could not particularly speak, but the words to
which he was to bear witness were spoken after the
last Parliament, and where the subject was offensive or
defensive war against the Scots. To the best of his
belief either these words, or words to that effect, were
spoken by the Lord Strafford : " Your Majesty having
tried all ways and being refused, and in case of this
extreme necessity, and for the safety of the kingdom,
you are acquitted before God and men. You have an
army in Ireland which you may employ here to reduce
this kingdom, *or some words to this effect.*" Lord
Clare, the brother of Strafford's second wife, then
advanced the weighty question : Whether by the expression " this kingdom," Lord Strafford had meant
the kingdom of England or Scotland ?

To this Sir Henry prudently replied, " it was far
from him to interpret the words."

Then came the question, did Strafford vote for an
offensive or defensive war with Scotland ? To this
Vane answered, that while he himself had counselled
a defensive, Strafford was for an offensive, war. On
this last phrase there was a general agreement. And
yet nothing is plainer than that a nominally offensive
may in reality be a strictly defensive war. In nothing
is it more necessary to interpret by the spirit rather
than the letter.

Thus in the late war between France and Germany,
nothing could be more easy than by following the
letter to represent the Germans as the offenders. They

 began the attack, they invaded the enemy's country, constantly they were the first to open battle, and finally dictated their own terms. The soil of Germany was untouched, while France was a prey to sword and flame. As invaders and conquerors the German armies trampled on the plains of France, while in no other guise than that of helpless prisoners did the French appear in Germany.

And yet the French were the real aggressors. They gave the challenge, and by their persistence rendered the concessions of the Germans vain. It was simply an act of good generalship, not provocative war, that placed the Germans the first in the field.

And thus it was intended by Strafford. The Scots had really commenced the war, and he plainly meant, that as the war had really begun, if it was to be carried on, it had better be done in a warlike and vigorous manner, and victory was more likely to be obtained by the English marching into Scotland than by waiting for the Scots in England.

Of course the original cause of the war, and whether the first beginners were justified in their outbreak, is altogether another matter. A similar question might be raised with regard to the battle of Dunbar. Cromwell marched into Scotland and began the attack. Yet it could not be called an offensive war on his part.

However, it was determined that these notes of Sir Harry Vane should do good service, and justify the Bill of Attainder. Before these words, so loosely reported, all the rest of the charge seemed set aside. On these the accusers dwelt, and insisted that they alone were fully sufficient to convict the utterer of High Treason. Hitherto the charge was taken article by article, no new one being entered upon till the previous one was disposed of. But now this order was put away. The accusers demanded and obtained the power of taking all the rest in a mass, and dealing with them as they pleased. To this the prisoner vainly objected. If taken, as before, singly, he said he could remember the circumstances and arguments applicable to each, but all thrown together it was impossible for him to do himself justice. But these single arguments were precisely what the accusers wished to avoid. Numbers taken separately looked insignificant: massed together they exhibited a power which was imposing. Their case was not legally strong enough to bear dissection.

Strafford was, therefore, compelled to take them on their own ground. He, at once, proceeded to deal with the notes of Vane.

And, first, he pointed out the weakness of the evidence.

Not one of the members of the Privy Council supported the testimony of Sir Harry Vane. The Earl of Northumberland, the Marquis of Hamilton, Bishop Juxon, Lord Treasurer of England, and Lord Cottington, were all examined on oath, and all alike denied the words as reported. But even if spoken, they rested on a single testimony, and according to the laws of England, even as late as the reign of Elizabeth and the present King, no man could be convicted of High Treason on the authority of a single witness.*

Then his words ought to be repeated in the sense in which he uttered them. God forbid any man should

---

* E. 6; Car. 12.

be judged for words taken by pieces, here a word and there a word, where the antecedents and consequents are left out, for then treason might be fetched out of every word a man speaks; as, for example, if one asks him, whether he will go to such a place?—he tells him by way of answer, he will kill the King as soon. The other swears he said he would kill the King. It is very true, indeed, but if the other words be added, it will then imply that he will be sure not to kill the King, and therefore he will be sure not to go to the place. So with the words he himself was said to have uttered, " that the King having tried the affections of his people, he was loose and absolved from all rules of government," &c.

What he meant was :—In case of absolute necessity, and upon a foreign invasion of an enemy, when all ordinary means fail, then the King was justified in using the only means in his power to disperse them. Such reservations had preceded his words, showing he meant the King must only use such power on a desperate emergency, and for the sole good of the Commonwealth, and if done for any other purpose than the good of the people, it would be oppressive and injurious.

Now there is no reason to doubt the sincerity of Lord Strafford in these words. And yet they contained the rock on which his whole career had broken itself. He was no vulgar tyrant of the Nero or Caligula species. He believed his measures were for the people's good; he thought that if the King saw the people could be benefited by setting the laws at defiance, he was justified in thus acting the part of a benevolent despot. Moreover, the King was to be the

judge of what was for the good of the nation. It was   1641.
against this principle that the English patriots were
resolved to wage war to the death. Their mistakes
consisted in the unfair means they used, and in con
founding the principle with those who professed it.
Consequently, they destroyed individuals, and allowed
the creed to survive, as it has done, down to our own
day. And the philanthropic preachers who still inculcate
in no mild or measured language the duty of the un-
reasoning obedience of the multitude to the absolute
authority of the few best and wisest are perhaps much
happier than they are aware of for not living in the
days of Pym and Cromwell, and the best and wisest of
the Puritan times. The next argument offered by Lord
Strafford was " that these words charged upon him were
not wantonly or unnecessarily spoken or whispered in
a corner, but they were spoken in full Council, where
he was, by the duty of his oath, obliged to speak
according to his heart and conscience in all things
concerning the King's service, so that if he had for-
borne to speak what he conceived for the benefit and
advantage of the King and people (as he conceived
this to be), he had been perjured towards God Almighty,
and now it seemed by the speaking of them, he was
in danger to be a traitor. But if that necessity was
put upon him, he thanked God he had learned not to
stand in fear of him that can kill the body. If he
must be a traitor to man or perjured to God, he would
be faithful to his Creator, and whatsoever might befal
him from a popular rage or his own weakness, he
must leave it to God and their lordships' honour and
justice. He had simply offered his opinion according
to his heart and conscience. An opinion might make

1641. an heretic, but he never heard before that opinion could make a traitor.

"Let it once be admitted that a councillor delivering his opinion under an oath of secresy and faithfulness at the council-table, *candide et caste* with others, shall, upon his mistaking, or not knowing of the law, be brought unto question, and every word that passeth from him out of a sincere and noble intention, shall be drawn against him for the attaining and convicting himself, his children, and posterity; after this, the speaker said, he did not know any wise and noble person of fortune that upon such perilous and unsafe terms would adventure to be Councillor to the King.

"If their lordships, therefore, put these hard strains and tortures upon those that were Councillors of State to his Majesty, when they spoke nothing but according to their hearts and consciences, it would disable them from those great employments to which their birth and thoughts did breed them, and make them more incapable than any other inferior subjects."

These arguments cannot be defeated. The usual answer to them is that Strafford had himself both at the councils of York and Dublin repeatedly set them at defiance. In the case of Mountnorris, especially, as well as that of others, he had exercised this very tyranny over conversation and opinion that he now so strongly condemned in his own case.

And this is true as the arguments themselves.

By a strange turn of fortune Strafford was suffering from the most bitter, if the most salutary, of all punishments. He was learning by personal experience the effects of the same injustice he had inflicted on others. Still it was injustice, and therefore cannot be quoted with approbation of those who inflicted it. 1641. Retaliation is no part of the English law, and that law alone was the standard by which Lord Strafford ought to have been tried. It is quite true that it is a clear part of the plan of Nature that men are to learn through their errors to feel their way from wrong to right, to know what obstacles exist simply by stumbling against them. But this principle never can be applied to human systems. The laws of Nature are perfect from the beginning. Once understood, they can always be obeyed. They are never created suddenly, and for special occasions, and applying to all alike, give all the same chance of benefit who learn to obey. But human codes continually change, and are affected by time, place, person, and circumstance. And because a man has broken a law to another, to punish him by breaking it towards himself, or by inventing one to suit his previously-committed crime, is about as great a contradiction of those natural principles to which Pym appealed as for the earth to change her course and the seasons to remain the same.

CHAPTER XV.

 THE 12th of April was appointed for the summing up of evidence on both sides.

Lord Strafford was first called upon to do his part, and on his asking if any new matter would be alleged, he was told that if it arose, of course, it would be brought forward. He then stated that he would confine his remarks to that already given, unless, in self-defence, he should be called on for more.

He then addressed the court in a speech remarkable alike for its close reasoning and pathetic eloquence.

Then, as before, he went over the articles that were said to amount to High Treason in the general sense of them, concluding his summary with these most rousing and suggestive words :—

" My Lords, that those should now be treason together that are not treason in any one part, and accumulatively to come upon me in that kind, and where one will not do it of itself, yet woven up with others it shall do it. Under favour, my Lords, I do not conceive that there is either statute law, or common law, that hath declared this endeavouring to subvert the fundamental laws to be High Treason.

" I say, neither statute law, nor common law, written, that I could hear of, and I have been as dili-

gent to inquire of it as I could be. And your Lord- 1641.
ships will believe I had reason so to do. And sure it
is a very hard thing I should be here questioned for my
life and honour upon a law that is not extant, that
cannot be showed! There is a rule that I have read
out of my Lord Coke, *non apparentibus et non exist-
entibus eadem est ratio.*

" Jesu! my Lords, where hath this fire lain all this
while, so many hundred years together that no smoke
should appear till it burst out now to consume me and
my children?

" Hard it is, and extreme hard, in my opinion, that a
punishment should precede the promulgation of a law:
that I should be punished by a law subsequent to the
act done.

" I most humbly beseech your Lordships take that
into consideration. For, certainly, it were better a
great deal to live under no law but the will of man,
and confine ourselves in human wisdom, as well as
we could, and to comply with that will, than to live
under the protection of a law, as we think, and then
a law should be made to punish us for a crime precedent to the law. Then, I conceive, no man living
could be safe if that should be admitted.

" My Lords, it is hard in another respect, that
there should be no tokens set upon this offence
by which we may know it; no manner of token
given, no admonition by which we might be aware
of it.

" If I pass down the Thames in a boat, and run
and split myself upon an anchor, if there be not a
buoy to give me warning, the party shall give me
damages, but if it be marked out then it is at my own

peril. Now, my Lords, where is the mark set upon this crime? Where is the token by which I should discover? If it be not marked, if it lie under water and not above, there is no human providence can prevent the destruction of a man presently and instantly. Let us then lay aside all that is human wisdom; let us rely only upon divine revelation, for, certainly, nothing else can preserve us, if you will condemn us before you tell us where the fault is that we may avoid it.

" My Lords, may your Lordships be pleased to have that regard to the peerage of England as never to suffer yourselves to be put upon those moot points, upon such constructions and interpretations and strictness of law, as these are when the law is not clear nor known. If there must be a trial of wits, I do most humbly beseech your Lordships to consider that the subject may be of something else than of your lives and of your honours.

" My Lords, we find that in the primitive time, on the sound and plain doctrine of the blessed apostles, they brought in their books of curious art and burnt them.

" My Lords, it will be likewise (as I humbly conceive), wisdom and providence in your Lordships for yourselves and posterity, for the whole kingdom, to cast from you into the fire those bloody and mysterious volumes of constructive and arbitrary treasons, and to betake yourselves to the plain letter of the statute that tells you where the crime is, that so you may avoid it. And let us not, my Lords, be ambitious to be more learned in those killing arts than our forefathers were before us.

" My Lords, it is now full two hundred and forty

years since any man ever was touched to this height, upon this crime, before myself.

" We have lived, my Lords, happily to ourselves at home, we have lived gloriously abroad to the world; let us be content with that which our fathers left us, and let us not awake those sleeping hours to our own destruction by rattling up of a company of records that have lain for so many ages by the wall, forgotten or neglected.

" My Lords, there is this that troubles me extremely, lest it should be my misfortune to all the rest (for my other sins, not for my treasons) that my precedents should be of that disadvantage (as this will be, I fear, in the consequence of it) upon the whole kingdom.

" My Lords, I beseech you, therefore, that you will be pleased seriously to consider it, and let my particular care be so looked upon, as that, you do not, through me, wound the interest of the Commonwealth. For howsoever those gentlemen at the bar say they speak for the Commonwealth, and they believe so, yet, in this particular, I believe I speak for the Commonwealth too. And that the inconveniences and miseries that will follow upon this, will be such, as it will come, within a few years, to that which is expressed in the statute of Henry the Fourth, it will be of such a condition, that no man shall know what to do or to say.

" Do not, my Lords, put greater difficulty upon the ministers of State, than that with cheerfulness they may serve the King and State. For if you will examine them by every grain, or every little weight, it will be so heavy, that the public affairs of the kingdom will be less weight, and no man will meddle with them that hath wisdom and honour and fortune to lose.

"My Lords, I have now troubled your Lordships a great deal longer than I should have done, were it not for the interest of those pledges that a saint in heaven left me. I would be loth, my lords "——

Here, overcome by the thought of the desolation of his children, and the memory of their mother, as well as too enfeebled by long speaking, in his present condition of health, to control his emotion, he was compelled to pause, and for a few moments was unable to control his tears. With a violent struggle he recovered his voice, but feeling himself unable to continue, he hastened to bring his speech to a close, thus :—

"What I forfeit for myself it is nothing. But, I confess, that my indiscretion should forfeit for them, it wounds me very deeply.

"You will be pleased to pardon my infirmity: something I should have said, but I see I shall not be able, and therefore I will leave it.

"And now, my Lords, I thank God, I have been by his good blessing towards me, taught, that the afflictions of this present life are not to be compared with that eternal weight of glory that shall be revealed hereafter.

"And so, my Lords, even so with all humility, and with all tranquillity of mind, I do submit myself clearly and freely unto your judgment; and whether that righteous judgment shall be to life or death.

"'Te Deum laudamus, te Dominum confitemur.'"

The effect of this speech upon the audience was great. But the accusers were relentless, and their vigilance still more excited by the signs of softening.

Their answer was given by Glyn, Pym, Maynard,   1641.
and St. John. The speech of Pym, contained as
before a mingling of the most masterly eloquence,
with a distortion both of the letter and the spirit of
truth.

It concluded with these terrible words.

"The forfeitures inflicted by treason, by our laws, are
of life, honour, and estate, even all that can be forfeited. And this prisoner having committed so many
treasons, although he should pay all these forfeitures,
will be still a debtor to the Commonwealth. Nothing
can be more equal, than that he should perish by the
justice of that law which he would have subverted.
Neither will this be a new way of blood. There are
marks enough to trace this law to the very original of
this kingdom. And, if it hath not been put in execution, as he allegeth, these two hundred and forty years,
it was not for want of law, but that all that time hath
not bred a man bold enough to commit such crimes as
these. Which is a circumstance much aggravating
his offence, and making him no whit less liable to
punishment, because he is the only man that in so long
a time hath ventured upon such a treason as this."

It has been related * that, as Pym uttered these last
tremendous and appalling words, he suddenly and in-
advertently turned his head and beheld the mournful
and mutely reproachful gaze of Strafford, fixed upon
him, as if in sad appeal against such merciless condemnation.

For a moment, the stern accuser was shaken, and
even his resolve quivered beneath the deeply thrilling

* Forster's British Statesmen, iii, p. 182. Also Howell's State
Trials, ii.

A A 2

and questioning look of his former associate and fellow worker, still, his countryman and brother before God. Better, a thousand times, have listened to the divine impulse that murmured mercy in his soul. Better for the sake of England, of liberty, of justice, of religion, to have hearkened to that voice that so surely spoke to him, which was no echo of weakness—such could never for one instant find entrance in the heart of Pym, but a whisper of the most celestial feeling, that can move the soul of man, to which no man ever regretted giving heed.

But it was not to be. For a few minutes, Pym was overcome by the surging tide, and a strange silence held possession of the whole assembly. Pym bent his head and feigned to search among his papers, while he struggled to regain his self-possession. It speedily obeyed his call. Once more, he raised his head and with unbroken voice, concluded with these words :—

"It belongs to the charge of another, to make it appear to your Lordships, that the crimes and offences proved against the Earl of Strafford are High Treason, by the laws and statutes of this realm, whose learning and other abilities are much better for that service. But, for the time and manner of performing this, we are to resort to the direction of the House of Commons, having in this, which is already done, despatched all those instructions which we have received. And concerning further proceedings for clearing all questions and objections in law, your Lordships will hear from the House of Commons in convenient time."

Meanwhile, in the House of Commons, the debate grew more exciting. The flimsy nature of much of the evidence, the absolute falsity of some of the

charges, the logical arguments of the prisoner,—above
all,—the clear impossibility of bringing the charges
under the definition of High Treason, without perversion
and distortion of the existing statutes, had had their
effect on those minds, ever a small minority, who, in
judging a question, refuse to be carried away by any
thought of the consequences of their judgment, any
personal feeling towards the object, or any other consideration than the pure spirit of truth.

Still, though increasing in number, the calmer and
more independent minded of the members of the lower
House, were few, in comparison with those who were
rather carried away by the words and influence of
their great leaders, than by any decided conviction of
their own. On the 14th of April, the Bill of Attainder
was read a second time and passed.

The rapidity with which it was carried through the
first and second readings, augured ill for the prisoner.
The reservation, that it should not be used as a precedent, seemed the only sign of consciousness of how
terrible a danger was involved in such a proceeding.
No tyranny more frightful can be conceived, than that
which leaves the actions of men undefined, and their
penalties unknown or unsettled until after the deed is
done. Better the vilest criminals that ever trod this
earth should escape untouched, than that such uncertainty in matters involving possible capital punishment, should ever be admitted into a code of law.

Happily, there was one man who saw this, who was
not carried away by the strong tide of passion, who
not only perceived the evil of the principle, but the
wrong to the prisoner himself. Every argument that
could be imagined has been brought forward to justify

1641.

1641. this Act of Attainder, and, again and again, the enormities of Strafford dwelt upon in the vain attempt.

To his immortal honour, Lord Digby saw through the error, and refused to lend his name to its sanction as a deed of right.

On the 21st of April, during the debate on the Bill, and before the third reading, Lord Digby rose, and most earnestly is the attention of the reader entreated, to the great lessons conveyed in the following extracts from his speech.

"Mr. Speaker,

"Truly, Sir, to deal plainly with you, that ground of our accusation, that spur to our prosecution, and that which should be the basis of my judgment, of the Earl of Strafford as unto treason, is to my understanding, quite vanished away.

"This it was, Mr. Speaker.

"His advising the King to employ the army of Ireland to reduce England.

"This, I was assured, would be proved before I gave my consent to his accusation. I was confirmed in the same belief during the prosecution, and fortified in it most of all since Sir Harry Vane's preparatory examination, by the assurances which that worthy member, Mr. Pym, gave me, that his testimony would be made convincing by some notes of what passed at that Junto concurrent with it. Which I ever understanding to be of some other councillor, you see now, prove but a copy of the same Secretary's notes, discovered and produced in the manner you have heard. And those, disjointed fragments of the venomous part of discourses. No results, no conclusions of counsels,

which are the only things that Secretaries should re- 1641.
gister, there being no use at all of the other, but to
accuse and bring men into danger.

"But, Sir, this is not that which overthrows the
evidence with me concerning the army of Ireland, nor
yet that all the rest of the Junto, upon their oaths,
remember nothing of it.

"But, Sir, this which I shall tell you is that which
works with me, under favour, to an utter overthrow of
his evidence, as unto that of the army of Ireland.
Before, whilst I was a prosecutor, and under tie of
secresy, I might not discover any weakness of the cause
which now, as a judge, I must.

"Mr. Secretary was examined thrice upon oath at
the preparatory Committee.

"The first time, he was questioned to all the inter-
rogatories, and to that part of the seventh which concerns the army of Ireland.

"He said positively in these words : '*I cannot charge
him with that.*' But for the rest, he desired time to
recollect himself, which was granted him.

"Some days after, he was examined a second time,
and then deposes these words concerning the King's
being absolved from all rules of government, and so
forth, very clearly. But, being prest to that part
concerning the Irish army, he said again : '*I can say
nothing to that.*'

"Here we thought we had done with him, till divers
weeks after, my Lord of Northumberland, and all
others of the Junto, denying to have heard anything
concerning those words.

"Of reducing England by the Irish army, it was
thought fit to examine the Secretary once more. And

 then he deposes these words to have been said by the
Earl of Strafford to his Majesty :

" ' *You have an army in Ireland, which you may
employ here to reduce* (or some words to that sense)
this kingdom.'

" Mr. Speaker, these are circumstances which, I confess with my conscience, thrust quite out of doors that
grand article of our charge concerning his desperate
advice to the King, of employing the Irish army here.

" Let not this, I beseech you, be driven to an aspersion
upon Mr. Secretary, as if he should have sworn otherwise than he knew or believed. He is too worthy to
do that. Only let thus much be inferred from it.
That he, who twice upon oath, with time of recollection, could not remember anything of such a
business, might well, a third time, mis-remember
somewhat in this business. The difference of one
letter, *here* for *there*, or *that* for *this*, quite alters the
case. The latter, also, being more probable, since it
is confessed of all hands, that the debate then was
concerning a war with Scotland, and you may remember, that, at the bar, he once said to ' employ
these.'

" And thus, Mr. Speaker, I have faithfully given you
an account what it is that hath blunted the edge of the
hatchet or bill with me towards my Lord of Strafford.

" This was that whereupon I accused him with a
free heart, prosecuted him with earnestness, and had
it, to my understanding, been proved, should have
condemned him with innocence. Whereas, now, I
cannot satisfy my conscience to do it.

" I profess, I can have no notion of anybody's
intent to subvert the laws treasonably, or by force.

And this design of force not appearing, all his other wicked practices cannot amount so high with me.

1641.

"I find a more easy and more natural spring from whence to derive all his other crimes than from an intent to bring in tyranny, and to make his own posterity, as well as us, slaves, as from revenge, from pride, from avarice, and insolence of nature.

"But, had this Irish army been proved, it would have diffused a complexion of treason over all. It would have been a withe, indeed, to bind all those other scattered and lesser branches, as it were, into a faggot of treason.

"I do not say but the rest may represent him a man as worthy to die, but perhaps worthier than many a traitor. I do not say but they may justly direct us to enact that they shall be treason *for the future*.

"*But God keep me from giving judgment of death on any man, and of ruin to his innocent posterity upon a law made à posteriori.* Let the mark be set on the door where the plague is, and *then* let him that will enter die.

"I know, Mr. Speaker, there is in Parliament a double power of life and death by bill, a judicial power, and a legislative. The measure of the one is what is legally just; of the other, what is prudentially and politically fit for the good and preservation of the whole.

"But these two, under favour, are not to be confounded in judgment. We must not piece upon want of legality with matter of convenience, not the defailance of prudential fitness with a pretence of legal justice.

"To condemn my Lord of Strafford judicially, as

1641. for treason, my conscience is not assured that the matter will bear it.

"And to do it by the legislative power, my reason, consultively, cannot agree to that, since I am persuaded neither the Lords nor the King will pass the bill, and, consequently, that our passing it will be a cause of great divisions and combustions in the State.

"And, therefore, my humble advice is : That, laying aside this Bill of Attainder, we may think of another saving only life, such as may secure the State from my Lord of Strafford, without endangering, as much by division concerning his punishment, as he hath endangered it by his practices.

"If this may not be hearkened unto, let me conclude, in saying, that unto you all which I have thoroughly inculcated to mine own conscience upon this occasion. Let every man lay his hand upon his heart and sadly consider what we are going to do with a breath,— either justice or murder. Justice on the one side, or murder, heightened and aggravated to its supremest extent. *He that commits murder with the sword of justice heightens that crime to the utmost.*

"The danger being so great and the case so doubtful that I see the best lawyers in diametrical opposition concerning it; let every man wipe his heart as he doth his eyes when he would judge of a nice and subtle object. The eye, if it be pretincted with any colour, is vitiated in its discerning. Let us take heed of a blood-shotten eye in judgment.

"Let every man purge his heart clear of all passions (I know this great and wise body-politic can have none, but I speak to individuals, from the weakness which I find in myself), away with all personal animosities, away with all flatteries to the people, in being the sharper against him because he is odious to them; away with all fears, lest by the sparing his blood they may be incensed; away with all such considerations as that it is not fit for a Parliament that one accused by it of treason should escape with life.

"Let not former vehemence of any be against him, nor fear from thence that he cannot be safe while that man lives, be an ingredient in the sentence of any one of it.

"Of all these corruptions of judgment, Mr. Speaker, I do, before God, discharge myself to the uttermost of my power.

"And do with a clear conscience wash my hands of this man's blood, by this solemn protestation, *that my vote goes not to the taking of the Earl of Strafford's life.*"

If anything in the shape of reasoning could have changed the minds of the Commons, it must have been this. But their minds had been made up from the beginning, and before the trial, which was really only to them a compulsory form to be gone through, rather to ratify, than to obtain judgment. It is quite impossible, even when, as in the present case, all the first motives and grounds of action are good and impersonal, to make the death or destruction of another an object to be pursued with all the energy which the belief in such necessity requires, and yet to remain unmoved by personal feelings. The lofty course invoked by Lord Digby had become unattainable to men who had worked for one end with such burning zeal as Pym and St. John, and Maynard, and those whom they represented. Up to a certain point, impartiality may

1641.   be preserved, but, after that, comes not only the need of punishment for the accused, but of justification for the steps already taken against him. It is quite possible to chastise another and yet to love him. But then it must be for his own good that the chastisement is inflicted. But when the culprit himself is ignored, or only regarded as a fit object of retribution, every blow is nerved by hatred, and all the more when the inflicter is not by nature cruel and morose, but, as Pym, indifferent in nothing, sacrificing himself as readily as the smallest trifle in a cause at heart. His cause was indeed holy, the liberty and prosperity of his country. Of that, he believed Lord Strafford was the most potent enemy, and not only did he desire his death as a needful deliverance, but he hated him with all the intensity of his soul, because he believed him an enemy. And that this personal hatred powerfully influenced him in the trial is as clear as daylight. It could not be otherwise. When he saw the condition of his beloved England miserable at home, despised abroad, when he thought of the fair promise blighted of early days, of Eliot dead in the very prime of life, the victim of that tyranny which had robbed the people of their dearest rights, and then beguiled from them the champion of their hopes, when he thought of all that Strafford might have been, and what he had been in the struggle, there need be no mystery in the relentless bitterness manifested even by so good and great a man. For Pym was a man, not a god, and, as such, needs the same allowance for his faults and errors that is due also to Strafford. He was unjust to Strafford, both through his hatred and from his being greatly mistaken in very much concerning him. His hatred had allowed him to listen far too eagerly and credulously to the falsest tales, to attribute wrong motives, and to close his ears to any good report. There is no need for far inferior beings to do the same in the present case.

In a passionate struggle, where incalculable interests hang on the balance, it is never to be wondered at that the combatants are carried by the excitement of their feelings far out of the realms of justice, of accuracy, and even of common humanity. But in history, precisely as in existing causes carried on by living actors, it is the most solemn duty of the spectator who watches both sides, himself free from the blinding clouds of the storm, to examine with religious impartiality into the facts and causes of errors which have led to such mournful consequences. It is not for him to erect himself into a flatterer of one side, a slanderer of the other, and wholly destitute of the excuse of the mistakes that really misled the original parties, or the burning sense of wrong that destroyed their powers of equity, to repeat with complacence the very falsehoods he is bound to expose. And justice must condemn the spirit in which the words of Lord Digby were received. If any proof were needed of the fact that passion and hatred, and not the high principles that alone ought to reign supreme in the highest tribunal of the kingdom, now governed the trial of Strafford, it is to be found in the treatment of Lord Digby. He certainly had a perfect right to express his opinion quite as freely as Pym. He was no friend of Lord Strafford, and had even been a foremost member of the committee for his trial. He had been as strongly prejudiced against him, as fully convinced that he had committed High Treason, and deserved death, as his colleagues. But he was open to reason, and not ashamed to acknowledge himself in error. He could have no possible motive but the very highest for changing his opinion beneath the force of evidence. And the more unpopular the prisoner, the mightier the force against him, the more honour was it to Digby that he refused to be borne along by the torrent himself, refused to see others swept away without a clear, unhesitating protest in the cause of right. His speech is the redeeming point in the trial; that is to say, that it is the only one in which all personalities are laid aside, and the desire to do right is made the ruling object. Yet " exceptions were taken by divers members," he was angrily called to account for many portions, and some time after, the whole speech having been printed like those of the other members, was declared " to contain matters untrue and scandalous in reference to the proceedings of the committees both of the Lords and Commons, and to the evidence of the witnesses produced in the case of the Earl of Strafford. Also that publishing the same after offence taken, and a vote passed for the Bill of Attainder, was scandalous to the proceedings of the House." Printer and publisher of the speech were also declared delinquents. The speech itself was ordered to be publicly burnt by the common hangman in Palace Yard, in Westminster, in Cheapside, and Smithfield, and the King was petitioned to confer no honour or employment on Lord Digby in future, who by this speech had deserved so ill of the Parliament. It is difficult for the accusers of Strafford to find among his deeds anything more arbitrary than this. The very alleged cause of offence, the publication of the speech, after the Act of Attainder was passed, was in itself necessary to clear Lord Digby's name from participation in that act. It is another proof of the unfitness of human beings, no matter how high their character, to be judges in any matter in which their passions are engaged, or to which they are individually a partisan.

Of course, the Bill of Attainder was passed on the third reading. On the very day of Lord Digby's speech it was carried by 204 against 59. It was then ordered to be immediately engrossed, and sent up to the Lords by Pym, who was commanded to signify how much it concerned the Commonwealth to have this matter expedited, as also that the Commons would be ready to justify the legality of it in a free conference when required by their lordships.

All this time, the King had not shown himself indifferent. At the trial, he had daily attended incognito in the private apartment prepared for him, and manifested so much interest as with his own hands to break down the screen that concealed him from the assembled multitude, who, though well aware of his presence, were so much more absorbed by that of the prisoner, that royalty in open daylight, and in loyal England, almost literally went for nothing.

But two days after the Bill of Attainder had passed the third reading, he gave a proof of his care for his devoted friend and servant by sending to him the following letter, the most creditable performance existing from his hand. Certainly, the lonely prisoner needed such a solace. Mercy was the undoubted prerogative of the King. Without any breach of the law, he could, even after the sentence of death was passed, interpose

1641.

and save the life of the worst criminal in his kingdom. And no human being could doubt that such a power would be eagerly asserted and maintained in the present case. Still, this written assurance must have carried comfort and certain hope to the prisoner.

" *The King to the Earl of Strafford.*

" STRAFFORD,

" The misfortune that is fallen upon you by the strange mistaking and conjuncture of these times being such that I must lay by the thought of employing you hereafter in my affairs; yet I cannot satisfy myself in honour or conscience without assuring you (now in the midst of your troubles) that upon the word of a King, you shall not suffer in life, honour, or fortune. This is but justice, and therefore a very mean reward from a master to so faithful and able a servant as you have showed yourself to be. Yet, it is as much as I conceive the present times will permit, though none shall hinder me from being,

" Your constant faithful Friend,

" CHARLES R.

" *Whitehall, April* 23, 1641."

Since the passing of the Bill of Attainder, the rage of the populace against Strafford had increased. They literally thirsted for his blood. It was not those who had really suffered by him, such as the landholders of Ireland, who had lost by the commission for disputed titles, &c., who were the most clamorous. Outside the Houses of Parliament his enemies were chiefly the

unthinking multitude, who always hunt down a fallen 1641.
minister, and whose fury was about as explicable and
as well-founded as that of a pack of hounds in full cry,
one bark being merely the echo of another. A petition
was got up, signed by twenty thousand Londoners,
recounting various grievances, and containing the following sentence :—

" Besides all which, from what strong and secret
opposition the petitioners know not, they have not
received what so much time and pains might give them
cause to hope, but still incendiaries of the kingdoms
and other notorious offenders remain unpunished. The
affairs of the Church, notwithstanding many petitious
concerning it, and long debate about it, remain unsettled ; the Papists still armed, the laws against them
not executed, some of the most active of them still at
Court ; priests and Jesuits not yet banished, the Irish
popish army not yet disbanded, courts of justice not
yet reformed, and the Earl of Strafford, who, as now
appears, hath counselled the plundering of this city,
and putting it to fine and ransom, and said, ' it would
never be well till some of the aldermen were hanged
up,' because they would not yield to illegal levies of
monies, had so drawn out and spent this time in his
business, to the very great charge of the whole kingdom, and his endeavours to obtain yet more, all which
makes us fear there may be practices now in hand to
hinder the birth of your great endeavours, and that
we lie under some more dangerous plot than we can
discover.

" And (the petitioners) do humbly pray that their
said grievances may be redressed, the causes of their
fears removed, justice executed upon the said Earl,

1641. and other incendiaries and offenders, the rather in regard, till then, the petitioners humbly conceive neither religion, nor their lives, liberties, nor estates, can be secured."

This petition was presented on the 24th of April, and on the 28th, Hyde, afterwards Earl of Clarendon, was sent up to the House of Lords to say that information had been received of a design of Strafford to escape, that he had ships at sea under his command, and that his guards were weak. The Commons, therefore, begged that he might be closely kept prisoner, and his guard strengthened.

Surely, never before were three nations in such terror of one helpless prisoner! Things must indeed be very far wrong in a government that can render any individual, whatever his talents and position, such an object of dread to a whole people!

On the 29th of April, Oliver St. John rose before the Lords, as the legal delegate of the Commons, to justify the Bill of Attainder. Nearly thirty folio pages are required for his speech. But a very few extracts will show how monstrous was the distortion of the simplest words from their original meaning in order to wrest them to the destruction of Strafford. No stronger argument against the Bill of Attainder can be brought than the fact that such perversion was required to support it.

After relating various cases of treason in different reigns, Lord Strafford was declared guilty of treason by compassing the King's death (!), by such an argument as this :—

"It appears," said St. John, "that it is a compassing the King's death by words, to endeavour to

draw the people's hearts from the King, to set discord
between the King and them, whereby the people
should leave the King, should rise up against him to
the death and destruction of the King."

As examples, he brought up various cases during the
wars of the Roses, in which the reigning king's title
had been denied by individuals of the opposite party;
and, as if the cases were exactly parallel, Strafford
was declared to have tried to disaffect the King and
people by his counsels. "And," said St. John, "to
counsel a King not to love his people is very unnatural. It goes higher (still) to hate them, to malice
them in his heart, the highest expressions of malice to
destroy them by war. These coals, they were cast
upon his Majesty, they were blown, they could not
kindle in that breast."

He then quoted the words ascribed to Strafford in
the articles, and said—

"We shall leave it to your Lordships' judgments
whether these words, counsels, and actions would not
have been a sufficient evidence to have proved an
indictment drawn up against him, as those before-
mentioned and others are, that they were spoken and
done to the intent to draw the King's heart from the
people, and the affections of the people from the King,
that they might leave the King and afterwards rise
up against him, to the destruction of the King. If
so, here is a compassing of the King's death
within the words of the statute of the 25th year of
Edward III., and that warranted by many former
judgments."

After a lengthy disquisition, illustrated in this manner, the speaker boldly asserted that, after all, a legal

 sanction was not needed in the condemnation of Lord Strafford.

"It hath often been inculcated," he said, "that law makers should imitate the supreme lawgiver, who commonly warns before he strikes. The law was promulgated before the judgment of death for gathering the sticks. No law, no transgression.

"My Lords, to this rule of law is *frustra legis auxilium invocat, qui in legem committit*, from the *lex talionis*. He that would not have had others to have a law, why should he have any himself? Why should not that be done to him that himself would have done to others?

"It is true we give law to hares and deers, because they be beasts of chase. It was never accounted either cruelty or foul play to knock foxes and wolves on the head, as they can be found, because these be beasts of prey. The warrener sets traps for polecats and other vermin, for preservation of the warren.

"Further, my Lords, most dangerous diseases, if not taken in time, they kill. Errors in great things, as war and marriage, they allow no time for repentance. It would have been too late to make a law when there had been no law."

What hope for any prisoner, even had he been perfect in his innocence, when such sentiments as these were allowed to pass unchallenged, uncriticised, while the wise and most temperate reasoning of Lord Digby was treated as we have seen!

By mute gestures, Strafford gave expression to an indignant protest against such language as this, and though he must have known it to be in vain, as it is expressed, "that he might not seem wanting to him-

self," * he petitioned that he might be heard in defence   1641.
against the Bill of Attainder. His request was refused.
Still, he had one strong hope. He had the promise of
the King that he should lose neither in life, honour,
nor estate. Even if he lost his titles and estates,
life, ever more precious as it becomes endangered, was
safe. The law itself sanctioned the King in sparing
that; and the unpopularity Charles had so long braved
for his own purposes, might well be borne to save the
life of his friend. Not yet would the young children
of the house of Wentworth be left orphans. A few
years, indeed, and this must be their fate. But a few
years would bring them to maturity. The son, to
whom Strafford had always taught that his proudest
and most worthy duty was to guard and cherish his
weaker sisters, would be a man able and rejoicing to
protect the rest.

That time arrived, Lord Strafford might gladly cast
off " this rag of mortality worn out with numerous
infirmities, which," as he had told the Lords, " if they
tore into shreds, there was no great loss." And none,
fettered as he was by ever-recurring attacks of bodily
torment, but must often wearily long for the final
peace.

His affections, not his ambitions, it was that now
bound him to the earth.

The next day, the King went unexpectedly in person to the House of Lords, and having sent for the
Commons, he thus addressed them :—

* Nalson's Collections, vol. ii., p. 186.

       "My Lords and Gentlemen,

"I had not any intention to speak of this business which causes me to come here to-day, which is the great impeachment of the Earl of Strafford. But now it comes to pass, that of necessity I must have part in that judgment.

"I am sure you all know that I have been present at the hearing of this great business from the one end to the other. That which I have to declare unto you is shortly this.

"That in my conscience I cannot condemn him of High Treason. It is not fit for me to argue the business. I am sure you will not expect it. A positive doctrine best comes out of the mouth of a prince. Yet I must tell you three great truths, which I am sure nobody can know so well as myself.

"1. That I never had any intention of bringing over the Irish army into England, nor ever was advised by any body so to do.

"2. There never was any debate before me, neither in public council, nor at private committee, of the disloyalty and disaffection of my English subjects, nor ever had I any suspicion of them.

"3. I was never counselled by any to alter the least of any of the laws of England, much less to alter all the laws. Nay, I must tell you this, I think nobody durst be ever so impudent (as) to move me in it. For if they had I should have put a mark upon them, and made them such an example that all posterity should know my intentions by it. For my intention was ever to govern according to the law, and no otherwise.

"I desire to be rightly understood. I told you in my conscience I cannot condemn him of High Treason.

1641.

Yet, I cannot say I can clear him of misdemeanour. Therefore, I hope that you may find a way for to satisfy justice and your own fears, and not to press upon my conscience. My Lords, I hope you know what a tender thing conscience is. Yet, I must declare unto you, that to satisfy my people, I would do great matters. But in this of conscience, no fear, no respect whatsoever, shall make me go against it. Certainly, I have not so ill deserved of the Parliament, at this time, that they should press me in this tender point, and therefore I cannot expect that you will go about it.

" Nay, I must confess, for matters of misdemeanour, I am so clear in that, that though I will not chalk out the way, yet let me tell you, that I do think my Lord of Strafford is not fit hereafter to serve me or the commonwealth in any place of trust; no, not so much as to be a high constable. Therefore, I leave it to you, my Lords, to find some such way as to bring me out of this great straight, and keep yourselves and the kingdom from such inconveniences. Certainly, he that thinks him guilty of High Treason in his conscience, may condemn him of misdemeanour."

Surely, this speech of the King was manly and to his credit. That he did not speak more strongly in behalf of his friend, and went even so far as to acknowledge him guilty of misdemeanour, may have been the most friendly act, as it was evidently done, not to go against Strafford, but to avoid provoking the jealousy of the Commons. As the King had said in his letter, it was as much as the present time would permit.

But the words of Charles had become a mere mockery in the eyes of the people. Not only had he so often deceived them that were every word he now spoke reasonable in itself, it would have turned to ashes as coming from him, but here even he could not refrain from palpable and useless lying. Were the memories of the Commons dead that he could tell them boldly " his intention was ever to govern according to law and no otherwise ?" But so it is. An habitual liar soon arrives at the point in which sin becomes disease, and he will tell falsehoods when they are not only useless but positively injurious to himself. But even with this unfortunate slip in it, we must look on this speech of Charles as coming from his better self.

But had it been perfect in wisdom and in truth, it would have had no better effect. The only result of any attempt to soften the Commons was to enrage them the more. When the King had finished, they returned to their own House, and with long cries of " Adjourn ! Adjourn ! " refused to discuss his proposals. " All that the King got by this free declaration of himself in favour of the earl," says a contemporary, " was to lose much of the affections of the people, whether he should pass the Bill or deny it. For if he passed it, then it was to be imputed to the necessity of his affairs, not his inclinations to the good of his subjects ; and if he denied it, then it must have been esteemed a denial of justice to his people."

Strafford himself, too well comprehended the spirit that was now abroad, and heard of the King's speech, which had been made without his concurrence, with the darkest forebodings. He felt truly that nothing could save him but the refusal of the King to pass the Bill of Attainder, or in the exercise of his regal prerogative to grant a pardon.

The King's speech was made on Saturday, and on

the following Monday a band of about six thousand of
the London roughs assembled in Palace Yard, and
posting themselves at all the entrances to the Houses
of Parliament, assailed the Lords as they entered, with
loud shouts of " Justice! Execution!"   When the
coach of Lord Arundel arrived, some of the mob
stepped up to the windows and told him insolently that
justice they had already: execution they desired and
would have it.

Arundel replied that they should have justice if they
would have patience. They answered, no, they had
already had too much patience, longer they would not
stay, and before he parted from them they would have
a promise of execution. He told them he was going
to the House for that purpose, and that he would endeavour to content them.

On this some of them, cried: " We will take his
word for once," and then with great difficulty he made
his way to the House.

The Lords sat till noon, when most of them returned
home by water to avoid the crowd. But when the
Lord Chamberlain and the Earl of Bristol, less pru-
dent, came out to their coaches, they were instantly
surrounded by ruffians, who especially clamoured at
Lord Bristol, crying, " For you my Lord of Bristol,
we know you are an apostate from the cause of Christ,
and our mortal enemy. We do not, therefore, crave
justice *from* you, but shall shortly crave justice *upon*
you, and your false son, the Lord Digby."

Besides this, they obtained a list of the members
who had voted against the Bill of Attainder in the
Commons, and placarded it in Old Palace Yard, with
the title attached of " Enemies of Justice and Straf-

1641. fordians," with the menace " that these and all other
enemies of the commonwealth shall perish with
Strafford."

A petition was also sent up to the Lords, saying,
that the people had just heard that the Tower was to
receive a hundred new men who were not, according to custom, drawn from the Tower Hamlets,
and that the captain being a confident of the Earl of
Strafford, their fears for the safety of the King and
country were greatly increased, and also lest some
plan should be formed for the escape of the Earl of
Strafford. They, therefore, prayed that the matter
might be investigated, and also that speedy execution
of justice might be done upon the Earl of Strafford.

On receiving this, the Lords sent six of their
number to the Tower to make inquiries, and found
that the King had sent orders to Sir William Balfour
to receive an additional garrison, chosen by him in
order to defend the Tower if need be against the increasing rabble. The Lords then ordered Balfour to
receive no new men except by their orders, and to
refuse the King's garrison if it should come. They
then informed the Commons of this, and at the same
time told them that the passing of the Bill of Attainder
was really hindered by the mob, who prevented them
from freely debating the subject. On this, the Commons
contrived to disperse the mob, and having appointed a
committee to inquire into what seemed to them the
suspicious appearance of the King's order to place new
men in the Tower, a plot was reported, involving the
King himself, for obtaining possession of the Tower.
Balfour also said that Strafford had endeavoured to
bribe him to let him escape, promising him the King's

pardon and £22,000, besides a good match for his son. <u>1641.</u>
This plot was denied, both by the King and others, and the King at once withdrew his order for the new men, whom he said he had only desired on account of the disturbed state of the city. There would have been no great harm, nor anything unjustifiable, if Strafford had tried to save his life and the King to help him. But notwithstanding the words of Balfour, there are two strong arguments in favour of the truth of the denial.

1. Why did not Balfour at once inform the Parliament of these attempts to tamper with him? Why leave it for a mob to give the first information?

2. On the very day that Lord Strafford is said to have proposed this matter to Balfour, he wrote his famous letter to the King.

After all the assurances of Charles, it was impossible for Strafford to believe that he would desert him. But as ever since the day he had undertaken to serve the King, he had fulfilled his pledge to the very letter, so now, at this dark and dangerous hour, he would still be true. He knew the manner in which the King was beset, and that having tied himself by a promise, he could not comply with the demands of the furious men who clamoured for blood—even if he would. If he would? Did Strafford ponder on that possibility? Could his idolized friend and master *wish* to break the bond by which he had bound himself to preserve the man who had sacrificed all for him? No. That could never be. To him, in prison and alone, it had been well indeed to send the letter as a reminder of what a rock he had to lean on through all things. But in a lofty friendship what need of written words? As the

1641. real life of man is not in the body which is seen and
felt, but in the impalpable and viewless spirit, so a
noble friendship builds itself not on written pledges
and spoken promises, but on that invisible attraction
that draws great souls together each by its own divine
impulse, watching ever over the welfare and happiness
of the other without one thought or calculation of cost
or profit or sacrifice to itself. And as to buying safety
or prosperity by the misfortunes of another, as to
escaping from present difficulty or danger by the
desertion of a friend—the bare suggestion was an
outrage. Yet, in the present terrific condition of the
country, who could say what might happen? Kings
had tasted a violent death before now, and from within
the huge walls of his prison Strafford could hear the
shouts and uproar of the infuriated rioters who, unre-
strained, wandered from east to west of the city and
round the palace of the King. The resolution of the
earl was taken—one worthy of so great a mind, so
passionate a heart. He would free the King from the
formal promise, release him from the chain of words,
and trust to himself alone. Should the struggle become so desperate that one life must be sacrificed to
save the other, then Strafford placed his in the King's
hand. But that anything less than the steel at his
own heart should allow Charles to accept the gift, no
soul with one spark of nobility could believe. Some
men, even then, would emulate Strafford in the strife,
and be themselves the victim. Still, under any circumstances, Strafford was right. The love that hung
on a promise alone was not for a soul like his. Amid
the weariness of imprisonment or exile, still he would
have the solace of the King's faith—faith proved by

the greatest of all tests, the test of perfect freedom. 1641.
And thus he wrote to Charles.

Lord Strafford to the King.

" May it please your sacred Majesty.

" It hath been my greatest grief in all these troubles
to be taken as a person which should endeavour to
represent and set things amiss between your Majesty
and your people, and to give counsels tending to the
disquiet of the three kingdoms.

" Most true it is (that this mine own private condition considered) it had been a great madness (since
through your gracious favour I was so provided) as not
to expect in any kind to mend my fortune or please my
mind more than by resting where your bounteous hands
had placed me.

" Nay, it is most mightily mistaken, for unto your
Majesty it is well known my poor and humble advices
concluded still in this, that your Majesty and your
people could never, never, be happy till there were a
right understanding betwixt you and them, and that no
other means were left to effect and settle this happiness, but by the council and assent of your Parliament,
or to prevent the growing evils of this State, but by
entirely putting yourself in this last resort, upon the
loyalty and good affections of your English subjects.

" Yet such is my misfortune, that this truth findeth
little credit; yea, the contrary seemeth generally to be
believed, and myself reputed as one who endeavoured
to make a separation between you and your people.
Under a heavier censure than this I am persuaded no
gentleman can suffer.

"Now, I understand the minds of men are more and more incensed against me, notwithstanding your Majesty hath declared, that in your princely opinion I am not guilty of treason, and that you are not satisfied in your conscience to pass the Bill.

"This bringeth me in a very great streight. There is before me the ruin of my children and family, hitherto untouched, in all the branches of it, with any foul crime. Here are before me the many ills which may befal your sacred person and the whole kingdom, should yourself and Parliament part less satisfied one with the other than is necessary for the preservation both of King and people. Here are before me the things most valued, most feared by mortal men, *Life or Death*.

"To say, Sir, that there hath not been a strife in me, were to make me less man than, God knoweth, my infirmities make me; and to call a destruction upon myself and young children (where the intentions of my heart at least have been innocent of the great offence) may be believed, will find no easy consent from flesh and blood.

"But, with much sadness, I am come to a resolution of that which I take to be best becoming me, and to look upon it as that which is most principal in itself, which, doubtless, is the prosperity of your sacred person, and the commonwealth, things infinitely before any private man's interest.

"And therefore, in few words, as I put myself wholly upon the honour and justice of my peers, so clearly as to wish your Majesty might please to have spared that declaration of yours on Saturday last, and entirely to have left me to their lordships, so now, to

1641.

set your Majesty's conscience at liberty, I do most humbly beseech your Majesty, for prevention of evils, which may happen by your refusal,—to pass this Bill, and by this means to remove (praised be to God) I cannot say this accursed (but I confess, this unfortunate) thing forth of the way towards that blessed agreement, which God, I trust, shall ever establish between you and your subjects. Sir, my consent shall more acquit you herein to God than all the world can do besides. To a willing man there is no injury done, and, as by God's grace I forgive all the world, with a calmness and meekness of infinite contentment to my dislodging soul, so, Sir, to you I can give the life of this world with all the cheerfulness imaginable in the just acknow-ledgment of your exceeding favours; and only beg that in your goodness, you would vouchsafe to cast your gracious regard upon my poor son and his three sisters, less or more, and no otherwise than as their (in present) unfortunate father may hereafter appear more or less guilty of this death.

" God long preserve your Majesty.

" Your Majesty's most faithful and humble
Subject and Servant,

" STRAFFORD.

" TOWER, *May* 4, 1641."

Had the Lords followed their own opinions and wishes they would have rejected the Bill of Attainder. But this they dared not do. Still, in order to escape the responsibility of the act, they applied to the judges for their opinion on its legality. The judges would at

1641.

this moment no more have dared to decide against it than to have challenged the Commons to combat. As a matter of course, the Lord Chief Justice of the King's Bench, in his own name and that of his colleagues, delivered it as their unanimous opinion: "that upon all that which their lordships have voted to be proved, the Earl of Strafford doth deserve to undergo the pains and forfeitures of High Treason." [*]

As an opinion in law, this decision is about as valuable as that, also of the judges, which decided against Hampden in the case of ship-money. But times had changed since then.

Nothing now remained to delay the Lords, and on Saturday, the 8th of May, they passed the Bill of Attainder by a majority of seven, twenty-six voting for it against nineteen who opposed it.

Alone between Strafford and the block stood the King. Was it possible that he could hesitate as to his duty in this matter? For matters of temper, of money, of power, again and again, he had braved all opposition. He had repeatedly set aside the law,—declaring himself accountable to God alone. Only a few days ago, to the assembled Parliament, he had solemnly pronounced Lord Strafford not guilty of High Treason. He had dwelt on the tenderness of conscience, told them that this was a case of conscience, and that, as such, no respect whatever should make him go against him.

Besides, there was his word to Strafford himself. That the magnanimity of the noble prisoner had unbound him from every tie, except that of the conscience on which he so impressively dwelt, did in no shadow

[*] Nalson, ii., p. 192.

of a degree alter his position. His promise was the mere messenger of honour, and the return of the messenger left the honour the same. His position was not altered. The desperate alternative of death or surrender had not arrived. The consequences of faith and valour were such as a man of very moderate courage might have braved. But Charles hesitated. He told the Lords he would give his answer on Monday. All Sunday was spent by this miserable creature in debating, whether or no he should with his own hand seal the death of his dearest and most devoted friend, whose very sins had been committed with the mistaken view of serving him, who had been true through all things, true even in the dark valley of the shadow of death!

He applied to various advisers and sent for the Lord Chamberlain, for the judges and the bishops. They were too much afraid of the mob to utter a word for the earl. The Lord Chamberlain told the King, that if he denied the people, it would be construed that he loved his enemies and hated his friends, and that if he did not speak comfortably to his people, they would desert him, which would be worse than all the evils that had befallen him in his life. Then he showed him how he might ease his conscience by casting all the responsibility on the judges. Taking up the Bible, this precious adviser opened it at the 19th of 2 Chronicles, and read from the 5th to the 8th verse to his royal client.

" And he set judges in the land throughout all the fenced cities of Judah, city by city.

" And said to the judges : take heed what ye do,

for ye judge not for man, but for the Lord who is with you in the judgment.

"Wherefore now let the fear of the Lord be upon you; take heed and do it: for there is no iniquity with the Lord our God, nor respect of persons, nor taking of gifts."

The Lord was with the judges in their judgment, and so the King was bound to follow it. No wonder that Charles needed the opinions of the bishops on counsel so blasphemous. But the bishops told him, that though he ought to judge by his own conscience in matters of fact, yet he ought to yield to the judges in matter of law. And so he must submit to the decision of the judges in the question of High Treason. So judges, bishops, and chamberlain all agreed.

But there was one noble exception, one brave man among them to redeem the honour of human nature. This was William Juxon, Bishop of London and Lord Treasurer of England. He, and he alone, told the King to obey his conscience only in this matter, and that whatsoever might be the consequences, he should be ruled by what was right. No wonder that in his own dying hour, it was to the brave and good Bishop Juxon that Charles turned for spiritual aid!

Too late, speaking of the rest, the King said : "they persuaded me to choose rather what was safe than what seemed just; preferring the outward peace of my kingdoms with men, before that inward exactness of conscience before God."

But what had he to do with persuasions of other men in such a matter, except that he wanted the excuse of the advice of others to do what was too surely prompted by his own weak and wretched heart? There is but one end to hesitation in such matters. The man who does not start back with inborn horror and shame at the bare thought of treachery and desertion, in the hour of danger, to a friend or a cause, needs no tempter to urge him down the path of dishonour.

And so it proved with Charles.

On the appointed Monday, the usher of the Black Rod came to the House of Lords, to tell them that the King had consented to pass the Bill of Attainder.

Notwithstanding the great pressure of public opinion and all that had been done to ensure the earl's death, that the King would pass the Bill was not believed. That he should do it without a deadly battle, without striking a blow, or maintaining even an attitude of resistance, overwhelmed all men with astonishment. Even the usher who brought the intelligence to the Lords was so bewildered, that he forgot his Black Rod and appeared without his insignia of office.

It was at first intended that the King should come in person to the House of Lords, to give his assent to the Bill. But that he should avoid this was not wonderful. He therefore granted a commission for giving his assent. As he signed the paper, that was to consign the earl to the scaffold, the tears gathered in his eyes, and he declared that Lord Strafford's condition was happier than his own. It was true, indeed.

Then the Bill of Attainder, with the name of Charles affixed, was carried to the House of Lords, and the Commissioners seated between the throne and the Woolsack waited the arrival of the Commons, who were summoned to hear their victory. When they had arrived with the Speaker, the clerk of the Parliament kneeling, presented the commission, to which

1641.   was attached the Bill of Attainder. The clerk of the Crown read the Bill, and the clerk of the Parliament pronounced the royal assent.

And thus was completed the last act of the trial.

But it was not in human nature even now to renounce a faint hope. Denzil Holles was one of the most zealous and popular members of the House of Commons. He had consistently opposed the encroachments of the King, and among the party represented by Pym and Hampden, &c., he held a prominent place. But as he was not only the friend, but the brother-in-law of Lord Strafford, being the brother of the Lady Arabella, the earl's second wife, the propriety had been recognised of his taking no part in the trial, and whenever that question came on, he left the House. For him the King now sent, and asked him if nothing could be done to save the life of his brother-in-law.

Holles told him that he had perfect legal power to grant the Earl a reprieve and save him that way, but he proposed a plan that he thought would be still better. This was, for Strafford to send him a petition for a short reprieve in order to arrange his affairs before death. This petition Charles was to take in person to the House of Lords, and laying it before them propose to commute the sentence to banishment. Meanwhile, Holles would not lose a moment in exerting his utmost influence in Parliament to persuade the members to consent.

This plan was then agreed on, and Holles hurried eagerly to his task. There seemed a prospect of success. His political position gave him a great advantage, while his friendship with Strafford afforded him authority to speak. He assured the members that

if Strafford were spared, he would follow a different   1641.
course for the future. His eyes had been opened and
he would become of infinite value to the Commonwealth. He would feel grateful for their mercy and
well repay it. And as a faithful servant, he would be
of far more use, than as an example of vengeance in
so many doubtful points of law.

The words of Holles rapidly made impression, and
the opinion of his contemporaries is, that he would
have succeeded and the Earl been saved, had the King
remained steadfast to his part of the plan. But it was
a very frequent practice with Charles to ask advice, to
form a project, and promise to follow a certain course.
Then, while the other parties were acting upon this
and incurring the responsibilities involved in it,
suddenly, without their knowledge, to strike into a
totally different path, and thus bring failure and disappointment in place of success. In such an awful
crisis as the present, it might have been supposed that
even the most unstable resolution would have been firm.
It seems incredible that the King could turn aside.
Yet so it was.

While Holles with trembling eagerness and newly
awakened hope was pleading and persuading, promising and convincing those whose sense of victory
was also likely to render them more favourable, the
Queen, with her usual ill-timed and mischievous interference, came to represent the danger to the King.
Little did she care for Strafford, whose only distinguishing characteristic in her eyes, had been his finely
formed white hands. What!—was it to be borne that
she and her children should be put in any risk, for the
sake of a man who was nothing at all in her eyes!

With petulant tears she had recourse to that most common weapon of women who, in other respects can prove themselves very selfish mothers indeed—her children. Like thousands of worldly beings, who would never dream of sacrificing their own vanities, or selfish tempers and propensities to the real good of their offspring, she clamorously urged her husband to renounce the highest and most solemn duties to this excuse. She soon conquered. Instead of sending to Strafford to prepare his petition for him to take to the Parliament, the King, setting entirely aside the plan on which Holles was so hopefully engaged, and without even letting him know of his changed mind, wrote to the House of Lords.

In the first part of the epistle, he tried to satisfy the voice of that conscience of which he had talked so piously, and which through all refused to sleep in silence. But by the unutterably shameful termination and the still more cold and cowardly postscript, he deliberately renounced the cause of Strafford, and with his own hand blotted out the last faint signal of hope.

The young Prince of Wales, in person, brought the letter to the House of Lords. Those who knew the plan of Holles, and were waiting the arrival of the King with the petition, prepared to second his promised proposal, gave up their last trust as they listened to the following words :—

*The King to the House of Peers.**

" MY LORDS,

" I did yesterday satisfy the justice of the kingdom, by passing the Bill of Attainder against the Earl
of Strafford.   But mercy being as inherent, as insepar-
able to a King as justice, I desire at this time, in some
measure, to shew that likewise, by suffering that unfortunate man to fulfil the natural course of his life in
a close imprisonment.   Yet so, if ever he make the
least offer to escape, or offer directly or indirectly to
meddle in any sort of public business, especially with
me, either by message or letter, it shall cost him his
life, without further process.   This, if it may be done
without the discontentment of my people, will be an
unspeakable contentment to me.   To which end, as in
the first place, I by this letter, do earnestly desire your
approbation, and to endear it more, have chosen him
to carry it, that of all your house is most dear to me.
So I desire, that by a conference, you will endeavour
to give the House of Commons contentment, assuring
you that the exercise of mercy is no more pleasing to
me than to see both Houses of Parliament consent, for
my sake, that I should moderate the severity of the
law in so important a case.

" I will not say that your complying with me in this
my intended mercy, shall make me more willing, but
certainly 'twill make me more cheerful, in granting
your just grievances.

" But, if no less than his life can satisfy my people,
I must say, *Fiat Justitia.*

* Nalson's Collections, vol. i., p. 197.

1641.   " Thus again recommending the consideration of my
intention to you, I rest

> " Your unalterable and affectionate friend,

> " CHARLES R.

" *Whitehall, May* 11, 1641.

" If he must die, it were charity to reprieve him till
Saturday."

Twice this letter was read before the Lords. It
simply confirmed the surrender, and showed the pro-
moters of the Bill how completely they had won. An
answer was at once returned to the King " that neither
of the two intentions expressed in the letter could
with duty in them, or without danger to himself, his
dearest consort the Queen, and all the young princes
their children, possibly be advised."

Henrietta Maria must have been contented indeed,
especially when the King, in reply to this message,
said :—

" What I intended by the letter was with an *if*—
if it might be done without discontentment of my
people : if that cannot be, I say again, the same I
writ : *fiat justitia.* My other intention proceeding out
of charity for a few days' respite, was upon certain
information that his estate was so distracted, that it
necessarily required some few days for settlement
thereof."

To this the twelve lords, who had waited on his
Majesty with the answer to his letter, replied with an
intimation on a subject on which he had not troubled
himself.

From the enemies of Strafford came the first sym- 1641.
pathy with his agonising anxieties for his children.

They told the King, " that their purpose was to be
suitors to his Majesty for favour to be shewed to the
Earl of Strafford's innocent children, and if himself
had made any provision for them the same might
hold." This was of course pleasing to his Majesty,
and with mutual courtesies the King and Lords separated.

A better comment on the conduct of Charles cannot
be given than in the language of the first of modern
biographers. Who will not endorse his words?

" It is a sorry office to plant the foot on a worm so
crushed and writhing as the wretched King, who
signed the letter, for it was one of the few crimes of
which he was in the event thoroughly sensible, and
friend has for once co-operated with foe in the steady
application to it of the branding iron. There is, in
truth, hardly any way of relieving ' the damned spot '
of its intensity of hue, even by distributing the concentrated infamy over other portions of Charles's character.

" The reader who has gone through the preceding
details of Strafford's life can surely not suggest any.
For when we have convinced ourselves that this ' un-
thankful King ' never really loved Strafford; that in
his refusals to award those increased honours, for which
his minister was a petitioner on the avowed ground of
the royal interest, may be discerned the petty triumph
of one who dares not dispense with the services thrust
upon him, but revenges himself by withholding their
well-earned reward; still does the blackness accumu-
late to baffle our efforts. The paltry tears he is said

 to have shed only burn that blackness in. If his after-conduct, indeed, had been different, he might have availed himself of one excuse—but that the man, who, in a few short months, proved that he could make so resolute a stand somewhere, should have judged this event no occasion for attempting it, is either a crowning infamy or an infinite consolation, according as we may judge wickedness or weakness to have preponderated in the constitution of Charles I." *

It is true. The relationship of blood is independent of the will, and the discords and alienations that often there take place may be the unavoidable consequence of unsympathetic temperaments struggling in a compulsory tie. But friendship, resting as it does on free election, drawing in the soul of another by the volunteered promises of a mutual choice, is a religion in itself whose claims are so solemn, whose duties so holy and so clear to every one of us, that all human nature rises in indignant protest against the profane breaker of its sacred laws. And thus it is that nothing in the whole life of Charles, not his broken promises to his Parliaments—his cruelties to the Puritan ministers—his plunder of his people—the blood poured out like water in the civil wars—have together made such an impression on the whole civilised world as his conduct to Lord Strafford. It stands alone in its infamy. Nothing can lighten it, nothing soften it. Time itself has been powerless to bid it fade from the memory, and down the ages to come the same true instinct of mankind, will sink the more common and less memorable sins of the tyrant King, beneath the ineffaceable and blasting shame of the perjured Friend.

* Forster's British Statesmen, vol. i., p. 403.

When the King had put his hand to the last form 1641.
of the law, the officers of the Parliament proceeded
to the Tower to bear the intelligence to the prisoner.
As Charles had never replied to his letter, or informed
him of the part he had acted, Strafford was taken by
surprise, and when told to prepare for death, he asked
if the King had really passed the Bill of Attainder.
When they told him that it was true indeed, that it
was the King's own hand that decided his death, a
pang of mortal agony, such as needs a soul intense as
his own to comprehend, thrilled through all his frame.
As if to hold down the tide of wild emotion that came
surging upward, he pressed his right hand upon his
heart, and from his lips burst forth the cry of tortured
love and confidence betrayed :—

" Put not your trust in princes, nor in the sons of
men, for in them there is no salvation."

Death was a very light matter now.

No record remains of any intercourse either by word
or letter between Strafford and the King after this—
not even the trace of a farewell.

Another day only was left, the 12th of May being
appointed for the execution of the sentence. Those
days were employed by the Earl in his cares for. his
children.

The promise of the Parliament to ameliorate that
part of the doom of High Treason which confiscates
every possession, and would have stripped the young
Wentworths of all, was kindly conveyed to their father,
and was now the greatest earthly consolation that
could be afforded him, and of his few remaining hours
he snatched time to write the following letter of thanks
to the Lords :—

        *The Earl of Strafford to the House of Peers.**

" Seeing it is the good will and pleasure of God
your petitioner is now shortly to pay that duty which
we all owe to our frail nature ; he shall in all Christian
patience and charity conform and submit himself to
your justice in a comfortable assurance of the great
hope laid up for us in the mercy and merits of our
Saviour, blessed for ever. Only he humbly craves to
return your Lordships most humble thanks for your
noble compassion towards those innocent children,
whom now, with his last blessing, he must commit to
the care of Almighty God, beseeching your Lordships
to finish his pious intentions towards them, and desiring that the reward thereof may be fulfilled in you
by him that is able to give, above all, that we are able
to ask or think, wherein I trust the Honourable House
of Commons will afford their Christian assistance. And
so beseeching your Lordships charitably to forgive all
his omissions and infirmities, he doth verily, heartily,
and truly recommend your Lordships to the mercies of
our Heavenly Father, and that for His goodness He
may perfect you in every good work. Amen."

Sir George Radcliffe was appointed by the dying
Earl his executor, and the guardian of his children.
In Radcliffe he could entirely trust. Through life none
had loved him more. Strafford's affection Radcliffe, to
his last hour, declared to have been " a treasure which
no earthly thing would countervail ; he was such a
friend as never man within the compass of my knowledge had : so excellent a friend, and so much mine."
Wandesforde had felt the same. He could not love
Strafford more than Radcliffe did, but his bodily frame

* Nalson's Collections, vol. ii., p. 196.

was less able to bear the blow, and, as we have seen, 1641.
he sank beneath the prospect of his loss.

Whatever were the faults of Lord Strafford, and in this record of him no attempt has been made to conceal or disguise them, there must has been much that was very glorious in his nature to kindle in others such a life-long, such a deathless affection. Perhaps, a part of it was that the love of Strafford himself was not of the exacting, jealous kind that watches for payment, and plays the part of a tyrant even over its object. No. Wherever his heart reigned, all his imperiousness vanished like a tale that is told. That haughty and overpowering pride, which elsewhere was his curse, seemed a thing heard of, not seen. Whom he loved he longed to bless. " He never," said Radcliffe, " had anything in his possession or power which he thought too dear for his friends. He was never weary to take pains for them, or to employ the utmost of his abilities in their service. No fear, trouble, or expence deterred him from speaking or doing anything which the occasions of his friends required. He was never forgetful, nor needed to be solicited to do or procure any courtesy which he thought useful for or desired by his friends. In his hands their interests were safer than in their own.

" God knows," adds Radcliffe, bitterly, " whether he was repaid again with the like kindness and fidelity."

By Radcliffe—yes. He well merited the trust bestowed, and proved a parent to the children confided to his care. *He* did not leave his friend to quit the world of earth without a fond farewell. " Dear George," as Lord Strafford called him, now wrote the following letter :—

        Sir George Radcliffe to the Earl of Strafford.

" God's arm is not shortened, nor his compassion straightened, but He knows what is good for us, and out of His infinite mercy makes all things work for the best to them that love him. Happy are we, if our light affliction, which is but for a moment, work for us a far more exceeding and eternal weight of glory.

" I am most confident that you have (and still do) diligently examined your conscience and whole life past; and by true repentance and lively faith made your peace with God in the blood of Christ Jesus. Having judged yourself, you shall not be judged; and yet chastened of the Lord, that you may not be condemned with the world. God makes you conformable to our blessed Saviour in sufferings; you have followed him in many of the same steps; you shall doubtless be glorified with him.

" I shall account it no loss if I do now shortly attend your blessed soul into the state of rest and happiness. But whatsoever small remainder of time God shall vouchsafe me in this world, my purpose is to employ it chiefly in the service of your children, the only means I have to testify my sense and acknowledgment of that great debt of duty and thankfulness to your memory, which I must be ever paying, but can never discharge.

" I most humbly beg your charity to my wife, your blessing to my son, your pardon to myself for all my negligences, ignorances, and infirmities.

" The Father of all mercies and God of all consolation be your peace and everlasting comfort."

This letter put to rest the last fears of Strafford for his children. He had the satisfaction of knowing that

the grinding pangs of poverty, at least, would not be   1641
theirs.   His wife had always treated them as her own.
Motherless, therefore, he would not consider them.
And though he had no reason whatever to doubt that
their numerous relations would also be kind to them,
still the feeling that Radcliffe lived was better than all
beside.

Then Lord Strafford wrote the following most beautiful and touching letter of advice to his son, reserving
his last words for his good and faithful Radcliffe :—

*The Earl of Strafford to his only son, William.**

"My dearest Will,

"These are the last lines that you are to receive
from a father that tenderly loves you.   I wish there
were a greater leisure to impart my mind unto you,
but our merciful God will supply all things by his
grace, and guide and protect you in all your ways.
To whose infinite goodness I bequeath you ; and therefore be not discouraged, but serve him, and trust in
him, and he will preserve and prosper you in all
things.

"Be sure you give all respect to my wife, that hath
ever had a great love unto you, and therefore will be
well becoming you.   Never be a wanting in your love
and care to your sisters, but let them ever be most
dear unto you.   For this will give others cause to
esteem and respect you for it, and is a duty that you
owe them in the memory of your excellent mother and
myself.   Therefore your care and affection to them

* Strafford Papers, ii., 416.

1641.   must be the very same that you are to have of yourself. And the like regard must you have to your
youngest sister; for, indeed, you owe it her also, both
for her father and mother's sake. Sweet Will, be
careful to take the advice of those friends, which are
by me desired to advise you for your education. Serve
God diligently, morning and evening, and recommend
yourself unto him, and have him before your eyes in
all your ways.

"With patience, hear the instructions of those friends
I leave with you, and diligently follow their counsel.
For till you come by time to have experience in the
world, it will be far more safe to trust to their judgments than your own.

"Lose not the time of your youth, but gather those
seeds of virtue and knowledge, which may be of use to
yourself and comfort to your friends for the rest of
your life. And that this may be the better effected,
attend thereunto with patience, and be sure to correct
and refrain yourself from anger.

"Suffer not sorrow to cast you down, but with
cheerfulness and good courage go on the race you
have to run, in all sobriety and truth. Be sure with
an hallowed care to have respect to all the command-
ments of God, and give not yourself to neglect them in
the least things, lest by degrees you come to forget
them in the greatest. For the heart of man is deceitful
above all things. And in all your duties and devotions
towards God, rather perform them joyfully than pen-
sively; for God loves a cheerful giver.

"For your religion, let it be directed according to
that which shall be taught by those which are in God's
Church, the proper teachers; therefore, rather than that

you ever either fancy one to yourself or be led by men that are singular in their own opinions, and delight to go ways of their own finding out. For you will certainly find soberness and truth in the one, and much unsteadiness and vanity in the other. The King, I trust, will deal graciously with you, restore you those honours and that fortune which a distempered time hath deprived you of, together with the life of your father, which I rather advise might be a new gift and creation from himself than by any other means, to the end you may pay the thanks to him without having obligation to any other.

"Be sure to avoid as much as you can to inquire after those that have been sharp in their judgments towards me, and I charge you never to suffer thought of revenge to enter your heart; but be careful to be informed who were my friends in this prosecution, and to them apply yourself to make them your friends also, and on such you may rely, and bestow much of your conversation among them.

"And God Almighty of his infinite goodness, bless you and your children's children; and his same goodness bless your sisters in like manner, perfect you in every good work, and give you right understanding in all things. Amen.

"Your most loving Father,

"T. WENTWORTH.

"TOWER, *this* 11*th of May*, 1641."

One most deep and galling pain was still reserved for Strafford. To these his latest hours he was pur-

1641. sued by the voice of one of his worst deeds. In the amount of work that he was obliged to crowd in the few hours that were allowed him between the passing of the sentence and its execution, he may well be pardoned for forgetting many an act of reparation he might have wished to make. But one he was not allowed to pass over. On his last day he received a letter from the injured Mountnorris. It was written in a deeply feeling strain, and while recounting the wrongs that had been inflicted upon him, Mountnorris besought Strafford not to leave the world without giving a testimony of his (Mountnorris') innocence. He implored pardon for thus disturbing the last hours of a dying man, and declared that nothing but the condition of his children, nearly ruined by the penalties imposed on himself, and which he had never merited, should have allowed him to speak at such an hour. He assured Lord Strafford of his complete forgiveness, and thus concluded:

"I do upon the knees of my heart, beseech my God, not to lay these wrongs to your charge, but to receive your soul into his glorious presence, where all tears shall be wiped from your eyes.

"Amen. Amen, sweet Jesus, which shall be the incessant prayer of

"Your Lordship's Brother in Christ Jesus,

"FRANCIS MOUNTNORRIS."*

No account has come down to us of Strafford's reply, or whether he even received the letter. The proba-

* Clarendon State Papers, vol. ii.

bility is that it never reached him, as the letter itself is   1641.
the only evidence of its having been written, and it was
not found among Strafford's papers.

And now the spring day drew towards its close. In
another part of the Tower, Laud awaited his trial.
How strange was the destiny that in life and death had
linked together beings so opposite! Laud was quite
an old man now, while Strafford was in the very prime
of his manhood. Yet but a few short months separated
them from the same untimely doom. Strafford now
asked the Lieutenant of the Tower if he might not
once more see his old friend and exchange a few
parting words.

"Not without an order from the Parliament," was
the reply.

"Mr. Lieutenant," said Strafford, "you shall hear
what passeth between us. It is not a time for me to
plot treason, or for him to plot heresy."

The Lieutenant told him he might petition Parliament for that favour.

"No," said Strafford, with a flash of his native
pride, "I have gotten my despatch from them, and will
trouble them no more. I am now petitioning a higher
court, where neither partiality can be expected nor
error feared." He then turned round to the Archbishop of Armagh, who was with him, and said : " But,
my Lord, what I would have spoken to his Grace of
Canterbury is this : You shall desire the Archbishop
to lend me his prayers this night, and to give me his
blessing when I go abroad to-morrow, and to be in his
window, that, by my last farewell, I may give him
thanks for this and all his former favours."

At once, Armagh left the room to carry the message

of Strafford to the poor old Archbishop. He soon returned with the answer of Laud. " That, in conscience, he was bound to do the first, and in duty and obligation to do the last, but that he feared his weakness and passion would scarce lend him eyes to behold his last departure."

> " Alas ! Life's little space forbids,
> My friend, our lengthened wish to greet.
> Soon night will press thy weary lids,
> And shades thy fleeting spirit meet."

Lord Strafford did not forget his servants. The exceedingly short time allowed him rendered it impossible for him to write to all he wished. But he still thought of others, and, fearing lest Guildford Slingsby, his private secretary might be in some danger, he hurriedly wrote a few lines, telling him to leave the country awhile, and " though never so innocent," to remain abroad till his own fate was forgotten.

" I am lost," wrote the Earl, " my body is theirs, but my soul is God's.

" God direct and prosper you in all your ways, and remember there was a person, whom you were content to call Master, that did very much value and esteem you, and carried to his death a great stock of his affection for you, as for all your services, so for this your care towards me all this time of my trial and affliction. And, however it be my misfortune to be decried at present, yet in more equal time, my friends, I trust, shall not be ashamed to mention their love to the children, for their father's sake."

But one duty now remained,—to answer the letter of Radcliffe. Once more, Lord Strafford took his pen in hand, and with these words to that faithful friend, he closed his work on earth :—

" DEAR GEORGE,

" Many thanks I give you for the great comfort you give me in this letter. All your desires are freely granted; and God deliver you out of this wicked world according to the innocence that is in you. My brother George will come to you and show you such things as, in this short time, I could think of. Imperfect they are, and therefore I wholly submit all to be ordered, as shall amongst you be thought most meet. And if the debts cannot otherwise be discharged, the lands in Kildare may be sold.

The King saith, he will give all my estate to my son, sends me word so by my Lord Primate. God's goodness be ever amongst us all, this being the last I shall write. And so blessed Jesus receive my soul!

" I leave it to your care that are trusted, that if you find the estate will bear it, to raise the portions of my daughters according as was intended by my will."

(No signature.)

CHAPTER XVI.

" 'Tis the morn, but dim and dark,
   Whither flies the silent lark ?
   Whither shrinks the clouded sun,
   Is the day, indeed, begun ?
   Nature's eye is melancholy
   O'er the city."   BYRON.

1641.

LONG before the dawn gave the first sad signal of the approach of day the capital was awake. It was not merely the lowest and most brutal of the populace who streamed from every part towards the east. Men of refined character, high education and position, formed a part of the multitude assembled to glut their hungry gaze with the spectacle of death. Among those awaiting the sight, was John Evelyn, the high-bred gentleman and suave scholar, friend and pupil of Jeremy Taylor.

The previous excitement of so many weeks had worked the populace to a dangerous pitch, rendering necessary every precaution to control the spirit abroad that day. All peaceful occupations were suspended. The train-bands were under arms, and with the irregular clamour of the crowd, mingled at intervals the roll of drums and the clatter of the troops of cavalry who patrolled the streets. Without, all was tumult, while steadily the living tide kept surging towards the east.

But there were other scenes that morning.

Westward of the city, now becoming fast deserted, so early had the egress commenced, was a house shrouded from the daylight, and hiding within its walls a group whose wild despairs no earthly power could soften.

Few seem to have thought of Lady Strafford and her children that morning. None mention them. Yet, we need no record of history, no document stamped with authority, to tell us what their condition must have been. And never ought such deeds as that of this 12th of May, no matter how just we may think them, to be dwelt upon without a thought of their saddest accompaniments.

In a room in the Tower overlooking the path to Tower Hill, sat the aged and trembling Laud. He was thinking of his last night's promise and trying to nerve himself for its fulfilment. And as we have not spared the poor old man our harshest condemnation for his past cruelties and follies, we can well afford our just sympathy and respect in this sad hour, when the highest feelings of his nature were called forth. The greatest man in the Long Parliament might have, at this time, regarded the Archbishop of Canterbury with reverence. All his own miseries, his wordly degradation, his ruined fortune, the long imprisonment he had endured, the prospect of what was to come,—all these were forgotten in the present grief. For Laud, also, loved Strafford, loved him to the end. Again, amidst all his faults, let us acknowledge with due honour this noble virtue of faithfulness in Laud. In his character, too, we find a light shining out of the darkness.

And in the palace of Whitehall? Who cannot see the chief figure there, pacing restlessly the gorgeous apartments, now looking from the casement upon the river that comes rolling from the prison walls, as if to bear a message to him from the Tower, now shrinking back as his eye falls on the unwonted swarm of boats and barges? If involuntarily in his confusion he turns to the opposite side of his palace,—with louder outcries and by a denser crowd, he is still reminded of what they go to witness.

O that the day were at an end! Perhaps, after all, fate may have been kind. Some means of escape may have been found. After all, the Parliament *may* have relented. They *could* do it so well. *He* had certainly done his best to persuade them. Why would they force him to sign the Bill? For he was compelled to sign it. All must acknowledge that. No one could blame him. Even Strafford himself had released him. If any should ever doubt that—there was Strafford's own letter to prove it. And then he had a duty to his wife and children. They were always the first claim on any man. Besides, the country demanded the sacrifice. What miseries other Kings had brought on England by refusing to surrender their favourites. Think of Edward the Second and Piers Gaveston for instance. What more could he have done? Even the judges and the bishops had told him he must yield.

Only Juxon said " No." If only he had listened to Juxon ! But he must silence that thought. For it was too late—too late.

Long before the hour appointed, every conceivable space within view of Tower Hill was seized and occupied. Not less than a hundred thousand persons

of all ranks were gathered together in one vast and
swaying sea of human life. As the Lieutenant of
the Tower beheld the immense concourse, and remembered the riots of the last weeks, he feared lest
even the soldiers should prove powerless against the
multitude, and counselled the Earl to take his coach
from the Tower to the scaffold, lest he should be torn
in pieces by the way.

But Strafford with calm and smiling scorn,
replied :—

" No, Master Lieutenant, I dare look death in the
face and, I hope, the people too. Have you a care
that I do not escape, and I care not how I die, whether
by the hand of the executioner, or the madness and
fury of the people. If that may give them better
content, it is all one to me."

And now the hour had come for Lord Strafford to
leave the Tower. As he drew near the window of
Laud's prison, he raised his eyes anxiously. The
Archbishop was not to be seen, and with an expression of disappointment and astonishment, the Earl
was passing on, when Laud, whose emotion alone had
been the cause of his momentary delay, appeared.

Then Strafford bowing his head reverently, almost
to the earth, supplicated :

" My Lord, your prayers and your blessing."

The Archbishop raised his hands in the form of
benediction and vainly strove to speak.

Mighty is the power of affection. Wonderful the
beauty of its holiness ! It dilated the soul of Laud,
and from the hitherto apparently fit object of cold
ridicule and pitiful contempt, it transformed him into
a being glorified with such poetry as could transfix the

1641.   imagination of a great artist, and live for ever on the canvass of Paul De-la-Roche.

Again, the old man struggled with the intensity of his feelings and in vain. Strafford understood him, but he could not stay. Perhaps it was better—with what was awaiting him; he must not be unmanned. Once more, he bowed his head and saying :—

" Farewell, my Lord, God protect your innocence," moved on—while Laud fell senseless into the arms of his attendants.

And now they arrived in full view of that ferocious and tremendous multitude, that had so awakened the apprehension of the Lieutenant of the Tower. But whither had vanished all their rage ?

As Lord Strafford appeared, dressed in the same deep mourning that he had worn since his misfortunes, divested of all outward sign of his rank and office, except his George, a deep silence fell on all the crowd. The native dignity of his form and face he could not lay aside. Now that to it was added the deep solemnity of the shadow of death that overhung him, and the expression of high command which was the necessary result of the terrible resolution he had brought to bear upon his feelings (for he had to rule the pains of the body as well as of the mind), all these blent together gave him the air not of a prisoner approaching the scaffold, but of a general marching to victory. Not a single word of insult was heard, nor sign of ribaldry from all that vast assemblage. The enormous masses of all that was lowest and most brutal in London were subdued and still. With grave courtesy, the earl raised his hat, and saluted, with the grace of a native gentle-man, the people on either side.

At the scaffold, waiting to sustain him and receive 1641.
his farewell, were his favourite brother, Sir George
Wentworth, the Earl of Cleveland, his brother-in-law
(brother of his first wife); the Archbishop of Armagh,
" a minister," probably his domestic chaplain, and
others of his friends.

When he had ascended the scaffold, he at once
began to take leave of his friends, when his brother
George burst into uncontrollable and excessive weep-
ing. Then Lord Strafford leaving the rest, at once
went to him, saying tenderly : " Brother, what do you
see in me to deserve these tears? Doth any indecent
fear betray in me a guilt, or my innocent boldness any
atheism? Never did I throw off my clothes with
greater freedom and content than in this preparation
to my grave. That stock," pointing to the block, " must
be my pillow; there shall I rest from all my labours.
No thought of envy, no dreams of treason, jealousies
or cares for the King, the State, or myself, shall inter-
rupt this easy sleep. Therefore, brother, with me, pity
those who, beside their intention, have made me happy.
Rejoice in my innocence."

He next addressed the people, protesting his innocence of High Treason, and his stedfast adherence to
the Protestant faith.

Now came the long farewell to all his friends ; each,
in turn, clasping his hand before joining with him in
the last petition to heaven. Then all knelt, and with
manly simplicity they gave their reverent testimony to
that inspired instinct deep in the human soul, which in
all generations has led man in his last hour to one
eternal refuge.

    When the little group had together repeated the Lord's prayer, they arose, and Strafford called to him his brother George. Though the eldest, and head of the family, and not sparing his time or his money for the advantage of his brother and sisters, Lord Strafford had never abused his superior position towards them, never in return for his boundless generosity, exacted servility or inspired the weaker members with fear. To part with this dearly beloved elder brother was too much for poor George. Though a strong man approaching the age of forty, he sobbed like a child.

When Lord Strafford had succeeding in calming him, he said :—

" Brother, we must part. Remember me to my sister and to my wife, and carry my blessing to my son, and charge him from me that he fear God and continue an obedient son of the Church of England, and that he approve himself a faithful subject to the King, and tell him that he should not have any private grudge or revenge towards any concerning me. And bid him beware to meddle not with church livings, for that will prove a moth and canker to him in his estate. And wish him to content himself to be a servant to his country, as a justice of peace in his county, not aiming at higher preferments.

" Carry my blessing also to my daughter Ann, and to Arabella. Charge them to fear and serve God, and he will bless them; not forgetting my little infant, that knows neither good nor evil, and cannot speak for itself. God speak for it, and bless it.

" I have nigh done. One stroke will make my wife husbandless, my dear children fatherless, and my poor servants masterless, and separate me from my dear

brother and all my friends. But let God be to them 1641.
all in all."

Then, still with a view to the feelings of George, as he began to disrobe, he said :—

" I thank God I am no more afraid of death, nor daunted with any discouragements arising from any fears, but do as cheerfully put off my doublet at this time as ever I did when I went to bed."

Not seeing the executioner, he said :—

" Where is the man that shall do this last office? Call him to me."

The man came and asked his forgiveness. Lord Strafford told him he freely forgave him and all the world. Once more the Archbishop of Armagh and the chaplain joined with him in prayer; then rising, he whispered a few words to the chaplain, who clasped both his upraised hands between his own, as if in faithful assurance of the fulfilment of a last request. The Lord Strafford knelt, and in a few minutes himself gave the signal of death.

A moment!——and life's fitful fever was over for him. Nothing could touch him further.

His remains were spared the indignities too often in that ferocious age inflicted on the body of one who had suffered death for High Treason. As a rule, the beheaded corpse of a peer of the realm was exempt from further insult.

The body of Lord Strafford was not deprived of the funeral honours due to his rank. It was first embalmed and then carried to Yorkshire, where it rests with those of his ancestors, in the church of Wentworth-Woodhouse.

The Earl left a widow and four children; William,

1641.   who eventually succeeded to his title ; Ann, Arabella,
and Margaret, the last a baby at the time of his death.
She alone, of the four, never married, but lived with
her widowed mother in close retirement in Yorkshire.

The Parliament fulfilled the promise made concerning these children.   Soon after their father's death his
estates were all restored to them, and in the reign of
Charles II. the attainder was blotted out and the
family restored in blood.

THE END.

BRADBURY, AGNEW, & CO., PRINTERS. WHITEFRIARS.

TINSLEY BROTHERS' TWO-SHILLING VOLUMES.

UNIFORMLY BOUND IN ILLUSTRATED WRAPPERS,

To be had at every Railway Stall and of every Bookseller in the Kingdom.

1. EVERY-DAY PAPERS. By ANDREW HALLIDAY.

2. THE SAVAGE-CLUB PAPERS (1868). With all the Original Illustrations.

3. THE SAVAGE-CLUB PAPERS (1867). With all the Original Illustrations.

4. THE DOWER-HOUSE. By ANNIE THOMAS (Mrs. Pender Cudlip), Author of "Denis Donne," &c.

5. SWORD AND GOWN. By the Author of "Breaking a Butterfly," "Anteros," &c.

6. BARREN HONOUR. By the Author of "Guy Livingstone, &c." &c.

7. THE ROCK AHEAD. By the Author of "A Righted Wrong," &c. &c.

8. BLACK SHEEP. By EDMUND YATES, Author of "The Rock Ahead," &c. &c.

9. MISS FORRESTER. By the Author of "Archie Lovell."

10. THE PRETTY WIDOW. By CHARLES H. ROSS.

11. THE WATERDALE NEIGHBOURS. By JUSTIN McCARTHY, Author of "My Enemy's Daughter," &c.

12. NOT WISELY, BUT TOO WELL. By the Author of "Cometh up as a Flower."

13. RECOMMENDED TO MERCY. By the Author of "Sink or Swim."

14. MAURICE DERING. By the Author of "Guy Livingstone," &c. &c.

15. BRAKESPEARE. By the Author of "Sans Merci," "Maurice Dering," &c.

16. BREAKING A BUTTERFLY. By the Author of "Guy Livingstone," &c. &c.

17. THE ADVENTURES OF DR. BRADY. By W. H. RUSSELL, LL.D.

18. SANS MERCI. By the Author of "Guy Livingstone," "Sword and Gown," &c.

19. LOVE STORIES OF THE ENGLISH WATERING-PLACES.

20. NETHERTON-ON-SEA. Edited by the late DEAN OF CANTERBURY.

21. A RIGHTED WRONG. By EDMUND YATES, Author of "The Forlorn Hope," "A Waiting Race," &c.

22. MY ENEMY'S DAUGHTER. By JUSTIN McCARTHY, Author of "The Waterdale Neighbours," "A Fair Saxon," &c.

23. A PERFECT TREASURE. By the Author of "Lost Sir Massingberd."

24. **BROKEN TO HARNESS.** By EDMUND YATES, Author of "The Yellow Flag," "Black Sheep," &c. &c.

25. **GRIF.** By B. L. FARJEON, Author of "Joshua Marvel," &c.

26. **GASLIGHT AND DAYLIGHT.** By GEORGE AUGUSTUS SALA, Author of "My Diary in America in the Midst of War," &c.

27. **PAPERS HUMOROUS AND PATHETIC.** Selections from the Works of GEORGE AUGUSTUS SALA. Revised and abridged by the Author for Public Readings.

28. **ANTEROS.** By the Author of "Guy Livingstone," "Barren Honour," "Sword and Gown," &c. &c.

29. **JOSHUA MARVEL.** By B. L. FARJEON, Author of "Grif," "London's Heart," "Blade-o'-Grass," and "Bread-and-Cheese and Kisses."

30. **UNDER WHICH KING.** By B. W. JOHNSTON, M. P.

31. **THE CAMBRIDGE FRESHMAN; OR, MEMOIRS OF** Mr. Golightly. By MARTIN LEGRAND. With numerous Illustrations by PHIZ.

32. **LOVER AND HUSBAND.** By ENNIS GRAHAM, Author of "She was Young and He was Old."

33. **OLD MARGARET.** By the Author of "Leighton Court," "Silcote of Silcotes," "Geoffry Hamlyn," &c.

34. **HORNBY MILLS; AND OTHER STORIES.** By the Author of "Ravenshoe," "Austin Elliot," &c. &c.

35. **THE HARVEYS.** By HENRY KINGSLEY, Author of "Ravenshoe," "Mademoiselle Mathilde," "Geoffry Hamlyn," &c.

36. **SAVED BY A WOMAN.** By the Author of "No Appeal," &c.

37. **A WAITING RACE.** By EDMUND YATES, Author of "Black Sheep," &c.

38. **JOY AFTER SORROW.** By Mrs. J. H. RIDDELL, Author of "George Geith," "City and Suburb," &c.

39. **AT HIS GATES.** By Mrs. OLIPHANT, Author of "Chronicles of Carlingford," &c.

40. **UNDER THE GREENWOOD TREE.** A Rural Painting of the Dutch School. By the Author of "Desperate Remedies," &c.

41. **THE GOLDEN LION OF GRANPERE.** By ANTHONY TROLLOPE, Author of "Ralph the Heir," "Can You Forgive Her?" &c.

42. **THE YELLOW FLAG.** By EDMUND YATES, Author of "Broken to Harness," "A Waiting Race," "Black Sheep," &c.

43. **NELLIE'S MEMORIES: A DOMESTIC STORY.** By ROSA NOUCHETTE CAREY.

44. **MURPHY'S MASTER; AND OTHER STORIES.** By the Author of "Lost Sir Massingberd," "Found Dead," "Cecil's Tryst," "A Woman's Vengeance."

45. **HOME, SWEET HOME.** By Mrs. J. H. RIDDELL, Author of "George Geith," "Too Much Alone," "City and Suburb."

46. **THE EARL'S PROMISE.** By Mrs. J. H. RIDDELL, Author of "Too Much Alone," "George Geith."

May also be had, handsomely bound in cloth gilt, price 2s. 6d. each.